T0380269

NITZEVET'S LEGACY

A MOTHER'S SIMPLE TRUST IN THE
FAITHFULNESS OF YAHWEH

LISA BETH TODD

WESTBOW
PRESS®
A DIVISION OF THOMAS NELSON
& ZONDERVAN

WestBow Press books may be ordered through booksellers or by contacting:

WestBow Press
A Division of Thomas Nelson & Zondervan
1663 Liberty Drive
Bloomington, IN 47403
www.westbowpress.com
844-714-3454

ISBN: 979-8-3850-3288-4 (sc)
ISBN: 979-8-3850-3289-1 (e)

Library of Congress Control Number: 2024918329

Print information available on the last page.

WestBow Press rev. date: 09/09/2024

CONTENTS

Introduction...vii
Prologue...ix

1 A Five-Year-Old Learns to Behave 1
2 Best Friends 8
3 Nitzevet Comes of Age 14
4 Birthday in Bethlehem.. 25
5 Passover... 36
6 Reu's Challenge... 46
7 Philistines in Bethlehem 50
8 The Feast of Tabernacles 56
9 A Bondservant.. 61
10 Father and Son 66
11 A Dilemma.. 74
12 Friends... 80
13 Tisha B'Av.. 91
14 The Secret Revealed 101
15 The Betrothal...112
16 Confronting the Jealous..118
17 The Preparation.. 126
18 Moving to Bethlehem..137
19 Relationships...143
20 A New Wife 148
21 Eli & the Ark 151
22 The Adventures of the Ark 160
23 Family 164
24 Rafi is Back 172

25 Preparation for Mizpah 179
26 Miracle at Mizpah...................................... 184
27 Shepherds and Sheep 191
28 The Year of Jubilee 205
29 A Reluctant King..211
30 Men to Battle.. 225
31 Zeruah... 234
32 Loss 236
33 Abigail Meets Her Prince............................ 241
34 Another Betrothal....................................... 253
35 The Plan 257
36 Joy in the Midst of Chaos............................ 261
37 The Seventh (Eighth) Son........................... 265
38 A Lesson from Jericho 272
39 David and the Lion 282
40 Yahweh's Regret... 284
41 The Ceremony 288
42 A Marriage Healed..................................... 298
43 The Tower of the Flock 305

Appendix A: Character List............................... 309
Definitions 313
Story Inspired by Real Events 315
Endnotes 317

נאמנות יהוה | The Faithfulness of Yahweh

INTRODUCTION

The Hebrew people arrived in the promised land over 300 years earlier. They had seen Judges come and go. Many of the people had forgotten their God, the one true God. Following the false gods of the people that surrounded them, their lives had become small, weak and without hope.

There was one family that did not forget. From the tribe of Judah, the ben Obed family followed the faithful example of their ancestors. They knew their God by name, Yahweh. They knew He protected them, lived in their midst, and wanted them to follow Him. They called themselves the Remnant. A small group of people who lived their lives with the joyous expectation and full confidence that their God would fulfill His promises to His people, in His time. They were patient followers of Yahweh.

The story starts with this family.

PROLOGUE

She was an only child of a widowed mother. But that did not mean she was not loved, cared for, and on occasion spoiled by those who knew her. But that was the problem. Her vivacious personality, coupled with her overly flexible boundaries provided the perfect opportunity for the perfect storm of a child, Nitzevet.

This precious little girl was part of Yahweh's plan for the redemption of a nation. Created in the image of God, at just the right time, to learn and grow and become a mother.

1

A FIVE-YEAR-OLD
LEARNS TO BEHAVE

THE WOMEN COULD HEAR HER exuberant yet piercing squeals echoing through the hills surrounding Efrat. Nitzevet was a young girl who loved life in a little town that embraced life. She was the talk of the town, the life of the town.

Situated about one parasang[1] from Bethlehem, Efrat was known for its aqueducts that supplied the nearby town Jebus with water. Typically, a quiet little town, an average-sized town among the towns nearby, Efrat was home to this sweet five-year-old anomaly who was creating quite a commotion among the town gossips. Sometimes, as the women gathered to draw water, one might hear the echo of these harsh sentiments: "Girls just do not act this way." To most of the people of the town, especially those who were not close to the Nitzevet bat Adael family, the consensus was that children, young and old, were "seen and not heard and rarely seen at that."

Nitzevet was oblivious to it all. Her joyful nature coupled with her tomboy antics made her the talk of the town but also endeared her all the more to those who loved her. You could not be in the presence of this energetic little one, with the mop of curly red hair, without letting out a giggle or a peal of laughter, as some of the seemingly stoic bearded elders were known to do at the sight of Nitzevet.

She was innocent, kind, generous, and full of life. Hard for her to sit still, Nitzevet, at the age of five, was always running through the herds of

1

sheep and watching them scatter, talking to her playmates, and climbing the few acacia trees that grew nearby. She always had a puppy in tow that needed a home, or another child who needed a drink of water and a fig cake.

"Gila, my daughter," sighed Dalit, "you should do something about our girl. She is the talk of the town!"

Gila smiled inwardly, trying hard not to let her amusement seep to her face. She knew that it was not good to be "the talk of the town," so she responded out of respect for her loving mother, "Yes, Mother, I know."

"She runs all over the place, free as a bird, wild as a donkey, and silly as a lamb. What are we going to do with my granddaughter? Her grandfather is not pleased at her behavior!" exclaimed Dalit, secretly suppressing a giggle at the picture appearing in her mind of Nitzevet's antics. But they both knew of the hidden smiles that her grandfather so desperately tried to hide from all of them. Nitzevet was the love of his life.

Sadly, Gila knew it was time to begin to reign in the little girl somehow, but how could a mother do this without crushing her spirit or dampening her joy? This precious child was Yahweh's gift to her; that was why she named her Nitzevet, meaning "thanks." A shadow of sadness crossed Gila's face, and her expression changed as she pondered the loss of her three babies before Nitzevet was born. Out of gratitude to Yahweh and the pure joy of motherhood, she had raised this precious gift with freedom and indulgence that not many children in the clan experienced.

It was becoming evident as her precious little one grew that people were recognizing the difference in her upbringing and were becoming more and more contrary to Nitzevet's joyful yet often out-of-bounds behavior. She just did not fit in traditionally with her own culture.

נאמנות יהוה

Gila's father, Shelach, was one of the elders of the town. While he came from the tribe of Judah, he considered his heritage not as important as that of his wife, the niece of Naomi. Everyone knew the story of Naomi, the mother-in-law to Boaz, one of the leaders of the tribe of Judah.

Shelach was pleased at how Yahweh had worked things out. The land that his wife had brought to their marriage was near the town of Efrat;

that was where he decided to sink his roots and raise his family. He was grateful that as a result of "his" wealth, he was appointed an elder in this little town. You could often find him sitting at the city gate where the elders met. Shelach did not mind being known as Boaz's cousin or his only son Obed's second cousin; he was privileged to be part of this great family.

Shelach, while he often voiced his displeasure at some of Nitzevet's antics, was positively smitten with his granddaughter. As with his wife and daughter, Shelach treated all women as equals; he was unique in that way. It was one of the reasons Dalit loved him so much, why she'd married him. She reveled in the respect that he gave her. The last thing Shelach wanted was for someone to criticize this bundle of joy that made him smile so many times a day. He was not sure how he would respond to such criticism. His desire to mold the behavior of this rambunctious child showed his wisdom and maturity. It was better to attend to discipline now when she was young, rather than losing control and cleaning up an unnecessary mess. The mess in this case was a wild child.

With her piercing blue eyes, this vivacious girl was not making it easy for any of them. Shelach, respecting Dalit's wisdom, had asked his wife to step in and let Gila know of his displeasure and allow Gila to pull in the reins, before someone came to him. Ultimately, Shelach did not want to have to discipline Nitzevet; as only a grandparent would know, that responsibility was mainly for parents. Deep down, he loved her as a father and wanted to rise up to guide her. He could not wait for a few years from now when he could start his role and privilege of instructing her in the things of Yahweh, especially all their God had done for the people. Not typically an indulgence extended to women in Israel; Shelach was indeed unique. Yahweh had given him girls, so he would teach his girls. Who knew why his God did what He did, but there must have been a reason that his girls needed to know the things of Yahweh among other things.

נאמנות יהוה

One evening, as Gila sat on the rooftop in the warm evening, a plan started to form in her mind. She would take Nitzevet on a journey to her cousin Leah's home in nearby Bethlehem. Leah was married to Obed, the son of Ruth and Boaz. Gila called Leah her friend and cousin, but it was Obed who was her grandmother's sister's husband's cousin's son's son … so a distant relative.

Leah had several children with a large house, and Gila knew that she could stay there for a while and, with Leah's help, take some time to teach Nitzevet how to behave and act more like a lady than a wild animal, as precious as she was.

Gila had heard that a caravan was coming by the next day on the way to Bethlehem as they often did, supplying the little towns with goods from afar. This was her chance, so she made reservations to join the caravan and then packed up a few things on one of her family's donkeys.

In the morning, after hugs and kisses from Grandma and Grandpa, Gila plopped Nitzevet on top of their belongings with a rope handle to hang on to and headed out to the village gate to meet the caravan. It was just over two parasangs to Bethlehem, not far at all, about a full day's journey, but far enough for Gila to know she needed protection from potential dangers.

Nitzevet waved goodbye with a giggle. She was so excited to be on a journey.

"Yes, we are visiting my cousins in Bethlehem," answered Gila after a fellow traveler welcomed her and questioned her destination. Not wanting to offer too much information, Gila smiled and walked on. As the cousin of one of the great men of the tribe of Judah, Gila knew it was wise to often keep her identity under wraps and not offer too much information.

Gila did not mind walking; it helped her mind to think, to ponder all that was going on in her life. Her husband, Gemalli, had passed on two years back. Nitzevet was only three, so she didn't remember him. Tears came to her eyes as she thought about how her father, Shelach, had taken the place of a father for Nitzevet and how her daughter loved him as much as he loved her. The sadness that had engulfed Gila for the past two years had slowly been lifting. As a child of Yahweh, she had a choice: to be bitter about her life or to trust Yahweh with the details and her future. She was so thankful to Yahweh for her precious Nitzevet. She had a life to live and hope for the future.

It was a beautiful crisp morning, and Gila could feel the presence of God. He was all around her. Gila was one of the remnant. These were the people who knew Yahweh in a deep and profound way. The remnant believed the ancient documents that said Yahweh had a plan to redeem the world through the coming of the "Son of Man." They believed Yahweh would use His people, the Israelites, to do this based on the covenant He made with them. These were special Israelites who followed the conditional covenant of Yahweh and understood the times as they walked with God and as He revealed it to them. They passed their knowledge and especially their love for Yahweh to their children and their children's children. This day, Gila, lover of Yahweh, simply relished the presence of her God.

"Ema, how much farther to Bet'lem?" asked Nitzevet.

"Not long, sweet girl. You are doing very well sitting up there. Would you like to jump down and walk a bit?" asked her mother.

"Yes, Ema!" squealed Nitzevet as fellow travelers giggled under their beards and scarves. Nitzevet had that effect on people.

Racing alongside the travelers, Nitzevet was sidetracked by the little flowers that grew sparingly along the road. Ever so tiny, she was so amused by their beauty. "Ema, the flowers are dancing with me! It is such a beautiful day Ema, come dance with me!" called the ever-effervescent youngster. Gila smiled and called Nitzevet to her, the caravan would soon stop for a midday meal and a short rest.

As she opened their food pack that Dalit had lovingly packed, Gila was once more overwhelmed with gratitude for Yahweh's provision, not just the food but the love of a mother and father who embraced and welcomed her after the death of her husband. Gila and Nitzevet bowed their heads and thanked Yahweh for their food as their fellow travelers wondered at this unique little girl and her reserved mama.

נאמנות יהוה

"She is a precious girl!" Leah commented after several days with Gila.

"Thank you, my friend," responded Gila sensing more she continued, "but I sense you have more to say."

"She is so full of life, how are we going to teach her how to be a calmer girl yet keep her who she is?" asked Leah. As a mother, Leah knew that it was often challenging to bring up children, but not impossible. As she lovingly watched this precious young mother and her sweet child, she knew that this would not be that difficult. She relished the opportunity to pass on some knowledge and watch Yahweh transform this little girl. "My dear, Gila, she is so precious … we will work with her."

"We have only been here for a few days; I can already see a tiny change," Gila observed.

Smiling, Leah knew what Gila had noticed, "Yes, I have seen the shy side come out when Jesse is around. She follows him around like a puppy dog. She isn't quite so rambunctious, but she does ask a lot of questions."

"As a thirteen-year-old boy being followed around by a five-year-old, he doesn't seem bothered by her and her questions," Gila observed.

"No, I think Jesse rather enjoys her attention. Her sweet demeanor and mop of red curls are quite endearing. Besides, I am a great believer that kids of various ages should enjoy one another's company. Jesse can learn how to be gentle with girls and Nitzevet will learn that sometimes she can and should listen quietly," Leah's wisdom was profound.

"Thank you, Leah. I knew that we would all learn something by coming here," Gila relaxed in Leah's presence.

נאמנות יהוה

"Jesse, do you like living in Bet'lem? Jesse, do you have lots of friends here? Jesse, what do you think we are going to have for dinner?" Nitzevet was notorious for peppering her victims with questions.

Not feeling like a victim at all, Jesse laughed, "Yes, Yes, and lamb stew?"

Nitzevet gave him a puzzled look which made Jesse laugh all the more. This little one was a precious girl.

Jesse looked down at Nitzevet and said, "Run home now, I am going to play a game with my friends. Can you tell your mother and my mother that I will be home for dinner?"

With the biggest, sweetest smile, Nitzevet responded, "Yes, Jesse!" and off she scampered to her Aunt Leah's home.

As the weeks passed, Gila and Leah were so pleased with the slight changes they were noticing in Nitzevet. She was a bit calmer and more eager to listen, yet she still had that twinkle in her eye.

It was probably time to go home, back to Efrat. Gila missed her mother and while Leah was a wonderful host and cousin and friend, it was time for her little family to get back to normal. Passover season is coming. She loved to help her mother prepare the house and she needed to help her pack for the journey to Shiloh where the Tabernacle was. Gila knew that the Passover celebration was really for the children, to teach them Yahweh's principles of redemption. This year was going to be so fun to begin to teach Nitzevet the steps of Passover.

2

BEST FRIENDS

IT WAS A SPECIAL DAY for Gila, her best friend was coming to Efrat for a visit with her family. Hannah was one of the best friends anyone could have. Their friendship was forged in the fire of struggle. Each had their unique trials, but both came through looking to their God as their foundation and hope. Not only kind and sweet, but Hannah was also wise beyond her years. It was always a blessing to have her around, to feel appreciated and honored, and to learn from her as well.

As Gila remembered the past, it was both sweet as honey and bitter as myrrh. Hannah had mixed that sweetness with the bitterness and become a person of even deeper character. It is Hannah who says, "There is no one holy like the LORD; there is no one besides you; there is no Rock like our God."[2] A person can tell that she lives by those words.

Hannah's story was both sad and unique. Her and Elkanah's wedding was romantic beyond all belief. Elkanah had loved Hannah at first sight, and she had responded in the same manner. They were married quickly and were … are … very much in love. There was only one problem. Hannah could not have children. After ten years of marriage and no children, Elkanah felt compelled to obey Hebrew oral law that said he had to take another wife to continue his line. So, he married Peninnah.

Hannah was only human, and it made her very sad. Not to mention Peninnah was as mean as she was fertile and by the fifth year of their marriage there were already four children and another on the way. The grief of not being able to conceive coupled with the comparison between her and Peninnah caused Hannah to almost crumble. But instead, she turned her heartache into prayer, and on one of the family's Passover journeys to the House of the Lord in Shiloh, she went into the Tabernacle to pray and petition Yahweh for a son.

Because Elkanah was from the tribe of Levi, and a descendant of Kohath, Hannah knew that if she had a son, he could serve in the temple of Yahweh as a priest. The Kohathites were specifically assigned by Yahweh to care for the vessels and objects within the sanctuary of Yahweh. Considering who she was, it seemed appropriate to ask Yahweh to give her a son in this place and she promised to give him back to God to serve Him all the days of his life as a Priest.

While she was in the temple praying fervently on her knees, her lips were moving silently. She was unaware of anyone observing her, so intent she was on communing with her God. Eli, the current high priest was sitting at the door post of the Tabernacle, and he was watching Hannah as she prayed and mistakenly thought she was drunk.

As Hannah tells the story, after Eli confronts her on her seemingly inappropriate behavior, she assures him that she is not drunk, only praying fervently. Eli realized his mistake and blessed her and asked that God grant her prayers.

After she went home, Hannah became pregnant and was so happy. She gave birth to a healthy baby boy, Samuel. And true to her promise, when he was weaned, she took him to Eli and he stayed there in the temple, living with Eli and learning from him.

Gila was humbled by Yahweh's gracious ways toward her friend. Not only did Yahweh give them Samuel, but He also blessed Hannah and Elkanah with several other children as well.

Gila's memories were interrupted by a noise at the gate. She looked up and there was Hannah. Gila ran to her friend with a warm embrace and said, "Shalom my friend, welcome," Hannah returned the hug but clung a little longer and tighter than Gila expected.

"Shalom Gila!" she whispered.

"Elkanah, Shalom!" said Shelach to his friend as he walked up behind Gila. "It is so good to see you, it has been too long."

"Where is Peninnah? Is she well?" asked Dalit concerned.

"She is with child and could not travel," Hannah responded with a slight grimace, "her daughters are quite old enough to care for her very well, so she decided to stay home and rest."

Hannah's youngest, Abigail, jumped down from her perch on the donkey and ran to Nitzevet who was hiding behind her mother. Abigail was just a year younger than Nitzevet. Hannah's visits were also special for Nitzevet because of Abigail. Gila had prepared everything the girls would need as they spent time together so that Gila and Hannah could have their own special time. Dalit had planned to entertain Peninnah to give Hannah and Gila time alone, but now that Peninnah was not among them, Dalit could be with the little girls and concentrate on domestic duties while the friends caught up. The women always had a plan in mind when Peninnah visited, so Gila and Hannah could make the most of their time together.

Gila urged Hannah to follow her to the cool roof top where they could sit and relax and talk after her long journey. She looked over her shoulder to her father and said, "Please come up Father with Elkanah when you want to rest."

After sitting, giggling, and pinching themselves to make sure they were really there and not dreaming, the women started sharing years of information.

"How is Samuel?" asked Gila first.

"He is well and thriving, thanks for asking," said Hannah. "He is my greatest joy and blessing. I do love all my sweet children; each is unique and a precious gift from Yahweh," she finished.

"The other boys, they stayed with Peninnah?" asked Gila.

"Yes, Gareb and Naharai stayed behind to watch their father's flock. Gila, I am going to have another child!!!" Hannah blurted out, surprising Gila with the information.

Gila squealed a little too loudly, "I am so happy for you Hannah, may Yahweh bless this child," she said graciously.

"Yes, this child of my old age," she laughed.

"I am surprised you traveled so far while pregnant," Gila admonished.

"Well, my friend, I am early on, and the journey was not that far. Elkanah takes such good care of me. He is a precious man," she smiled at the thought of her husband even after twenty-five years of marriage.

Gila could only imagine - her husband had died so long ago; she would like to think that her marriage would have been like Hannah's. Indeed, it would have been. Gila knew her husband was a very good man, and she was very much in love with him.

"I see that Nitzevet is quite the little lady these days!" giggled Hannah knowing that Gila would understand. Hannah was one of the few that Gila had confided in about Nitzevet's wild younger years.

"Yes, my friend, she is the most precious daughter, better than I could have imagined or dreamed. Yahweh has truly been good to me."

"I am so sorry you lost Gemalli when you were so very young," Hannah sighed.

"I know, but Yahweh is my portion. "My heart rejoices in the Lord; my strength is exalted in the Lord," Gila smiled as she quoted Hannah's prayer. "I am content and satisfied."

"After our evening meal, after we help Mother clean up of course, shall we tell the girls Samuel's story?" asked Gila.

The moments turned into hours and the sun was setting when Dalit called everyone to dinner. What a feast it was, a feast of family, of friendship, and rejoicing for all that Yahweh had done for these two families.

Abigail and Nitzevet snuggled in together among the blankets and pillows on their sleeping mats, ready for the promised story. Hannah began, "I am going to tell you the story of when Yahweh spoke to Samuel."

Nitzevet looked at her mother, "Really Ema? Yahweh spoke out loud to Samuel?"

"Yes dear, quiet now, listen to the story," Gila gave her precious daughter a big smile.

The girls knew that Hannah had left Samuel at the Tabernacle with Eli, and they mostly understood why, but Hannah began with a few details, "You know that Samuel lives in the Tabernacle with the priest Eli, right? I left Samuel with Eli when he was five years old. It was the hardest thing I have ever done. At the same time, Yahweh made it one of the best. Eli has taken very good care of Samuel over the past fifteen years. At first, I thought, how could this old man care for such a small boy? But the truth is girls, when Yahweh calls us to do something, He equips us. He gives us the tools, knowledge, and ability to do what he is calling us to do. I believe he equipped Eli. Maybe because Eli knew he had failed with his first two sons, he felt Yahweh had given him a second chance."

"Anyway, when Samuel was eleven years old, he told me the story of how Yahweh spoke to him. He typically slept near the ark every night. One night while he was fast asleep, he heard a voice call out to him.

Samuel assumed it was Eli, so he got up and ran into Eli and said, 'Here I am, for you called me.'"

"Eli responded to Samuel, 'I did not call, go back and lie down.' Samuel told me that it seemed like Eli was not too happy that he had been awakened." At this Hannah smiled, the girls giggled picturing the sleepy grumpy old man in their minds.

She continued, "So Samuel went back and laid down. Again, he heard someone call, 'Samuel.' He jumped up quickly and ran back to Eli and said, 'Here I am, you called?'"

"Eli, more than a little upset for being woken up twice now, responded to Samuel again and said in a rather harsh tone, 'My son, I did not call you, now go back and lie down.'"

"Samuel obeyed, but he was a little confused. When Samuel told me the story, he said that the voice was as clear as day and he knew it had to be Eli. But he went back and laid down again, as instructed."

"The voice came again, a third time clear and loud, 'Samuel.' My boy was so startled that he jumped up and ran to Eli yet again, now a little annoyed himself, and said, 'I am here, you called.'"

Hannah leaned in and whispered to the girls, "It was then that Eli realized that it was Yahweh calling Samuel. Eli quickly got over his annoyance and gently told Samuel, "Go and lie down, and if He calls you, then you shall say, 'Speak Lord, for your servant is listening.'"

"Samuel, still confused, went again and lay down in his place. It was then that Yahweh came and stood and called again, just like the last three times, 'Samuel, Samuel?'"

Samuel said to him, "Speak, Lord, for your servant is listening."

"What happened next, Aunt Hannah?" asked Nitzevet, barely able to contain her excitement.

"Well, something pretty incredible happened that changed Samuel forever," she paused as the magnitude of what she was going to say weighed on her. "Yahweh stood before Samuel," she said in awe and reverence. Hannah continued, as the girls listened with rapt attention, "It was a hard thing for a young boy to hear, but he listened ... Yahweh said, 'I am about to do a shocking thing in Israel. I am going to carry out all my threats against Eli and his family, from beginning to end. I have warned him that judgment is coming upon his family forever because his sons are blaspheming their

God, and he hasn't disciplined them. So I have vowed that the sins of Eli and his sons will never be forgiven by sacrifices or offerings.'"

"That must have been both amazing to speak to Yahweh himself and yet hard for Samuel to hear," said Abigail wise beyond her years.

"Yes, my sweet, it was hard for Samuel to hear but harder for him to tell Eli. He told me he was afraid to say anything to Eli. He was so young. Samuel went about his chores in the morning, opening up the temple and doing what he was supposed to, trying to avoid Eli. But Eli called to Samuel and asked him to tell him everything that Yahweh had told him, not even to hide a single word."

Hannah paused, looked the girls in the eyes, and said, "Samuel told Eli everything Yahweh had said."

"What did Eli say to my brother, Ema?" asked Abigail with big eyes.

"Eli loves Yahweh, so he said to Samuel, 'It is the LORD's will,' Eli replied. 'Let him do what he thinks best.'"[3] Hannah responded.

She continued, "Samuel told me that he was so very sad for Eli's sons, Hophni and Phinehas, he knew them and worked with them. But he knew that they did wrong things and that Yahweh was displeased, so was Eli. But Eli never really did anything about it. He did not give them consequences for their actions as their father."

Abigail was sad, she knew Eli and liked him. He was to her an elderly grandfather full of love and kindness. She knew that Yahweh was judging Eli for his inability to control his sons. She did not know what they did, only that her brother had told her they were bad and did not obey Yahweh and brought great dishonor to their father Eli and to the People.

As Gila kissed Nitzevet and Hannah kissed Abigail, Gila smiled and said to both the girls, "That is why we must discipline and instruct our children. It honors Yahweh and pleases Him because discipline produces children that honor and please Him."

After their mothers left the room, Nitzevet whispered to her friend, "Can you believe that Yahweh spoke to Samuel?" Both girls lay snuggled together silently thinking about how that was possible, wondering what that would be like. Their God cared enough about his people to visit them and lead them and speak to them. A tear escaped from each little girl as they fell asleep pondering the awesomeness of their God, wondering if Yahweh would ever speak to them.

3

NITZEVET COMES OF AGE

TWELVE WAS A BIG BIRTHDAY for Hebrew girls. Gila was determined that it was going to be special for her daughter. There was a big party and sleepover planned in Efrat for Nitzevet and her girlfriends and then a mother-and-daughter picnic the next day. As a special surprise for Nitzevet, the morning after the picnic, Gila had booked transportation for herself, Nitzevet and Dalit to go to Bethlehem to spend yet another couple of days to celebrate her birthday with the rest of the family.

The day came when Nitzevet's friends finally arrived around noon to begin preparing for the dinner and sleep over. Nitzevet was beside herself with pleasure. Gila and Dalit had planned to involve the girls in cooking the meal together and then eating together as well. Dalit was in charge of cooking the main course with the girls, and Gila was ready to prepare the vegetables and bread. Shelach had already killed the lamb and butchered it according to custom. While Dalit was busy preparing the lamb for roasting, she instructed the girls on what to do next. They chattered like hens and giggled like birds; it was way too much for Shelach in his old age.

After delivering the main course of the meal, Shelach had plans to sit late at the city gate and then partake in an evening meal with his friends. They were more than willing to accommodate him when he explained how things were playing out in his home with the gaggle of girls.

The lamb portions were gently roasting over the open fire when Gila called the girls over to start the bread. She assured them there would be plenty of time to talk while the meal was cooking as she hushed them and encouraged them to pay attention. Having already milled the wheat grain, Gila had each girl mix up a separate portion of bread. They mixed their grain with water and began to knead it. Gila was so pleased, that not much instruction was needed as she realized that Nitzevet had surrounded herself with girls who already knew how to cook and bake. They were raised in families where their mothers took the time to teach and then allowed the girls to do their part in making the meals.

Dalit brought the seor over and Gila measured out a portion of barley flour for each bowl. This would allow the dough to rise and give it a bit of a sour flavor. To make the meal special, each girl was allowed to choose a different spice to knead into their bread. Nitzevet chose to knead grape juice into her flour instead of water and then added raisins at the end, it was her favorite, and with a dash of cinnamon, it was perfect. Nitzevet was known for her sweet tooth. Another girl chose to add some fennel and yet another cumin and garlic. It was going to be a lovely dinner. After much giggling and nonsense, the bread was finally set aside under a cloth to rise. Gila shooed the girls away, off to Nitzevet's room where they could have some privacy and talk like girls do.

Dalit handed Gila a cup of wine as she plopped down on the cushions in the cool shade of the courtyard, "what a wonderful group of girls! Did you see how they made the bread without much instruction?" Gila smiled and continued, "Yes Mother, it was wonderful. I was thinking how blessed we are that our daughter has chosen such wonderful friends to be near her through life."

"It is true that our character is partially developed by those we surround ourselves with," said mother to daughter."

"Yes mama, you are correct, and Yahweh is good."

Dalit laughed inwardly; Gila always gave Yahweh the credit. She truly loved Him.

Giggling and whispering, Nitzevet heard her friend ask, "There must be someone you are interested in romantically. Or at least someone interested in you?" Nitzevet's friend asked.

"You are 12 now and marriage is not that far away, do you have plans?" demanded another friend.

Nitzevet giggled, "You are all so silly. Yahweh has a plan for me and my family, He will bring the right man, the perfect man to me. I do not have to worry. I am so pleased to be here with you all, celebrating. But tell me Asenat, we know there is someone special waiting for you!"

Asenat blushed and remained silent. It was all so new to her, she did not want to stumble over her words, nor did she want to give away secrets.

To Asenat's relief, Gila called the girls over to bake the bread. It has risen well, and they only needed the girls to put it on the rocks to bake. The meat was ready and was being taken off the spit to rest.

Gila had made tasty date cakes for the girls to finish their meal with. Everyone was so happy and blessed to be a part of the celebration of this young girl's passage into womanhood. None of them would forget it.

The next morning, the girls woke up sluggishly, having whispered into the wee hours of the morning. But that was all part of the plan. They enjoyed their morning porridge with dates and figs and fresh cool goat's milk and then packed up their things and headed home.

Gila encouraged Nitzevet to go back to her bed and get a couple more hours of sleep before they set off for their mother-and-daughter adventure that afternoon. Nitzevet yawned and complied.

In the meantime, Gila sliced up some thin slices of lamb to warm up over the fire this afternoon as well as some of the delicious bread the girls had made. Dipped in olive oil and garlic, it was so amazing. She even packed a couple of date cakes for the end of their meal. Now to wait for Nitzevet to wake up.

נאמנות יהוה

Time was coming in Nitzevet's education where she needed to learn important principles that would keep her heart close to Yahweh. Gila's desire was to impart some of this knowledge so that her daughter would never fall into the trap of distancing herself from Yahweh and following or even acknowledging foreign gods as was the pattern of so many. While Gila had willingly imparted knowledge of housekeeping and how generally things worked, she had even included the basics of metals and science to her daughter with the help of her father. Gila had intentionally left out things that would cause her daughter stress. Things that she felt Nitzevet did not need to worry about at a young age.

Now that she was 12 and the recent crisis with the Philistines and Samson, Gila felt it was time to share the details. Gila slung the lunch bag over her shoulder and handed Nitzevet the skin of cold goat's milk, opened the gate, and said, "My daughter, tell me what you know about the Philistines?" Gila asked as they walked, to get a sense of what her daughter knew.

Nitzevet adjusted the goat skin on her shoulder and replied, "Well, mama, I know that they live near The Great Sea and that they do not follow Yahweh."

"Go on my dear," she encouraged.

"I know that they have made our lives difficult in the past, they have attacked towns and our men have fought back. I also know that Yahweh has protected us from them, I heard the elders talking about it. Once when I went to the city gate with my grandfather, I heard that there was a new Judge, I think his name was Samson. But I sensed that the elders were not pleased with him. They thought he was a fraud," Nitzevet responded thoughtfully.

"I do know Ema that I have heard rumors that he has superhuman strength. But I am not sure what that means or why," Nitzevet gave her mother a puzzled look.

Gila knew that Shelach would often take Nitzevet to the city gates but had not realized that her daughter might hear and retain information like this. She trusted Shelach and knew that he would not speak of things in her presence that she should not have heard. Gila used the knowledge that Nitzevet already knew and expounded upon it. "My daughter, you are correct he did have extraordinary strength. He was chosen by Yahweh to punish the Philistines, which he did. And I must tell you that Samson recently died."

Nitzevet was saddened by the news. Any person's death was a tragedy, but especially someone whom Yahweh had chosen to be a leader of the people. "How did he die, Ema."

"Samson lived a tragic life, and he died a tragic death. One of the saddest stories early in his life involved a riddle. There were other times when Samson endured much hardship. I am sure if you were to ask him, there were good times too. He did have Yahweh's spirit with him, and he did accomplish some amazing things for Yahweh."

Gila paused; they were almost at their picnic destination. She pointed to the horizon, and they made their way to the spot. "This is so beautiful!" exclaimed Nitzevet. "You knew that my birthday would not be perfect without wandering and picnicking in the fields, right?" she asked and giggled at the same time.

"Yes, my dear, I knew. But I also wanted to spend time with you, just the two of us, talking about things. I am always here for you," declared her mother.

They spread out their picnic on the soft blanket that Nitzevet had carried. As the sun warmed their backs and the girls nibbled on the delicious food that Gila brought, they continued the conversation.

"What was the riddle?" asked Nitzevet.

Gila laughed, it was so like Nitzevet to not forget a detail like that, "I do not know my daughter. Let's ask your grandfather. If he doesn't know then we will ask Obed when we get to Bethlehem tomorrow."

"Behind us is the Great Sea and the coastal plains where the "Sea People" live," said the teacher to her daughter. "They have been there as long as we have been here. It seems that some of our ancestors think they arrived at the same time, but since we were not here it is hard to know. Our relationship with them has never been good."

Gila continued to tell Nitzevet the intertwined story of the Sea People and their People. As the story goes, these Sea People sailed across the Sea from Crete, Cyprus, and the Aegean and colonized the coastal lands along the Mediterranean Sea, with the aid and permission of Egypt. The cities they settled in were known as the Pentapolis of the Philistine Confederacy. From the north to south the cities were Ekron, Gath, Ashdod, Ashkelon and Gaza.

For years the Israelite people have had a love-hate relationship with these people. Forbidden to have blacksmiths by their Philistine overlords, Israel did not have weapons. And the tools that they used daily had to be sharpened by the Philistine blacksmiths. Consequently, they were superior in arms as well as in their military organization. The Israelites were forced to interact with the Philistines for some of their basic needs. Yet, Gila explained that not all of them were evil. There were even times when some of the People got along with some of the Philistines. Gila would remember the admonition from the Priests about how Yahweh used the

Philistine people to punish the People when they were disobedient and followed idols and other gods. She could not imagine why her people would so often abandon their true God for these stone, wood, and metal idols who seemingly hated their people. The people seemed to think they had to do awful things to please their gods. It disgusted Gila, to think of the children that were sacrificed and the lives that were ruined because of the worship of these evil gods. But she would leave that discussion for another day.

"Someday, my dear, I will ask your grandfather to tell you why the Philistines have the technology of metal that they have and why we don't. But it is a story for another day and best told by my father," she said.

Gila continued the story of Samson. "He was chosen by Yahweh and ultimately did a great deal on behalf of Yahweh. The people wondered if he could have done more as they look back on his life." From the pieces of the story that Gila gleaned from Shelach and listening to Obed on her visits to Bethlehem, she knew quite a bit. There was the wedding feast and the riddle that spoiled everything including Samson's marriage.

"After a few years, he fell in love again. This woman's name was Delilah. But the Philistines were still mad at Samson, for the things he was doing to them. They knew wherever he went there was trouble. Because of his great strength, they feared him and were always seeking a way to get rid of him. The Philistine rulers went to Delilah and told her to find out what the secret of Samson's great strength was. They gave her a lot of silver. She did what they asked because she was not a nice woman. She never loved Samson, if she would so willingly give him up for silver."

"As the story goes, when Delilah asked, Samson told her that his strength would disappear if they tied him with seven fresh bowstrings that had not been dried. After he fell asleep, they came in and did exactly what he said. Then Delilah proclaimed, 'Samson, the Philistines are upon you.' But he snapped those bowstrings as if they were nothing. But he did not leave."

"Delilah asked again. Samson told her that if they bind him with new ropes that have never been used, he would be as weak as any other man. Soon he fell asleep, they did just what he said and again Delilah proclaimed, 'Samson, the Philistines are upon you.' He got up and snapped the ropes as if they were threads."

"Please tell me he left, he left and never came back, right?" Nitzevet asked.

"No, my daughter, he stayed. Delilah was mad at him and accused him of making a fool of her," Gila said, shaking her head, "it was Samson who was the fool."

"Then she asked again, and he told her if she braided his hair and wove the 7 braids into the fabric on the loom and tightened it with the pin that he would be weak. She did it. Again, she called out, 'Samson, the Philistines are upon you.'"

"He pulled up the entire loom and fabric when he awoke. This time Delilah accused him of not loving her. She continued to nag him and nag him and beg him to tell her. He got so sick of it, that he actually told her the truth - 'if you shave my head I will lose my strength.'"

"As was the pattern, when Samson fell asleep, Delilah called the rulers and they brought the silver. They shaved his head and then Samson was weak. He thought he would jump up as before, but he had indeed lost his strength. They blinded him and took him to Gaza. He lived in prison grinding grain for quite a while. It seemed as if Yahweh had forgotten about him."

"It seems to me that he wanted to lose his strength! After all those attempts you would think that he would assume that Delilah was going to do what he said. So why would he tell her?" Nitzevet's anger was obvious, she was not sure who she was angrier at, Delilah for being so evil or Samson for being so foolish.

After a few moments of thought a tearful Nitzevet asked "What happened to him Ema?"

"His hair began to grow," smiled Gila.

"Oh! Then what happened?" Nitzevet sat up straight sensing a twist in the plot.

"The Philistines were getting ready to have a big party to sacrifice to their god Dagon. They believed that their little god had delivered Samson into their hands. During the party, they called to have Samson brought out to entertain them. They chained him among the pillars. He told the servant to put him where he could feel the pillars of the great hall. The servant led him over to the pillars and chained him up there."

"Samson then asked Yahweh to strengthen him one more time so he could get revenge for his two eyes. While all the rulers of the Philistines and 3000 men and women were gathered to watch, Samson pushed against the pillars and killed more people in this one act that also resulted in his death than he did while he was alive."

Nitzevet was a little shocked and even a little horrified at her age by such a tragic story. But the ever-hopeful person she was saw her God's hand in it all. Samson had often disobeyed Yahweh, but Yahweh still chose to use him for his purposes. At the same time, Samson lived the tragic life that his actions brought him to.

"Yahweh will always be a loving and great God. But He does not always save us from our actions and our choices. Sometimes in His wisdom, he allows us to reap the consequences of what we choose to do. The sadness that comes as a result breaks his heart as much as it does ours. And yet, He still loves us. As Hannah says, 'He is our Redeemer'," Gila said as she hugged Nitzevet close.

Gila and Nitzevet packed up what was left of their picnic lunch and walked back to town thinking of Samson and wondering who would lead the people next. Then Samuel popped into Gila's mind, he talked with Yahweh. Maybe it will be him!

נאמנות יהוה

"Grandfather?" questioned Nitzevet as Shelach walked through the gate, "What was Samson's wedding riddle?"

Shelach. taken aback a bit by the abrupt question, looked around the room and saw the smiles on the women's faces. He knew it had begun. It was his turn to begin instructing Nitzevet. He had waited a long time. He loved knowledge and teaching. Even though he did not have a son or a grandson, he had a beautiful granddaughter. If she were anything like her mother, she would indeed be a challenge to keep up with. She was smart, kind, intuitive, and questioning, all the best qualities of a good student.

"Come my granddaughter - let's leave your mother and grandmother to finish preparing for dinner and we will have a cool drink in the shade and talk," he was quite pleased that she had asked him the question, Nitzevet could tell.

"So, your mother has told you about Samson?" Shelach questioned as they walked to a cool spot in the yard to talk.

Nitzevet handed him his drink and took a seat beside him, "Yes, Grandfather, she told me that he was a judge of the people and that he recently died. She also told me of some of his conquests."

"Well, the riddle was actually one of Samson's experiences that he had while visiting the Philistine woman that he wanted to marry. He was on his way to Timnah to meet the woman with his parents. While he was on the path, a lion attacked him. It was near the vineyards and apparently, his parents were not close by, so they did not see what happened. However, the other young men that were with him saw the attack. They said that it was amazing, the Spirit of the Lord came upon Samson, and he attacked the lion and as if it were a young goat, with his bare hands he ripped the lion's jaw apart. The men were all shocked, even Samson, for it was the first time he had felt strength like that. But he did not tell his parents.

Later, on the second journey on the way to the wedding, Samson stopped by that spot to see if the lion carcass was still there. In the carcass a hive of bees had made a nest and to his surprise there was honey. Samson, not stopping to think, scooped some out and ate it and took some back to his parents, who gladly ate it with him. But again, he did not tell his parents where he got it.

When he arrived at the wedding, he was appointed thirty companions by the bride's parents. These were not his friends. Samson threw a party and during the party, Samson suggested that he tell them a riddle. If they guessed it then he would give them thirty fine linen robes and thirty sets of festive clothing. If they could not guess it, then they would give him thirty fine linen robes and thirty sets of festive clothing."

"What was the riddle, grandfather?" asked Nitzevet.

"My sweet girl, I will tell you, but let me finish the story first. Samson was married, and as you know, weddings last about a week. After three days, the thirty companions had not yet guessed the riddle. They then went to Samson's wife and told her they would burn down her father's house with her in it if she did not get the answer to the riddle for them," Shelach paused.

Nitzevet was a bit shocked at the thought. "They really said that?" she asked.

"Now you understand, they were not Samson's friends, nor were they friends of his wife. She knew how serious this was, so for the rest of

22

the celebration she cried whenever she was with Samson. And finally, on the seventh day, he was so exasperated that he told her the answer to the riddle. And she told the wedding guests."

Shelach paused because this was the hard part of the story to tell a young girl. But truth, even hard truth, is instructive, so he tried to make it understandable to her age and her gender. "My dear, Samson was so angry, that he now had to pay the price since they 'guessed' the riddle. In his anger, he went to a nearby Philistine town, Ashkelon, and killed thirty men, took their clothing, and gave it to the men. But Samson was still so angry about what had happened, he went to live with his parents. His wife was given to the best man at the wedding."

"Why would Samson want to marry a Philistine woman and associate with people who would threaten to kill his wife and treat him poorly as well?" Nitzevet asked.

"Good question. It seemed that was one of Samson's flaws, he consistently made bad choices and associated with the wrong people," replied Shelach, as he glanced at Nitzevet, he knew she was waiting for the riddle.

"Before I tell you the riddle, what was one thing that Samson might have done to walk more closely to Yahweh?" he asked.

"It seems that he did not talk much to his parents. Maybe they would have given him insight or guidance had he consulted them?" she said.

"Exactly! Now for the riddle," Shelach paused for impact ...

"Out of the one who eats came something to eat; out of the strong came something sweet."

Nitzevet thought for a while, and knowing the story she knew the answer to the riddle, it seemed so easy to her:

"One who eats refers to the lion, honey refers to what is sweet," she said. "It seems easy."

"But if you did not know that Samson had killed the lion and that bees had made a hive in the carcass - could you have guessed the answer?" he asked.

"Probably not," Nitzevet admitted, then said firmly, "No, I could not have guessed."

"The other thing that you must know is that Samson was a Nazarite, he was never supposed to touch a dead animal or person," Shelach explained.

"But he touched the lion!" Nitzevet was shocked at the disobedience.

"My dear granddaughter, I think the lesson from Samson's life teaches us to be careful with whom we associate and be obedient to Yahweh, even in the small things. Samson was born to be a special tool in the hand of Yahweh to punish the Philistines. But he associated with his enemies and lusted for things he could not have, mostly women. He did not love Yahweh enough to be obedient, enough to keep himself separate. It is a good lesson to remember my dear," Shelach admonished.

4

BIRTHDAY IN BETHLEHEM

THE MORNING CAME EARLY AS they prepared for their special journey to Bethlehem. The three of them had to be at the city gate by daybreak to meet the caravan that was passing from town to town. Nitzevet was eager to get to Bethlehem to see her extended family and friends. At twelve it was always an adventure to go to Bethlehem, even if it was close. She pondered how interesting it is that she had so many friends in both towns, it was as if she had two homes. Each group of friends was special and unique, and she loved them all.

Spending time with her mother and grandmother, having them all to herself was very special to Nitzevet. The journey was a gift in itself. She could almost feel herself growing up, chatting with these beautiful women who had poured into her life, she was grateful for their love and care and was beginning to understand what that meant. Nitzevet knew the journey was drawing to its end when she could see the busy gate of the beautiful little city ahead with the well nearby. This was always one of her favorite moments, knowing she was almost there. She could almost touch the massive wooden gate at the entrance of the town and taste the cool clear water from the ancient well. Everyone stopped at the well near the gate of Bethlehem, the water tasted so good as if it were designed to be longed for.

Since they were still a few hundred yards out, she could watch the people as they approached. The city was bustling with traders and buyers as well as a group of elders off to the side, these were the leaders of the town who regularly sat at the city gate discussing the business of the town. She could see little children darting in and out among their parents. Not too long ago she was one of those children. She noticed a shrewd woman haggling for a good deal as the seller, with an exasperated look acquiesced and gave the woman what she wanted, obviously at the price she wanted.

Nitzevet giggled, she remembered, not so long ago, her Ema doing that very same kind of haggling, the wise woman that she was. She quickly smothered the giggle not wanting to explain to her Ema what she was thinking about.

This was her time, her birthday, her adventure. She was planning on running to the hills first thing after greeting her family. They were early enough in the day so that she could spend a few moments in the hills before dinner. Her mother had assured her.

Leah was waiting in the courtyard of the ben Obed home when she saw them walking down the narrow lane. She knew how special this time was for Nitzevet so the first words out of her mouth were: "Welcome, my sweet girl! May Yahweh grant you the most blessed birthday."

"Thank you, Aunt Leah, He already has, I am here with you and Uncle Obed," smiled Nitzevet, knowing how to say just the right thing to solicit a smile and hug from her Auntie.

"Run along, my girl, you have until the sun is almost on the horizon, then come back. Please be here before it dips below the mountains," admonished Gila with a smile.

Dalit could never understand Nitzevet's need to run, "Why do you encourage her so? She is now twelve, shouldn't she be concentrating on what women should be doing rather than running the hills?"

Gila smiled at her mother and winked at Leah who was watching the family drama unfold, "I know Ema, but she loves the hills and the quiet. I will never take that away from her. There are enough hours in the day to accomplish what needs to be done and still leave time to wander the hills with Yahweh if one is efficient. Besides, it is her birthday!"

Dalit smiled at her wise and wonderful daughter. What a shame she did not have a dozen children, she was truly a wonderful mother.

נאמנות יהוה

Nitzevet ran straight to the tower. It seemed to be calling her. She had been coming here for a long time. Longer than she could remember. She was five when her family began their frequent journeys to Bethlehem, only glimpses remained from her memory of that time, but the tower was always there.

Built long before her people returned to the land, the Tower of Migdal Eder was to Nitzevet, a place where she most felt Yahweh's presence. She could never explain it, even to herself. But it was simple, when she was a little girl, she felt peace here. Comfort and contentment were also among the feelings she most often felt when she was in this place. When she was younger and would wander the fields, she would end up here, lay down and take the most restful of naps. Looking back now she couldn't explain why.

Even at such a young age, Nitzevet knew that Yahweh was a merciful God. Her mother and grandparents had reminded her often what He had done for the people by bringing them out of Egypt with His mighty hand and parting the Red Sea so they could escape the evil pharaoh. Their God had led them to this very land that he had promised Abraham would be theirs. She knew that Yahweh had made a covenant with Moses as a representative of the People and given them statutes to live by. The covenant was a bilateral conditional covenant where Yahweh had promised that if His people lived by the statutes and feared the Lord they would prosper and be preserved. Yahweh said that righteousness would be theirs if they were careful to follow every one of the commands that He had given them.

Just as Abraham had believed Yahweh and it was counted to him as righteousness, Nitzevet knew that her God loved her and cared that she believed as well. So she believed. In her twelve-year-old mind, it was uncomplicated. This was why she longed to be in His presence in this place, she could trust Him.

The tower was located in Obed's pastureland near Bethlehem, passed down to him by his father Boaz. Obed owned a considerable plot of land, where he raised thousands of sheep. This family was actually known by many far and wide for the quality of their sheep.

Nitzevet found her favorite spot, a dip in the small patch of soft grass near the foot of the tower. Dew on the grass made her treasured retreat cool, even refreshing, especially on a hot day. She lay down, as if cradled in the hand of God and looked up at the tower. She loved to ponder life with her God. With thoughts of Samson on her mind and feeling the presence and love of Yahweh, she began to quote her favorite song that Moses had written:

> Lord, you have been our dwelling place throughout all generations.
>
> Before the mountains were born or you brought forth the whole world, from everlasting to everlasting you are God.
>
> You turn people back to dust saying, "Return to dust, you mortals."
>
> A thousand years in your sight are like a day that has just gone by, or like a watch in the night. Yet you sweep people away in the sleep of death— they are like the new grass of the morning:
>
> In the morning it springs up new, but by evening it is dry and withered. We are consumed by your anger and terrified by your indignation.
>
> You have set our iniquities before you, our secret sins in the light of your presence.
>
> All our days pass away under your wrath; we finish our years with a moan. Our days may come to seventy years, or eighty, if our strength endures;
>
> But the best of them are but trouble and sorrow, for they quickly pass, and we fly away. If only we knew the power of your anger!
>
> Your wrath is as great as the fear that is your due.
>
> Teach us to number our days, that we may gain a heart of wisdom.
>
> Relent, Lord! How long will it be? Have compassion on your servants. Satisfy us in the morning with your unfailing love, that we may sing for joy and be glad all our days.
>
> Make us glad for as many days as you have afflicted us, for as many years as we have seen trouble.

*May your deeds be shown to your servants, your splendor
to their children.*
*May the beauty of the Lord our God rest on us; establish the
work of our hands for us- yes, establish the work of our hands.*[4]

Nitzevet loved to daydream about her future. What did Yahweh have for her? Who would be her husband? Where would she live?

"Yahweh, my King," Nitzevet prayed, "I love you with all of my heart. I love you with all of my soul. I love you with all of my strength." She smiled as she quoted the Torah and thought to herself how good it was to be in the presence of her one true King.

"My dear child," said a gentle but strange voice.

Nitzevet turned and saw a man standing next to her. Her first response was fear mingled with confusion. Having never experienced someone so handsome, yet seemingly kind and gentle and overall otherworldly, she did not know what to think or do or say. She just looked at him and trembled.

The man smiled at her and gently encouraged her, "Do not fear little one, Yahweh has sent me to tell you that He has great things planned for you."

"Who are you?" asked Nitzevet in a small voice.

"I am a messenger of the One, sent to tell you of His love for you," he responded.

"Oh!" replied Nitzevet, waiting for the messenger to go on.

He smiled, "Dear one, I cannot reveal to you what our King has in store for your life, only that you are never alone. All that will come to you comes through His hand and he walks the path with you."

In wisdom and courage beyond her years, she responded, "I am so grateful for Yahweh's love. Thank you for telling me," a tear slipped down her young innocent face.

The messenger smiled as he wiped the tear with his hand, "You bring joy to the throne of the One, as you follow the path He has set before you. He hears all of your prayers, spoken and silent. Call upon Him when you are in need. You are never alone." And with that, the beautiful messenger was gone.

Nitzevet continued to cry. Not from fear or sadness, but from pure unspeakable joy. Her King loved her. He loved her so much he sent a messenger to tell her … here at the foot of her tower. What an incredible gift. Lost in her thoughts Nitzevet knew her life would never be the same. She knew that their God tabernacled with them and that somehow and in some way, He was present with them. Remembering the stories of Abraham and how Yahweh walked into his tent and ate with him. She remembered Moses when his God passed by him, and Yahweh covered him with his hand and Moses saw his back. She knew that Yahweh had promised that there would be a Redeemer, to rescue them from the plight that Adam and Eve and subjected them to by their choice in the garden. There was so much she did not understand.

Most of all Nitzevet wondered about what Yahweh had planned for her. She knew instinctively that her life would never be dull. It never had been and now, having spoken with a messenger from her God, she was convinced it never would be. Feeling content in the moment, Nitzevet repeated the words of the messenger over and over so she would remember them, *"Dear one, I cannot reveal to you what our King has in store for your life, only that you are never alone. All that will come to you comes through His hand and he walks the path with you."* Then she drifted off into one of those deliciously restful sleep for a late afternoon nap.

נאמנות יהוה

… what was that? Nitzevet sat up, awakened by something, something very quiet … there it was again, a soft whimper, almost a cry. Quickly and quietly, she arose and carefully stepped around the tower. It took her a few moments to get to the backside of the tower, but when she did, she saw him. A young boy, quietly weeping into his hands. He was a bit younger than Nitzevet, maybe ten years old and his clothing was torn and dirty. His legs and feet were caked with mud and his hair was disheveled. He whimpered again and it was a desperate kind of anguish, that sounded as if he was almost at the point of giving up.

"Shalom!" greeted Nitzevet gently with a whisper.

Her voice startled the young boy, but when he saw her, she could tell he was not afraid, although he seemed a bit nervous. "Shalom!" she said again.

"Hello," said the boy.

Nitzevet smiled. "Why are you sad my friend? Are you lost? Can I help you find your way?"

"I am not lost. I am here because I have no other place to go or to be ..." the boy stumbled on through his words, "I have no one and nothing. I am no one. I am nothing."

Nitzevet's heart was broken over such sadness and anguish of soul. She crept over and sat next to the boy, hoping her presence would comfort him so she could help in some way.

"My name is Nitzevet, what is your name?" she asked.

"Reu," responded the boy quietly.

"Well, Reu, I would like to hear your story, if you would like to tell me," Nitzevet nudged.

"It is not much of a story. My family is gone, and I don't know what to do. I am from the town of Gaza. I heard all my life about the people of Yahweh. How they loved their God and He loved them. I wanted to come here and find out for myself. My Parents were in the temple of Dagon when Samson made the building fall," Reu paused.

"I am sorry," Nitzevet said.

"I do not blame your people or even Samson. My people treated him horribly. He didn't deserve it. But I am now alone in this world." He paused as another tear slipped silently down his cheek as he sat there drawing a line through the dirt. Nitzevet could tell he was overwhelmed with grief.

"I heard from my friends and relatives in Gaza about the Hebrew people. They often spoke of your people's desire to follow their God. I thought that by coming here, I would find people who were like their God, people who would let me work for them. But people are mostly afraid of me. And those who are not afraid are mean and chase me away. I don't know what to do," his head returned to his hands, and he continued to sob as a fresh wave of grief rolled over him.

Nitzevet was quiet. Because of whom the Philistines were, it was no wonder that this young Philistine in front of her was feared by the people and sadly she understood the meanness toward him as well. Yahweh had commanded the Israelites to dispossess the Philistines of the land that he had promised to Abraham. But, in the end, her people were not obedient and were paying the price with the constant harassment from these people.

She pondered this new perspective on how her people did not match their God. Yes, Yahweh wanted them to be removed so that His people could possess the land that He had given them. But he had also commanded his people through Moses to be a light unto the nations as a kingdom of priests. Yahweh was also gracious and kind to the least of these, especially the young. Her understanding of what her God was like and what He expected was remarkable for one so young.

Reu had heard of how Yahweh led his people and saved them on many occasions. That is what the world around them experienced and heard about when they encountered the Israelite people. Sadly, that is not how the Israelite people treated strangers among them, even the littlest of these like Reu.

Just then Nitzevet looked up to the horizon and she saw a figure moving toward them. It was Jesse. She could recognize his gait from a long distance, and it made her smile. Just then she had an idea. "Reu, see that man coming?" as she pointed to Jesse.

Reu for the first time in her presence showed fear and slipped a little closer to Nitzevet. "Yes, what shall I do?"

"He is the great-grandson of my great Aunt." Reu looked at her with a puzzled look unable to follow the family tree. She laughed and continued, "He is my cousin. His name is Jesse, and his family owns this land. I believe Yahweh brought you here for a reason. Let's talk to Jesse. Will you trust me?" Then she added, "Will you trust Yahweh?"

If there was anything that Nitzevet knew, it was the character of the family of Obed and his sons. They did match their God. She waved at Jesse and called out, "Hi Jesse!" Reu peaked out from behind her.

Jesse had seen Nitzevet and her young friend and was watching as he walked up. He had slowed down a bit so that he could surmise the situation and evaluate what might be going on. His first concern was for Nitzevet's safety, which he could tell she was fine. Now, who was this young boy?

"Hi Nitzevet, your Ema and grandmother sent me to find you. It is your big night. I thought I would find you at the tower, so I came here first and here you are," he paused, "Who is your friend?"

"Jesse, meet Reu, Reu meet Jesse," she introduced them.

"Shalom Reu, welcome to Bethlehem," Jesse greeted them, knowing immediately by Reu's mannerisms and dress, that he was speaking with a young Philistine boy.

Reu smiled, for the first time. He had finally met two people who were gentle and kind. He heard Nitzevet explaining his situation.

"He is alone, Jesse. What do you think we can do for him? Do you think there is a job that he could do for food and a roof over his head? Do you think your father would be ok with him coming with us?" she asked.

"Come Nitzevet, come Reu, let's walk and talk," Jesse turned to lead the way back to Bethlehem, even at twenty years old he was the consummate shepherd, leading not forcing. "Just this morning I was telling my father that I needed help in the north pasture with the sheep. I need someone who will go before them, search out weeds that might be harmful, and then on occasion stay with the sheep when needed," he looked questioningly at Reu.

Reu seemed pleased but said honestly, "I do not know anything about sheep or weeds or anything."

"But are you willing to learn?" asked Jesse looking directly at Reu appreciating his forthright honesty, and somehow already knowing the answer to the question.

"Yes, sir, I am willing to learn," Reu responded and then added eagerly, "I would love to learn."

Jesse smiled at his eagerness, knowing eagerness and honesty were the first and most important qualities of a hard worker. "Then I am willing to teach."

"There is one other thing I would like to learn," Reu asked.

"Sure, if I know anything about it, I will teach you," Jesse was eager to learn the thoughts of this young man.

"Will you also teach me about your God?" he asked.

That was the first time for Jesse. Never had he been asked to tell a foreigner about Yahweh. Jesse perceived this was the beginning of a great relationship, he could feel it in his bones. "Yes, my lad, Nitzevet and I will both tell you all that we know about Yahweh and all that He has done for us, and what He can do for you!" Jesse wiped the tear that was forming in his eye.

Nitzevet followed Jesse's instructions to go and tell the women all about Reu. In the meantime, Jesse proceeded to search for clothing and other essentials that Reu might need and then he would supervise a bath in the spring.

The kitchen was busy preparing a feast, so Gila put Nitzevet in the corner where she was close enough to enjoy the fellowship, but far enough so she did not have to work … this was her birthday celebration. She sat out of the way, sipping a warm cup of spiced milk, and told them all about Reu. They asked a lot of questions, as wise women do. Not only were they listening for the answers to their questions about Reu, but how Nitzevet was giving the answers, her tone, and inflection, and the words she chose. Convinced that this was a good thing and that Nitzevet and Jesse and even these women could see Yahweh's hand in this young boy's life, they agreed to welcome him.

Nitzevet did not mention the visit of the messenger. It seemed to her now that it was a dream, but deep in her heart she knew it was not. Someday she would share, but right now it was a gift from her God, and she would replay it over and over in her mind.

By the river just across the knoll, Jesse was sitting on the bank waiting for Reu to finish bathing. Jesse had brought a towel, and soap. He hoped that he did not have to tell the boy HOW to bathe. With relief Reu popped up over the riverbank, he was clean. Jesse handed him a tunic not unlike the one he wore, just much smaller.

"Reu, we have lots of clothing. My Ema has insisted that we keep everything and hand it down or give it away. I have gathered other things you might need that will fit you and I will put them on your bunk where you will sleep with the other shepherds and workers. Does that sound good?" Jesse asked.

Reu did not answer but lifted his head and gave Jesse the most amazing smile with eyes again filled with tears, this time tears of joy. He couldn't speak so he just smiled. As he slipped on the new sandals, he whispered to Jesse, "Thank you!"

"You are welcome, my young friend! You are so welcome. Let's go celebrate Nitzevet's birthday!" Jesse jumped up and started to jog to town with Reu not far behind. 'It was going to be a great birthday celebration for a wonderful girl,' Jesse thought to himself.

5

PASSOVER

PASSOVER SEASON WAS ONCE AGAIN upon them. At the age of thirteen Nitzevet was truly beginning to understand the significance that the Feast of Unleavened Bread and Passover played in the life and history of her people. All the details had meaning both past and future. All the little rituals were not done for ritual sake itself, but to point out what Yahweh has done and what He is doing, and most importantly what He will do, for Israel.

"Ema, I have searched the house for hametz. I even found the morsel of bread that Grandma left on the back of the shelf," Nitzevet announced, smiling as she glanced over at her grandmother and winked at her while repeating the mantra, "No yeast allowed in the house for Passover!"

"Why Nitzevet?" Asked Gila, ignoring the silliness, she wanted to hear the answer from the lips of her daughter.

Nitzevet rolled her eyes, she had been quoting this same answer for at least four years, "We celebrate Pesach meal without yeast because our people had to leave Egypt in haste," Nitzevet realized the importance of the remembrance and her attitude changed, she continued to explain, "At midnight on the day of the angel passing over, Pharaoh demanded the people leave. They picked up their dough wrapped in cloth and carried it in the kneading troughs on their shoulders," Nitzevet thought for a while as a new dimension of understanding flowed through her mind.

"So that is why for seven days we must not eat leavened bread, because the people were on the move, no time to let the bread rise, they had to

36

eat flat bread every night," she had not put this particular piece of the puzzle in place.

"What about the lamb, Nitzevet, what role does the lamb play in Passover?" Gila gently questioned her daughter.

"Ema, you know how sad this makes me. We have to bring in a little lamb, a one-year-old, into our home on the tenth day of Nisan, and then on the 14th day we must kill it according to the Threshold covenant," Nitzevet paused, contemplating the facts. "After we kill the lamb, we take some of the blood in a bowl, and dip a sprig of hyssop in the blood and wipe it on the doorposts as well as the beam above the door.

"Nitzevet, why do we put the blood of the lamb on the doorposts and the beam above the door," Gila asked.

"We do this to honor Yahweh because He passed over the houses of the Israelites who had this blood on the doorposts. He killed the firstborn of every house that did not have the blood. But he spared those who did. Many Egyptians died," Nitzevet explained.

"What about the lamb?" Her Ema continued the questioning.

"We must attach it to a cross and roast it over the fire, not boil it or eat it raw," Nitzevet looked sad, knowing that this was all going to play out before her yet again this year.

Noticing her sadness Dalit encouraged her granddaughter, "I think that is Yahweh's point. We are to wrestle with the sadness of the sacrifice. Go on, precious one,"

"We must eat it all, and if we cannot, we must burn what is left over. Nothing must remain till morning," responded Nitzevet.

All these little details puzzled Nitzevet. There must be a reason that God had outlined them and demanded that they be followed, a lesson perhaps, maybe a picture of what is to come. 'Why the lamb on the cross, why the blood on the door, why the three days?' she continued to ponder.

Breaking away from her pondering she asked, "Mama, when do we leave for Bethlehem?"

Leah and Obed had once again invited the small family of a mother and daughter and grandparents to share Passover with them in Bethlehem, "We are leaving tomorrow morning, early. I am so glad that Yahweh said that we could share with our extended family because we could not eat a whole lamb," Gila told them facts they already knew.

Nitzevet slipped away after her question. She knew she was ready to go. Secretly she had been ready for several days. Going to Bethlehem was beyond doubt one of her favorite things to do. Yes, cousins, yes Aunt Leah, yes, a beautiful city, but also ... Jesse.

Nitzevet woke up early, and the morning was beautiful. Nitzevet was always ready for adventure, even if it was their routine journey to Bethlehem. The little family had made the journey many times and every year there was always a caravan, a rather large one, going to Bethlehem on the ninth of Nisan. This gave them plenty of time to participate in the selection of the lamb for Passover and the ultimate sacrifice on the fourteenth at dusk.

As they journeyed Nitzevet noticed what a beautiful time of year it was. Beautiful, not only because Spring had just arrived and the rather mild climate in Israel was just beginning, its most beautiful season, but also because the people anticipated the Passover season with respect and joy. It was a weeklong time of remembering what Yahweh had done for them. A miracle, so significant, it changed the trajectory of an entire people group numbered in the millions. Only, Yahweh, Lord of heaven and earth could cause the plagues and change the heart of Pharaoh. Only, the God of the Universe could part the Red Sea and save His people.

נאמנות יהוה

The next morning Nitzevet woke up in Bethlehem next to her Ema. After breakfast, she had the morning to do whatever she would like. First, she planned to visit Rebekah, also thirteen, and one of her closest friends who lived just around the corner from the ben Obed family in Bethlehem.

Nitzevet found Rebekah just coming back from getting water at the well. Rebekah was so pleased to see her wonderful friend waiting on her doorstep.

Squealing with delight, the girls embraced and greeted one another with joy and love. "Shalom Rebekah, it is so good to see you, it has been so long, how are you?"

Rebekah carried the water into her home and motioned for her friend to sit down, "I have been waiting to see you," Rebekah said as she reached behind the partition in the wall and pulled out a small package, "I made you something" she said as she handed the package to Nitzevet.

Nitzevet was so pleased, she loved receiving gifts and she loved that Rebekah remembered. As she gently opened the package, she gasped as she found a beautiful pair of earrings, delicate and lovely, something that only Rebekah could make. Three thin strips of delicate leather braided with strands of gold thread and a single shell hanging from the strings.

"Remember how I did not have a present for you on your birthday?" Rebekah said, "Well, I was waiting for my father to go to the shore of the Great Sea to find these tiny little shells that were just perfect. I am sorry you had to wait."

"Rebekah, your presence at my birthday was enough. I did not need a present. But I love these beyond measure. Thank you!" Nitzevet hugged her closest friend, treasuring the gift.

The girls talked for several hours and then Nitzevet suddenly remembered that she had promised to help choose the lamb with Keturah. She kissed Rebekah goodbye for the day and ran back toward her home. A smiling Keturah greeted her on the path, "Good timing sister, I was just coming to look for you. Shall we go and choose the lamb?"

Nitzevet nodded and took her cousin's hand and relished her family bonds. Keturah was the wife of Obed's second son, Jephanneth. Since the sons of Israelite families lived with the family, building on to the family house for their new wives, Keturah had become an important person in the household, learning well the ways of her mother-in-law, Leah, who was matron of the household. Keturah was also fiercely protective of Nitzevet. She loved teaching Nitzevet and caring for her slightly younger cousin.

As they approached, they could see that Jesse was busy with people crowding around him as he helped them choose their Passover lambs. As the leading sheep herding family in Bethlehem, Obed and his three sons were all very busy during the Passover season.

The family flock of Boaz had been passed down through many generations from Jacob, who was a truly amazing sheep herder and breeder. Everyone knows the story of when Jacob asked only for the spotted sheep and his father-in-law quickly gave him the spotted sheep thinking this was a sweet deal to offload the unwanted sheep. Then as Jacob continued to care for the flock of pure white sheep, they kept coming up spotted, because Yahweh was taking care of Jacob.

The breeding tips and tricks were passed down from Jacob through the line of Judah. When the people returned to the land, it was Bethlehem that became the center of the flocks of Jacob, currently, owned and run by Obed and his sons.

Jesse, earlier in the day, had carefully selected the lamb for his family. There would be eleven family members present for Passover this year at his house. He saw his sister-in-law approaching and went and untied the lamb for her. As Jesse was about to hand the rope to his sister-in-law, he noticed the beautiful girl standing next to her. Nitzevet was older. It had been a year since he had seen her, and he was again taken back by her unique beauty ... her uniquely beautiful eyes. She gently took the rope from his outstretched hand, petted the lamb and nodded with a sweet smile to Jesse.

As they walked away Keturah smiled at Nitzevet, "What was that all about?" she asked.

"What was what all about?" responded Nitzevet, with a pink tinge slowly moving across her face.

"What was all that going on between you and Jesse?" she questioned.

"Please don't say anything Keturah, please ... I care for your brother; I hope and pray that someday he will care for me too," begged Nitzevet.

Keturah nodded and smiled, never would she betray the feelings of a companion, especially not this sweet girl, but she knew more than she let on, for it was obvious that Jesse was also smitten.

נאמנות יהוה

The table was set, pillows were laid out, wine was cooling, and the goblets were on the table. The food was prepared, and the lamb was about ready to eat.

"Leah, where would you like us to sit at the table?" Called Keturah.

"Please have each spouse beside their mate and Gila and Nitzevet are to be beside Dalit. Please place Dalit and Shelach across from your father and me," responded Leah.

Keturah was careful to do just as Leah had asked, but at the end of the table, she placed Nitzevet next to Jesse.

Nitzevet was pleased but shy. Jesse was reserved, but content as they listened to Obed recount the "retelling" of the story of the exodus starting with Moses in the basket floating down the river.

Remembering the Exodus and the Passover was not the only thing that Nitzevet will be remembering this year. This was her first time at the Passover table seated next to Jesse, surrounded by the people she loved. Could it get any better?

נאמנות יהוה

Early the next morning, a Shabbat day, after the Passover meal, Nitzevet quietly dressed and snuck out of the house. She was on her way to her tower, to spend some time with her friend, her confidant, and her God. After the appearance of the Messenger last year, she had been anticipating her return. She had packed her breakfast of cheese and unleavened bread with some goat's milk in a bag last night. All she had to do was sling the pack over her shoulder and take off.

The shepherds at the tower had come to respect and love the little girl that had grown up among them. Because they were Obed's shepherds, caring for Obed's sheep on Obed's land, they had been carefully instructed to care just as much for this sweet girl as she wandered among them. For years, they had watched over this fatherless child as if she were their own. Truth be told, it was not hard to care for Nitzevet. Her kind ways only deepened with age as she developed wisdom. The bonds of friendship and family grew stronger with her and the shepherds … her shepherds. She was truly their little lamb.

As they saw her approaching their fire near the tower, Maharai jumped up and threw another log on the fire for Nitzevet. They had just finished their morning meal and were about to take the sheep to the northern pasture. Rather than let the fire die, he knew Nitzevet would enjoy its warmth in the early spring morning until the sun was higher in the sky.

"Thank you Maharai!" greeted Nitzevet smiling as she noticed his efforts. "You knew I was going to make some warm spiced milk for my morning meal?"

"Just wanted to make sure you were warm enough, metuka. Sometimes the dew on the grass makes the morning air chilly," he said speaking from experience.

"Shalom and bless you, my friend," smiled Nitzevet.

Abiezer approached Nitzevet with a smile, "Anything new young lady?"

"Nothing new Abiezer, I just wanted to spend some time with my Friend," she replied.

Abiezer knew who she spoke of, they all knew and marveled at the simple profound faith of such a young girl. "Abiezer, I heard there was a cave near here where sheep were kept warm?"

"Yes, if you stand here," Abiezer said, pointing to a spot near the fire. Standing behind her, he pointed over her shoulder with his finger, "Look yonder to that hill, imagine going down the other side and about 1000-foot falls past the top. There you will encounter a path that actually takes you back toward the city and straight to the entrance of the cave."

"Is it safe to visit?" she asked.

"Yes, it is still on Obed's land, although on the very edge where his land wraps around and meets Bethlehem," he explained.

"What is it used for?" asked Nitzevet.

Sibbecai answered the question as he packed his gear, "It is where we take the newborn sheep and their mothers as well as the sick or weak animals when it is very cold at night. We feel they should get accustomed to the cold weather slowly, rather than have to experience it so young."

"You care so well for the sheep! Thank you for showing me, I might go visit today."

"Have a wonderful day of adventure!" Abiezer called as he and Sibbecai and Maharai proceeded to gather up and call the sheep and lead them off in the direction of the north pasture.

Nitzevet unfolded her pack, took out her little pot, and poured the milk from the goat skin into the little clay pot. The pot fits perfectly on the stone Abiezer had placed next to the fiery log as if he knew her little pot would need a resting place to warm the milk. She smiled at his thoughtfulness. She then took out the small packet of spices and sprinkled some into the milk as it warmed. Leah had taught her how special spices added to various foods made what they ate and drank so special and memorable. Forever, when she would drink spiced goat's milk she would think of the Tower and her friendship with Yahweh.

After munching on her food and sipping her milk tea, Nitzevet laid back on her cloak and quoted her favorite Poem ... *"Satisfy us in the morning with your unfailing love, that we may sing for joy and be glad all our days."* [5] ... It was good to be in the presence of Yahweh. She stayed in that position for quite some time.

She heard his footsteps and then the breeze brought the gentle smell of a shepherd her way and Nitzevet knew that Reu was close. He was always so quiet, but he could never fool her. She pretended to be startled when he pounced next to her like a little lamb.

"Good morning my friend," She greeted him. "I am so glad to see you. It has been almost a year since I have been here. Sip my tea, it will warm you on the inside."

The pleasant look on his face told her that he indeed was pleased to see her, and he liked her tea. "I will teach you how to make it, but you will have to get more spices from Aunt Leah, she has plenty."

Reu slowly sipped the warm and tasty milk tea, while they chatted and enjoyed the warmth of the fire. Nitzevet remarked to herself how he had grown. It was as if Reu had become different, he was confident for a little boy and ... happy.

As the sun warmed up the day, Nitzevet asked, "Reu, would you like to go on an adventure with me? There is something I want to explore and until I do, my curiosity will never be vanquished!"

"Yes, of course, I am always up for an adventure. Jesse gave me the morning off from watching the sheep, to do whatever I would like to do. Let's go - which way?"

Nitzevet gathered her pot and cup and stuffed them into her sheepskin bag and then stashed it in the hole of the sitting log by the fire. She stomped out the fire, so it would not spread and then tidied up the area of the shepherd's camp.

Pointing to the hill that Abiezer showed her, she said, "Over the hill, let's go!"

The two friends skipped and ran and flitted through the grass, free as birds and happier than any two friends could be. Sure enough, when they got to the hill they counted 1000 footfalls. But Nitzevet realized that

1000 of her steps were not equal to 1000 of Abiezer's, especially on a cold night when he wanted to get to the warm cave quickly. They decided to add about two hundred- and fifty more-foot falls to their count and sure enough - they encountered the path just as he had said.

Up the path they went toward the town of Bethlehem, the grade was not that steep, but it was up, just as Bethlehem was up. The area around the town had been terraced for raising and pasturing sheep, for growing gardens and for general ease of crossing the land. As the city of Bethlehem grew, so did the need to terrace the surrounding area.

There it was. They had to crouch a little to enter the cave, Nitzevet more than Reu since she was taller. Something told her that she would not be taller than him for much longer. He was growing, especially since he had been under the care of Jesse and his family.

In the corner of the cave, Nitzevet noticed a pen of sorts. She pointed out to Reu that it looked like the shepherds would move the larger animals to the back of the cave with lots of straw to lay on and then put the gate up so that they would not move around much in the interior of the cave. She could imagine how the body heat from the animals would probably warm up the cave nicely.

To the left she saw a cleft in the rock hewn out of the stone wall of the cave. It was filled with fresh straw which they probably used as a type of manger. There were other wooden managers around the open floor as well. She could see in one of them an indentation where a young lamb had lain, warm in the bed of straw. In the other far corner was a huge stash of hay, ready to feed any animals who sought shelter in the cave. For some reason, tears came to her eyes at the sight of the indentation of the little lamb's head in the straw and the thought of it lying warm and secure with the caring shepherds around.

It was Nitzevet's way to settle herself in a corner and look around at every detail, familiarizing herself with everything as if she were memorizing the details to share with someone. Then she would imagine all the ways this place could be used, who would be there, who would appreciate the simple warm yet rustic beauty of the place. Sometimes she would invent a story to go along with her imagination, to help her remember and appreciate it.

At that moment, with her young friend next to her, in silence learning how to appreciate as she did, she sensed that this would indeed be a place where Yahweh would be. Someday she knew He would use this place to bless the world. How she knew that was beyond her. She just knew and told no one.

"This is truly a place of Shalom, Reu!" she said.

He whispered back to her, "Yes, I feel it too!"

After quite a long time pondering and enjoying one another's company, they were back on the path toward the tower. Nitzevet looked back at the cave wondering why she felt so drawn to it.

Back at the shepherd's campfire, she picked up her bag, hugged Reu and made her way back to Leah's home where her Ema and grandmother would be waiting for her. She cherished her adventure in her heart. Someday, she would have children to share her adventures with, she knew it.

6

REU'S CHALLENGE

THE FAMOUS 'SEA-PEOPLES' HAD COME to Israel's promised land referred to by the locals as Canaan. They were not a large conquering population, rather they had arrived on the coast in small mobile groups of men who could travel light and take over the small cities that were scattered up and down the coast of the great sea.

The Philistines, as they came to be known, conquered five cities along the coast of the great sea, Ashkelon, Ashdod, Ekron, Gath, and Gezer. The pentapolis, the governmental confederacy of these five cities, was ruled by the five kings called Seranim, one from each city. Each of the five cities enjoyed great autonomy, despite the confederation. Because of their superior fighting ability and advanced arms technology, they were able to insert themselves as a new layer of nobility in the region quickly and without much resistance.

While this area was previously characterized by a thriving urban culture, once the Philistines conquered the area and dominated as rulers, the cities gradually began to resemble villages. These villages showed a decline in the civilized elements of life as well as a decline in living standards. It was as if a dark age had followed in the path of these conquering people, bringing instability to a land where the people had existed and thrived for hundreds, even several thousand years.

נאמנות יהוה

For Reu, life in the pasture was pleasant. He learned quickly and well, Jesse was so pleased, not only to have such a good worker but a good friend. He could always count on Reu to be ready and willing to do what needed to be done and to do it well.

Little did he know that Reu's life was about to be challenged.

No one knew the full details of why Nitzevet found Reu sitting at the Tower in tears a few years ago, only that he had 'escaped' the collapse of the temple of Dagon in Gaza and that his parents had died in the rubble. At that time out of fear, Reu had neglected to add that he and his parents were not free men, they were slaves to one of the largest families in Gaza. The family of Horam was one of the Seranim rulers of the five cities of the Philistines. As time went on, Reu had always intended to tell Jesse the full story of his past life, but the past faded as the present enveloped him with love, kindness, and the knowledge of Yahweh.

As history goes, Horam was killed in the collapse of the temple, but his wife survived, barely. After the rubble had settled, she languished in grief for several years. Everyone and anyone of importance was dead, her husband, her children, her friends, everyone.

After the allotted time of mourning in the Philistine tradition, Horam's wife began looking for the slaves that were lost or had escaped. Reu's body was never found among the ruins, so he was on the list. Since Bethlehem is only a couple of days' journey from Gaza, it was only a matter of time before Horam's family began looking there for the missing slaves.

Reu was resting by the fire with the other shepherds enjoying the respect and comfort of comradery that he had never known existed. He was now twelve years old; he had been in the employment of Obed for almost two years. Happiness could not begin to describe how he felt.

"I heard there were Philistine men in town today," Abiezer mentioned looking at Reu.

His tone was gentle as if he were probing to see what Reu knew. "I did not know," responded Reu quietly, visibly shaken at the news.

For a while now the shepherds had suspected that Reu was hiding something. An average ten-year-old boy does not take to hard labor with relish as Reu did. They do not have the efficient manner and quick step that this young boy exhibited day in and day out. Nor does the average-year-old boy take orders without question. These shepherds had sons and nephews, so they knew. The consensus was that Reu had been a former slave and indeed had been set free in one way or another when the temple was destroyed. Because they cared so much for him, they never pushed for more details, they accepted his word.

Abiezer noticed that Reu looked a bit nervous after the exchange so he spoke up, "Is there something we can do for you?"

Reu had never really trusted anyone since his life had changed so dramatically. Before that he had really only trusted his parents who cared for him well. But he also knew that eventually there was an element of faith in trust. These men had not only welcomed him, and taught him, they had cared for him emotionally and physically as if he were a brother or son. Taking that leap of faith he decided to trust. "Please, if you don't mind, keep my presence a secret?"

Sibbecai and Maharai nodded affirmatively as Abiezer responded smiling, "Your will is our command, young man."

Sibbecai, the oldest shepherd, spoke up, "Reu, we need someone to go with Paarai and take the older flock toward the far eastern pasture of Obed's land. Do you think that you could do that? You will need to be gone for about two weeks."

Reu looked up abruptly and smiled. "Yes sir, I would be glad to."

Sibbecai motioned to Maharai, "Could you help them separate the sheep at dawn and send them on their way? Abiezer, could you pack their supplies, so they have food for fourteen days?"

The next few minutes were spent giving Reu and Paarai some direction regarding local caves near the pasture, and how to get there without much of a path. They were told that there were very few travelers, and they would not see anyone. The older shepherds knew Reu could handle the task and the journey. Boys become men at thirteen in Israel, Reu was almost there. This was a good test for their young friend.

As the shepherds tucked in early for the night, expecting to arise at dawn, Reu quietly spoke with Yahweh, "Thank you for my new family and friends."

"Sir?" Reu tapped Sibbecai on the shoulder.

"Yes?" asked a sleepy Sibbecai.

"Thank you for letting me trust you ... thank you for caring about me," he said as a silent tear slipped down his cheek glistening in the moonlight.

"You are blessed my son and you are welcome," he responded gently. The shepherds slept well that night, especially Reu.

They woke early and separated the sheep that the boys would take from the flock. Gathering their bed rolls and supplies that Abiezer had put together, Reu and Paarai flung their packs over their shoulders, smiled at the shepherds, and then stepped eagerly in front of the sheep to lead them East.

'I am blessed!' he echoed Sibbecai's words in his heart. 'I will be back.'

7

PHILISTINES IN BETHLEHEM

THE TRIBE OF DAN INHERITED the southern coastal plain near the five Philistine cities. After Samson, who was a Danite, destroyed the temple of Dagon in Gaza, some of the Israelites who lived near the Philistine towns grew nervous. Even though they were a war-like tribe they were unable to fully conquer the land they were allotted. They claimed this was due to the superior weaponry of the Philistines and the iron chariots that they used to defend their cities. It was the opinion of other tribes, however, that they would have been able to conquer the land because Yahweh had promised he would be with them and help them.

The leaders of the tribe thought it would be a good idea to send some of the more military-minded families north to conquer other towns. The ben Tzuri'el family was one of these families. After the Danite soldiers conquered the northern town of Laish several families moved up. To please his parents and help them move, Uzzi, his wife Chazael, and their daughter Ednah, made the long journey up to the new town renamed 'Dan', in their new territory at the foot of Mt Hermon at the head of the Jordan river.

After a few months in the little town in the northernmost part of the land of Israel, Uzzi and Chazael felt uncomfortable. They did not know whether it was the rural location or the lack of friends for their daughter since most of the people that moved were soldiers. Uzzi was never really afraid of the Philistines, nor did he understand why he shouldn't pursue a business relationship with them. Uzzi decided to relocate his wife and daughter to Bethlehem, just twelve parasangs away from their original home in the territory of Dan.

Uzzi immediately made himself known throughout Bethlehem as a businessman. He was willing to talk to anyone and give his advice to all who would ask, even those who didn't.

One morning, while sitting at the city gate, Uzzi was supplying the elders of the town with a wealth of knowledge about the metal capabilities of the Philistines. It was new information to Obed since he spent most of his life raising sheep. In the middle of the conversation, Jesse walked up to ask his father a question.

While the father and son talked, Uzzi noted the handsome features of the young man, the strength and boldness of his stride, and the evident confidence that radiated from his presence. 'This man would make a good son-in-law!', he said to himself. It became a mission.

נאמנות יהוה

After Reu and Paarai left, and the morning meal was finished, Sibbecai left Maharai and Abiezer with the flock. He headed to town to talk to Jesse about his decision to send Reu away for a couple weeks.

"Jesse!" called Sibbecai as he saw Jesse walking across the great courtyard near his home.

"Shalom Sibbecai is all well?" worried that something bad had brought Sibbecai in from the fields.

"All is well, but I need to talk to you about Reu," he said as Jesse stiffened. Jesse had developed a bond with the boy but had always been waiting for the other shoe to drop so to speak, since certain things did not add up in Reu's life.

"No, all is well sir. I just made a decision to help the boy and wanted to tell you and to have your blessing," Sibbecai then proceeded to tell Jesse about the Philistines in town who were asking questions. He told Jesse of Reu's response and his gratitude for being able to be far from town.

Sibbecai took this opportunity to share with Jesse his suspicions about the past of their young shepherd. How he was too good of a worker and too efficient and willing to be anything other than a trained slave. Jesse had had the same thoughts, so this was not news. But somehow, these men were relieved to be discussing it together out of their genuine love and respect for such a young boy.

"Sibbecai, I am going to look into the Philistines in town and see what I can find out. I will try to dissuade them from looking further, maybe I could point them in another direction," Jesse pondered his next move.

"I will head back to the flock; we will think about it as well and let you know if we come up with something. Can we speak this evening?" Sibbecai asked.

"Yes, at sunset, here, I will meet you," Jesse responded.

Jesse chided himself for not thinking ahead. He had heard about the Philistines. Bethlehem was a very small town, something like that doesn't go unnoticed by anyone - even the smallest observer.

He headed back to his home and found his sister-in-law Keturah. He had a plan.

"Shalom Keturah. Would you help me this morning?" he asked.

She smiled, "Yes, brother, I would love to help you."

"Will you go to the well this morning and listen for any information about Philistines in town, what they are looking for, and what they have found?" he asked.

Keturah knew what he was asking and surmised why. She liked little Reu and with the wisdom of a mother she had guessed as much that Reu had a past of some kind. Without asking questions she responded, "Yes, I am on my way now," She picked up the water jug, ready to be filled, and walked toward the well.

Jesse decided to go talk to his father and let him in on the conversation and what was taking place, so they could be united and not be caught off guard by lack of knowledge.

Keturah walked up to the well. She noticed that several women were standing around. She could also tell that there was something wrong. It wasn't the calm happy conversations she was used to. There were more concerned looks and whispers.

"Shalom Rebekah how are you?" she asked.

Rebekah smiled as she responded, "Fine Keturah, how is Nitzevet?"

"I haven't seen her in a few weeks, but I think she may be coming to Bethlehem next month ..." Then she asked as she continued to observe the women around them, "Rebekah, why is everyone worried?"

"There are five Philistine men in the city, and it makes everyone uneasy," she whispered.

"Do you know why they are here or what they want?" she asked.

"Something about missing slaves from Gaza. When Samson destroyed the temple of Dagon two years ago, apparently several slaves ran away, and they are out looking for them," Rebekah responded.

They both nodded to each other because they knew that Reu was probably one of those slaves, but he had crept into their hearts and both Keturah and Rebekah were very fond of Reu. They did not even mention his name to each other.

Moving to the next group of women, Keturah forced a smile and greeted them, "Shalom ladies."

"Shalom Keturah," they responded. "Has your family been questioned by the Philistines yet?"

"Questioned?" asked Keturah.

"Yes, they seem to be going house to house, to see if they can find any of their missing people," said Shoshannah.

The ladies all turned to see Ednah approaching, most of them rolled their eyes knowing that Ednah did not fetch water, she fetched information.

"Shalom Ednah!" Keturah stepped up to head her off.

"Hello Keturah, how is your family?" she said.

"Well, thank you! How is your family, Ednah?"

"We are enjoying the news from the coast. New things are happening in Gaza. Ever since moving here, we have not heard what is going on in the world around us. We have enjoyed gathering news from our neighbors," said Ednah.

"Neighbors or Overlords?" asked Keturah.

"Now now, Keturah, just because they are more powerful and skilled craftsmen in bronze and metals, doesn't mean they are our overlords," explained Ednah ignorantly repeating talking points from her father.

"They may be neighbors, Ednah, but they are not good neighbors. They often attack small towns like Bethlehem and take over, enslaving our people," Keturah admonished.

"Tisk tisk, you are so narrow-minded, look at what they provide for us. My father says that they have invented a special metal, that they will sell to us," she said mockingly to Keturah.

Keturah decided to get some information from Ednah for once, "Why do you think they are here?" she questioned offhandedly.

It seemed as if Ednah was pondering, "I am not sure. It seems they are looking for someone. But no matter, my father will get all the information he needs from them about their metal. You will see," She moved on from Keturah to talk to the other women.

Keturah looked at Rebekah and nodded and then filled her jug with water and went through the gate back toward home. She was convinced that Ednah did not care much about why they were in Bethlehem, but she did get some useful information from her.

She encountered Jesse in the courtyard, "They are looking for lost slaves and questioning each family, but it seems that most people do not know about Reu. We have kept him busy and far from the center of things. Those that do know, would never give him up."

Jesse listened and nodded. He knew that Reu was "shepherding" but just realized that Sibbecai had never told him where Reu was, or what his plan was, only that he had one. "Keturah, thank you. Reu is safe, but honestly, I do not know where he is. And you do not know either. Continue to do whatever you can to not acknowledge anything. And thank you!"

Keturah did not need to be thanked; she was fond of Reu, and Jesse knew it.

נאמנות יהוה

As chance would have it, or maybe more than chance, Uzzi spent the next morning with the Philistine men discussing metal and production processes. They were more than willing to discuss.

"The metal workers live in the five cities of the Pentapolis. Do you have metal workshops outside the cities?" Uzzi asked.

Rafi, the most talkative of the soldiers, responded, "No the Rulers do not allow any forges outside the cities. They are hard to keep track of. If we become suspicious of anyone smuggling weapons, we simply shut the city gates and search everyone," Rafi said, not knowing he was giving away military secrets and protocol.

A distracted Rafi winked at Ednah, who sat quietly in the corner having donned her best dress and applied eye makeup as she knew the Philistine men liked. Ednah blushed at his wink.

Uzzi, oblivious to the flirting going on, proceeded to ask more questions, "Do you think the Rulers would be open to another metal forging location if they had ultimate control and a large stake in the profits?"

"I am unsure, I think control over metalwork is of more concern than profit to the rulers," Rafi responded, "at least that is what I have observed."

"Enough talk of metals!" Nerhad, the obvious leader, demanded. "We leave early in the morning to continue our search. We will take our leave now. Thank you, Uzzi, for the meal and conversation."

Rafi reluctantly stood with the rest of his comrades and bowed to Ednah, indicating that he liked her. He stepped closer and said, "I will be back to visit if that is ok with you?"

Even though Ednah knew that approaching her before asking her father was disrespectful, she was beyond pleased and shyly nodded her head and extended her hand. Rafi took her hand and kissed it and then followed the others out into the street.

Uzzi was disappointed. It seemed that a metal forge, sponsored by the Philistines, was out of the question. He knew he could make it work and make it profitable. But he also knew that metal would then be in the hands of the Israelite people, which the Philistines were trying to prevent.

Soon, Ednah would find out that her father was not the only one disappointed by the Philistines. Rafi never returned. She waited day in and day out. Finally, the memory of the flirtatious Philistine was just that, a memory.

8

THE FEAST OF TABERNACLES

DAILY LIFE FOR NITZEVET IN the small town of Efrat was both busy and yet at times lonely. Not having any siblings, Nitzevet's closest confidants were her mother and her grandmother. This was actually an advantage to someone like Nitzevet because her character as well as her understanding of things around her was much more advanced than her friends that lived in Efrat. Her days were filled with walking beside these two women who taught her everything and engaged with her in conversation as if she were a friend.

Nitzevet, however, often lamented the negative side of this arrangement, especially when she was with her friends. As she grew, she had less and less in common with girls of her age. At home, Nitzevet was involved in the conversations of Yahweh, and national and town politics. She would often hear Shelach expound on the evils of the sons of Eli, Hophni, and Phineas.

These two men kept coming up as the topic of conversation in many Hebrew households. Because Eli was the high priest and judge of Israel, it was obvious that people would be concerned when his sons were so evil. Hannah would often visit her friends and share what she learned from Samuel about the state of the leadership of Israel. Since he lived with Eli as a priest in training, he had a front-row seat to the antics of these two priests who did not know Yahweh, and their lifestyles proved it. Samuel's life was often impacted by their evil behavior, and he could see the toll it was taking on his mentor Eli.

נאמנות יהוה

It was time to celebrate the Feast of Tabernacles. Nitzevet was fifteen and her little family decided to celebrate the Day of Atonement in Efrat on the tenth day of the seventh month and then make the journey to Bethlehem on the fourteenth, the day before the first day of the seven-day Feast of Tabernacles. Nitzevet loved this festival because it coincided with the completion of the harvest and was a wonderful opportunity to give thanks to Yahweh for providing for them. There was also lots of delicious food. The Torah had instructed them to celebrate God's blessing on the seven major crops: grapes, figs, pomegranates, olives, honey, wheat, and barley. One of the special ways Moses commanded them to observe this holiday was to sleep in homemade booths under the stars for seven nights. These 'tabernacles' were to remind the people of the forty years in the wilderness, where their ancestors lived, when their God had provided food, water, and protection.

The little family left Efrat early in the morning and arrived in Bethlehem that afternoon. After spending the night at the Obed home, the whole family packed up their booths and food supplies and set up their living space by the Tower to spend the next seven nights camped on Obed's land. The shepherds loved this tradition when the family joined them and celebrated the feast while they enjoyed a wonderful time of friendship, stories, and food enjoyed by everyone with thanksgiving.

One of the highlights were the stories that Shelach prepared each year to share with the group, special stories from their ancient past. There were some younger children among them who were now of the age to hear these stories. Reu and Nitzevet were among those who were younger.

The meal of warm stew and unleavened bread somehow tasted better under the stars in the shadow of the Tower, thought Nitzevet. Maybe it was the presence of her family and her shepherds, maybe it was the laughter that was shared and the joy that was present. It all made for a wonderful time together.

Gila and Leah passed out cups of warm spiced milk while Shelach moved his stool closer to the center of the group and the fire so that everyone could hear and see him as he told the stories.

Finally, the group settled. Rebekah and her family had joined the ben Obed family by sleeping under the stars, as did many of their neighbors. Rebekah snuggled in with Nitzevet and they prepared to listen.

"Yahweh is the highest among the gods. He is good. He is the God of gods. He is the Lord of Lords. He alone does great wonders, who by his understanding made the heavens, who spread out the earth upon the waters, who made the great lights—the sun to govern the day, the moon and stars to govern the night; to him who struck down the firstborn of Egypt and brought Israel out from among them with a mighty hand and outstretched arm; to him who divided the Red Sea asunder and brought Israel through the midst of it, but swept Pharaoh and his army into the Red Sea; to him who led his people through the wilderness; to him who struck down great kings, and killed mighty kings—Sihon king of the Amorites and Og king of Bashan—and gave their land as an inheritance, an inheritance to his servant Israel.

My friends, the angels who we call 'Watchers' were part of Yahweh's council. Yahweh chose to operate in a bureaucracy with a counsel of angels, whom He called the Benei Elohim. These angels were the watcher angels set over humanity to watch them. But these angels, long ago, did not keep their positions of authority and righteousness but abandoned their proper dwelling. Two hundred of these celestial beings conspired together to come to earth to take the human women as their wives. They came to earth at Mt Hermon which is located to the north of our brothers of Manasseh. These evil elohim had offspring with the women on earth and produced the Nephilim.

These wayward celestial beings along with their vile offspring corrupted the whole earth with their evil ways and spread knowledge that was never intended for mankind. Yahweh sent the flood to destroy everyone, except Noah and his wife and three sons and their wives. Yahweh imprisoned the two hundred watcher angels until the end of the age.

The sad thing as you all know, is there were more fallen Watcher class angels. Remember the Tower of Babel after the great flood, when mankind conspired to create a one-world government under the control of Nimrod? Yahweh confused their languages and divided mankind into seventy nations to prevent them from ever creating a one-world government again. As a punishment, He set over each nation a watcher angel to watch each nation. These were not righteous angels. They have caused much grief. They defend the unjust and they show partiality to the wicked. Ultimately friends, Yahweh will destroy them.

Yet we can rejoice because Yahweh reserved for Himself Abraham. Yahweh alone rules over the descendants of Abraham. We have Yahweh, He is ours," Shelach bowed his head for a moment to silently thank Yahweh for His gracious provision for Israel. With his knowledge and understanding of the evil of these angels, Shelach knew what it meant to belong to Yahweh.

He continued, "We have struggled so much when we came into this promised land, because of the Nephilim. After the flood, Moses told us that these Nephilim were still on the earth, some people call them Anakim. Remember my beloved friends what Joshua said, "There were none of the Anakim left in the land of the people of Israel. Only in Gaza, in Gath, and in Ashdod do some remain."

Several people stole a glance in Reu's direction, not with judgment but with compassion. They knew that he understood more than any of them what the descendants of the Nephilim were like. Reu felt their attention and in a motion of hopelessness shrugged his shoulders.

Shelach smiled at Reu in encouragement then continued, "We are never to fear these people, never. Yahweh commanded us through Moses, 'See, the Lord your God has set the land before you. Go up, take possession, as the Lord, the God of your fathers, has told you. Do not fear or be dismayed.' However, we are to take seriously the damage that they can do to our culture and our faith if we allow them even the slightest opening."

Shelach loved talking about Yahweh and His special purpose for His People, Israel. He was saddened that on so many occasions, the Hebrew people did not respond in the same manner toward their God.

Reu leaned back as Shelach was talking and remembered his experiences. When he lived in Gaza, his mother would take him to the marketplace on occasion to purchase supplies for the household. On several occasions, he caught a glimpse of giant people, men, who were walking through the marketplace. His mother explained that they were another race, but that is all she would say. They were very large and very scary. He shivered thinking, 'I am glad that I never encountered one of them alone.'

Rebekah saw Reu shiver and surmised what he was thinking about, suddenly she realized there was more about Reu that she did not know.

Rebekah's heart filled with compassion as she pondered the young man sitting a few yards from her. How frightening for him, she was glad that he was here now, with the people who had become his new family.

Obed asked the question, "So the watchers over the seventy nations were not the same watchers who created the Nephilim before the flood of Noah?" He knew the answer, but he thought Shelach would give a good answer for the listeners.

Shelach smiled, knowing what Obed was doing, "No. Actually, our God did not spare these evil angels when they sinned but cast them into Tartarus and committed them to chains of gloomy darkness forever. The seventy Watchers who were put in charge of the nations at Babel were different angels, some were equally as evil and their fate is the same, death like man."

Shelach realized it was late and the men had allowed the fire to die down a bit, so he stood up to pronounce the blessing as was his usual practice every night of the feast of Tabernacles: "The Lord bless you and keep you; the Lord make his face shine on you and be gracious to you; the Lord turn his face toward you and give you peace."[6]

He slowly picked up his stool and walked to his sleeping mat in his booth. The mothers roused the little children and prodded the adolescents onto their bed rolls. Soon the whole camp was asleep, apart from a few appointed shepherds to watch the flock which grazed nearby.

Nitzevet could smell the sheep as the breeze ruffled her hair. It was a welcome smell for her, sheep were a comfort to her. She snuggled next to Rebekah and was soon lost in her thoughts about Watchers and Nephilim. Her last thoughts landed on the gracious provision of Yahweh and His graciousness, and the shining face of the heavenly messenger who visited her three years ago on her twelfth birthday, in this very spot.

9

A BONDSERVANT

EDNAH'S BIRTHDAY WAS SUPPOSED TO be a joyful occasion. Her mother had planned for this day for quite some time, hoping to make her eighteenth birthday a special celebration. Chazael knew her daughter was frustrated that she was not yet married or even engaged. As her mother, Chazael knew there was not much she could do, deep down she knew Ednah had yet to become the kind of person that a young man would desire as a wife.

As Ednah prepared for her party her character was reflected in her demeanor. Rather than celebrating, she was frustrated and bitter about her single state. She wanted to be married. She wanted to have wealth and prestige. She had neither.

"Come along my dear, your friends are arriving for your party," Chazael coaxed her from her room.

"Friends, what friends!" the petulant young woman responded.

"Don't be bitter, Ednah. These are your friends and they have arrived to celebrate this special day with you. Put on a smile and come out now," Her mother was losing patience.

Ednah stepped out of her room and surveyed the group of girls who were gathering. She noticed Rebekah among the young women, she barely knew her, it might have been more truthful to say she knew of her. Ednah thought to herself 'mother was really reaching to invite people that I don't even know to my party'. Then the thought occurred to her, she knew that Rebekah was close to the ben Obed family ... and Jesse. 'Maybe if I make friends with Rebekah, it will give me an introduction to Jesse.'

'This is going to be better than I thought!' Ednah again thought to herself and put on a smile as she walked over to the unsuspecting Rebekah.

נאמנות יהוה

It was late fall; Jesse was wrapped in a sheepskin to ward off the chill in the air. As he sat next to Reu he was lost in his thoughts as he watched the flock and pondered his life, one of his favorite things to do. A deep thinker who loved to commune with Yahweh. He was twenty-four and knew that he needed to choose a bride soon. It was expected. But he just didn't feel as if the time was right, he was not one to rush into things. He wanted to admire and cherish the woman he would choose like his dad cherished his mother. Like his grandfather, Boaz cherished his wife Ruth, what a love story that was. He longed for the same, he had to admit he was a romantic.

"Jesse, why did you take me in?" Reu blurted out in the darkness. Reu's puzzled look was obvious to Jesse. The two friends were alone with the flock that was starting to get restless, they needed water. Jesse surmised that this was an important conversation, so he stood up and started to walk through the flock to lead them to water, Jesse could always think better while walking.

Jesse looked over at Reu who was following him and paused for a moment, thinking. Most of Jesse's friends were comfortable with the walking and thoughtful pauses, Reu, one of Jesse's closest friends understood more than anyone. They all knew, having spent time with Jesse, that waiting patiently would produce a good answer.

"Because of Nitzevet," said Jesse continuing to amble through the pastureland. "Because when Nitzevet speaks, she speaks with wisdom, kindness, justice, and compassion. Those of us who are blessed enough to know her and grow up with her, have learned to listen well and observe what she says."

Reu had never been part of a culture where women were respected. All cultures put men above women and to varying degrees disrespected them. Not these people, Yahweh's people. It was as if they considered their women as precious and worthy of protection.

"I have a lot to thank Nitzevet for, don't I?" asked Reu.

"Yes. But also remember, that once I did listen to Nitzevet, I learned to cherish you as my own brother. You are a good friend Reu, I am glad you are here with us," Jesse said.

As Reu nodded and walked back through the flock toward home, Jesse knew that Reu turned so his tears would not show. He felt blessed to have such a good and loyal friend. All those around Jesse and Reu had learned to appreciate their relationship. They saw an example of a selfless friendship of two very unequal and unlike souls who just loved each other, maybe because of Nitzevet, who was like an older sister to one of them and maybe something else to the other.

As Reu grew and learned and followed Jesse everywhere he was known far and wide as a "shepherd of the tower". Only a few knew that not only was this where he met his destiny with Yahweh and the family of Jesse and Nitzevet, but where he felt most at home, most loved in this world. Reu listened well, especially to Jesse and Obed. But one could often find Reu sitting in the corner of the kitchen and listening to Leah talk and sing about Yahweh.

One of the reasons that Reu grew and flourished was because these people lived and breathed their God. They truly loved Him as a guide and friend, not just a deity to give them what they wanted or to be afraid of. Reu, as a Philistine child, was taught only to fear the god dagon.

One morning, several months after the incident with the Philistines, Reu knew what he must do, what he wanted to do. After spending all day with the flock and with Yahweh, he made his way to the river, bathed, and put on a clean tunic. He proceeded to go in search of Jesse.

"Jesse!" Reu called from across the pasture.

Jesse smiled, "Shalom, shalom, Reu!"

Walking right up to Jesse he blurted out in all seriousness, "Will you allow me to be your bond servant?"

Jesse stepped back and observed his friend, what a strange request. "Reu, what an odd request, you are a free man. You are my valued worker and treasured friend, why do you want this?" asked Jesse bewildered.

"Jesse, I have come to love your family. You are my brother, beyond what I could have imagined a brother to be. I want to forever be a part of this family, to pledge my life to live here. To protect your flocks, your family and you," Reu explained.

"But Reu ..." Jesse stammered.

"Let me continue, Jesse. I have always been a slave; it is what I am and what I know. I will always be looking over my shoulder for the Philistines to find me." For impact he repeated himself, "They will always be looking for me. But if you claim me as your bond servant, and mark my ear, they cannot argue. I was very young when I came here, and you took me in and made me your servant. They respect the laws of slaves." Reu looked up at Jesse hopeful.

"I cannot argue with your logic, Reu. But you must know, you will have the mark of a bond slave, forever," Jesse explained.

"I understand," Reu said.

"You will always be my brother and my friend," Jesse smiled.

"And Jesse, I want your God, Yahweh, to be my God. I want to serve Him as you do."

Reu could tell that Jesse was blessed by this request and by his friendship. Jesse's hug was warm and welcoming, like a hug from a long-lost brother. Jesse granted him his wish, "Yes Reu, you can pledge yourself to my family, if that is truly what you want."

Jesse and Reu went home for dinner and then Jesse indicated to his father that there was something he wanted his help with. As they walked Jesse explained to his father what Reu had asked for. Obed had grown close to the boy as Jesse had.

"Are you sure he knows what he is asking for?" questioned Obed.

"He knows that he will never be free of his Philistine overlords unless he is bound to another family. He also knows that being a slave to the ben Obed family is more like being a part of a loving family than a slave. You can't deny it, Father, all the people of town know that our slaves and servants really are our family," laughed Jesse.

Obed smiled, "Yes son, I know. Yahweh has shown us that we are to love one another and that all people are equally valuable no matter their station in life. If there are those of us who have the power and authority to be over others, we might as well use that power and authority to make their lives better, not worse."

"I am fine with Reu becoming your bondservant. As long as he knows that may mean something different to others than it means to our family," said Obed.

"Thank you, Father, we will have the ceremony tomorrow evening after an evening meal, by the Tower," Jesse informed his father.

"Why by the Tower?" asked Obed.

"It is what Reu has requested. It was there he ended up when his world fell apart and where he met Nitzevet and I. It was there he was welcomed by the Shepherds. It is there where he wants to become part of our family," explained Jesse. Obed smiled as tears clouded his eyes.

The next evening the men gathered. The shepherds were there as well. Reu knew that at this ceremony would be those men who cherished him. He knew that pledging his life to someone forever was serious. But he also knew the kindness, generosity, and character of the family of Obed went deep to the bone. He rejoiced with his new family and after his ear was pierced and Jesse put on the salve, they all sat down by the fire to enjoy the evening of fellowship and laughter together.

10

FATHER AND SON

OBED MADE IT A POINT to seek out each of his sons and talk to them individually. He loved these moments with each, knowing that this is where he would learn the details of their lives and the secrets that they wished to share with him. At this time, he was seeking out Jesse. It has been a few months since he had the opportunity for a father-son conversation with his youngest son and he had something on his mind. Not an easy thing to bring up to your son, a suggestion for a wife, and not even a suggestion that settled well with Obed. Ednah was not exactly what Obed was looking for in a daughter-in-law.

"Shalom, Jesse," Obed greeted his son.

He could see Jesse's smile, "Shalom father!" Obed knew Jesse loved these moments with him.

Obed decided to start the conversation with a question rather than jumping in with his own agenda straight away, "I have noticed that you have been more pensive as of late. What is on your mind son?"

"Father, you know I am in my twenty-fifth year," Jesse began. Obed nodded, willing to let his son continue without interruption. "It is time I found a wife," Again, Obed nodded, hoping to control his exuberance as Jesse brought up the very subject on his mind before he had to.

"Father, I know who I want as my wife," proclaimed Jesse.

Obed could not keep silent, for this was news to him, "Who son?"

"Nitzevet!"

Obed thought for a long moment, and all the past ten years finally made sense to him. Things he had noticed in the moment finally had meaning that coalesced into an understanding that this was not a new conclusion that Jesse had come to. This match has been in the making for some time.

This, however, did not bode well for what Obed needed to discuss with Jesse, but there was no time like the present to get it all out on the table. "Son, I have been in communication for the past year with Uzzi ben Tzuri'el, about his daughter Ednah," He paused to see if there was any response from Jesse.

"Is that the family from the tribe of Dan that moved here a few years back?"

"Yes, how did you know they were of the tribe of Dan?" he asked.

"I heard talk in the town, they are from the north originally. There is quite a lot of animosity toward the Danites not only because of their blatant idolatry but that they rejected the land that Yahweh gave them and went north. I am not sure why her family moved here."

Obed forged ahead, "Anyway, Uzzi's daughter has come of age ..."

Suddenly, Jesse leaped up from his perch on the rock he had been sitting on and stood staring at his father, realizing now why he had brought up Ednah in the midst of a conversation about marriage.

Obed recognized the look on his son's face and knew that Jesse was not pleased. He could see that his son was biting his tongue because he knew that it would be difficult to take back words spoken in haste.

"I know that I should have come to you sooner," he said with a tone that he hoped would calm his son down. "But to be honest, I was hoping the whole thing would go away. Maybe he would find someone else for his daughter. He is taken with your character, so he says. I, however, think he is more taken with your position and inheritance, not to diminish your character, my son."

Jesse was calming down a bit. He recognized that his father had been put into this position and had done nothing wrong. "I am sorry for my hasty reaction father. I am just not used to finding out information long after I should have known about it."

Obed, nodded, "Point taken son," Obed had a way with his sons. Treating them like men when they were very young enabled them to grow into manhood with grace and wisdom.

"Father, how do we make this go away? I do not want to humiliate or alienate anyone."

"Let me think about it, son, and we will see what we can do," Obed smiled reassuringly.

As a man of Yahweh, Obed knew that Yahweh himself was the orchestrator of these things.

"Father, what do you think of MY choice?" questioned Jesse, "Do you approve?"

Obed clapped his son on the back and with a wholehearted reply said, "Absolutely!"

Obed was very pleased. He loved Nitzevet as his own daughter and she and her family were closer to his family than anyone. Obed had always left these matters to his sons, to make their own choices. More importantly, he trusted in Yahweh to lead them to the right wife. He had learned this from his mother. Having been raised in a culture of false gods, his mother, a Moabite woman choosing to follow the Israelite God Yahweh, had uncommon insight into the leading, guiding and blessing of Yahweh.

Leah had been searching for her husband all morning. She was supposed to tell him of a large order for lambs from a neighboring tribe. It really was getting warm, and she needed to get back to her chores. Typically, she would find him in the stables on the way to the Tower, but not there, she decided to wander out to the field where he often would sit and think. She noticed from a distance that Obed was with Jesse, and they were talking. Not wanting to interrupt their conversation, she quietly approached and waited. And it was in that moment when she overheard Jesse proclaim who he wanted for a wife.

After the shock of the instant knowledge, she also had the same reaction as Obed. So many things made sense. Quietly, Leah backed away from the men. Forgetting her purpose for being there, she made her way back to the village, letting the men discuss this very important matter alone. The sky was so blue, the trees were so green, and she could hear the bubbling of the not-so-far-away brook, there was just something about good news like this that made the day better.

Leah, stepped through the door of her home and after kneeling beside her bed she quietly thanked Yahweh. This was wonderful news, and she was pleased to know that Yahweh had allowed her to know. Leah believed that nothing was ever out of the scope of Yahweh's knowledge. Even allowing her to know of her son's desire to marry Nitzevet was God's gift to her. She prayed that it would all come to be according to her God's plan.

Remembering the promise of Yahweh to bring forth a Redeemer, Leah, a romantic at heart and a lover of God, also part of the Remnant would always think, could this be the way her God would bring forth His Redeemer, through Jesse and Nitzevet? Those who were taught about the expectation of a Messiah, an anointed one, were often called the Remnant. They knew that in the Torat Moshe, it stated that Judah would be the tribe that produced the Messiah:

"The scepter will not depart from Judah, nor the ruler's staff from between his feet, until he to whom it belongs shall come and the obedience of the nations shall be his."[7]

Leah remembered when her father-in-law, Boaz would often quote the "blessing" that Yahweh spoke about for Israel would be the coming Messiah:

"I will make you into a great nation, and I will bless you; I will make your name great, and you will be a blessing. I will bless those who bless you, and whoever curses you I will curse; and all peoples on earth will be blessed through you."[8]

Leah sighed a sigh of joy, only time will tell.

נאמנות יהוה

Jesse was glad that his father had taken the responsibility of informing Ednah's father that he was off the market for a wife. Ednah was not the kind of woman he was seeking. He remembered hearing bits and pieces of information about Ednah, that this particular young woman often got her way. It is difficult to live in a small town and not know some of the character flaws of those living in close proximity. He secretly prayed that Yahweh would help his father take care of what might be a very sticky situation and then thanked Yahweh for allowing him to choose Nitzevet as his wife. She was the woman he desired.

A bit old-fashioned in his thinking about marriage he believed it was the man that chose his wife. Yet, being the gentleman that Obed raised him to be, Jesse also was seeking a woman who actually wanted to be his wife. He felt very strongly that marriage was a mutual endeavor, created by Yahweh to bring joy to everyone. Working together, raising a family with a wife you truly loved and who truly respected her husband in return was something that Jesse cherished in his parent's marriage and longed for in his own marriage.

He thought of Nitzevet. Beyond her beauty, she was sweet and kind and ... full of life. Nitzevet did love life. She embraced every moment with passion. Whether it was the animals and nature, cooking and creating delicious food, or discussing politics and the law, he was amazed at the depth of her understanding of all things. He laughed as he imagined raising a family with her at his side, what joy they would have. He prayed that he would never disappoint Nitzevet.

His thoughts turned back to the problem at hand, maybe he had it wrong about Ednah, maybe she wasn't even involved yet in the matchmaking. Maybe, all would be well, and Uzzi would seek a suitable mate for his daughter from another family. Jesse was still worried.

נאמנות יהוה

Dalit was so excited; Leah was coming to Efrat for a visit. She was so pleased to be able to host her friend and niece. Gila too was exuberant, she considered Leah her best friend as well as a cousin. The three women had such a close and unique relationship that Dalit had observed the other women in Efrat speaking of their friendship with respect and sometimes jealousy.

But it went deeper than that, not only were they cousins, and friends, but they were united in their closeness to Yahweh. When they got together, they would talk about what Yahweh was doing and they would pray for one another and for their people.

Leah arrived in the warmth of the afternoon, tired and dusty, and was greeted by her cousin Dalit.

"After you get settled Leah, please come out and we will have refreshments," Dalit was always a gracious hostess. "We have sent Shelach off to his friend's house for evening meal, so that we will have girl time - just the four of us."

"I will be right out!" It was obvious that Leah was eager to speak with her friends.

Dalit knew that Leah had something special to share with them. She could sense it and told Gila. They chatted quietly as they waited patiently on the shady roof of the house for Leah.

"I am so excited to share with you some very delicate news," began Leah. "Please remember, I am sharing this with you so that we can pray for Yahweh's will and purposes."

"Please continue, we understand," said Dalit.

Leah looked around and asked, "Where is Nitzevet?"

"I think our girl is in the fields roaming as usual."

Leaning over to Gila and Dalit, Leah said, "Jesse wants to marry Nitzevet."

Dalit gasped and looked over at Gila whose face was bright with a knowing smile.

"You knew?" Leah asked, looking at Gila.

"Yes. Not because anyone has told me anything, only as a mother knows instinctively the heart of her daughter," Gila responded smiling and looking at her mother. "Just as you have always known mine."

"The looks that I have seen from Jesse, the blush that I noticed from Nitzevet in Jesse's presence. Yes, I knew 'something'," laughed Gila.

Dalit interjected, "Well, I am just pleased as I can be. We love Jesse."

The women continued to talk into the evening. They agreed that their Yahweh had His hand in this, and they would leave all the details to Him. They talked about how they would not mention it to anyone, and they would try to act surprised when they were told. Dalit knew that her job now was to bring the whole situation before Yahweh, asking Him for His blessing and presence.

נאמנות יהוה

The weight of this delicate situation made it difficult for Obed to find a way forward.

He knew he needed to solve the issue and shut it down, so Obed invited Uzzi over to speak with him about the marriage situation. Silently,

Obed prayed that Yahweh would work out the details and help him find a way to appease Uzzi without hurt feelings and grudges.

Uzzi approached the house of Obed and Leah with a smile on his face. As Obed watched him approach, he sighed, it appeared to Obed that Uzzi was expecting good news regarding the marriage plans between Jesse and Ednah.

"Greetings neighbors!" Uzzi said warmly as he embraced Obed in the courtyard and nodded at Leah.

"Shalom, Uzzi" Obed responded.

"Shalom," offered Leah.

"Please come take a seat, Leah has prepared some refreshments of cool goat's milk and her renowned date oat cakes, help yourself," Obed passed the basket of oat cakes and then proceeded to pour a healthy goblet of cold milk for each of them.

As Uzzi took a big bite of date cake and savored the sweetness, he sat quietly waiting for Obed to start the conversation. Obed cleared his throat and prayed for courage, "I have invited you here to give you some news. After speaking with Jesse, I have come to the knowledge that he has a maiden in mind that he would like to marry."

Obed could visibly see Uzzi's face go white as he processed the information. It wasn't so much anger he could see wash across his face in that instant as it was a disappointment and maybe even a hint of fear. Uzzi took a long drink of his milk, using the pause to stir up courage, he set the glass down and looked at Obed. "I am so sorry to hear that. I thought we had an agreement. I thought you were the leader of this household, and that Jesse would do as you say."

Now Obed was not easily rattled, and so rather than take offense immediately, he began to explain the situation. "Uzzi, we are different, in our family, we …" Uzzi rudely lifted his hand and waved him off, obviously not wanting to hear an explanation.

"Your family may be different, but it is of no concern to me. Your promise was made."

Not being able to tolerate people who do not listen well, Obed began to let Uzzi know exactly the state of the situation. Changing the tone of his voice, he continued: "In no way did I promise you anything. If you remember every conversation, we had you will notice that I never even implied a promise or the hint of a promise," Obed continued to raise his voice as he slowly stood, "In fact, my exact words were, "let me speak with Jesse', at every turn, in every conversation. Now that I have spoken with Jesse, you have my answer. Nay, you have more than that, you have my promise, Jesse intends to marry someone else," Obed extended his arm, pointing to the door with firm encouragement for his visitor to leave.

It was obvious that Uzzi was not willing to make an enemy, especially of Obed ben Boaz, and leave on such abrupt terms, so he calmed his voice and bowed to Obed, "I am sorry to have made assumptions. Please forgive me for my haste. I remember, you never made a promise, I think it was my wishful thinking and hope that implied the promise. Please forgive me and let us remain friends?"

Always willing to redeem a friendship, Obed agreed and patted his friend on the back saying, "All is well, all is well."

Obed watched as Uzzi left differently than he had come, dejected, sad and disappointed, still holding half his date cake as if it was the only token of value he had. Obed wondered what the hint of fear that he sensed was all about.

11

A DILEMMA

MONTHS HAD GONE BY SINCE her birthday and acquaintance with Rebekah. Every day, every week, every month brought hope to Ednah's heart that she would someday be Jesse's wife. Her father had all but promised that he would make it happen. And Ednah made sure that what she was promised, she received.

What a handsome man, she thought to herself. At eighteen years of age, she had hoped to have already been married for the past few years. It was her one goal in life, to marry well. To Ednah, "to marry well" meant wealth and respect. Jesse's family had both and more. The leading sheep herding family in the area, the son of Obed, the grandson of Boaz, who at one time for a short time judged Israel.

'Could she ask for more?' She smiled. He will be mine and we will be rich and respected.

"Ema, when did Papa say he was going to talk to Obed?" she sweetly asked her mother.

Chazael responded, "I believe it was this very afternoon he was invited over for refreshment," apparently perceiving precisely what Ednah was up to.

Ednah knew that her mother also wanted a son-in-law that brought great respect and a sizable bride price known as a mohar. She watched as her mother went to the hidden shelf in the wall of their home. Glancing behind her to make sure that no one else was watching, an old habit as an Israelite living in a theocracy, she quickly removed the little icon from the hidden alcove and handed it to her daughter.

"Go put this under your pillow. It might bring us luck," her mother told her.

Ednah obediently, without a second thought, took the little dagon image and put it under her pillow. It was a common practice in her house to ask the grain god for what they wanted. Sometimes for a good harvest, sometimes for restoring health. Why not ask for a good marriage? She needed all the help she could get if she was going to pull this off. Ednah knew that she was not the prettiest of girls in Bethlehem and a stranger for the most part. She knew she wasn't the brightest either, men were always rambling on about something she couldn't fathom, but when did men every marry women for their minds?

Ednah fondly remembered the stone arches of her second home in Laish, the beautiful little town in the shadow of Mt Hermon. A chill went down her spine at the thought of Mt Hermon, as beautiful as it was ominous, like there was an evil presence there. She shook the feeling away and went back to her pleasant thoughts. The silver idols from Micah were still there, proudly displayed for all to worship. Unlike this dumpy little town of Bethlehem, Ednah couldn't believe there were no idols set up so there was more of a choice for worship. The priests of her town willingly and proudly served the idols and Yahweh at the same time. Nobody in Dan seemed to be bothered by the combination of gods like they were here in Bethlehem.

נאמנות יהוה

"NOOOO!" screamed Ednah as she threw the clay cup she was holding across the room, smashing it into little pieces as it hit the floor. "I want Jesse as my husband! Father, you promised!"

Uzzi had just returned from Obed's home and decided to share the news immediately and get it over with. Ednah continued to rage for a while, he knew her disappointment was real but still manipulative. Typically, her tantrums eventually got her what she wanted. Uzzi usually gave in when the rage of his daughter reached a certain level, but this matter could not be resolved by him caving to her wishes. He could tell even now that she began to switch tactics, and he watched as she melted into a heap of tears and anguish. In the past, he could have never resisted that tactic. But this was a different matter.

"My daughter, there, there, my daughter, if it were in my power to grant your wish, I would do it in an instant!" He tried to console her.

"But at last, we are dealing with other people, another family, who have desires and wishes of their own. Jesse already has a wife in mind," Uzzi spoke those last few words very quietly hoping to slip them in.

Sitting up quickly, Uzzi could see the tears drying on her cheeks as his daughter questioned him, "What did you say?"

This is what Uzzi had feared when he was told that Jesse had a wife chosen, that Ednah would find some way to make this poor girl's life miserable. "He has a wife in mind," he sighed.

"Who is it, I must know!" Ednah demanded with a calculating tone.

"I do not know. I did not ask. It is not my concern," he reluctantly sighed.

"I will know. I will find out. I will make it my concern!" hissed Ednah mockingly, as she stomped out of the room, into her small room.

נאמנות יהוה

She was not getting any younger, everyone knew it, she could hear the whispers between her parents. Every moment was spent thinking of ways to find Jesse's love interest. She must stop this infatuation; she must have Jesse for herself. Ednah had started going to the well for water every morning a few days ago, getting up was so hard, but she must.

Shuffling her way to the city gate where the well for the residents of Bethlehem was, Ednah hoped to find someone to question. 'I have to be careful,' she thought to herself, 'I can't be too obvious.' Pleasantly surprised she saw Rebekah, remembering that she would probably know who Jesse is intending to marry, "Hello Rebekah, how are you today?"

"Shalom Ednah," Rebekah responded without much enthusiasm, yet with a gentle smile to be polite.

"Have you heard of anyone engaged yet in town? Any news at all, even whispers?" nudged Ednah her manipulative tone was obvious to all who were listening.

Ednah was hoping that Rebekah didn't know what she was up to, but she could tell Rebekah was suspicious.

Rebekah responded simply, "No. I have not," To steer the conversation she continued, "It seems that people are not so interested in getting engaged during this time of the year. The month of Av is a rather somber time of year," explained Rebekah.

Ednah looked puzzled, unaware that Rebekah had so adeptly turned the conversation, "We did not celebrate Av in Dan."

"Ednah, you do not 'celebrate' Av," Rebekah explained. "We 'observe' Tisha B'Av. We meet on the ninth of Av in the evening and fast and pray while we listen to the reading of the scroll," instructed Rebekah.

"How dreadfully boring. Fasting, as in not eating? Why would anyone want to fast?" questioned Ednah.

The whole town had heard the rumors that the family from Dan had moved down from the north and that they did not fit well into the culture at Bethlehem. It was becoming more and more obvious that they were woefully uneducated as to the standards of conduct and rules of observance in a normal Israelite town. Anyone could tell that Rebekah was a bit shocked that even though they had been residents for a few years now, the family of Uzzi had not yet observed the ninth of Av.

"Ednah, would you like to come over for refreshment after I draw the water? You could walk with me!" invited Rebekah as she pondered how to educate this unsuspecting girl.

Not having anything else to do and growing weary of the dust and heat, Ednah agreed that she would go with Rebekah.

As the girls walked, Rebekah began to talk about the feasts of Israel. She told Ednah which was her favorite and why. When she saw Ednah raise her eyebrow on a particular topic, she would question her and find out what exactly she did not understand and then explain it. Rebekah was only a few months older than Ednah, so at the age of eighteen, she was wise and kind. Not only that, as a lover of Yahweh, she knew that He loved Israel and that He had a special purpose for them in history and even walked with them on a personal level.

When they reached Rebekah's home, she put down the water jug and invited Ednah into the cool interior of the house so they could quench their thirst.

Ednah licked her lips as she saw Rebekah put out the date cakes on a small platter and pour the cool goat's milk into jars. She was hungry and thirsty.

Rebekah continued, "One of my favorite passages in the scrolls is the first part of the last scroll of the Torah. It is Moses' writing, and he says,

> 'See, I have taught you decrees and laws as the Lord my God commanded me, so that you may follow them in the land you are entering to take possession of it. Observe them carefully, for this will show your wisdom and understanding to the nations, who will hear about all these decrees and say, "Surely this great nation is a wise and understanding people." What other nation is so great as to have their gods near them the way the Lord our God is near us whenever we pray to him? And what other nation is so great as to have such righteous decrees and laws as this body of laws I am setting before you today? Only be careful and watch yourselves closely so that you do not forget the things your eyes have seen or let them fade from your heart as long as you live. Teach them to your children and to their children after them.'" [9]

Rebekah took Ednah's silence for interest and continued, "My life's goal is to have children and teach them about Yahweh."

Ednah was not in the least interested in Rebekah's carefully chosen passage of the Torah or her words. She was thinking about Jesse and what her next step should be. Then she heard Rebekah's comment about children and stopped short.

Looking at Rebekah with suspicion she narrowed her eyes and asked, "Are you planning on marrying anyone in particular?"

Rebekah paused and replied, "No actually, no one has asked for my hand, and since we are not wealthy nor have great standing, I am not sure anyone will."

Ednah was not even aware of the sadness that had come over her 'friend'. Her voice smacked with relief as she blundered on, "I am so glad to hear …" and then catching herself in a rare moment of self-awareness continued, "I mean … maybe during this month, it is not best to think about such things," she stuttered, as she stumbled over a few details of her newfound knowledge.

Rebekah wiped the tear that had escaped and questioned Ednah, "Why are you so interested in people getting betrothed right now?"

Ednah had not expected the question and hemmed and hawed - she had not expected to be asked outright what she was up to and had not prepared an answer. She blurted out, "I was just wondering who Jesse ben Obed was going to be betrothed to," Ednah figured she might as well tell the truth since befriending Rebekah was turning out to be so much work.

"Well, Ednah, I guess I can't help you much in that area, I just don't know Jesse that well. It has been lovely chatting with you. I do need to get to my chores before the day wears on and it gets too hot to do them. Thank you for stopping by," and with that she ushered Ednah out of her home still holding half of her date cake.

As Rebekah pondered the conversation with Ednah that afternoon, it all made sense as she put the pieces together. Jesse was a friend, his family was well known to be friends with everyone, as well as leaders in the community. It was not yet common knowledge that Jesse and Nitzevet were courting. In fact, as close as Rebekah was to Nitzevet, and as often as they had talked about Yahweh and His plans, she did not know for sure. She suspected. She had seen the looks between them and the beaming face of Nitzevet when Jesse was around, it was hard to miss. But this was something she was going to protect from anyone who did not love Nitzevet and Jesse as she did, especially someone with seemingly nefarious intentions.

12

FRIENDS

A FEW DAYS LATER REBEKAH eagerly awaited Nitzevet's arrival. It was the morning before the evening of the Tisha B'Av remembrance and Nitzevet and her family were to arrive in Bethlehem that day. Whenever Nitzevet came to Bethlehem, Rebekah was the happiest, at least that is how she saw it. There was no closer friend than Nitzevet. Every moment that Rebekah had with her friend was precious and she did not want to waste not even one second. Rebekah knew she would have a few hours of time with Nitzevet all to herself since her mother and grandmother sheltered during the heat of the day in Leah's home, while her grandfather Shelach spent the afternoon at the gate with the elders of Bethlehem. After setting everything up for the visit she pondered whether she should tell Nitzevet about Ednah and her quest to marry Jesse. She decided that she would not cast a shadow over her time with her friend with news that might upset Nitzevet. It is best to leave that for another day.

Rebekah's heart raced as she heard her friend's footsteps on the path outside her home. The girls embraced for a long time, cherishing the momentary closeness of this unique long-distance friendship. After they had settled down in a cool corner sipping their chilled spiced milk, they caught each other up on all of the things that had occurred in the absence of each other. As they were just stirring to refill their cups, they heard more footsteps outside the gate, and then someone timidly called out "Shalom, it is I!"

They opened the door to find Reu smiling at them. "Shalom Reu, it is so good to see you!" they said in unison.

"Please come in and join us for a cup of cold spiced milk," Rebekah reached for his hand and pulled him into the cool house.

"I would love to!" He responded, stumbling over the threshold.

Rebekah poured their friend a cup of the sweet delicacy, knowing that Reu added to the friendship rather than detracting.

"I don't really know what Av nine is," Reu commented to Nitzevet.

"It is tomorrow, the day after today," Nitzevet laughed at her simple answer, she knew she was being silly.

Reu gave her a puzzled look that indicated he thought he missed something.

"Just making fun, Reu, seriously, what would you like to know about Tisha B'Av which is tomorrow and begins today at dusk?" She made a point as she filled her cup again.

Reu looked puzzled, "Usually, I am in the fields caring for sheep while you all attend the ceremony. This year, now that I am a member of the ben Obed household, Jesse gave me the afternoon and evening off. He says I need to attend so I will get a better understanding of what Yahweh did for the people ... uh, my people. What is so important about the ninth day of this month?" he asked.

"Our God is all about remembering and telling the stories of old. Yahweh has instructed His People to teach our children and sojourners among us, like you Reu, about His holiness and His goodness. And you are right, my friend, it is not a celebration, it is a ceremony of remembrance," she explained.

> *"Only be careful and watch yourselves closely so that you do not forget the things your eyes have seen or let them fade from your heart as long as you live. Teach them to your children and to their children after them."* [10]

Rebekah quoted her favorite passage from the Torah, for the second time in as many days.

Reu pondered the passage quietly and then said, "I was told there was fasting?" he asked wrinkling up his nose at the thought as any teenage boy would.

Rebekah laughed and explained, "Yes, we fast for twenty-four hours. Make sure you eat enough before sunset tonight to last you until after sunset tomorrow." Rebekah got up to place several date cakes on a platter along with some cheese, bread, and grapes. She set the platter between Nitzevet and Reu.

Nitzevet continued as she munched on grapes. "Not every tribe and town celebrate Tisha B'Av like we do. Because Grandpa Boaz's parents Salmon and Rahab settled here, they wanted their children and their children's children to remember all that Yahweh had done for them. As a result, they established the ceremony as a town mandate. We have been celebrating it ever since."

"Boaz ben Salmon was your grandfather?" Reu asked, having heard many stories about the great man.

"No actually. He is Jesse's grandfather. But he was my great-great aunt's daughter-in-law's husband. It's complicated," she said brushing the air with her hand not wanting to unravel all that relationship right now. "But I refer to him as Grandfather as Jesse does."

As usual, they found themselves discussing Yahweh and His plans. Specifically, they were pondering the twelve observers that Moses sent into the land of Canaan and why ten of them rejected Yahweh's plan to take the promised land that they had inherited from Abraham. They explained the details to Reu as his questions came up.

Having approached the Jordan River, Moses sent in twelve advanced observers on a touring mission into the land known as Caanan, their promised land. The eager group of over five million Israelites eagerly waited for the return of the observers.

After forty days the twelve men returned from their tour. Joshua and Caleb told the people of the beautiful land and showed the produce they had brought back. All the men confirmed that it was indeed a beautiful land flowing with milk and honey.

Rebekah paused for a moment for the next part of the story is the very reason they instituted the somber ceremony of Tisha B'Av. Nitzevet noticed the pause and gave her time before they continued. Reu sensed that the girls were somber because of the story.

Rebekah explained to Reu that ten of the observers that returned started to speak evil of the land their God had given them. "In fact," she explained, "Joshua called it a slanderous report. Only Joshua and Caleb were positive and determined that they could take the land through the power of Yahweh."

Adding to the story, Nitzevet explained that the report included seeing the sons of Anak living there. All three of them knew who those people were, the descendants of the Nephilim.

Reu shivered, he had seen some of these people. There were a couple of them that lived in Gaza, his hometown. He understood the fear that the Israelite observers experienced. Nine feet tall, very strong men with six fingers and toes on each hand and foot. There were rumors that they were cannibalistic too, which terrified Reu.

Nitzevet saw the shiver and the look of fear on Reu's face, so she moved on to explain why Yahweh was so angry. The people said, "If only we had died in this wilderness."

"It was on Tisha B'Av when they said that" Rebekah explained.

"Moses and Aaron realized what the people were saying to Yahweh, and they fell face down in front of them. They pleaded with the people, but the people wanted to stone Moses and Aaron and Joshua and Caleb."

"They wanted to kill Moses?" Reu exclaimed.

Rebekah looked at Reu, realizing that he was shocked at the lack of trust that the Israelites had in their leader. His shock is what everyone should feel when they hear this story. "Yes, they wanted to kill both Moses and Aaron because they did not trust them or God to lead them in victory over the people in the land."

"Did you know that Yahweh's glory was visible at that moment to all of Israel?" asked Rebekah.

"Really? Why did Yahweh show Himself?" asked Reu, again stunned.

Rebekah pondered the question, "We have talked about this before, but the consensus is that Yahweh was angry and was protecting Moses and Aaron."

"Because of his anger, Yahweh told Moses that instead, He was going to kill all of the Israelites. But Moses pleaded with Yahweh for the lives of the People based on Yahweh's reputation among the nations and Yahweh relented and instead, He granted their wish 'if only we had died in the wilderness.' He made them wander for forty more years before they as a people could enter the promised land, so that every person older than twenty years old on the day that the spies returned was dead, except for Joshua and Caleb. All the current living adults who grumbled and refused to go into the promised land would die in the desert and not see the land that they had longed to inhabit."

Rebekah pondered out loud, "So during the forty years, Yahweh condemned those over twenty and showed mercy to those under twenty years of age. The same forty years were to one group of people the terrible punishment and the other group a testimony of grace and protection. Yahweh is so complex." It was so like Rebekah to understand the holiness and complexity of her God.

Reu was having a hard time comprehending the magnitude of the anger of Yahweh and at the same time the great mercy of their God, to such a sinful people. He counted himself among them, and he was grateful for such a compassionate God. It was obvious to Reu that there was much he needed to learn about God.

Nitzevet could see Reu wrestling through everything in his mind and said, "We don't always understand the ways of Yahweh. But we trust Him completely. If He says go, we go, if He says fight, we fight. But we have not always been so trusting, and I somehow feel that we will not always trust Him in the future."

Nitzevet sensed that the conversation had turned toward sadness and not wanting to leave the conversation there, Nitzevet said, "My Ema said the grapes that the twelve observers brought back after their mission were so big that it took two men carrying a bunch on a stick between them. Can you imagine tasting one of those grapes, it would be a whole meal!" Nitzevet laughed at Reu's longing face as he held up a seemingly tiny grape. Rebekah instinctively went to the kitchen for another bunch of grapes and handed them to Reu.

While he munched on the sweet grapes he told them, "My ancestors also loved this land. But my ancestors made treaties with the giants that were here, and we adopted a lot of their beliefs and technology as well."

"Are you talking about the technology of metal and making weapons?" asked Nitzevet.

"Yes, I do not know much about it, but I was interested in it. I was very isolated, and my life was very hard. Living in the palace I had to be quiet and then when I was old enough to do chores, I worked all day from sunup to sundown. It was not a very happy childhood; I cannot even remember a time when I did not have work to do. However, my mother was very kind and good to me. She is what I miss most about my past. Actually, she is the only thing I miss," he confessed.

The girls could only imagine how hard it must have been for a little boy to grow up as a slave for the Philistines. Reu did not often share much about his past, so Nitzevet and Rebekah were sensitive to not move past his vulnerable moment too fast. Their pause indicated that they wanted him to know they had heard him.

"We are sorry for the loss of your mother and your childhood, Reu," Rebekah said kindly.

"Thank you, Rebekah," Reu responded, returning her look as well.

Rebekah sipped the last of her spiced milk and said, "We should be going!" She wrapped up two more date cakes, handed them to Reu, and admonished him to finish them before sunset.

נאמנות יהוה

Eli was pleased to be invited to Bethlehem this year to hold the ceremony. Eli loved Yahweh. He wanted the people to remember the good things and especially the bad things that had taken place ... and also why they had happened! The story of the twelve leaders Moses sent into the land and the subsequent decision by the people to reject their God's plan to enter the promised land was definitely one of those things he wanted Yahweh's people to never repeat. As a Judge and Priest appointed by Yahweh, he could choose which town he would be in each year on the Ninth of Av, this year it was Bethlehem.

"I know it is a small town," He told his young apprentice Samuel when questioned about his decision. "I know that there are many other larger, more worthy places that I could be, but somehow, I am being drawn there," He saw Samuel's puzzled look and responded, "No, no, not a word from God, more of an impression. I feel good about my decision to go there, so that is where we are going."

Samuel at the age of twenty-five, was satisfied with that answer. God was present, even now with Eli, the High Priest of Israel.

Samuel was excited to be going to Bethlehem. He did not often go out to visit friends and family because of his Temple duties in Shiloh. But Bethlehem is where his mother's best friend Gila would be with her relatives and family. It was always good to see them, they treated him like family, and he always felt welcome around them. He remembered the kindness of Gila. Even though they were not related, Gila was like his favorite aunt. Often, she would come up to Shiloh when he was just a boy and bring him special treats. He had always looked forward to his Ema and Gila's visits. She did not have children until he was about eight years old. Once she even came when she was pregnant.

Eli and Samuel were going to be staying with the Obed ben Boaz family. He knew most of the family, but not the wives of Obed's sons. As they approached Bethlehem, Samuel could see the well at the edge of town by the city gate. A drink of cool water from the well would definitely be welcome about now.

He looked at Eli and realized that the elderly man really needed to rest. "We will soon be there; I will go ahead and get a cup of cool water for you."

Samuel picked up his pace and quickly made it to the well. The women from the town were there getting water for the evening since the Ceremony was not too far off. "Shalom!" Samuel greeted the women. "I am Samuel with the priest Eli, could I please have a cup of water for Eli?"

Keturah quickly gave Samuel a cup of water, "I am Keturah and you and Eli will be staying with my husband and my family."

Samuel was pleased to have met one of his hosts so quickly, he could get Eli into the shade and resting soon. "Thank you, Keturah, bless you!" and he ran back to Eli with the water.

"Eli, we have accommodations settled, we are to follow Keturah," he said pointing to the young woman with the water jug standing by the well.

Keturah led them to the gate of their home. "Welcome, Eli and Samuel!" Obed said as he greeted his tired and dusty guests. Obed's greeting came with a big bear hug for Samuel, he loved that boy. After greeting Eli warmly, he said, "Your accommodations are here," as he led them to the room with a sturdy bench and two mats where they would sleep.

Eli slipped down on the bench exhausted. Mostly because of his weight, yet combined with his age, it must have been a very difficult journey. Obed observed this and was grateful to Yahweh for this man and his sacrifice.

Samuel handed Eli another cup of water and a cool wet cloth for his face and stepped out of the room with Obed. "We will let him rest in the cool quiet room for a while."

Obed took Samuel out to the courtyard where they took shelter in the shade. "Thank you for coming, Samuel. We are so grateful to be blessed this year by you and Eli!"

"We too are glad to be here. Do you know when Gila and her family will arrive?" he asked.

"Yes, they are already here resting before the evening ceremony," Obed explained.

"It will be nice to catch up with Gila," Samuel smiled.

"Nitzevet is out visiting friends, I believe she will meet us at the ceremony this evening. Let me bring you some refreshment before the fasting starts," Obed rose to tell one of the servants to bring food and drink to Samuel, also to bring enough for Jesse who would be coming in from the fields soon to eat.

Jesse walked into the courtyard just after his father left and saw Samuel sitting in the shade alone. "Shalom … Samuel!"

"It is so good to see you, brother," Samuel responded. When they met years ago, it seemed as if there was an immediate bond between these two men that went beyond human understanding, even then as boys they both knew it and felt it. Their infrequent reunions were always sweet fellowship for the men who were like brothers.

Jesse had bathed quickly in the stream and come in from the fields a bit early hoping to have a quiet moment with his best friend, so he blurted it out … "Samuel, I am going to ask Nitzevet if she will be my wife tonight, Yahweh willing, and I would like you to oversee our betrothal, if she says yes."

Samuel seemed taken aback and stood there in silence. His face did not reflect what was in his heart. He was overjoyed that Jesse wanted to marry Nitzevet, but as usual, he was in awe of how Yahweh always worked things out. He now understood why Yahweh prompted Eli to come to Bethlehem.

After big hugs and generous good-natured teasing, Jesse explained what he wanted Samuel to do, "Could you and Eli stay with us through our Sabbath and participate in our betrothal ceremony on the afternoon before Shabbat?"

Samuel smiled, "Let me check with Eli, but I believe we were going to stay until the day after Shabbat anyway."

Obed came back with the servant behind him carrying the bountiful pre-fast meal that they were going to take together. "The women are inside eating their meal; we can take it together out here. I had the servant provide Eli with his meal inside while he prepared for the evening. What is going on, you are both beaming?"

Jesse cleared his throat, smiled at his father, and began, "Remember our discussion in the field a while ago, and I told you my intentions and who the object of my intentions was?"

"Yes, son, I remember with great joy," he responded.

"Samuel has agreed to officiate our betrothal ceremony on Friday afternoon, to be followed with the feast on Shabbat. Is that ok with you Father, can we have the celebration in two days?"

"Has she said yes?" Obed asked.

"Not yet, but I am asking tonight," Jesse responded.

Obed glanced at Samuel and then at Jesse and with a big robust laugh, "Of course my son, of course … if Nitzevet says yes, we will have a celebration for sure."

The rest of the meal was spent discussing the details of what was necessary. Samuel would write up the marriage contract with Eli's help. Of course, Jesse would ask Nitzevet the most important question and Obed would help his wife put together the makings for a wonderful betrothal celebration at the end of the week.

נאמנות יהוה

Nitzevet was in a somber mood as the three friends made their way to the center square where the solemn remembrance would be held. She wondered if Jesse would be there, would he remember that she was coming? As a seventeen-year-old girl and Jesse being a man of twenty-five, she was a bit shy around him as their customs dictated. She had so many memories of her childhood and visiting Bethlehem. The many hours her family spent with the ben Obed family provided many opportunities for her to get to know her distant relatives, especially Jesse.

נאמנות יהוה

In the quiet of Obed's cool guest bedroom, Eli's thoughts turned dark. Sometimes Eli wondered why he bothered. Will Yahweh's people ever learn? They have been in the promised land for over three hundred and fifty years now. Joshua brought them in with fervor and high hopes and the promise of a land of their own. But from his perspective, the High Priest of the people of Israel, they were no further on their journey than if they were sitting on the East side of the Jordan River. In fact, in his opinion, they were worse off. Some of the people had adopted the gods of the people in the land. They had simply added them to a collection as if Yahweh would tolerate being part of a collection.

He often sat in his home and people came to him wanting to know what Yahweh was doing. They would confess that they were asking all the little gods to help too, just in case Yahweh had forgotten them.

It angered him so that they could not remember all the things that Yahweh had done for them. Yahweh chose them, not because they were special in any way, or that they merited being chosen, but because Yahweh himself wanted to bless all peoples of the earth ... the EARTH ... through them. "Stubborn people!" he whispered.

The stress of his position, the sadness that it brought led Eli to neglect things in his own life. Eli was a man of great girth. He could not stop eating. He wasn't hungry, he was sad. Not only that, but his sons were evil men. He hated to admit it to himself, but they were. 'They cared only about profit and what the priesthood could bring them ... yes, they were priests ... PRIESTS!'

Eli gently unrolled the scroll and marked the place where he would begin the ceremony. Eating the last morsel of the prefast meal and drinking the last of the cool goat's milk, he was ready.

The last remnant of the hot afternoon was dusty and dry as Eli made his way with Samuel to the city square in Bethlehem to start the ceremony. Every movement, every engagement was a work unto itself, just getting there was a taxing experience, physically for sure, but mentally as well. This year he had an impression that something was going on … 'What was God up to?' he thought.

13

TISHA B'AV

EDNAH HAD DECIDED TO ATTEND the ceremony as Rebekah had suggested. Her parents chose rather to relax in their cool quiet home than to brave the dusty crowds in the warm evening.

She found Rebekah who had brought two friends. Ednah nodded as she took a seat next to Rebekah. Leaning over she asked Rebekah, "Have you seen Jesse?"

Rebekah, inwardly rolling her eyes, responded, "No." And then purposely locked her eyes on Eli who was stepping up to speak so that she would not even encounter a glimpse of Jesse and have to tell Ednah.

Gently, Rebekah put her finger to her lips to silence Ednah as she leaned in with another question as Eli began to speak.

Rebuffed, Ednah pouted. She did not relish being shushed, 'who did Rebekah think she was? And who was this old fat man getting ready to speak? He was standing up there in such a somber mood. It was not like this in Dan. Her tribe knew how to throw a party. Sure, they did not have these luxurious buildings and town center for meetings, but they had fun!'

Then she spotted him. Jesse stood at the back of the crowd off to the side. He was so handsome; his beard was neatly trimmed, and his hair was slicked back as if he had just bathed. His tunic looked new, and he stood straight and tall, how she longed to be his wife. It just wasn't fair, she saw him first, her father promised, it wasn't fair. She noticed that he was looking around as if he were looking for someone. Then he stopped and she saw a slight smile take over his face. She traced his line of sight to see if she could see what or ... who he was looking at. But her vantage point just was not good enough, it was someone near her, directly behind her maybe. She knew she could not stand up without drawing undue attention. 'I will follow him after the ceremony ... maybe he will lead me to someone.' Ednah settled back and decided not to listen but to feed her fantasies of being a rich, connected, young wife in Bethlehem.

נאמנות יהוה

Eli was grateful to sense the cooling of the breeze as the sun slowly disappeared behind the hills to the west of Bethlehem. The people had gathered, as the children were being hushed into silence, everyone took their seats. Just as three stars appeared in the sky, signifying it was now the Ninth of Av, Eli began the evening of the new day by opening the scroll to the fourth section, he found his way to the beginning of the story that Moses had written down for them.

Clearing his throat to get the attention of the people, lifted his chin and began to read the well-known story:

> *"The Lord said to Moses, 'Send men to explore Canaan, which I'm giving to the Israelites. Send one leader from each of their ancestors' tribes. So at the Lord's command, Moses sent these men from the Desert of Paran. All of them were leaders of the Israelites.*
> *These are their names:*
> *Shammua, from the tribe of Reuben;*
> *Shaphat from the tribe of Simeon;*
> *Caleb, from the tribe of Judah;*
> *Igal from the tribe of Issachar;*
> *Joshua from the tribe of Ephraim;*
> *Palti from the tribe of Benjamin;*
> *Gaddiel from the tribe of Zebulun;*
> *Gaddi, from the tribe of Manasseh;*
> *Ammiel from the tribe of Dan;*
> *Sethur from the tribe of Asher;*

Nahbi from the tribe of Naphtali;
Geuel from the tribe of Gad.

These are the names of the men Moses sent to explore the land.

He told them, "Go through the Negev and then into the mountain region. See what the land is like and whether the people living there are strong or weak, few or many. Is the land they live in good or bad? Do their cities have walls around them or not? Is the soil rich or poor? Does the land have trees or not? Do your best to bring back some fruit from the land." (It was the season when grapes were beginning to ripen.)

So the men explored the land from the Desert of Zin to the border of Hamath. They went through the Negev and came to Hebron, where Ahiman, Sheshai, and Talmai lived. They are descendants of Anak. (Hebron was built seven years before Zoan in Egypt.) When they came to the Eshcol Valley, they cut off a branch with only one bunch of grapes on it. They carried it on a pole between two of them. They also brought some pomegranates and figs. So they called that valley Eshcol [Bunch of Grapes] because of the bunch of grapes the Israelites cut off there.

Forty days later, they came back from exploring the land. They came back to Moses, Aaron, and the whole community of Israel at Kadesh in the Desert of Paran. They gave their report and showed them the fruit from the land.

This is what they reported to Moses: "We went to the land where you sent us. It really is a land flowing with milk and honey. Here's some of its fruit. But the people who live there are strong, and the cities have walls and are very large. We even saw the descendants of Anak there. The Amalekites live in the Negev. The Hittites, Jebusites, and Amorites live in the mountain region. And the Canaanites live along the coast of the Mediterranean Sea and all along the Jordan River."

Caleb told the people to be quiet and listen to Moses. Caleb said, "Let's go now and take possession of the land. We should be more than able to conquer it."

But the men who had gone with him said, "We can't attack those people! They're too strong for us!" So they began to spread lies among the Israelites about the land they had explored. They said, "The land we explored is one that devours those who live there. All the people we saw there are very tall. We saw Nephilim there. (The descendants of Anak are Nephilim.) We felt as small as grasshoppers, and that's how we must have looked to them."

Then all the people in the Israelite community raised their voices and cried out loud all that night. They complained to Moses and Aaron, "If only we had died in Egypt or this desert! Why is the Lord bringing us to this land—just to have us die in battle? Our wives and children will be taken as prisoners of war! Wouldn't it be better for us to go back to Egypt?" They said to each other, "Let's choose a leader and go back to Egypt."

Immediately, Moses and Aaron bowed with their faces touching the ground in front of the whole community of Israel assembled there."

Eli paused, not for effect, but because he was overcome with emotion. He could only imagine the sadness and anger they caused Yahweh with their distrust. As a leader of these people, he could uniquely feel the grief of Moses and Aaron as they bowed to the ground. As the current leader of Israel with two wayward sons, he had his share of rebellion.

Nitzevet heard a sniffle and glanced at Reu. She saw tears in his eyes. What a gentle soul, surely, he loved Yahweh, he was impacted by the sin of Israel as were the rest of the Remnant.

After a few moments, Eli lifted his head and continued:

"At the same time, two of those who had explored the land, Joshua (son of Nun) and Caleb (son of Jephanneth), tore their clothes in despair. They said to the whole community of Israel, "The land we explored is very good. If the Lord is pleased with us, he will bring us into this land and give it to us. This is a land flowing with milk and honey! Don't rebel against the Lord, and don't be afraid of the people of the land. We will

devour them like bread. They have no protection, and the Lord is with us. So don't be afraid of them."

But when the whole community of Israel talked about stoning Moses and Aaron to death, they all saw the glory of the Lord shining at the tent of meeting."

This time Eli paused for effect. So many of the people passed over this statement. He said very slowly … "The glory of the 'I Am' appeared to all the people. Yahweh was so angry that they were about to kill his representatives, Moses and Aaron that he stopped them with His glory."

"The Lord said to Moses, "How long will these people treat me with contempt? How long will they refuse to trust me in spite of all the miraculous signs I have done among them? I'll strike them with a plague, I'll destroy them, and I'll make you into a nation larger and stronger than they are."

But Moses said to the Lord, "What if the Egyptians hear about it? (You used your power to take these people away from them.) What if the Egyptians tell the people who live in this land? Lord, they have already heard that you are with these people, that they have seen you with their own eyes, that your column of smoke stays over them, and that you go ahead of them in a column of smoke by day and in a column of fire by night. But if you kill all these people at the same time, then the nations who have heard these reports about you will say, 'The Lord wasn't able to bring these people into the land he promised them, so he slaughtered them in the desert.'

"Lord, let your power be as great as when you said, 'The Lord … patient, forever loving … He forgives wrongdoing and disobedience … He never lets the guilty go unpunished, punishing children … for their parents' sins to the third and fourth generation … ' By your great love, please forgive these people's sins, as you have been forgiving them from the time they left Egypt until now."

The Lord said, "I forgive them, as you have asked. But as I live and as the glory of the Lord fills the whole earth, I solemnly swear that none of the people who saw my glory and the miraculous signs I did in Egypt and in the desert will see the land which I promised their ancestors. They have tested me now ten times and refused to obey me. None of those who treat me with contempt will see it! But because my servant Caleb has a different attitude and has wholeheartedly followed me, I'll bring him to the land he already explored. His descendants will possess it. (The Amalekites and Canaanites are living in the valleys.) Tomorrow you must turn around, go back into the desert, and follow the road that goes to the Red Sea."

Then the Lord said to Moses and Aaron, "How long must I put up with this wicked community that keeps complaining about me? I've heard the complaints the Israelites are making about me. So tell them, 'As I live, declares the Lord, I solemnly swear I will do everything to you that you said I would do. Your bodies will drop dead in this desert. All of you who are at least 20 years old, who were registered and listed, and who complained about me will die. I raised my hand and swore an oath to give you this land to live in. But none of you will enter it except Caleb (son of Jephunneh) and Joshua (son of Nun). You said your children would be taken as prisoners of war. Instead, I will bring them into the land you rejected, and they will enjoy it. However, your bodies will drop dead in this desert. Your children will be shepherds in the desert for 40 years. They will suffer for your unfaithfulness until the last of your bodies lies dead in the desert. For 40 days you explored the land. So for 40 years—one year for each day—you will suffer for your sins and know what it means for me to be against you.' I, the Lord, have spoken. I swear I will do these things to all the people in this whole wicked community who have joined forces against me. They will meet their end in this desert. Here they will die!"

So the men Moses sent to explore the land died in front of the Lord from a plague. They died because they had returned and made the whole community complain about Moses by spreading lies about the land. Of all the men who went to explore the land, only Joshua (son of Nun) and Caleb (son of Jephunneh) survived." [11]

Nitzevet was enraptured by the words shaping the story of her people. As tears slipped down her face, she silently prayed to Yahweh for forgiveness, not only for her own sins and shortcomings but for those of her people. She quoted: "By your great love, please forgive these people's sins, as you have been forgiving them from the time they left Egypt until now."

As the ceremony was coming to a solemn end, she slipped away to wander in the fields and ponder all that she had heard. It was her natural tendency to verbalize her prayers to God out loud, that is why she sought the quiet, secluded hills around Bethlehem.

"Yahweh, we are such stubborn people. We seek our own way without trusting You. After all the things you have done for us: preserving our race over four hundred years in Egypt, then bringing us out of Egypt at the right time, providing food and water in the wilderness, going before us in a cloud by day and a pillar of fire at night," Nitzevet paused as she pondered all that God had done.

"Yet we are a … What did you call us Lord, oh yes, a stiff-necked people," Nitzevet could not help but smile, picturing a stubborn ox who was unwilling to obey the guidance given by its master. That is what we are, she thought, stubborn and unwilling.

Nitzevet looked up and found herself in the evening shadow of the Tower, her tower. Nitzevet felt the presence of Yahweh. She loved the nearness and companionship she felt with her Maker. She sat down and wrapped her arms around her, simply enjoying the moment. For some reason, she knew this thin place, where heaven and earth seemed so close, would be a very special place in the future.

Right now, it was the pastureland of Jesse's family. Maybe that is why she loved being there, in addition to the presence of Yahweh, it was owned by her special friend's family. Nitzevet was unsure if Jesse knew that she considered him a special friend. As far as she knew, he barely knew her and probably never thought of her.

נאמנות יהוה

Jesse had seen Nitzevet toward the back of the crowd to his right. He admired her red curls that seemed to be all over the place, but at the same time beautifully shaped to cascade down her back. There was a glow all around her. 'It is probably the glow of the sun bouncing off the red of her curls, but the glow made her all that more beautiful. He was going to go say greet her as soon as the ceremony was over. He too was enraptured by Eli's reading of the scroll. Jesse knew that his people had sinned greatly in the wilderness and had suffered for their sins. He wondered, would he have been one of the two or one of the ten? Would he have rallied the cry to take the land with God's power or would he have seen the giants and longed to shrink back to the safety of Egypt? Lost in his thoughts he looked up to see where Nitzevet was, and she was gone.

It was dark. Jesse knew that Nitzevet loved to wander in silence. It was one of the things that he loved about her … she was not bound by the need for the presence of others as most girls were. She was not afraid to be in the fields alone. He laughed at the thought, maybe she was given too much freedom as a little girl, but it made her who she is now. And she was lovely, mind, soul and body.

Jesse slipped away to the Tower; he knew that is where she would probably end up. He had often followed her and watched as she ended up sitting in the shadow of the Tower. Typically, he would leave her alone with her thoughts and keep watch a way off. He had always had a special desire to keep her safe.

This evening, however, Jesse wanted to talk with Nitzevet. So he slowly approached her and called out in a soft voice, "Slicha, Nitzevet! How are you?"

Her smile was radiant, even in the moonlight. He was pleased.

"Shalom Jesse!" she responded with maybe a little too much excitement in her voice she thought.

"I hope I am not intruding on your quiet time?" responded Jesse.

"No, you are welcome, I am just pondering the reading this evening and wondering about all of it. I welcome your thoughts."

Jesse thought for a moment, "I know what you mean. It is so important for us to remember what our ancestors did so that we will not repeat their mistakes. Seeing Yahweh's response to their unwillingness to take the land, makes me understand just how angry He was with them."

"He has done so much for us, Jesse. We are so blessed to be Yahweh's chosen people. I pray that I will be like Joshua and Caleb when Yahweh calls upon me to do hard things for Him," Her sincerity was clear to Jesse.

They sat quietly for a few minutes. Then Jesse gently broached the subject that was on his mind, "Nitzevet ... do you think you would ever want to be my wife?"

The shock was obvious on her face. Jesse feared he had just made the mistake of his life. But what he did not know is that the shock was because she had never thought Jesse would ask that, in spite of all her dreaming that he would.

Just as quickly as the shock came, it left and was replaced by a sweet smile and a quick shy nod. That was all that Jesse needed. He knew that Nitzevet was willing to be his wife. As a man of twenty-five years, people were wondering why he had not yet chosen his wife and settled down. But deep down, ever since that first summer when Nitzevet visited she had a hold on his heart. At first, it was as a little sister and sweet friend, but as she visited over time, the spark of love gently grew into a flame. Jesse knew she was the one for him.

Couples did not often discuss marriage themselves, typically, marriage was arranged. But never forced. Jesse knew he must now speak with Shelach since Nitzevet's father had died many years ago. Her grandfather would step into her father's place.

Jesse, now a bit shy himself, smiled at Nitzevet. "Would you be willing to have our betrothal ceremony this Shabbat? We will start the Kiddushin then," he questioned.

Nitzevet, again a little shocked at the quick timing, but pleased, smiled her radiant smile with sparkling eyes while nodding yes again. Her beauty was not lost on Jesse. Her red hair and beautiful blue eyes were often the talk of people around him. He had heard his friends and even his brothers mention her beauty. But he had never responded, for to him Nitzevet was more than her beauty. She was special, unique, full of life and intelligent, a characteristic not typically sought after in a bride.

Jesse smiled as he enjoyed being near Nitzevet ... 'his bride', he relished the thought. The years will never be boring with Nitzevet by his side. He looked up at the tower and felt that special Presence. He knew this would be a special place for many years, a place where things were revealed, and people encountered God.

Pondering his ancestors, Jesse silently prayed that he would be a faithful husband to Nitzevet as his grandfather Salmon had been to his great-grandmother Rahab and as his grandfather Boaz had been to his grandmother Ruth and as his father Obed had always been to his mother Leah. Who knew that he would ask her to be his bride on the most unlikely day of the year, the Ninth of Av. Truly this day would also be remembered through the years.

Jesse and Nitzevet walked back to town the appropriate distance apart. While they were almost betrothed, a status as committed and serious as marriage, they understood the customs of their people and knew that they would wait to even hold hands until they were betrothed.

14

THE SECRET REVEALED

TRUE TO HERSELF, EDNAH FOLLOWED Jesse after the terribly long ceremony. He was heading out to the fields. As far as she could tell he wasn't following anyone, but it seemed by the cadence of his steps that he had a destination in mind.

Keeping to the shadows Ednah followed as far as she could. Being out in the fields like that at night in the dark, she could feel the fear creeping up the back of her neck. She kept looking around, wondering if there was anyone or anything lurking in the shadows.

Thinking it better to ease her fear, she decided to retrace her steps to the safety of the town and then wait for Jesse to return, if indeed he did return.

Settling down on a bench in the shadow next to the furthest outbuilding in Bethlehem, Ednah shivered, not so much because of a chill, but because deep down she knew she was spying, and it gave her a creepy feeling.

About the time of the first watch, Ednah stirred from dozing because she heard voices coming out of the darkness. She sat up and looked intently hoping to be able to recognize who was coming. She distinctively noticed Jesse and then heard his laugh; she knew that laugh anywhere. Then she looked hard at the shadow next to him. As the person turned to face Jesse, the moonlight reflected on her face and Ednah saw the beautiful young woman walking next to Jesse. The same person who was sitting next to Rebekah that evening during the ceremony. She also saw the radiance and joy that was on her face.

Shocked, Ednah sucked in her breath. Immediately hoped no one heard. It seemed they didn't. They were not holding hands, just walking in from the fields. This must be the person Jesse is going to marry, why would he spend time with anyone else … she could totally see why, she was beautiful.

נאמנות יהוה

The remembrance in Bethlehem was not over that evening. The people were expected to return to the town center early in the morning to conclude the special time. While they all left in silence the night before, they knew that the morning would bring celebration.

Eli decided that Samuel should lead this portion of the remembrance. As Samuel stood up in the center square, he raised his head and smiled at the people gathered.

"You all know that Yahweh did not leave us in the wilderness." The people let out a loud 'teruah'. Samuel smiled.

Eli marveled at the presence that Samuel had before the people and the respect that he received from them. He could feel the presence of God in Samuel, not unexpected knowing that Yahweh had spoken to Samuel when he was a boy. Eli pondered that Yahweh had never spoken to him audibly.

Samuel continued, "He brought His people to the Jordan river after forty years in the wilderness. The only people who had been at this point before were Joshua and Caleb." Samuel paused, thinking how much he loved this part of the story. He began to read from the Scroll of Joshua:

> "After the death of Moses the servant of the Lord, the Lord said to Joshua son of Nun, Moses' aide: "Moses my servant is dead. Now then, you and all these people, get ready to cross the Jordan River into the land I am about to give to them—to the Israelites. I will give you every place where you set your foot, as I promised Moses. Your territory will extend from the desert to Lebanon, and from the great river, the Euphrates—all the Hittite country—to the Mediterranean Sea in the west. No one will be able to stand against you all the days of your life. As I

was with Moses, so I will be with you; I will never leave you nor forsake you. Be strong and courageous ..."

"Be strong and courageous ..." the people responded as Samuel paused for them.

Reu looked around at the people, he had not expected the response.

"...because you will lead these people to inherit the land,
I swore to their ancestors to give them.
"Be strong and very courageous ..."

"Be strong and VERY courageous ..." the people in unison replied again.

"Be careful to obey all the law my servant Moses gave you; do not turn from it to the right or to the left, that you may be successful wherever you go. Keep this Book of the Law always on your lips; meditate on it day and night, so that you may be careful to do everything written in it. Then you will be prosperous and successful. Have I not commanded you? Be strong and courageous ..."

"Be strong and courageous ..." again in unison. This time with Reu joins in with a loud voice.

"Do not be afraid; do not be discouraged, for the Lord your God will be with you wherever you go."
So Joshua ordered the officers of the people: "Go through the camp and tell the people, 'Get your provisions ready. Three days from now you will cross the Jordan here to go in and take possession of the land the Lord your God is giving you for your own.'" [12]

Here is where the story gets good, thought Samuel as he paused and smiled at the people before him. This was the point he wanted the people to really understand.

נאמנות יהוה

"There, there," consoled Chazael, "it will be alright."

"No mama, she is beautiful, and it is over for me. I will never get married!" whaled Ednah.

Chazael hated to see her daughter so sad. She wanted to fix this for her sweet daughter. 'Why,' she thought, 'why did the gods not fix this!'

A mother should always be able to step in and solve the problems of their children. What else were mothers for, if not to pave the way and make it easy for their children? Besides, after moving to Bethlehem she had very little to do. The people here were too … too … focused on their God. It is as if everything they did, most of them, was in relationship to what He expected of them. They obeyed all the feasts, even the sad ones. Back in Dan, her tribe had decided to only celebrate the happy feasts where there was a big party and lots of food. Sure, there were holdouts who gathered for the fasts and the remembrances, but none of them were her friends. Now here in Bethlehem, roles were reversed, and she was the outsider.

As she held her weeping daughter in her arms, a plan began to formulate in her mind. If she could smear the character of this girl that Jesse was interested in, somehow, maybe Jesse's parents would relinquish and force their son to marry Ednah. It sounded outlandish, but she had been privy to things like this in the past.

First to find out who the girl was, and then get the rumors out.

Her daughter had mentioned that she saw them coming in from the fields together at first watch. Chazael was pretty sure that this girl's parents, whoever they were, would not approve of this unchaperoned behavior of their daughter. The plan began to unfold. Before Chazael was able to gather all the facts, she set her daughter on a mission to discredit Jesse's choice.

Ednah had wholeheartedly agreed with the plan her mother had set up. She was going to slip a few words of gossip here and a few there. "Maybe, I could make it look like I was concerned for this girl's reputation when I let the comment out?'"

"Very good," commended Chazael, "and remember do not look too eager to provide the information, we want them to use their own imagination along with your words."

It was decided then, between mother and daughter, to do the very thing that caused the Israelites to wander and die in the wilderness, intentionally spreading lies to thwart Yahweh's plans.

The next morning it was time for the morning trip to the well. Awkwardly carrying her bucket, Ednah made her way to the community well. She slipped up next to one of the girls she had spoken to before and greeted her sweetly. The girl was pleased to be noticed by an older girl, having seen Ednah on occasion, so she responded hopeful of a friendship, "Shalom Ednah, I am well."

Ednah asked, "What is your name?"

The girl responded eagerly, "Shoshannah."

"Shoshannah, how is your family? Any news of any kind to share?" she smoothly engaged.

"My family is fine, thank you for asking, I have no news," Shoshannah was so pleased to be asked.

"What about engagements in Bethlehem? Is anyone getting married," asked Ednah of her unwitting accomplice.

Shoshannah laughed, it really was the talk of the town, the fresh news that Jesse was seeking someone's hand in marriage, so Shoshannah relayed this information to Ednah.

Pleased to be getting somewhere, Ednah prodded more, "Who is this wonderful person, I would love to meet her and congratulate her?"

Shoshannah was happy to pass on the happy news, "It is Nitzevet bat Adale from Efrat."

Ednah now realized why she did not know who this was, Nitzevet bat Adale was not from Bethlehem. She felt relieved that she wasn't so much out of the loop that a romance had gone on in the same town under her own nose with her own man.

Proceeding with the plan, Ednah dropped a few words, "That reminds me, someone told me that they saw Jesse, way past first watch walking into town with a young woman, that must have been who it was," there the hint was dropped.

Shoshannah thought nothing of it and proceeded to babble about weddings and such. How exciting there was going to be a wedding soon.

Disguised at her slowness to recognize a juicy bit of gossip, Ednah moved to her next victim, a woman she had not yet encountered at the well. "Good morning how are you and what is our name?" she asked.

"Shalom, I am fine and my name is Shifra!"

"Any news with you or your family Shifra?" Ednah asked, not really interested. Her only desire was to drop a few more words about Nitzevet and then move on for the day.

What Ednah did not know is that she had just approached the wrong person. Shifra was Obed's second daughter-in-law, married to his second son Vophsi. Shifra was shy and typically stayed at home caring for the children of their clan. Keturah had three boys and Shifra had two girls. Today was a unique day, Keturah was very pregnant with her fourth child, so Shifra was busy gathering the water for the day's needs.

"No news," Shifra said, smiling sweetly. Shifra had heard the conversation with Shoshannah, and she was a wise woman, she knew what Ednah was up to. Obed had told the family of the encounter with Ednah's father and the fear that he had walked away with at the encounter. Now she understood. There was a young woman here up to no good.

Ednah turned to Shifra and dropped her tidbit adding to the gossip, "I wonder if the parents of Jesse's intended would be very happy knowing they were together in the fields, alone without a chaperone," and then she added for effect, with a very concerned look on her face, "I am worried for her reputation."

Shifra was steaming. She knew very well what Ednah was up to now, and it wasn't because she was worried about Nitzevet's reputation. The fact was, that everyone in the town of Bethlehem who knew Nitzevet, also knew her character. Having come to Bethlehem often since that first journey, she had found her way into most of the hearts of the towns' people. Only the newcomers, like Ednah and her family and those offended by a vivacious bubbly little girl, did not truly know Nitzevet.

This kind of insidious gossip is what ruins lives. Shifra would be no part of it, but neither did she feel confident to confront Ednah. She decided she would let someone with more authority do that for her. Putting a smile on her face she said, "look at how fast the moments pass, I must get home with the water before breakfast," she turned quickly and went home.

Rebekah was standing in the shadow of the gate near the well, listening to the conversations around her. She heard everything that

Ednah said to both Shoshannah and Shifra. Silently she thanked God that it was Shifra who heard the rumor and that she knew Jesse's sister-in-law. Something must be done. Sometimes it is not enough to just close our ears and not spread rumors, sometimes we have to encourage others not to spread them, as seemingly innocent as they intend to be.

נאמנות יהוה

Jesse was nervous as he prepared his speech for Shelach. Since the family was in Bethlehem for the Ninth of Av, he knew he had to act quickly so that they could be betrothed before Shelach and his family as well as Samuel went home. Typically, they stayed until the day after Sabbath to journey home.

Knowing he would find Shelach at the gate of Bethlehem with the elders, he found Reu who would be going with him as his witness, and off they went to the city gate. Jesse smiled inside as he saw his father there, knowing that he had probably planned to be there to give Jesse a little boost of courage. Jesse walked up to the elders, greeted everyone, and then asked to have a conversation with Shelach.

Shelach was neither blind nor dumb, and Nitzevet was as much to him as a daughter could be, so he knew why Jesse was there. But according to the custom, he did not let on. "Shalom, Jesse!"

"Shalom …!" Jesse mumbled as he stumbled over his word, not knowing what to call this man before him.

Dripping with sweat, he just blurted out, "I would like to ask for Nitzevet to be my wife."

Shelach laughed, "You just get right to it, don't you son?"

Jesse nervously laughed in return and responded, "Yes sir, when it is an important matter!"

"Good answer! You have my blessing, Jesse; I have known for a while of your intentions and have had plenty of time to consider. So yes!" a very gracious Shelach responded.

Jesse was so happy, he leaped into the air and hugged Reu who was standing next to him. Turning to Shelach he asked, "Is it alright with you if I leave the mohar between you and my father?"

Shelach glanced at Obed knowingly and said yes and then pushed the boys back through the gate to go tell Nitzevet the good news.

Nitzevet was glowing as she saw a beaming Jesse and happy Reu walking up to the Obed home. She knew that Jesse had asked Shelach for her hand in marriage. When the men arrived, her two favorite men, she was overjoyed as she witnessed Jesse's beautiful smile filled with love and Reu's genuine affection as if she were truly his older sister.

"Your grandfather said yes!" Jesse beamed.

Nitzevet did not know what to say in the midst of her joy. Jesse took her hand and kissed her palm in an intimate gesture to ease the awkwardness of the moment. It was the first time Jesse had ever touched her and it was such a gentle touch that Nitzevet was overwhelmed and did not know how to react, so she ran into the house in tears, overwhelmed.

Gila was watching the whole scene from the window and noticed Jesse and Reu's confusion as Nitzevet bolted. Gila quickly slipped into the courtyard to waylay the boys.

Smiling, she walked up to Jesse and gave him a big hug and kiss on the cheek, "Shalom, my son!" she greeted.

"What have I done, Gila, to offend Nitzevet?" he asked.

"Nothing my dear, nothing. Your kindness and gentleness overwhelmed her, and she was unprepared for how to react. She has never been touched by a boy, nor been loved in the way you love her. She is fine and I will go to her now. We have already begun preparations for the ceremony tomorrow afternoon. Do not worry yourself over anything," Gila slipped away to go to her daughter.

נאמנות יהוה

Tomorrow afternoon was the betrothal followed by Shabbat dinner. They only had twenty-four hours to prepare. Fortunately, Jesse knew his mother, Leah, was a master ceremony and feast planner. She had planned many of the betrothals in the village including her own. Jesse, taking his soon-to-be mother-in-law Gila at her word, grabbed Reu and headed to the pastureland. He needed to think. What needed to be done before he could take Nitzevet as his wife? It will probably be six months ... his father needed to tell him when he could go … he needed to build a home … there was so much to do … he could not wait to get to the fields where his thoughts would flow freely.

Reu followed, relishing that he could be such a vital part of such an important and exciting event in Jesse's life.

נאמנות יהוה

Nitzevet was indeed overwhelmed by the gracious, kind, loving man that Jesse was. Not knowing how to respond she just ran. Through her tears, her mother comforted and encouraged Nitzevet, telling her that she had explained to Jesse why his beloved had run, and Jesse totally understood. Soon Nitzevet was giggling about her foolishness when Rebekah walked in squealing as only girls do when they find out a wedding is about to happen.

"Jesse's Ema came to get me to tell me the good news," she bubbled with her cheeks rosy from the rush over to Nitzevet's house. "How can I help you prepare for the big night tomorrow?" asked Rebekah.

Hugging her friend, Nitzevet replied, "I am so glad you are here; you can help us plan!"

The girls and Gila spent the afternoon planning and giggling and just having a wonderful time. As they were discussing what to wear the next day a gentle knock was heard. Gila jumped up to see who it was. She came to Nitzevet and told her that her groom was looking to speak with her.

Nitzevet was glad to have a moment with Jesse after her foolishness and running from the courtyard earlier. "We will only be a moment, Ema."

After Nitzevet stepped into the courtyard, Jesse handed her a beautifully made leather bag and said, "It is a gift, your mattan."

She had not expected this, it was a beautifully made bag, she knew that Jesse had made it and that it had taken quite some time to make. "Open it," Jesse urged. Nitzevet gingerly opened the precious bag and pulled out a beautiful white wedding garment, exactly her size. Tears formed in her eyes. It was a beautiful betrothal gown, she knew that Leah had made it, but it also had taken quite some time to make. She was so blessed. This wedding had been under planning for quite some time.

Jesse took her hand and kissed it again gently and then he was gone.

Nitzevet showed the ladies the wonderful gift that Jesse had given her. The leather bag and beautiful gown. Walking over to her cabinet in her room, Nitzevet gently pulled out a small fabric bag and unrolled it. Opening the flap, she pulled out the delicate shell earrings that Rebekah had made for her several years before for her birthday. "I shall wear these with the lovely dress that Jesse gave me. Ema, I must thank Aunt Leah for the gown?" she said, looking knowingly at her mother.

Gila smiled, "Yes my dear."

Opening the door just a crack, Nitzevet peeked out and saw her aunt on the other side of the courtyard. She called out "Aunt Leah, could you please come in here," called Nitzevet.

Leah walked in wiping her hands on her apron with a quizzical look on her face. "Thank you, Aunt Leah, for the beautiful dress. I know you made it; the size, color, and fabric are absolutely perfect and exactly what I love."

"You are welcome, dear daughter, very welcome. And I have known for a few weeks about Jesse's intentions," Leah wiped a stray tear as she hugged her new daughter.

The girls spent the rest of the evening dreaming about the event that would take place the next evening. They knew this was not the 'formal' event that started the wedding feast that was months away, but this betrothal was important to them, and they wanted to look their best. Laying out their dresses they made their plans. Rebekah would come over early in the afternoon and they would help Leah in any way they could and then get dressed together.

נאמנות יהוה

It was late that evening when Leah sought out Shifra. She knew there was something bothering this sweet girl. She loved her daughters-in-law as much as any mother would. Never having daughters of her own, she loved these two girls, soon to be three, so very much. When they were hurting, she was hurting.

"My dear daughter, what is bothering you?" she asked. This is a joyous time, there is so much to do, and I want you to celebrate also.

Laying on the hammock, Shifra was resting for a moment from a long day of chores, despite the fact that she was a few months pregnant and tired. Shifra knew it was time to share her burden with her husband's mother, one of her best friends.

"Yes, something is bothering me, but I am at a loss as to how to handle it. Maybe you can help me figure out what the right thing to do would be."

"Yes, my dear, I will try," responded Leah.

Shifra proceeded to tell Leah all about the conversation at the well. How Ednah had first approached Shoshannah and dropped a nugget of "concern" about Nitzevet, and then proceeded to engage her, not knowing she was Jesse's sister-in-law. Disgusted at Ednah's behavior, Shifra admitted that she did not confront her at the moment, but decided to find someone who had more authority and could deal with the situation without making Ednah and her family enemies.

Shifra had learned, living with Obed and Leah, that harsh words were never the first choice. Words spoken in anger or frustration were usually not carefully chosen and were impossible to take back, like scattering feathers in the wind.

Leah sat quietly for a moment after hearing the burden that Shifra was bearing. She agreed with Shifra, that these are the kinds of situations that can ruin relationships and families if not handled properly. "My daughter, I will handle this. We are bringing our precious Nitzevet here to Bethlehem to live with us, we cannot knowingly bring her into a hostile environment of neighbors. We must seek to solve the issues at hand as best as we can. We cannot ignore this. Jealousy only festers if not dealt with, it doesn't go away."

Grateful that she could unburden Shifra, yet the sadness that she experienced over having to confront a neighbor, drove Leah to her knees late into the night to ask Yahweh to prepare the way before her.

15

THE BETROTHAL

THE COURTYARD WAS TRANSFORMED INTO a beautiful destination, by the hand of a very talented woman. Leah knew exactly how to arrange things to make people feel welcome, as well as transform an ordinary place into a paradise.

Nitzevet and Rebekah wandered around the courtyard wanting to remember every detail. The tables were scattered around the edges of the courtyard with several candles on each. A delicate piece of fabric rested under the candles surrounded by bunches of bright pink Tamarisk flowers. A couple of deep red pomegranates were nestled among the candles and flowers to bring out the depth and variety of colors. Nitzevet could smell the spicy aroma of the myrrh oil that Leah had sprinkled on the fabric under the candles. Leave it to Leah to think of a way to enhance everything from the beauty of the flowers to the fragrance of the Myrrh to the taste of the food creating remarkable beauty from ordinary things close at hand.

Nitzevet and Rebekah were tasked with placing a bowl of figs and dates and nuts on each table, so the guests would have something to munch on before and after dinner. Nitzevet knew that her soon-to-be mother-in-law had asked her to do this so that she could take in the beauty and check all the details of the decorations before they needed to get dressed.

There were candles on the stone walls illuminating the shadows and spreading the golden glow over the nooks and crannies of the beautiful courtyard. Under the shade tree, there was an arch of muslin fabric with candles spread around. On the opposite side, there was a buffet like no other. An endless stream of servants was bringing out the food and placing the platters on the table.

Nitzevet could smell the fragrant roasting lamb, and the stewed vegetables from the garden seasoned with herbs and spices. The freshly baked bread made her mouth water like never before. The garlic and olive oil were ready to dip the fragrant bread, it made her stomach growl. She was so grateful for the quiet moments she was given to drink in the beauty of the place. But now it was time to get dressed.

The girls returned to their room and got dressed together, helping each other put the finishing touches on their evening attire. Nitzevet had not seen Jesse since he had kissed her hand, although she had sent several messages to him through Reu, just to make sure he was aware that she was over the moon to begin their betrothal.

The messages she received in return were so sweet. Reu gently knocked on the door in the early afternoon and told Rebekah that Jesse said to … "Tell Nitzevet, my love, that tonight is the beginning of a great adventure."

Nitzevet treasured the words with all her heart. Now, as dusk was setting, she could hear the men in the courtyard, Samuel's distinctive joyful voice. She could hear Jesse's rolling laughter, Obed's deep voice, and Shelach's admonition in jest. It made her heart full of joy to hear her favorite men enjoying life and each other.

There was a knock on the door, Rebekah opened it to let Gila in. She walked in and embraced her beautiful daughter, "My dear daughter, you are lovely," she said in astonishment.

Nitzevet noticed the lilt in her voice, "Are you surprised mama?"

"My sweet girl, I am never surprised at your beauty, only that today, I am giving you away. You are no longer mine. I never imagined the finality of this moment," she said as she wiped away a few tears.

"My sweet Ema, this is only our betrothal. I have to wait many months before I am fully Jesse's wife. Besides, I will always be devoted to you even though I belong to Jesse. I can and will do both, it is easy to be devoted to both of you," she smiled.

Nitzevet noticed that her mother was dressed in a long flowing teal gown with a simple muslin sash. "You look so beautiful and young Ema. I am so proud to be your daughter."

"It is time for us to go, my daughter. Your grandfather is waiting outside. He insisted that we both walk you to the arch to meet Jesse." Gila turned to Rebekah and instructed, "Rebekah, you will go before us and meet Reu just outside the door. The two of you will walk together to the arch and then Rebekah will stand to the left of the arch and Reu will stand behind Jesse to the right of the arch," Rebekah nodded with understanding.

There was another knock on the door indicating that everyone was in place, and it was time. Rebekah opened the door to see the beaming face of her friend Reu holding out his hand to take hers. Rebekah took his hand and he wrapped it around his arm and they walked together through the house into the courtyard and slowly up to the arch. She was overwhelmed by the beauty of the place and the smiling joyous faces. She was especially cognizant of the handsome young priest standing under the shade tree, under the canopy of muslin gazing at her as she walked up. Reu gently led her to her place beside the arch and then went and stood on the other side behind Jesse. After taking his place, Reu winked at her for encouragement, for this very wise young man had noticed the blush in her cheeks when she saw Samuel, and he had seen the twinkle in Samuel's eye at the sight of Rebekah.

Jesse could hardly behold what he saw. She took his breath away. A beautiful woman with wistful red curls peeking out from under the white linen veil. A beautiful smile radiated from beneath her delicate nose and glowing eyes. Nitzevet was dressed in all her glory in the beautiful dress his mother had made. A beautiful gold sash with shells and earrings that matched. He even noticed her delicate feet shod with the most intricate of sandals. This was his bride ... his bride. He had waited so long for her, and he must wait even longer.

Gila and Shelach walked on either side of the bride, guiding her to her place next to Jesse. As Nitzevet stood beside Jesse she noticed a tear trickle down his cheek. She reached up without thinking and with an intimate gesture gently wiped the tear away. He leaned over and whispered in her ear, something no one could hear.

Samuel cleared his throat and smiled, to move the attention of the gathered loved ones from the display of genuine affection back to the task at hand. "Dearly beloved, friends, family, relatives, everyone who knows and loves this couple, we are here to announce and celebrate the betrothal of these two beautiful souls."

Samuel read the customary contract that he and Eli had written up together.

Leah stepped up and together with Gila lifted Nitzevet's veil while Samuel poured two glasses of wine and handed them to Shelach.

Shelach then handed one glass to Jesse and the other to Nitzevet and both drank deeply from the delicious wine to seal their covenant vows. The veil was replaced by Leah and Gila to signify that Nitzevet was not fully a wife yet.

At that moment a huge shout went up from the guests and there was cheering and clapping. After a few moments Obed, standing in the center of the courtyard, cleared his throat loudly to get the attention of the people, and lifted his voice in prayer, "Yahweh, Lord our God, we celebrate today the betrothal of this wonderful couple, bless them in the coming months and bless this food we are about to consume."

At that moment, everyone was reminded of the amazing aromas coming from the food table and the kitchen. Reu led Rebekah to the head table while Jesse, in an unexpected bold move, but not out of character, swept Nitzevet off her feet with his strong arms as if she were but a small child, and carried her to her chair at the table.

Nitzevet took mental pictures of everything that night. She would remember in the many years to come, the beauty and joy surrounding her on this night, it would never leave her and prove to bring her great hope in times of sadness.

נאמנות יהוה

Nitzevet and her mother and grandparents returned to Efrat the next day. Now she only had to wait, Jesse said maybe six months. She knew he would be building a home for them attached to his parent's house in Bethlehem. It was typically the custom for the new couple to live with the groom's parents. Sometimes they lived with the brides. But since Jesse was very much involved in the shepherding business of his father, Nitzevet knew he would be needed there. It was fine with her, living near her sisters-in-law would, could, only be the best experience of all, only that she would miss her mother and grandmother.

"My daughter, I am so happy for you!" Gila approached Nitzevet one morning, "We have much to do, we have to prepare your dowry."

"A dowry Ema, you are giving me a dowry?" questioned a puzzled Nitzevet.

"Of course, precious one. You are getting married!"

Nitzevet knew that dowries came from the father of the bride as something that she took into her marriage, so she had just assumed that she would not have one. As unpresumptuous as she was, her family had been preparing for this for several years. The only living offspring of Dalit and Shelach, they wanted to lavish her with all that they had. In the days ahead, Nitzevet would come to understand just how precious she was to those who loved her.

Your Grandfather has asked me to make you a whole new wardrobe befitting the wife of a leader in the community as Jesse is. It will take us quite a few months to get everything finished. Our first order of business is to go to the marketplace and choose the fabric you would like for these gowns. So tomorrow morning we will go and meet the caravan that arrives at the same time every week - they will have good material.

נאמנות יהוה

Gila and Dalit were ready to go when they woke Nitzevet. It took her only moments to get ready and take a few sips of her hot spiced milk. After a couple of bites of bread, she was ready. The women headed to the marketplace.

"My dear, you are to choose whatever fabric you see that you really like. Your grandfather has told us to spare no expense," Dalit said.

"I know your favorite colors are teal and scarlet. I also know that you like delicate and flowing linen-type fabric," smiled her mother, remembering how Nitzevet always looked like a princess in the right dress.

'Yes, Ema and Grandma, I will choose some nice fabric. Look at this one!" Nitzevet held up the simplest yet most delicate of teal fabrics. It was truly lovely. "We will need some white silk for undergarments for this fabric. It is too thin to wear without silk," she said while falling in love with the fabric herself.

The women walked away that day with enough fabric for ten dresses. A whole new wardrobe for Nitzevet and her new life.

נאמנות יהוה

A few days after Shelach and his family left to return to Efrat, Obed knew it was time to get to work helping Jesse plan for his home so the marriage feast could occur. Obed was so pleased to be bringing yet another lovely daughter into his household. He was trying to think what a good bride price would be for Nitzevet. Typically, the bride price was paid at the betrothal, but because it was 'rushed' due to Samuel and Eli needing to get back to Shiloh, Obed had agreed with Shelach to put off the actual payment till later.

"Leah, you know I cherish your opinion. Tell me what we should give to Shelach and the family," he gently inquired of his wife.

"My love, think, they have property to pass to Gila, they are a small family not in need of much, so our gift should be of great meaning and bring them great joy and reflect our gratitude for giving us their precious daughter," Leah responded.

"What if ..." The wheels were turning in Obed's mind. Leah was pleased because she knew it gave Obed great pleasure to give gifts.

"What if ...?" she asked.

"Let me do some thinking and you will be the first to know what we will give; do you trust me?" he asked.

"Yes!" she said wholeheartedly, having been on the receiving end of Obed's exceptionally thoughtful gift-giving for more than fifty years.

16

CONFRONTING THE JEALOUS

LEAH WOKE EARLY THE NEXT morning, hoping to have a few moments in prayer. The Lord had given her an idea about how to proceed with Ednah and her family. After her time with Yahweh in the cool crisp morning, Leah began the preparations for a wonderful picnic lunch for three. Aged cheese, special unleavened barley crackers, grapes, cool goats' milk, and her special date cakes. She packed a blanket and napkins.

When the lunch was ready, she set out for Ednah's home. Knocking on the door, Leah prepared herself.

"Good day," greeted Chazael.

"Shalom," responded Leah with a smile. "I have come to take you and Ednah on a picnic. I know we don't know one another well, but I thought a chat over a bite to eat on a beautiful day would be just the way to get acquainted."

Chazael was taken back and more than a bit suspicious, as well as she should be, after plotting against this woman's family. But the offer to get out of the house and chat with another woman outweighed the suspicion and was too inviting to say no. "Let me see if Ednah is available to go," leaving Leah standing on the doorstep, Chazael went to petition her daughter.

"Of course, Mama, maybe we could get more information about Jesse," she smiled mischievously with a knowing look.

The door opened and Chazael and Ednah were ready to go. Leah led the way, "I have a lovely little spot just outside the city where there is a rocky alcove, and we can picnic in the shade."

"Sounds lovely!" said Chazael. But Ednah was more cautious, "How far is it? Are there bugs? Are there wild animals?"

Leah smiled, as she took a good long look at Ednah. "No, my dear, it is quite close and very safe. It is our land, and everyone knows that."

Satisfied, Edna proceeded to follow.

After they found a rock outcropping, which was truly lovely overlooking the city of Bethlehem, Leah spread out the blanket with Chazael's help and proceeded to unpack their lunch.

"How long your family has been in Bethlehem?" asked Leah.

"About three years now," responded Chazael.

"Do you like living in our little town?" she asked, noticing that Ednah made a sound with her mouth indicating that she may have something to say on the topic.

Not waiting for Chazael's response, Leah turned to Ednah, "Ednah, how do you like Bethlehem?"

"There are not a lot of parties here. It seems that people just work and eat and sleep and then do it all over again the next day, week after week. The last party was the Tisha B'Av which did not include food at all," Ednah's voice sounded a bit whiny.

Leah was beginning to understand why Ednah would never be a match for Jesse, even if Nitzevet was not in the picture. Jesse despised complaining and bad attitudes.

"We are a very traditional town. And yes, living life takes a lot of work, day in and day out, but we share the load. And we try to make our evening meals fun and full of laughter. But you are correct, for the most part, we work hard."

"What are some things that would bring you joy, Ednah?" Leah asked.

Thinking for a moment, Ednah thought she would drop a hint, "I would like to get married soon," keeping her eyes on Leah to see her reaction.

"I can understand Ednah. I believe that is in the heart of most young women," Leah responded as if she had no clue Ednah was interested in her son.

"My mother was a wise woman and she taught me something that made a remarkable difference in my life," pausing for effect, Leah continued after a moment, "Remember, that seeking to become the best wife you can be is the best way to find a good husband," Leah wanted her words to sink in.

"When we make it our goal to 'find a husband,' we are focusing on the wrong thing. We use all our energy looking around and looking at the qualities of others. What Yahweh would prefer is that we look inward and while living our lives among our family and friends, we learn to be the best person, the kindest person, so that the young men look our way and want to get to know us."

Chazael was impressed with Leah's wisdom. She knew that her Ednah could use some education on how to be a good wife. As far as she knew, Ednah did not know even the basics of how to be a wife. Could she run a household? Could she care for all the things that are necessary? Typically, Ednah spent most of her time in her room brooding. Maybe that was her fault. She did not demand that Ednah participate in the family chores. Usually, it was just easier to do them herself rather than fight Ednah and then have to redo the work because she did the job poorly.

Chazael had a novel thought, maybe letting Ednah do the chores was more about teaching her to be a wife than it was to get them done or done in the right way.

Leah continued, "When I was your age, my mother took every opportunity to teach me a new task that would be vital to know when I got married. In fact, I was so busy learning things, and improving on them, that when Obed walked into my life, it was very unexpected."

"In fact, I had actually spent so little time engaged in contemplating marriage that my teen years went really fast."

Ednah was listening. Something was melting in her heart. She knew that she spent way more time evaluating the qualities in others than she spent working on her own thoughts and abilities. She was starting to become quite ashamed at her behavior, especially of late, scheming and plotting to destroy a relationship between two people she did not even know, just for her own gain. Yes, she was ashamed.

The two older women continued to talk and chat about lighter things, truly enjoying the day and the lunch and the view of their beautiful town.

Chazael noted to herself that Leah had opened up a whole new view of life, that she had not considered. Work and life and teaching were fun and should be embraced with one's whole being, so as to not miss a moment or an opportunity.

As the ladies walked home, there was the hint of a new sense of friendship between them and they could all feel it, each to themself hoping it would be a new beginning of something really special.

"Shalom my friends," Leah said as they parted ways, "May Yahweh bless your evening."

"Shalom!" the mother and daughter called out in unison to their new friend.

Leah was content. When Yahweh was at the center of a plan, it just worked out and you could trust Him to use your word in His way.

נאמנות יהוה

Keturah had the evening meal started and only needed Leah to put the leavened bread into the oven.

Leah smiled. This is exactly what she was talking about with Ednah, women who knew how to be a blessing to others and who took great pride in their work.

"Ema, why are you smiling?" Keturah asked.

"Just thinking how wonderful you are and how much I appreciate you!" she replied.

"You really are the best Ema and grandmother," her daughter-in-law raved.

Leah gathered all five of her little grandchildren like ducklings in her arms and kissed them all and then shooed them out of the kitchen area so she could make the bread.

"Oh, Ema, Father said he wanted to take a walk with you this evening after our meal. Shifra volunteered to clean up after. She is resting now so she can work later."

"Thank you my dear. I think I know what he wants to talk about. But you need to get off your feet, that little one will be coming soon!" she said, always the concerned mother.

נאמנות יהוה

121

"My love, I wanted to pass my idea by you before I told anyone. But you knew that didn't you?" Obed lovingly looked at his wife as he grasped her hand "Let's take a walk under the stars."

"Sweet Obed, always the romantic, yes I knew, that is why I trust you; you always think of me first and consider my feelings," she gazed into his eyes.

"Well, when we work together, whatever we accomplish is so much better, I am compelled to include you!" he responded.

"Tell me then, my dear, I am anxious to hear."

Obed began to tell Leah of his wonderful plan to help Jesse build a double house for his bride who shares their courtyard. It would be a home for Nitzevet and Jesse, but it would also be the mohar because it would contain special rooms for Gila, Dalit, and Shelach whenever they came to town. It would be as if they had a second home.

Leah was so pleased, what a wonderful and generous gift to give. Not only blessing Jesse and Nitzevet, but their sweet friends. It is always hard to give a gift to someone like Shelach and Dalit, they have land, they have servants, and they have livestock. But a room of their own to visit their daughter is the perfect gift.

Obed explained that they could all pitch in and make the home for their friends special and beautiful.

"My husband, I love that you have included all of us to join you in creating this gift, it will be a work of our hands, for our special friends," Leah explained.

"Exactly!" said Obed. "Do you have any thoughts or suggestions?"

"How long do you think it will take to build?" she asked.

"If we plan it right, I believe about thirty days to plan and gather supplies, ninety days to build. Maybe a few more."

"Then I suggest you make all the plans and then after Sukkot, we will begin. That way, if Dalit and Shelach come to Bethlehem for the feasts next month, they will not know anything of our plans," Leah said.

"Good idea my dear wife."

"Also, tell only Jesse. The others may not be able to keep a secret while our guests are here. But then after they leave, we can tell them all the plans."

"Another good idea, my dear," said Obed.

They finished their evening walking hand in hand in the pastureland. Their own thoughts occupy their minds. Leah of how to decorate the home for her beloved son and friends, and Obed thought of the structural elements he would need to plan out to make it secure and unique.

נאמנות יהוה

Now that Leah was on board with the bridal gift for Nitzevet and her family, he needed to inform Jesse of the plan. Typically, according to tradition, the father of the groom directed the construction of the newlywed home that was attached to the family home. Obed knew that Jesse had a special ability to engineer and design, so he wanted this gift and their home to be a reflection of Jesse.

"Son, we need to talk!" Obed said as he encountered his son early one morning.

"Yes, Father, is everything ok?" he asked, hoping there wasn't a problem.

"Of course, my son, we need to talk about your new home with Nitzevet," Obed said with the biggest grin Jesse had seen in a while.

"Of course, Father, when would you like to speak?"

"Let's get some breakfast and head out toward the field. Bring a writing instrument and some parchment, you will have an assignment," Obed smiled.

Jesse laughed and went to gather the tools while Obed gathered up their breakfast.

They headed out to the field side by side, each lost in their own thoughts. Jesse was excited to hear what his father had to say, and Obed was calculating the cost and need for materials.

As Obed poured a cup of hot spiced milk for Jesse, he said, "Your mother and I have come up with a wonderful idea. We would like to build a house for you that is big enough to have a living space for Shelach, Dalit, and Gila. The house will be your new home for your bride but also include rooms for your in-laws that will be the mohar."

Jesse was blown away by the generosity of his father. "That, that would be amazing Father. Nitzevet will be so pleased!"

"You know how much we enjoy having them come and stay with us. If we design it in such a way that we can use your room and build on from there we could have a wonderful home for you and our extended family," Obed beamed.

Jesse was pulling out the drawing tools, "I have already guessed, my homework is to design this massive addition," he said with a grin.

Obed relished that his son knew him so well, "Yes, please design it. We would like it to reflect you and your talents and abilities. Can you have the list of materials and supplies needed ready so that I can purchase them through my suppliers?" his father asked.

"Absolutely, Father, give me a few days," he said as he sipped his warm spiced goat milk, he snickered at the thought of how his mother had shaped and molded his father even to the point of getting him hooked on this spiced milk concoction that he knew even his bride loved.

"Oh, and Jesse, tell no one until after Sukkot. That way no one will let the secret slip while Nitzevet and her family are here next month. After they leave you can tell the others and we will start the building project," Obed instructed.

Jesse spent all day in the field watching the sheep and designing his home addition. Just like his father suggested he used his own room as the jumping off point for the addition. A new entrance would be constructed from the courtyard that would lead into spacious living quarters with a kitchen to one side and a great room. Off to the right was Jesse's room, which would become the room for Shelach and Dalit. Straight ahead and slightly to the right was a staircase that led to an upstairs bedroom where Gila's room would be. There would also be a door on the second floor that would lead to the rooftop area that will extend over the entire house. On the main floor to the left of the staircase, Jesse designed a large room for himself and his new bride. It featured a private sitting area and a window that looked off to the hills. From that angle, the top of the Tower would be visible from the window. He knew that if his wife ever needed to stay home, she could at least sit by the window and look over the hills.

Reu was coming over the hill, and Jesse was so excited to share the plans with him. "Shalom Reu."

"Shalom Jesse. I noticed you took the day watch shift for yourself. Either you have thinking to do or planning?" he surmised.

"How well you know me, my friend. I am designing our new home addition as a bridal gift for Nitzevet and her family," Jesse explained, and then suddenly remembered the admonition from his father to tell no one. "Reu, I was not supposed to tell anyone for fear they would accidentally tell Nitzevet. We want it to be a surprise, can you keep it a secret until after they leave next month?"

Reu smiled, knowing that Jesse knew he could and that he would keep his 'master's secret.

Jesse showed Reu the drawings and explained each and every corner and how the structure would be strong and reinforced to hold the weight of the rooftop as well as the second story bedroom.

"That is shaping up to be an amazing home, Jesse. I would be honored if I could help you build it."

"I was counting on your help Reu, you are invaluable when it comes to getting things done efficiently. Thank you for offering before I could ask. I can always count on you. And thank you for keeping my secret!" Jesse squeezed Reu's shoulder in a gesture of friendship.

Reu took his leave from Jesse and wandered back to town, pondering the goodness of Yahweh. How could a foreigner, a slave no less, as a young boy encounter such a good and loving family? How could this be his fate? Ah, but it was not his fate, it was God's plan, and he was so blessed by it. Yet again he praised Yahweh. What was Nitzevet's song? "I thank you, Lord, with all my heart I sing praise to you before the gods. I face your holy Temple, bow down, and praise your name because of your constant love and faithfulness because you have shown that your name and your commands are supreme."[13]

If there was anyone who understood the difference between Yahweh and the gods, it is me, thought Reu. All my life all I knew were evil gods who cared nothing for me, and only wanted sacrifice after sacrifice of everything. On top of that they relished evil and ungodly things. Yahweh is so different. He is holy and gives guidelines for his people to be holy, so they can approach him and love him. I will always praise Yahweh above all gods.

17

THE PREPARATION

GILA FELT THE PROMPTING OF Yahweh to talk to Nitzevet about the intimate details of marriage. Deep down she never wanted Nitzevet to get married, but she knew that was unrealistic and unfair to expect her to stay with her always. A wise mother, she decided to expound on Nitzevet's knowledge by telling her about the great women of her past.

"Nitzevet, can we take a walk this afternoon?" asked Gila of her daughter.

"Yes mama, that would be lovely," responded Nitzevet.

Gila remarked to herself, that Nitzevet was never one to assume that the conversation would be a reprimand or a confrontation. Her genuine love for people always puts her on the best terms. She resolved issues as they came up and never left hard feelings unresolved.

"Wonderful, my daughter, I will prepare some refreshments to enjoy on the journey."

Nitzevet met her mother at the edge of the field closest to town. They just instinctively knew where to meet and when. It was probably the substance of their unique relationship, a friendship with deep mutual respect.

"What did you want to talk about Ema?" asked Nitzevet.

"I wanted to tell you the full story of Ruth and Boaz, all the parts together. I know you know quite a bit about them, but I am not sure you have heard it all, told without pause and with the reasoning behind what was done," explained Gila.

"I suppose you are right Ema, I would love to hear the whole story, beginning to end."

Gila knew her daughter would relish the details of the love story, especially the role that Yahweh played in bringing Boaz and Ruth together.

"Your great aunt Naomi left Bethlehem with her family during the great famine. Naomi, Elimelech, and their two sons, Mahlon and Chilion traveled to Moab where there was plenty of food and land. After a few years, both sons had married and then all three men died. Saddened, hopeless, and lost Naomi decided to return to Israel," Gila paused, feeling her own pain at the loss of her husband.

"What you might not know is that Mahlon married a woman named Ruth and Chilion married a woman named Orpah."

"I do know that mama," said Nitzevet.

"Yes, that you do know, but do you know who Ruth and Orpah were?" she asked.

Nitzevet had not thought about that and smiled, "I am listening."

"Ruth and Orpah were the daughters of King Eglon of Moab," Gila paused.

Nitzevet looked a little shocked. How that secret had been kept she did not know. Maybe she was the only one that did not know?

Gila continued, "So Mahlon and Chilion both married daughters of the King of Moab. Naomi encouraged her daughters-in-law to stay in Moab and remarry. As the King's daughter, Naomi was sure there would be a future there for them. Neither Ruth nor Orpah had children yet.

Orpah decided to do what Naomi suggested and she stayed in Moab. Ruth however said, "no, I will not stay." And in the famous words that had been handed down through the family, she said, "Do not urge me to leave you or to turn from following you. For wherever you go, I will go, and wherever you live, I will live; your people will be my people, and your God will be my God. Where you die, I will die, and there I will be buried. May the LORD punish me, and ever so severely, if anything but death separates you and me."[14]

"Naomi could not argue with her plea, so she embraced Ruth and the great gift of friendship and service she gave and returned to Israel.

One of the reasons that Ruth's true heritage was 'forgotten' was that she truly embraced Yahweh. Not while she was married to Mahlon as much as when she chose to come to the land of Israel with her mother-in-law. She put a stake in the ground and made a promise to follow Yahweh.

But, Ruth, a Moabite widow living in the heart of Israel after the death of her husband, had little hope for a future. I think that Naomi had some idea of the truth of this. Ruth had married young and to a foreigner. Now she herself was a foreigner. Even though Naomi's husband had vast properties in Israel, she as a woman, had no access to them without a husband. So she and Ruth were destitute and hungry.

But one day, after living in Israel for a few days, Ruth was gleaning wheat behind the harvesters as the poor were allowed to do, each hoping to gather a handful of grain for their supper. While gleaning, Ruth noticed a man at the edge of the field, he had come to inspect the harvest. She could tell that he was the landowner and the boss. She kept working, but she noticed that he was looking her way and asking questions about her. A little fearful, she was nervous when the man, who she later came to know as Boaz, came over to her and told her to stay on his land and continue to harvest wheat with the other women.

Ruth told Naomi that night of her encounter and how Boaz had been kind to her. Naomi knew that Boaz was not only an elder of the town but was known to many as a judge of the People. He was also a relative of Naomi's husband Elimelech ... he was one of the Kinsman Redeemers of the family. Naomi encouraged Ruth to do what Boaz said and continue to glean in his field and under his protection.

Because of Boaz' kindness, Naomi had a plan to let Boaz know that Ruth was in need of a Kinsman Redeemer."

"What was so important about Boaz becoming a Kinsman-Redeemer, I don't fully understand who that is?" Nitzevet asked.

"Naomi and Ruth were destitute. They had no money, no land, because they were women and Naomi knew Ruth had no future. In the Torah, there was a law written that a woman who had no children whose husband had died, could marry her husband's relative and have children to carry on the family line. The man was then acting as the redeemer and vindicator of the family. It is so like Yahweh to write this provision in His law to protect women.

But as the story goes, Yahweh was way ahead of any of Naomi's plans. By putting Ruth on Boaz's land and putting a spark of love in Boaz's heart. He brought Ruth and Boaz together in a great love story.

Naomi told Ruth to go to the threshing floor where, after the day's work there was always a festival and then the men would lay down and sleep so they could work the next day. She told Ruth to note the place where Boaz laid down and then go uncover his feet and lay down. Then, to do whatever Boaz said. Ruth said yes and obediently went to the threshing floor that night.

"Wasn't she afraid Ema?" asked Nitzevet.

"I am sure she was. But remember, Boaz was a kind and just man, who loved Yahweh and was loved by Yahweh. Did I tell you he was one of the Remnant? When he saw Ruth lying there at his feet, he was immediately impressed by her character and her sacrifice. He knew she was the daughter of a King, who left it all behind. She did not demand riches or young men or privilege, she obeyed her mother-in-law and Jewish custom and risked her reputation to seek a kinsman redeemer. He blessed her and commented on her character, Boaz knew he could not find a better wife, then he encouraged her to stay till the early morning when she could then get up and leave before anyone recognized her."

"I forgot she was a princess. She was gathering grain as a princess," Nitzevet pondered the concept with awe and even greater respect for this woman who humbled herself before Yahweh.

"Ruth went home and told Naomi that Boaz was a kinsman redeemer but not the closest. He had explained to Ruth that he had to go ask another man if he wanted to be the kinsman redeemer first before he could say yes."

"Can you imagine, Ema, waiting to see who your husband would be … the great Boaz or some other man?" asked Nitzevet a bit horrified at the thought. She had never considered marrying someone she didn't know or wanted to marry.

"Yes, my daughter, I can only imagine. But as the story goes, Boaz went to the city gate where you know all the business of the town takes place and Boaz knew the other man would come by and he did. Boaz asked him to come and sit for a while and he invited ten elders to come as well. He informed the man that Naomi's property was up for sale and that he was first in line to redeem it. The man said yes - he would be glad to redeem it. Then, that is when Boaz told him he would also be redeeming Mahlon's wife, Ruth the Moabite woman as well, to carry on the family line. But the man said no, he could not put the rest of his property in jeopardy by taking another wife. Boaz then took off his shoe and made the deal with the man in front of ten witnesses. Ruth was to become Boaz's wife.

Boaz had his own family inheritance and because he had chosen to be Ruth's kinsman redeemer had also inherited Elimelech's vast properties when he married Ruth. Being the kind and generous man that he was, he gave the largest portion to Naomi and a rather large portion of Elimelech's land to Aliza, Naomi's sister who lived in Bethlehem, and your great-grandmother, Nitzevet. Your grandmother inherited it, and I will inherit it and then you and Jesse.

I tell you this story, my daughter because I want you to understand fully that when Yahweh is allowed to guide our steps, He takes us to places that may be hard, but those places will bring the greatest joy. Leaving her family and her people was hard, but Yahweh brought Ruth to Boaz, who became the love of her life. More importantly, Yahweh brought Ruth to Himself. Do not be afraid to do hard things for Yahweh and then trust Him for the results, even if it may take time to realize them.

Marriage is about trust and sacrifice. Follow your husband, be kind, gracious, and forgiving, and let him know how you feel. Let him know how his actions make you feel. If you hold a grudge against him because of something he did, how will he know how he hurt you unless you tell him kindly how his actions made you feel? This will allow your relationship to remain intimate and open and you will never regret that kind of a relationship."

נאמנות יהוה

Six months had passed and the addition to the Obed household was truly amazing. Some even called it a work of art. Jesse, Obed, and Reu had put their hearts and souls into the design, and Leah and her daughters-in-law had put their hearts into the finishing touches.

The ladies enlisted Shoshannah to plant several planters under the windows and beside the door of the attached dwelling. She was known as the town gardener. Shoshannah knew every plant and what it produced and what it could be used for. She planted puvvâh so that Nitzevet could harvest the crimson red seeds for dying fabric. She planted Shikkeron in the window boxes because the vibrant yellow blossoms would make Nitzevet happy. And of course, no house would be complete without a healthy herb garden for all the wonderful meals that a new wife will make for her husband. The women were so pleased with Shoshannah's work that she was being asked by many other women to build flower and herb gardens for them.

Reu noticed the beauty that Shoshannah naturally left behind wherever she went. He was intrigued. How could one girl so sweet and so small leave such a lasting impact. He wanted to know more about her.

נאמנות יהוה

Jesse had been pondering for a while how he was going to pull off the traditional wedding procession if Nitzevet lived in Efrat. The tradition was very important to the tribe of Judah, they would never consider any other way than following the wedding traditions of their ancestors. To them it had a deeper meaning, even though they could not fully grasp it. They knew that these traditions were one of the primary ways that Yahweh instructed about the past and foretold of the future. Jesse consulted the one woman in his life that could help with this kind of thing. She might even pull off a miracle.

"I just don't know how I am supposed to go get Nitzevet when Father says and bring her here on the same night, with all of our friends and family. Mother, you have to help me devise a plan," Jesse lamented.

"My son, I have been thinking of this for a while. I did not want to make a suggestion until you asked. But I do have a plan, would you like to hear it?" she asked with a smile.

"Of course, Mother, what is the plan?" he begged.

Leah furrowed her brow in thought as she pondered the plan, "So, we will send Rebekah to Efrat to stay a few days and then have her bring Nitzevet here to Bethlehem under the pretense of a short visit. She will stay with Rebekah in her home and be none the wiser. Shortly after they leave Efrat on their journey, Gila, Dalit and Shelach will follow and arrive here at their new home. Then on the evening of your Father's choice, you will "go and get your bride" at Rebekah's home and the parade will begin," she explained.

"Oh, and her parents will bring all her wedding attire with them, and we will put it in Rebekah's closet so that when they hear the shofar - Rebekah can help Nitzevet dress and be prepared for the wedding and the feast. We will leave the details of how that will be accomplished to Rebekah and Shoshannah," Leah had thought of every detail.

"Ema, I knew you would know exactly what to do. Thank you!" Jesse said as he hugged his mother.

The plan was set in motion, with Obed's permission of course. He, as the Father, was the only one who knew the day or the hour that he would send his son to get his bride. It was important that their plans be within the parameters of his plan.

Leah asked her husband one more time, "Are you sure, my love, that you are fine with the plan that Jesse and I have concocted?"

"Yes, my dear. Jesse has worked so hard on the home addition, and it is beautiful. It has been long enough for him to wait for his bride, and he isn't getting any younger," Obed laughed.

"Rebekah is excited to leave, we will send her tomorrow to Efrat. I will send with her a letter to Gila and Dalit with all the plans so they will be ready and prepared for a wedding any day or night after they arrive here in Bethlehem.

The journey seemed long to Rebekah, but it only took four hours. She stepped off the donkey she was riding just as they arrived at the gate to the town of Efrat. Shelach was there and was surprised to see her. He knew Nitzevet's friends well.

"My dear Rebekah, what brings you to Efrat? We did not expect you," he questioned.

Rebekah stepped closer to Shelach and whispered in his ear. She did not want to risk exposing the secret plan to anyone else. She showed him the scroll that she was going to give Gila and Dalit. He nodded with approval and sent her on her way to Nitzevet.

Nitzevet was shocked when her best friend knocked on her door. Rebekah quickly told her all was well so that she did not worry and told her that she had missed her so much she had to visit, which was true. So Nitzevet thought nothing of the surprise visit.

Gila and Dalit secretly prepared everything as Leah had outlined in the message. They were ready to go two days later. When Reu showed up at the door, asking for Rebekah, indicating that her parents had requested that she return home. Knowing this part of the plan, Rebekah begged Nitzevet to come with her for a few days to help her if she needed it. Nitzevet, always up for an adventure and a visit to Bethlehem, went with her friend.

The girls enjoyed the journey, Nitzevet, unaware of anything other than a fun visit, and Rebekah filled with joy that her friend would soon be married. They arrived in Bethlehem and went straight to Rebekah's home. She insisted that they go and help prepare dinner, there was no time to stop by Jesse's home and see Leah.

Gila, Dalit, and Shelach arrived a couple of hours after the girls and immediately went to the home of Obed. As they rounded the corner, they were shocked at what they saw. The home was different. They had expected a small addition for Jesse and Nitzevet, but this massive extension with an upper floor was amazing. Obed and Leah met them at the gate of their home with a twinkle in their eyes.

"I can see that you are puzzled at the size of this addition," Obed chided his friend. "Shelach, Dalit, Gila, in lieu of a traditional Mohar of silver or wealth, which you do not need and would be reluctant to accept, our family built the ben Shelach family this home for you here in Bethlehem."

Leah hugged her closest friends as they wiped the tears from their eyes. Gila and Dalit did not know how to respond to such a generous, kind gift given from the heart. They truly felt like instead of giving away their daughter they were gaining a whole family. Shelach just remained quiet, overcome with emotion at the generosity of his friend.

As they walked through their new rooms, they were amazed at the quality of the workmanship and the beauty of everything. Gila thought how pleasant it would be to visit Nitzevet whenever she wanted and not be in the way.

Obed said to them all, "You are giving us your only daughter, your only granddaughter. The only thing we can do is invite you to join her and stay whenever you want as long as you want. The rooms are yours."

נאמנות יהוה

Rebekah kept Nitzevet busy all the next day and into the evening. She did not know when Obed would tell Jesse to come, it could be this night or the next or even the next. But she wanted Nitzevet to be prepared. After inviting Shoshannah to join them for an evening of girl time, Rebekah decided that they would 'practice' fixing Nitzevet's beautiful curly red hair for her eventual wedding night. Rebekah decided not to tame the flaming curls, but to create a crown of flowers instead. She then took some small white flowers that Shoshannah was cultivating for just this occasion and made a beautiful crown intertwined with gold thread. She combed through her curls and then placed the flowers on the top of her head.

It was truly beautiful. Even Nitzevet, unaccustomed to looking into the mirror, for she did not have a vein bone in her body, admired the skill of her sweetest friend. Rebekah's mother brought them each a cup of warm spiced milk. They enjoyed sipping their tea and chatting about the things they would do together when Nitzevet came to live in Bethlehem. Nitzevet watched and laughed as Shoshannah practiced with Rebekah's hair and Rebekah did the same for Shoshannah. The girls were very pleased with what they had accomplished.

It was getting late, so they decided that it was time to get ready to sleep. While Nitzevet was pulling out her bag, she heard a noise far in the distance. Rebekah and Shoshannah heard it too. Suddenly, Rebekah and Shoshannah knew what it was and were surprised. There were several other couples engaged in Bethlehem, but none of them were close enough to their wedding day. "What do you think the event is?" asked Nitzevet, for she assumed it was not for her, she was not at home.

Rebekah and Shoshannah smiled. Nitzevet looked at them puzzled, as she slowly came to the realization, "No, it is not Jesse. I don't think he is coming for me so soon."

Rebekah hugged her friend and said, "Hasn't it been long enough? Where did you think the wedding would be?"

Shoshannah said, "What if Jesse heard you were in town and Obed sent him to get his bride?"

Nitzevet was almost in tears, "But my dress, I am not prepared?"

Rebekah walked across the room saying, "Your hair is beautiful! And ..." Then she opened the closet and pulled out Nitzevet's wedding dress, once again made by Leah specifically for Nitzevet.

She had never seen anything so beautiful. An ankle-length gown of snowy white, soft and flowing, so delicately made. She traced her fingers over the delicate gold strands woven through the hem and sleeves of the gown. These were distinctive to a bride's gown. They were also distinctive of the talent of Leah. Shoshannah located the beautiful sandals and the golden sash that were meant to go with the gown that Reu had dropped off in secret that afternoon. "Suddenly, all the details of the past few days came into focus for Nitzevet. She now understood the visit by Rebekah and the surprising journey to Bethlehem, the visit by Shoshannah, fixing her hair. She was slightly embarrassed that she had no clue. "It has to be Jesse then. Obed had decided to send his son!" she shouted.

נאמנות יהוה

The girls got dressed. Shoshannah had brought her wedding garments just in case. Always be prepared was her motto.

As the girls were getting ready, they heard the Shofar getting closer and closer as Jesse was walking through the streets of Bethlehem waking up the neighbors and friends. By blowing the horn, the wedding party was inviting all who heard and were prepared to join the bride and groom for the wedding feast.

Finally, the crowd that had been gathering as Jesse and his family paraded through the streets, arrived at the door of Rebekah's home. Rebekah's father threw open the door and stepped aside to show the beautiful bride and her bridesmaids waiting just inside the door.

Nitzevet stepped forward and Jesse, speechless and motionless, was amazed at how beautiful his bride was. He could see her sweet smile in the darkness. Reu nudged him out of his paralyzed moment and indicated for him to help Nitzevet into the litter. Her two new brothers-in-law Jephanneth and Vophsi along with Shelach and Rebekah's father, carefully picked up the litter and proceeded to "fly the bride to her groom's home".

Back through the streets of Bethlehem, they paraded, Jesse at the front, full of smiles, blowing the shofar every now and then glancing back at his bride, followed by Leah, Dalit, Gila, Keturah, Shifra, Shoshannah, Rebekah, and many others who would not think of missing the wedding of the most prominent man in Bethlehem. When they arrived at the ben Obed family home, Jesse helped his bride from the litter, picked her up and carried her through the gate into the courtyard and through the door and the whole procession of people proceeded to follow them into the home of Jesse. Part of the tradition was that the door was shut firmly behind the last guest and locked. If you did not enter with the whole group, you did not enter.

As Jesse carried her, Nitzevet looked up at the expanse of the ben Obed home and how it had changed. She was shocked. Of course, she had expected something, but nothing this grand. As she wandered around the new expansive addition her mother explained to her that it was the mohar, the bride price. A new home for all of them. Nitzevet wept. Obed and Leah must have known how much she would miss her mother and grandmother, to give her such a lavish bride price.

Then the party started. The food was wonderful, aromatic and warm. Roasted lamb, fresh cheese, Leah's date cakes. It was the perfect wedding feast.

18

MOVING TO BETHLEHEM

JESSE AND NITZEVET'S WEDDING FEAST lasted the traditional seven days. Most of the guests, who were friends and neighbors, went home during the day and returned in the evening. It was the grandest party Nitzevet had ever known.

Her family had packed most of her things quickly after she left to go to Bethlehem with Rebekah, so during each day she was busy with her mother and grandmother moving her things into her new home and getting settled.

During the seven days of the feast, Jesse would escape for a few hours at midday to attend to the family business, but he would return as quickly as he left, to spend as much time as he could with his new wife. It was a time of relaxing and getting to know one another. They spent hours and hours in their well-decorated comfortable room gazing at the fields through the picture window and loving every moment just being together while they made plans for the future.

"Jesse!" Nitzevet exclaimed on the third morning of their wedding, "I can see the top of the Tower from my window!"

Jesse rolled over and gathered his precious wife into his arms, "I wondered how long it would take you to notice" he said smiling.

"It has been quite a busy few days, my husband," she said, blushing at the thought.

Nitzevet kept thinking in her heart that her life was too good to be true. She went from wondering if this man even noticed her, to being engaged and now lying in bed next to him. Sure, they had had many conversations during their betrothal, in the courtyard among the family. But this was so new to her. It was so wonderful.

A wonderful family, a wonderful husband, and plenty of time to get to know him. There were so many things she did not know about Jesse; she was sure that it would take a lifetime to really know him well.

Samuel had spent the whole week at the ben Obed family home in their guest room. When building the new addition, Jesse and Obed had made a special room for Samuel, considering him a close family friend. Hoping that as High Priest of Israel, he knew he had a place to call his own while in Bethlehem. They wanted him to be able to get away and pray and fellowship with people who loved him as family.

Obed made every effort to spend time during the week to discuss the things of Yahweh with Samuel. He was impressed with the wisdom and knowledge of such a young man. God was present in Samuel. Obed often noticed Rebekah conversing quietly in the shady courtyard with Samuel each afternoon, sipping on spiced milk. He found Leah one day, "have you noticed the budding friendship?"

Leah laughed, "Of course my husband, we have all noticed. Their laughter is beautiful and inspiring. They truly enjoy talking and being together. They are good friends, and I think we may have another wedding in the future. Let's keep quiet about it so that Yahweh has His way in their hearts."

The very next afternoon Samuel took Obed, Leah and his mother Hannah and sister Abigail, who had also stayed for the whole wedding feast, for a walk and a conversation. Samuel broke the news of his wedding plans with these special people in his life. His father, Elkanah had passed on a few years back and out of respect he had already made Eli aware of his intentions, but he considered Obed more of a father than anyone. Obed and Leah were overjoyed for they loved Rebekah as a daughter, being Nitzevet's best friend. Hannah could not have been happier, her heart was full of joy and her eyes were full of tears, she would gain another daughter.

On the seventh day of the feast, everyone knew the grand party was about to end. The group was a bit sad, but down deep they all knew that life had to get back to normal. As they stood out in the courtyard waiting for the final feast to be ready, Samuel stood up and pronounced boldly,

"I would like to make one final blessing on the new couple, 'Blessed art thou, O Lord our God, King of the universe, who hath created joy and gladness, bridegroom and bride, mirth and exultation, pleasure and delight, love and brotherhood, peace and friendship. May there soon be heard in the cities of Judah, and in the streets of Jerusalem, the voice of joy and gladness, the voice of the bridegroom and the voice of the bride, the jubilant voice of bridegrooms from the wedding canopy, and of youths from their feasts of song. Blessed art thou, O Lord, who gives the bridegroom joy in his bride'."[15]

He paused for a moment, looked over at Rebekah and smiled. He reached for her hand and continued, "My friends, I now would like to make an announcement … by the grace of Yahweh we would like to announce that this evening Rebekah and I will be betrothed."

A cheer went up from the whole wedding party as they rejoiced. The men each gave Samuel a big bear hug and the women cried. Nitzevet jumped up and hugged Rebekah. She had no clue their relationship had progressed so far. She was so wrapped up in her own wedding that she did not even notice the budding romance right under her nose, and Rebekah had not discussed it with her.

"My dear friend, may I be as wonderful of a friend to you while you wait as Samuel's betrothed as you were to me," Nitzevet said to her friend, as she noticed Rebekah's beaming face. At that moment she treasured the joy of her friend deep in her heart.

Rebekah spoke with hesitation, "I hope you don't mind us using the last day of your wedding feast as our betrothal?"

Nitzevet laughed so loud others looked her way, then after hugging her gracious friend she said, "You could not have given me a better wedding gift than to choose this day and my home to host your betrothal. I am just sad that I did not know earlier so I could help with the plans."

In the corner of the courtyard Gila looked over at Leah and asked, "You knew?"

"Of course, my dear," Leah laughed. "We have been planning this for a few days. Did you notice the few extra guests from Shiloh? Samuel's close friends from his childhood have traveled with Ahitub, Eli's grandson, to witness the betrothal," she responded.

A few moments later, the people gathered by the arch and Obed stepped up to the front to lead the betrothal ceremony. Hannah stood beside Samuel and Rebekah's father and mother stood beside her. Obed poured the wine and led the young man and the young lady through the ceremony.

Jesse and Nitzevet stood holding hands in the crowd, happy to share their joy with their closest friends. However, not paying close attention to the ceremony, Jesse nibbled on Nitzevet's ear and whispered, "You were a beautiful bride," she giggled and blushed. Jesse had his arms wrapped around her waist as if to never let her go. She sighed a contented sigh; it could not get any better than this.

As the final feast for Nitzevet and Jesse became the betrothal feast for Samuel and Rebekah, Nitzevet noticed how the table decorations and the lighting, and the food were just that extra special. It could not have been planned more perfectly, but then it was Leah and her two daughters-in-law pulling off this event, Jesse's wonderful family.

Samuel walked Rebekah back to her home that evening pondering his life. He was thirty-three years old, and soon to be married to this beautiful young woman walking beside him. Certainly, Yahweh was good. He gently hugged his bride-to-be and as he left her at the door of her home, he reminded her, "I will be back for you, my love. It may be any time. I have my own home, so I don't need to build one. Will you be ready for me?"

Rebekah's heart was full, "I will be ready every day from now until you come. Even now I am ready!"

Samuel smiled at her youthful exuberance and turned to leave; he planned to return to his home in Shiloh the next morning with Ahitub and his friends, but he longed to stay here with his beloved.

נאמנות יהוה

Nitzevet blinked open her eyes just as the sun popped over the horizon through her window. As the brain fog eased, she realized today was Shabbat, Nitzevet's favorite day. Literally, it meant 'to stop'. The ben Obed family for many years had made it a mandatory practice for all the members of their clan from Boaz to the youngest shepherd. This custom made Nitzevet so happy, her family in Efrat had also celebrated Shabbat like the ben Obed family.

Food for the day was prepared on the day before and tucked away for 'grazing' as Jesse liked to refer to it, they could eat when and where they pleased.

The shepherds did not move the flock on Shabbat but rather joined them in the fields resting in the quiet sunshine or laughing with their friends over a simple meal.

Nitzevet's new routine, now that she was Jesse's wife and lived in Bethlehem, was different than most people. Typically, everyone would sleep in and approach the day slowly, she however, would wake up early, pack up her snack, and head to the pasture where she could be alone with her God. She knew that this pattern would not always be possible, someday she would have children to care for, and sleeping in would be a blessing.

The air smelled wonderful as she lay hidden in the tall, sweet grass looking up at the clouds as the sun warmed her toes. There was so much to enjoy about life when one takes time to slow down, stop, and delight in Yahweh's creation. As she pondered Shabbat, she thought about its origins, she knew that it was started in the Garden after Yahweh had created all things, he rested on the seventh day. It was what God had asked the people of earth to do on the seventh day and so her people taught it to their children. God had built into creation a rhythm of life ... six days of work and then one day to stop and rest and delight in creation and more importantly to delight in Yahweh Himself.

She marveled that God had mandated this 'stopping', this rest was one of His 'words' that he gave Moses. She remembered something that her grandfather had taught her. The original words of Yahweh given on Mt Sinai said, 'Remember the Sabbath'. But forty years later after their sojourn in the desert, Moses retold the law to the new generation and he said, 'observe the Sabbath'. It was as if Moses knew the people needed a mandate, a command and the reason that Moses gave for the observance was different too. The original mandate said to remember the Sabbath and keep it holy because God rested on the seventh day, but Moses gave a different reason to this new generation. God grounded his instructions in the story of Israel's exodus from Egypt. Nitzevet thought, 'it was as if God knew this generation, scared by the horror of slavery, needed to know that they were truly free and that they could indeed stay that way. An illustration of this freedom that God wanted them to see was the freedom to rest and delight and find joy … people who can do that are truly free.'

Nitzevet smiled, "What a good God you are!" a tear of joy rolled down her face as she worshiped the one true God.

Jesse knew he would find her here in the pasture near the tower. The grass was so tall, she was harder to find than usual, but then he saw the wisp of her scarf blow in the wind just above the top of the grass and his heart skipped a beat, his love.

Slipping into the grass next to her not to disturb her thoughts he lay there on his side looking at her beautiful face enjoying the warm breeze and the warmth of his love next to him, grateful for simple, quiet moments.

"Jesse, why did God call Shabbat holy?" Nitzevet asked.

Jesse smiled at her inquisitive mind, "My grandfather told me it was because the gods of this world were to be found in space, not in time. So you could find them in their holy temple or a holy mountain or a holy shrine, but our God, Yahweh is not found in a place but in a day. He said that if we want to meet our God we don't have to make a pilgrimage or go to Him, we just stop long enough to experience Him, so He set aside a day for us to do that and made it one of His laws. My father said that enjoying God is so important to Him and to our own emotional health that He mandated it."

"Is that why I always feel refreshed and full of joy after Shabbat?" Nitzevet asked as she mentally put the pieces together.

"Yes, my love," Jesse said as he reached for his bride and pulled her close, feeling her melt into his embrace. The embrace of love is also part of the experience of Shabbat.

19

RELATIONSHIPS

THE COOL MORNING BREEZE CAUGHT the three women by surprise as they walked through the field where the dew lingered at the tips of the long blades of grass. They often walked and talked together about how their lives were changing and what the future would hold.

"Rebekah, let's invite Ednah to your wedding!" Nitzevet said with a singular boldness. Rebekah smiled, how like her sweet friend, "Yes, let's do it!" Shoshannah was pleased with the thought, "Let's stop by her house on the way back and let her know that we want her to come."

The girls were very happy that they could at least seek to include this rather sad girl in their group. Whether she would respond was anyone's guess, but they would try.

Rebekah had a thought, "Let's actually stop by and invite her to your house for a noon meal today and then we will talk about Rebekah's wedding and invite her."

"Best idea ever!" exclaimed Nitzevet.

After their morning walk the girls, true to their word, stopped by Ednah's home and knocked on the door.

A very shocked, shy, and still a bit ashamed young woman answered and graciously invited them in. "Ednah", Rebekah spoke up, "We were stopping by to invite you to Nitzevet's home for noon meal today, are you busy? Can you join us?"

Her face revealed further shock at the kindness and gentleness with which they addressed her. Ednah was so unused to this level of kindness. Never would the women in her previous town ever speak with such grace, especially after the things that Ednah had perpetrated on them. She could do nothing but accept. As she closed the door, a particular warm feeling settled in her chest. 'Is that what joy feels like?' she thought.

נאמנות יהוה

Sitting in the green grass in the pasture near the tower, Nitzevet pondered her life so far. A few months of marriage can truly change one's perspective about life, having a companion to share your every struggle, and joy. She marveled continually at the grace of God to provide such a precious institution as marriage that would establish a sacred space for two people to grow in the presence of Yahweh while walking the journey of life together. Yahweh knew what he was doing. She pondered that maybe this was what her God meant when he said, "Let us create man in our image ..." It seemed to her that her marriage to Jesse was a picture of the relationship that Yahweh longed for with His people. 'Maybe,' she pondered, 'Yahweh created marriage for that specific purpose, to image His relationship with His people?' How she longed for the world to experience Yahweh as she did. Maybe He does have a plan someday to redeem the world. Didn't Yahweh tell Moses, "And in you all the families of the earth shall be blessed."

"Where are you?" came a high-pitched voice of an excited woman. Nitzevet knew it was the voice of Rebekah, but she didn't sound worried.

"Over here, my friend. Is everything alright?" Nitzevet asked.

"My dear friend, he is coming! Samuel is coming!" she said, catching her breath.

"I thought it was supposed to be a surprise?" her puzzled friend asked, leading her friend to the blanket in the grass to sit and rest.

"It still is, I don't really know when he is coming. You know Samuel, always thoughtful of others. He did not want me to be caught off guard. He sent a servant from Ramah to tell me to expect him within the next few days. He wanted me to know the general season of his arrival if not the exact date or time," Rebekah explained, smiling at Samuel's kindness.

"Wonderful! We have everything ready; we just need to wait for the trumpet sounds," Nitzevet said excitedly. "You do realize they will probably be in the evening," Nitzevet smiled.

The girls hugged each other, and tears of happiness flowed down their cheeks. Nitzevet was so glad to have a friend with whom she could discuss the joys of marriage. Rebekah will begin her life with her Love forever. The girls stayed in the shadow of the tower for a while longer as Nitzevet shared her insights from that morning about marriage. She could see the joy in Rebekah's face as she eagerly lapped up the information like it was food for her soul. She was so excited to experience this with her beloved.

Samuel arrived two days later with his closest friends from Shiloh and Ramah. Hannah had arrived a day earlier with Samuel's close friends from Ramah. The thoughtfulness of Samuel to inform his sweet mother. He wanted her presence at this very special event. Of course, Leah had everything ready. Keturah and Shifra had been working long days with Leah to prepare the feast for the wedding and decorate the courtyard for the seven-day party.

Samuel and Jesse were busy preparing Samuel's room where Samuel was to bring Rebekah that night or early morning after the wedding procession and first feast. He placed fresh flowers from the garden on the small table, and a dish of dates and fruit to nibble on, not that they would need that or even remember it was there after the feast. "I never knew you had such cultured decor talent!' Jesse teased, "for a priest, you sure do know your way around flowers," Samuel tossed him a frown face; Jesse was always the jokester.

Jesse's brothers had been put in charge of the children (their children) during this busy time and like most men, they found the most skilled person to actually do the work of caring for and playing with the children, Reu. Mostly they chose him because he loved the children, and they loved him. Keturah and Shifra had noticed how he was so kind and gentle but a leader as well. They trusted him with their children like they trusted their own husbands, 'maybe even more', about which they would often tease their husbands.

At Rebekah's house, they knew Samuel had arrived and suspected that tonight was the night he might come. Nitzevet was busy helping her prepare. Shoshannah had joined them. "Rebekah, your hair is so lovely," Shoshannah remarked. She had decided that a long braid starting at the front and top of her head and winding on each side toward the back would be stunning. "Your silky black locks contrast beautifully with the gold thread that I have weaved through the braid," Shoshannah had planted the Star of Bethlehem in Nitzevet's garden for just this purpose. Reu had brought her a few sprigs that morning and she gently tucked the delicate flowers into the braids and then stepped back and said with a quiet voice, "You really are a star of Bethlehem!!!"

Nitzevet could not contain her tears, for before she stood one of the most beautiful women she had ever met. Not only on the outside but on the inside ... Rebekah was lovely.

Rebekah's mother brought in a tray for the girls to nibble while they waited. As she caught a glimpse of Rebekah she smiled and said, "What a lovely young woman Yahweh has given me." It was obvious to all that the overflowing joy in Rebekah's heart made her strikingly beautiful. Her mother hugged her daughter, as her eyes welled up with tears, she explained that they were bittersweet tears of joy and sadness. Joy for the wedding day of her precious daughter and sadness that she would be giving her away.

"Ema, this is the best day of my life. Yahweh has given me a beautiful childhood with wonderful parents and friends in a beautiful little town. Now He is sending me on a journey into a new chapter of my life. As the wife of a priest of Yahweh. I know it will be challenging, but you have raised me well, and I am prepared. I hope I can still count on your sage advice from time to time?" Rebekah asked.

Her mother responded with a big hug and kiss. The ladies all sat nibbling on the food and chatting while they patiently awaited the sound of the trumpet. They knew he was coming, he said he would, and they were confident.

Then they heard it, the distant sound of a trumpet and they all smiled, every one of them knew what this was. Rebekah was ready.

Samuel knocked boldly on the door of Rebekah's home and was greeted by a jubilant father of the bride who greeted Samuel with a big bear hug and proclaimed, "Let the adventure begin!" in a very loud voice.

Samuel's two friends from Ramah and Vophsi and Jephanneth put the litter on the ground so that Rebekah could step into it, just as Nitzevet had done four months earlier.

When Rebekah appeared at the door of her home at Samuel's call, everyone could hear the gasp from the crowd. They had all noticed the remarkably beautiful bride standing before them. Everyone but Jesse, who was standing next to Samuel, and when the girls came into view, he could only see the beauty of his own bride standing just behind Rebekah. Jesse caught Nitzevet's eyes and winked at her, making her blush.

Rebekah, not accustomed to the attention of so many people, also blushed a deep red, she had never given her appearance a second thought. This is probably what made her all the more beautiful. Meanwhile, her father, sensing her discomfort from all the focused attention and knowing what his daughter was thinking as she blushed, leaned over and whispered in her ear, "You are lovely and it is a gift from Yahweh, embrace it and give Him the glory my daughter," she hugged him and graciously stepped into the litter.

While all this was taking place, Samuel, like Jesse a few months earlier, just stood frozen in place. He could not believe this lovely girl was going to be his wife today! In his young life, having lived in the place of worship at Shiloh and in his home at Ramah, he had not had a lot of contact with women. In this moment it hit him that this amazing woman who was a gift from Yahweh stood before him, and he silently prayed that he would be worthy of her and that he would always live up to his responsibility and commitment. Jesse nudged Samuel with a snicker and said, "We have to walk back now brother, you think you can do that?"

Samuel smiled at the good-natured ribbing from his friend and proceeded to put the horn to his lips to lead the way back to the wedding feast, after of course, smiling and winking at his bride who blushed an even deeper red if that were even possible.

Nitzevet noticed that Ednah had quietly joined the throng of people, slipping in between her and Shoshannah as they walked back to the ben Obed home. She smiled to herself, thanking the Lord that Ednah had been ready and wanted to join them.

Obed flung open wide the door of his own home as he heard the procession approach. He welcomed all the guests that had joined the wedding parade. When the last guest had passed the threshold, he shut and locked the door.

20

A NEW WIFE

PASSOVER SEASON IS HERE AGAIN. It had been eight months since her wedding, so this was Nitzevet's first Passover as a married woman. She fondly remembered the Passover when she was eight, it was the best. She had learned so many things about what Yahweh had planned for His people. Now that she was eighteen and married, she was expected to play a larger role in the preparations and ceremony with Jesse's family, which she was so glad to do.

Leah, Keturah, and Shifra had always had a picnic lunch before the Passover season started to plan the events. This year, Nitzevet was included in the special preparation picnic. They decided to go to the shade of the tower, they knew Nitzevet loved it here and it was cool and shady. These ladies never missed an opportunity to make an event truly special by making even the planning of it a special treat as well.

Leah suspected that there might be some news coming from Nitzevet soon, she sensed a change in her sweet daughter-in-law that only a mother would know and sense. But she would wait patiently for Nitzevet to reveal her news when she herself figured out there was news to share. As mother-in-law and knowing the special bond that Nitzevet had with Gila she did not want to spoil that surprise and memory by usurping her position.

Leah started the discussion, "Obed went over the requirements with me again last night. But it was not necessary, I have hosted Passover for thirty years, I don't even need to think about how to do it anymore."

"Ema, besides the traditional lamb, unleavened bread and bitter herbs, was there anything special you wanted to include on the menu this year for Passover?" Keturah asked. The other women nibbled on the delicate picnic treats as Leah pondered the question.

"Girls, I was talking with our neighbor the other day and she has been adding Charoset to the Passover feast," Leah mentioned it as she took a bite of a beautiful date.

"What is that? I have never heard of it," Shifra questioned.

"It is a mixture of figs, dates, and nuts. The ingredients are chopped very fine and mixed with a little fruit juice to make a thick paste. Can any of you think of what it might represent from the time of the Exodus?" asked Leah, always looking for a teachable moment.

"We don't know, please tell us!" asked Shifra.

"Yes, my daughter," Leah said smiling, "It represents the mortar that was put between the bricks that our ancestors made to build buildings".

"Oh!" All three girls said in unison. "It sounds really yummy, and meaningful," replied Nitzevet, "let's include it, I know Jesse would love it," she said smiling. The other women present rolled their eyes at her comment. It was always about Jesse.

Nitzevet spoke up, "I know the bitter herbs remind us that our ancestors were unable to offer sacrifice and worship to God, and that was even more bitter than the slavery of Egypt."

Keturah added, "The Lamb is to be roasted, and no bones are to be broken in this process. Why do you think that is Ema?"

"I think Yahweh has a reason, and it will eventually be revealed, right now we just obey the instructions and wait to see what Yahweh has prepared for us," responded Leah.

"We will probably need to make extra Matzah because the men love to eat Matzah. Why do you think we were instructed to put stripes on it?" Shifra asked Leah.

"My daughter, again I do not know, but I have a notion that Yahweh will eventually reveal that too. He never requires anything from us that does not lead to or represent a significant purpose or plan," Leah responded.

"Today is the ninth of the month, tomorrow is when we need to get our family lamb from Jesse, can we leave that to you Nitzevet?" Shifra said, smiling again along with a good eye roll.

A beaming young bride responded, "Yes, of course!" just as she turned a lovely shade of green.

"Nitzevet, are you all right?" asked Shifra.

"Yes, I just got a little nauseous, it might have been the fourth date that I ate in a row, on top of the curds. But it was so delicious," she responded.

Leah smiled as she thought, 'Soon Nitzevet will know why she is nauseous. It's just as I had thought.'

נאמנות יהוה

"Why am I sick Ema?" Nitzevet asked Gila as she lay on her bed in the darkened room with a cool cloth on her forehead.

Leah had sent word that maybe Dalit, Shelach, and Gila could spend the upcoming Passover with them in Bethlehem. They had arrived the day before Passover and had a lovely meal. Gila smiled to herself, after seeing Nitzevet's glow, she knew immediately why Leah had asked, and what was really going on with Nitzevet.

"My daughter, you are not sick," Gila said as a matter of fact, with a very big smile.

Nitzevet sat up and looked at her mother. Instinctively, she knew what her mother was implying. "Really! You really think I am pregnant!" she exclaimed.

Then she sighed a huge sigh of relief. "I thought I had a terrible disease. I feel miserable sometimes, especially in the morning," then she giggled while turning green again, she felt dumb, not having recognized all the symptoms. She had seen both of her sisters-in-law go through this numerous times.

"Ema, can you go get Jesse? I think there is something I need to tell him," she said as she smiled a radiant smile.

21

ELI & THE ARK

NITZEVET WAS JUST DOWNRIGHT UNCOMFORTABLE.
Her mother had never told her that being pregnant was so very ...
uncomfortable. It seemed as if her huge belly just led the way in front of
her wherever she went. But she was so excited to welcome her little one
into this world.

"What did you say his name was going to be Nitzevet?" Jesse asked.

"His? What if it is her?" she responded.

"I will love whoever comes," Jesse smiled as he wrapped his wife in
his arms.

Looking up into his face Nitzevet explained, "I want us to remember
that Yahweh brought us together, that we are married because Yahweh
has a special plan for us, I know it in my heart. That is why I want to
name him Eliab."

"God is Father! I like it. So it shall be," replied Jesse. "And if it is a girl?"

"I am just not sure. I may have to wait on that," she responded.

"Very well, my love. I am off to the fields to check on the shepherds.
It is a shearing season, and they are very busy. They could probably use
some encouragement," he pondered.

"You are kind Jesse, tell Reu hi from his nephew Eliab!" she laughed.

Jesse kissed her forehead and said teasing, "What if it is a girl?" As
Nitzevet rolled her eyes, he noted how soft her skin was. He was so
blessed.

He was whistling as he walked out the front gate of the courtyard,
thinking how just a year ago he had brought his lovely wife through that

gate as his bride. What a celebration it was. It was seven days that he would never forget.

"Shalom, shalom!" Jesse heard the cries of someone near the gate of the city. He started to pick up his pace in the direction of the noise to see what was going on. A few men were there, and more were coming as Jesse arrived.

A very tired and dusty tall Benjamite messenger had come from Aphek. He had just witnessed a battle. He was running from town to town to tell the story. In short sentences, trying to catch his breath the messenger told the tale, "The Israelite army was camped in Ebenezer. The Philistine army is camped at Aphek. The two armies prepared to do battle. We were confident that we would win. At the end of the battle, and after the dust had settled, we realized ... we realized ... that the Philistines had killed four thousand Israelites on the battlefield."

Shocks and bewilderment swept through the growing crowd, "what happened next," several called out.

The young messenger continued, "The commanders of our army were trying to figure out what to do. Someone had the thought of bringing the Ark of the Covenant from Shiloh to the battlefield."

"Why would they do that? Did Yahweh tell them to take the ark? Did he speak to Samuel or Eli?" asked Obed who had been sitting at the city gate since early in the morning.

"No. I think they were so upset at losing, it was as if they were trying to compel Yahweh to fight for them," he paused.

"I heard one of the commanders tell the soldiers not to provoke Yahweh in this manner. He encouraged the impulsive young men to take a step back from this rash decision and consult Eli and Samuel first to see what Yahweh's will was." The tall runner slowed down a bit and continued his story, "They ignored the commander. It took two nights for the Ark to arrive, Hophni and Phinehas, the Levite brothers in charge of caring for the Ark came with it. It is almost three parasang from Shiloh to Aphek. When the Ark arrived, there was a great and mighty shout from the soldiers. I am sure the other army heard it and were wondering what had happened." The messenger was really slowing down. The adrenaline from his run was subsiding and he looked very weary.

A young girl from the crowd noticed his weakened state and brought him a cup of water from her water jar.

While he refreshed himself, men standing in the gate were shocked and wondered why their God had seemingly forsaken them. Some of the people standing around the messenger whispered that it was about time Yahweh got into the fight. "Didn't he promise to go before us and win our battles?" they asked.

The messenger ignored them and continued the story. "The enemy army went out to fight again against our soldiers and now the Ark of the Covenant was there ..." he stopped as if the rest of the story was too hard to tell.

The eager Bethlehemites encouraged the messenger to continue.

The tall messenger stood up, looked at his fellow Israelites, and told the rest as tears rolled down his face, "The defeat was great. We lost an additional 30,000 men."

The shock was obvious. Everyone fell silent. They had thought they would hear of a great victory because of the circumstances, but a defeat.

Jesse spoke up in a somber voice, "Where is the Ark now?" Jesse could feel the thickness of the silence and the grief that came with it all around him.

The Benjaminite lowered his voice, "In the hands of the Philistines."

An even greater shock rippled through the crowd. The story kept getting worse. There were many tears, some moaning, and a lot of wailing. The Ark had been with them for hundreds of years. Crafted by Moses, it was the place where Yahweh resided. It was His seat among them, His presence in the midst of His people, and now it was gone, now He was gone, so they thought.

Not having fully thought through the emotional response of the crowd, the messenger looked at the grieving crowd and thought to himself, 'Should I tell them now that Eli is dead? Should I tell them that I watched him fall off a bench and die? Should I tell them that Hophni and Phinehas died when the ark was captured?' He decided to wait till the next morning, he needed rest so he could continue his journey.

Jesse debated whether or not to tell Nitzevet in her condition. But he knew his wife, it would be better to come from him rather than others, besides their marriage was built on trust and no secrets. He also knew the strength and calmness of her great faith in Yahweh would help all of those around. Running back to his home, he paused at the gate asking his God for help in telling Nitzevet.

Nitzevet was shocked, saddened, discouraged, and puzzled, but uniquely undefeated as the others were. She knew that Yahweh was bigger than the Ark. She knew that Yahweh was never confined to a tent and a box. She knew that He was with her. He was with His people. Actually, she was mostly disgusted that the Israelites thought they could compel their God to do their will. And that dragging the Ark around would be the instrument to force the Almighty Creator of the Universe to bend to their will. Now 34,000 men are dead.

Nitzevet needed to walk, so once again, she found herself at the base of the Tower. She prayed to her God, truly seeking answers, "Why would You abandon us? Why would You allow your Ark to be captured? The Ark that was the first to cross the Jordan River, the Ark that houses without decay a jar of manna, the Ark that holds Moses' rod that turned into a serpent?" Her questions were honest and bold yet humble, she was truly puzzled at the turn of events.

As she thought, Nitzevet realized that Yahweh had done so many things for them, raising up Judges and rescuing them from their enemies. It was all so amazing and unpredictable. She recounted to herself the story of how her God raised up Deborah and then gave into her hands the life of the commander of the army Cissera. Then Yahweh raised up Gideon and whittled his army down to 200 - the number of sufficiency, and Gideon was victorious. Then Samson, as wayward as any man could be, Yahweh still used him to defeat their enemies. The Philistines have never again held the amount of land they had before Samson.

She realized that with all of these events, Yahweh had led His people, not the other way around. They were victorious because they asked and obeyed, not because they demanded.

It was Nitzevet's custom to put into poetry her thoughts for events like these, even in times like this. Nitzevet thought these words on that day sitting beneath the tower:

"My God, forever your word is firmly fixed in the heavens. Your faithfulness endures to all generations; you have established the earth, and it stands fast."

This young mother, the daughter of a single mother, knew deep in her being that Yahweh, the only father she had ever known, had a special plan for the world. While her people, the Hebrews, were His chosen, they were not chosen because they were special, they were special because they were chosen.

After the stories of the past three hundred years flashed before Nitzevet's eyes, including the most recent, loss of the Ark of the Covenant, it was never clearer to her how "not special" the Hebrew people were. 'Could any other people be more sinful?' she thought.

"But God," she said out loud.

Shoshannah was slowly approaching, and having heard Nitzevet's words, and asked, "What do you mean my dear?" She had come to check on Nitzevet, worried about her being alone and so very pregnant.

"Shalom, Shoshannah. Despite our foolishness as a nation, despite of our sin as a people, despite of our lack of trust as individuals, Yahweh Himself is faithful. We would not exist, except for our God. Our God is faithful," she said.

The friends snuggled together, sitting quietly pondering the events of the day. Praying that Yahweh's will would be done.

נאמנות יהוה

Several weeks passed and life in the town of Bethlehem almost went back to normal. Except for the cloud of gloom that hung over all of Israel, knowing that their Ark of the Covenant was in the hands of a foreign power.

Nitzevet's time had come to give birth. Jesse was so pleased, he knew he would love this child, male or female.

After many hours, Gila finally came out of the apartment where Jesse and Nitzevet lived and announced to Jesse that he had a beautiful baby boy named Eliab.

Jesse was a lover of Yahweh. He could not help but know his God. As the son of Obed, he had an amazing father figure who set Jesse up to understand who a father is and what his responsibility is as the leader of his family. More than that, a good father gives their children a view of who their God is, and how their God interacts with and loves people.

Jesse had of this knowledge and understanding for sure. As the husband of Nitzevet, he had gained yet another perspective of who Yahweh was, a Friend and companion.

נאמנות יהוה

"My love, I am so grieved that we cannot perform the ceremony of redemption where the Ark of the Covenant is," Jesse snuggled his wife close with their newborn between them, sleeping soundly.

Nitzevet paused before speaking, pondering her words carefully, "My dear husband, you know that Yahweh is with us even here, even now. Wherever we have the ceremony, our God is there."

Jesse loved her faith. "Yes, my sweet one, you are correct. Why don't we have Samuel come here and invite the whole town to the redemption ceremony?"

Nitzevet's face beamed with joy as she thought about the event. It was a once-in-a-lifetime event for a mother, only the first-born male would go through this ceremony on the thirty-first day of his life. "But that is only ten days away!" Nitzevet proclaimed, suddenly concerned that their newly formed plans would be shattered.

"You talk to my mother about the feast, and I will send a messenger to Samuel about the ceremony, we will see if we can make it happen in ten days." Jesse kissed this beautiful young mother beside him and then gently kissed the top of Eliab's head so as not to wake him. Leaving the darkened room, he was on a mission to contact Samuel.

"My precious daughter, you know we can and will make that happen!" Leah responded with enthusiasm. She loved parties; moreover, she loved making them happen.

Nitzevet's eyes filled with tears, "You are the most wonderful Ema! Thank you for caring for me."

As Nitzevet sniffled through her tears of joy and gratitude, Leah remembered the vivacious redheaded five-year-old that came to her house to learn how to 'behave'. How that amazing little girl became a beautiful young woman, holding her own child, certainly made Leah tear up.

Wiping her moist eyes, Leah responded "Let's see what Samuel says after he gets the message from Jesse, and then we will begin the plans for 10 days from now."

נאמנות יהוה

Jesse walked to the city gate the next day with his father discussing the redemption ceremony. As they reached the gate Jesse looked down the road and there was the messenger on his way back from Shiloh with Samuel's response. He read Samuel's message as a smile spread across his face: "Yes, my friend, Rebekah, and I will come to Bethlehem and perform the Redemption Ceremony for Eliab. It has been so sad here since the death of Eli and his sons. We need family and friends. We will be there in five days."

Jesse went back to Nitzevet and his mother to let them know that the ceremony would indeed happen, and that Samuel and Rebekah would be there in five days. This event will have a dual purpose, Eliab's ceremony and encouraging Samuel and Rebekah.

נאמנות יהוה

"He is so lovely," Rebekah whispered as she kissed Eliab's soft head and snuggled him even closer. Sitting in Nitzevet's spacious apartment, she relished these moments with her best friend and this sweet baby.

Nitzevet smiled, "I know!"

"My dear friend, how are you? How is Samuel? What is your life like with Eli and his sons gone?" Nitzevet asked.

"Samuel is deeply grieved. He knew that Phinehas and Hophni were not good or wise men, but he loved Eli as a father. They had a deep and abiding relationship after many years of living as a family," Rebekah sighed.

She continued, "But he is slowly improving, he knows Yahweh does not leave us in the midst of our grief for long. Samuel spends long hours talking with Yahweh and asking what it is that Yahweh is planning.

157

The Ark is gone, and that may grieve Samuel as well, but he knows that Yahweh does not rely on the presence of physical things to commune with His chosen. We will wait to see what He has planned."

"Thank you for coming here and spending time with me. I wanted you to be here for the ceremony anyway!" Nitzevet said. "You stay here and settle in and I will go get us some food. It is about mid-day and I am in need of food."

נאמנות יהוה

"We are gathered here to celebrate with a ceremony and a feast, the redemption of a first-born son," Samuel began as he stood before a rather large crowd. He looked over the people, as a great sadness overwhelmed him. He knew they were here for Jesse and Nitzevet's firstborn, but he also knew they were there for encouragement from him. He needed to let these people know that Yahweh was undeterred in His love for them.

Jesse stood before Samuel holding Eliab with Nitzevet by his side.

"Jesse, is this your first-born son?" Samuel asked.

"Yes!" Jesse responded looking at Nitzevet and then at his son.

"Which do you prefer, to give me your firstborn or to redeem him?" Samuel asked, looking over at his mother as he said this.

"We will redeem him!" Jesse said, rather somberly, as Samuel continued with the blessing:

"Blessed are You, Lord our God, King of the Universe, who sanctified us with His mitzvot, and instructed us regarding the redemption of a son.

Blessed are You, Lord our God, King of the Universe, who has kept us alive, sustained us, and brought us to this season."

Jesse then reached toward his father who placed 5 shekels of silver in Jesse's hand. Placing the shekels into Samuel's hand, he smiled and said, "Thank you."

Samuel took the coins, smiled, and then blessed Eliab. He then proceeded to hold up a cup of wine and read the word of Moses:

"When he gives you the land where the Canaanites now live, you must present all firstborn sons and firstborn male

animals to the LORD, for they belong to him. A firstborn donkey may be bought back from the LORD by presenting a lamb or young goat in its place. But if you do not buy it back, you must break its neck. However, you must buy back every firstborn son.

"And in the future, your children will ask you, 'What does all this mean?' Then you will tell them, 'With the power of his mighty hand, the LORD brought us out of Egypt, the place of our slavery. Pharaoh stubbornly refused to let us go, so the LORD killed all the firstborn males throughout the land of Egypt, both people and animals. That is why I now sacrifice all the firstborn males to the LORD—except that the firstborn sons are always bought back.' This ceremony will be like a mark branded on your hand or your forehead. It is a reminder that the power of the LORD's mighty hand brought us out of Egypt." [16]

22

THE ADVENTURES OF THE ARK

IT HAD BEEN SEVEN MONTHS since the Benjaminite messenger had told them about the capture of the Ark. Another stranger came running into the little town of Bethlehem. He ran through the gate, past the elders, and headed straight for the town square, calling people to join him as he ran. Quickly, a group of people assembled. Some of the older men standing nearby encouraged the runner to take a seat, have some water, and wait for the elders of the town before he began.

Soon, Obed, Jesse, and Shelach, who were visiting his granddaughter and great-grandson, arrived along with several other elders of the town.

The messenger began his tale, it was the tale of where the Ark had been.

"The Ark arrived first in the city of Ashdod after it was captured," the messenger explained. "The Philistines, as usual, thinking the Ark was but another idol, put it into the temple of their gods next to their idol Dagon. The next morning, they found the idol of Dagon face down before the Ark of the Covenant."

The gathering crowd looked at one another with puzzling looks and encouraged the messenger to explain.

"The Philistines knew that we considered the Ark sacred, so they assumed its rightful place was alongside their gods in their temple. They set the statue back up and then again, the next morning not only was the idol of their false god face down, but the head was detached as well as the hands."

The Bethlehemites were all shocked. They knew what this meant. It was common practice for the pagan armies to cut off the hands and

160

heads of their enemies conquered in battle. Yahweh was making a very clear statement to Israel's enemies. More importantly he was making a statement of His power over all other gods. Hope sparked in the hearts of the crowd as they listened.

The messenger continued, "As the days went by, the townspeople as well as people in villages surrounding Ashdod started to have tumors develop all over their bodies. They knew instinctively that it was because the Ark was in their presence. In an effort to save themselves, they sent it off to Gath where not only did the people suffer tumors, but great confusion as well."

Pausing to take a breath and drink cool water, the messenger considered the details of his story. "I should also tell you that there was an infestation of rats in the land of the Philistines, so they considered that to be a plague sent by our God."

"The Ark was then sent on to Ekron and as it rolled into town the people cried out: 'They have brought the Ark of the God of Israel around to us, to kill us and our people.' It was even worse there - people died and those who didn't die, suffered greatly from the tumors."

"They had had enough so the Philistines gathered their five lords together and demanded that the Ark be sent back to us. We don't know why for sure, but they included five golden replicas of mice and five golden replicas of what we think are tumors. The elders in Beth-Shamash are speculating that they dared not send the Ark back to us empty, so as a kind of guilt offering, they put in the golden replicas of tumors and mice, the number of the lords and the types of plagues," the messenger paused to take a breath.

Chuckling to himself he pondered out loud, "Had they really known Yahweh they would have known that replicas, like idols, are not among the approved offerings acceptable to Yahweh."

Obed was amused as well and said, "They were probably thinking what their god would want, more idols, more gold, and then acted accordingly."

The messenger had finally settled down and the long run had taken its toll on his body, but the people would not tolerate a break in the story.

The messenger continued, "The lords of the Philistines took a cart and two oxen that had just calved and had never been yoked. They yoked the oxen together, penned up the calves, put the Ark along with the box containing the gold tumors and rats on the cart and sent it off. With this test they were trying to discern if these plagues and trials were caused by the God of the Israelites or if it was just a coincidence: Would the oxen return to their lowing calves and reject the yoke, or would they go against their natural tendencies and go straight into the Land where Israel lived? As they watched the oxen, they knew beyond doubt that it was the God of the Israelites that had done these things to them. The oxen went straight on leaving their calves behind."

"The men of Beth-Shemesh were in the fields harvesting their wheat and when they saw the Ark on the cart they knew what was happening and they rejoiced. The oxen stopped next to a large rock in the field of Joshua. The Levites who lived in the town took the ark off the cart and then used the wood and the oxen to make a burnt offering to Yahweh."

"I know Joshua," Jesse said, "He is a good man. What happened next?"

"Several of us noticed that there was a group of Philistines at our border, including soldiers. We confronted them and found out they were the five Philistine leaders and their guards. They had followed the Ark to the border. This is how we learned the story of where the Ark had been and what had happened. The rulers explained to us that they were simply returning what was ours and meant no harm, so we let them go. Besides, had we attacked them, we would be dead because they had quite a few soldiers with them."

"Many Philistines died?" asked Reu.

"Yes, they died from the tumors. But that is not all who died," the messenger's demeanor changed; Jesse could see tears forming in his eyes. "My brother along with sixty-nine other men from our village decided that they would take this opportunity to see what was in the Ark. Late last night they snuck out to where the Ark was and we assumed they tried to look inside it. We found their bodies this morning with the lid of the Ark askew. We knew what had happened."

Jesse, touched by the emotion of the young man, reached out and put his hand on the shoulder of the messenger; he knew that he was suffering right now, yet despite his suffering, this young man had volunteered to be the messenger to tell Israel what had happened. "I am sorry for your loss," Jesse said quietly.

Reu too identified with the young man, knowing what it means to lose family.

"Thank you. Joshua said you were a kind man. Ultimately, we asked the people from Kiriath Jearim to come and get the Ark. They took it to the Levite Abinadab's home on a hill and consecrated his son Eleazar so that he could guard the Ark."

Nitzevet and Gila had joined the crowd as the messenger was recounting his story. While they were pleased that the Ark was returned, they mourned for the lives lost. 34,000 now 70 more. Nitzevet looked down at her sweet little son as he lay in his basket smiling up at her. Someday he would be a man and may have to fight for the Lord. She prayed as only a mother could.

נאמנות יהוה

"Nitzevet, we are moving to Ramah!" Rebekah exclaimed.

Nitzevet was carefully folding Rebekah's cloak as she packed it for their journey, as she pondered Rebekah's statement. When the realization struck her that Rebekah would be a few hours away rather than all the way up in Shiloh, she was overjoyed. "Why, what happened?"

"Since Eli died and the Ark is in Kiriath Jearim, Yahweh told Samuel to return to Ramah where he was born, and we will live with Hannah," Rebekah beamed.

"I am so happy for you! And Hannah! And me!" Nitzevet squealed.

"What is going on in here?" Leah and Gila burst through the door.

After the girls explained the reason for their excitement, there was much rejoicing all around. Rebekah explained what Yahweh had told Samuel, "My husband is to start the judge's circuit of Bethel, Gilgal, and Mizpah, and we are to live in Ramah."

Leah processed the information and said, "So Samuel is to be not only a Priest of Yahweh but a Judge too?"

23

FAMILY

JESSE WOKE UP EARLY, AS was his custom, ready to get to the fields, there was much to do. He took a moment to gaze at his lovely wife laying in their bed with their children. Her beautifully wild red hair spread over the covers, and her soft face relaxed from a good night's sleep. What a beautiful picture she was, the mother of his children.

"You are an amazing mother," Jesse whispered as he kissed her forehead. "I don't know how you can so adeptly chase a one-year-old around and all the while carry and then give birth to another beautiful boy."

"I am glad I am young, if we have more children, I am going to need lots of strength," Nitzevet commented as she observed the sweet face of her newborn son, Abinadab, kissing his nose and snuggling her napping first son, Eliab.

"If?" Jesse quietly chuckled to himself as he left for the fields, knowing full well he intended to have a basket full of children.

Nitzevet, having heard his under-his-breath comment, rolled her eyes as he left, knowing that if she were to have more children, her heart would be full.

נאמנות יהוה

Shoshannah and Nitzevet were walking in the field by the tower enjoying the warm morning sunshine as they watched Eliab chase the little lambs that had just been born a few weeks ago. Seven-day-old

Abinadab slept soundly snuggled securely against Nitzevet with a piece of cloth.

It was quite the show, watching the hysterics as Eliab tried to pet the cute little lamb and for his effort got a headbutt and a mouth full of hair. Surprising to both women, it did not make Eliab cry, but rather made him all that more insistent that he was going to pet the little creature.

Shoshannah burst into laughter while watching. Nitzevet observed her younger friend and pondered the twinkle in her eye and a bounce in her step as they made their way to their picnic, so she asked, "What new thing has come into your life Shoshannah? Something is stirring. You must tell me."

"Yes, my dear friend, that is why we are here, I need to tell you … Reu and I are to be betrothed!"

Once again, the squeal of joy peeled from Nitzevet's lips, not unlike that of Eliab who was busy chasing two lambs now. She put baby Abinadab down in his blanket and rushed to Shoshannah to give her a warm embrace. "I am so happy for you, friend. I have longed for this day. In fact … it is about time! When will you have the ceremony?"

Shoshannah, pleased to be finally sharing her news, continued, "Reu wants a quiet ceremony, soon, with a few people, only your family, and my family. He still fears the reprisal of the Philistines if they were to hear of him," she said, her tone suddenly taking a sad turn.

Nitzevet longed to be a source of encouragement for her friend, "We will keep it quiet and at the same time, celebrate with great joy. I am sure Leah will make it just as you wish."

"Your family has cared so much for us; do you think that Leah would prepare the wedding supper?"

"My dear Shoshannah," Nitzevet began and then said with confidence, "you are precious to us. Reu is precious to us. You are already family, so yes, we care for you. And Leah would have it no other way!"

She hugged her 'sister to be', Nitzevet had always considered Reu her little brother since the first day they met. One who enjoyed the precious relationships that she had, Nitzevet knew this sweet, innocent girl who loved Yahweh and saw the good in everything and brought beauty to everything would bring great joy to Reu's life.

"Reu wants Jesse to lead the betrothal ceremony," Shoshannah looked at Nitzevet with a question in her eyes.

"Of course, I am sure Jesse would be honored, why do you look so unsure of the request?" Nitzevet asked.

"Because Reu is not a son, but a bond servant," Shoshannah looked more worried now that she had voiced the words of her concern out loud.

"My dear, you know that Reu is a bondservant because he requested it, not because Jesse demanded it. Besides, Jesse has always considered and treated Reu as a younger brother, not a servant," Nitzevet instructed.

"Yes, I have always known that, but I was worried about how Jesse felt."

"Jesse is as he acts, as he talks, as he thinks, there is nothing hidden with Jesse. He is very transparent," she paused as thoughts of her beloved traveled the familiar path through her mind, then continued, "You will know if something worries him, and he will act accordingly. Which isn't always the best thing," Nitzevet smiled as she revealed to her friend some of the faults of her husband. Even his faults made him all the dearer to her.

Shoshannah visibly relaxed in front of Nitzevet. Sometimes, knowing the truth about someone helps understand how they will respond. She was so grateful for Nitzevet. The girls continued their chatter, making plans for the betrothal and the eventual wedding all while watching the two little boys.

"I wish Rebekah could come to our betrothal," Shoshannah sighed.

Nitzevet smiled, "I think Rebekah is a little busy with Joel. Not only was he a difficult pregnancy, but also a difficult birth. Thank Yahweh they are both doing well and are healthy. But you are right, I don't think they can come to the betrothal. But the wedding, I am sure that Rebekah will not want to miss it."

נאמנות יהוה

At the same time, Reu was in the northern pasture behind the shepherd's cave that he and Nitzevet had explored years ago. Enjoying the morning sun and quiet conversation with Jesse, Reu sensed it was a good time to ask something of his friend and master.

"I want to marry Shoshannah, Jesse. Will you lead our betrothal ceremony?" he asked.

Jesse immediately jumped up and let out a whoop, realizing too late the consequences of his loud response as the sheep scattered in fear. He grabbed Reu in a big bear hug and said, "It is about time, my brother!"

Reu could not believe that Jesse knew.

Jesse saw Reu's puzzled look and having perceived what he was thinking explained, "We all knew! You follow her like a puppy dog. We all see you plant flowers for her and hang on every word when she talks of "star of Bethlehem' and 'Myrrh'." Jesse made a face as he adolescently mimicked Reu's infatuation with Shoshannah, "it is about time! And yes, I would be honored to preside over the ceremony."

Reu smiled. He felt loved and accepted, even with all the good-natured teasing, maybe because of it.

"I want it to be very quiet and small because of my past," Reu said.

Jesse thought for a while, "Yes, I think that would be wise, but it will still be very special and meaningful. You better talk to my mother first about both the betrothal meal and the wedding feast. And don't even think about NOT talking to her. Can you imagine if you did not ask the premier party planner of Bethlehem to plan your wedding? I wouldn't want to be that person," Jesse teased.

The men were lost for a few moments in their happy thoughts of their women and weddings. Jesse needed another piece of information, "When will the wedding happen?" knowing that Reu wanted to follow Hebrew customs but did not have a father.

"I have spoken with Shoshannah's father. We are going to build a room in his house for us to live in, so he will play the role of my father, and let me know when it is time to get my bride," Reu beamed at the thought. "In fact, it will appear as if I am simply helping him build an addition. No one really needs to know that it is for Shoshannah and I. We just don't want the 'news' of a wedding between a Philistine and a Hebrew to be broadcast throughout the land."

"Yahweh has brought you to us and made you one of His own. There have not been many people who have come from nations outside of Israel and joined us so wholeheartedly as you. But because you recognized the one true God and have desired to follow His ways and His statutes, with everything you have, you are unique. Remember what Moses wrote? 'The stranger who resides with you shall be to you as the native among you, and you shall love him as yourself, for you were aliens in the land of Egypt; I am the Lord your God.'"[17]

"Thank you, Jesse!" Reu was moved by Jesse's words.

"Excellent! Better go now! Find my mother. I don't want to be the son who knew before she did," Jesse demanded.

Reu laughed and started gathering his bag to head back into town. "I will go now!" he said, chuckling as he walked.

Leah was overjoyed when Reu asked her to plan both the betrothal meal and the wedding feast. She immediately found Keturah and Shifra and they began planning. It was Shifra's job to go and find Shoshannah and find out all the special things that she wanted to include. "Oh, and when you do talk to Shoshannah, make sure her mother is there and knows that she is a big part of the planning. No wait, let me go first and talk with her mother and make that very obvious. Then you can go talk with her and Shoshannah and make plans."

Shifra smiled at the care her mother-in-law showed for other people's feelings and how they may or may not perceive things. She always went out of her way to make sure they felt included and were comfortable with the choices and plans being made.

נאמנות יהוה

"But I am sure the wedding is only a few days away," Nitzevet told Gila as she lay in bed desperately ill from her third pregnancy. She was already six months along and the morning sickness had not dissipated in the least. After the simple betrothal ceremony, they all waited eight months for Reu to build his home. The whole family had heard rumblings of the completion and inspection of the home, so they secretly knew there would be a wedding soon, but the day or hour was yet unknown.

Holding the cool cloth to her daughter's face, Gila comforted her, "I know how important it is that you attend Reu and Shoshannah's wedding feast. And you will attend. There will not be a procession, just a quiet gathering of friends for dinner here. When the time comes you can stay up as long as you are comfortable and then Jesse can bring you to your room when you need to lay down. Don't worry, we will keep you informed of every detail."

Nitzevet felt comforted. She knew that she needed to take care of herself and ultimately it was not her wedding. But she so much wanted to be a part of everything and not miss a single detail. It was a good thing that Leah and her sisters-in-law were the ones doing all the work for the meal, she was no help at all.

נאמנות יהוה

Seven days later Keturah gently knocked on Nitzevet's door and came in to tell her that the wedding meal for Reu and Shoshannah would be soon, preparations were underway.

Gila came later in the afternoon to help Nitzevet get dressed, just in case Reu came for his bride. It would not be large or sophisticated, they did not want any rumors of a wedding feast to spread so they were treating it as a dinner among friends.

"What will Shoshannah wear Ema?"

"Leah made her a lovely little dress that matches her sweet personality. It does not have all the marks of a wedding dress, but it is precious, and she will look beautiful in it," Gila responded.

"Who is helping her get dressed?" a worried Nitzevet asked.

"My dear, her two sisters arrived last week for a 'visit'. Shifra has gone to help her, and Rebekah will be there. All is well. Those girls are good friends and are having a lovely time. Stop worrying. You are caring for the little life inside of you and that is what would make Shoshannah happy right now."

Fully dressed, and looking beautiful as usual, Nitzevet was relaxing on the cushions talking with her beloved, as they waited for Reu and Shoshannah to arrive. "Jesse, do you really think Shoshannah's father will tell Reu to get his bride tonight?"

"We don't know 'for sure' but we have a lovely meal prepared for our family if not," Jesse smiled, knowing this is how wedding feasts were done, no one really knew the day or the hour for sure. They continued to discuss the unique situation of Reu and Shoshannah.

"Yes, I know it is different, my love," Jesse explained, "It is unusual for the son-in-law to build the room attached to the home of his bride, but since Shoshannah's parents have three daughters, there would never be a son to build an addition to their home. They decided that it was the perfect idea for Reu to build on to their home since he has no family. It is a beautiful little cottage attached to the back wall of her parent's home."

"I can't wait to see it, Jesse!" Nitzevet sighed knowing it would be a while before she could tour the new home.

Reu and Shoshannah walked quietly hand in hand down the path toward the ben Obed home. It was a bit out of character, no flying the bride, no trumpet, but this was their wedding day, even though no one could really know. Reu had planned to have his friends inform the wedding guest to assemble at the ben Obed home when Shoshannah's father told him it was time. All of the guests were already at Jesse's home, waiting for the young couple.

After all the guests and Reu and Shoshannah stepped through the doorway, Shoshannah's father shut and locked the doors. It was time for feasting.

The meal was delicious, as are all of Leah's feasts. But the depth of friendship and understanding of redemption, from foreigner to follower of Yahweh, that permeated this celebration could be felt by all. There were more than a few tears of joy in the room. Leah fussed over the food making sure each guest was satisfied, Jesse laughed at Reu's jokes. Shoshannah sat back on the cushions next to her new husband on one side and her best friend Nitzevet on the other thinking this was the best day of her life.

They all knew how special this was and each was grateful for the role they had played in Reu's life and the role they were excited to play in the future of this new little family, whatever that looked like.

נאמנות יהוה

Nitzevet gave birth to a tiny little girl a month early. Her family was worried about her, it was always possible to lose a child, it happened more often than anyone wanted to admit, but each had made it their mission to pray fervently for this tiny little soul and for Nitzevet. Reu and Shoshannah had taken Eliab and Abinadab to their home for a couple of nights the past few weeks. Keturah had bunked them with her children on the other nights so that Nitzevet could rest and hold on as long as she could. Yahweh's hand of protection and these efforts were probably what pulled everyone through this difficult pregnancy and birth. They named their baby girl Zeruiah. Jesse wondered why his wife would want a name that meant 'tribulation from the Lord'. It seemed rather sad.

"Because we must remember the difficult times as well as the good times," Nitzevet explained. "And how Yahweh is present in both and shows us His hand of love and grace and healing in the difficult times too."

This made sense to Jesse, and he knew that Zeruiah would grow up knowing that she was blessed because she was protected by the Lord. He knew that she would understand the pain and the plan of their God and how He would always be with her.

24

RAFI IS BACK

AT THE AGE OF TWENTY-THREE most Hebrew girls were considered past their prime for marriage. Parents typically made every effort to arrange a marriage while their daughters were young. But the ben Uzzi family was different. It wasn't that Uzzi had not tried, rather Ednah was unique. While pretty in her own way, as a typical Hebrew girl, there was something about her character and her demeanor that most mothers did not want for their sons. Ednah lamented her old age and longed to be married yet with no hope on the horizon. Then, one day, he returned.

Rafi stepped out of his chariot. As he tossed the reins to a local shepherd boy walking toward the well at the city gate, he was reminiscing about the young, too young, girl he had met in this small backward Hebrew town about ten years ago. He wondered if she was still here. 'Probably married her off to a local goat herder.' he thought. His condescension toward the Hebrews oozed from his being even as his military cadence demanded respect, or so he thought. As he walked through town, the reflection of his round metal shield caught the eye of several of the elders of the town. He noticed the concern, etched on the faces of the oldest of the men, and that his presence was alarming to the younger men in the crowd. 'Apparently, Rafi thought, it has been a while since a Philistine, military at that, had walked through their town.' He picked up his steps as he boldly walked through town.

Reu, watching the sheep in the fields south of Bethlehem had noticed the plume of dust as he noticed the chariot coming from the south toward

Bethlehem. He knew the shape of the chariot well; it had wheels with six spokes and was drawn by two horses. The great "Sea Peoples" as they liked to call themselves, were known for their chariots. Reu wondered why a Philistine would be coming to Bethlehem. Now that he was a bondservant of Jesse and so many years had passed, he did not worry so much about himself. But he knew that where there was a Philistine there was bound to be trouble.

"Jesse, wait up!" Reu called as he ran to catch up with Jesse's quick pace as he walked toward Bethlehem from the area of the Tower. "There is a Philistine soldier in town. I just wanted you to know."

"Really? How do you know?" Jesse asked.

"I saw him coming down the road in his chariot, I assume that means he is a higher-ranking officer. He was alone. Other than that, I don't know much else," Reu informed him.

"I will head up and see what is going on. Don't worry, friend. Our God is good!" His smile and words encouraged Reu.

Reu always appreciated Jesse's thoughtful encouragement. He quickened his pace as he headed home to his wife and the sanctuary of their home.

Rafi had come to do random reconnaissance for the kings of the Pentapolis. It was their custom to periodically send out scouts through the land of Israel to gather information and bring it back to the kings. Rafi had volunteered to go to Bethlehem. He knew he could get information from the sniveling little man Uzzi and was hoping to also get a glimpse of that youngish girl.

Uzzi got up to open the door after the loud knock had awakened him from dozing on his cushions. 'Who would be knocking in the heat of the day?' he thought.

He blinked as his eyes adjusted to the brightness of the afternoon sun flooding the house through the open door, he slowly recognized the older version of the young Philistine that had been in his home ten years prior. "Rafi?" Uzzi asked.

"It is Commander now!" Rafi said rather harshly, annoyed at this little man.

"Come in Commander, how can I be of service to you?" Uzzi asked.

"Information. I have only come for information," he demanded. "Then I will leave," he said as he scanned the darkened corners as he stepped into the room. A flash of color caught his eye from the furthest corner.

As the figure moved slightly in the shadows, he noticed a rather lovely woman standing there. Pleased that Ednah was still there, he also noticed that just after he acknowledged her, she had pulled the veil over her face. Knowing enough about the Hebrew culture, Rafi recognized that this was an indication that she was yet unmarried. 'This is good.' he thought as he turned and smiled at Uzzi, the crease in his forehead softening a bit.

Uzzi invited Rafi to have a seat. After providing him with refreshments, he proceeded to answer all of his questions, without hesitation. Uzzi, while assuming the role of a smart businessman, was often naively unaware of the nefarious motives of others. He never once during the conversation thought that maybe he was offering too much information about his town or friends to this 'stranger'.

Rafi smiled as he remembered this loose-tongued quality of Uzzi. Nodding politely as Uzzi provided a vast amount of information he thought, 'This is why I came straight to this house. Well, at least one of the reasons.' he thought as he glanced over at Ednah, now seated just outside the doorway of the other room, glancing every now and again in his direction.

נאמנות יהוה

"What?" questioned Obed in a loud voice as he stared at his wife in the courtyard. He was hot and tired from a long day of managing the massive sheep business that just kept growing. This news was not making him happy.

Leah worried that all the neighbors could hear him, made a motion with her hands to quiet him, and then took him by the hand to sit on the bench. She could tell this would need to be a longer conversation.

"My dear, she is not our daughter, nor is their family under our purview. We need to be calm about this and not overreact," she tried calming her husband as she poured him a cup of warmed milk. As she added the spices slowly and made him watch her simple actions, she knew he was calming down. She handed him the milk tea. "Ednah will marry Commander Rafi next month."

Obed was dumbfounded that Uzzi would allow this. But as he began to consider the character of this man and the things that he had done over the few years he had been in Bethlehem, he realized allowing this marriage between his daughter and a Philistine soldier was not so out of line with his character.

"I fear for the girl. I am also worried about bringing the element of the Philistine military into our little town. It will make us all nervous. Do you know their plans for the future? Where will they live?" The questions spilled out of Obed's mouth like water from a jar.

Leah paused, considering what she should do. "Let me go talk to Chazael and see what I can find out. Will you promise to wait for me before you do anything rash ... or SAY anything rash?" she asked, smiling at her husband, as she patted his hand in a loving gesture.

"Yes, my love, I will wait," he turned and looked at her raising his eyebrows and smiled saying in a pretend gruff voice, "But don't make me wait too long!" he kissed her forehead as he rose and left, returning to the fields to think.

Leah knew that she needed to go immediately to talk to Chazael, but she needed to seek guidance first. Yahweh must go before her and guide her words and actions.

נאמנות יהוה

The street sloped gently up toward the ben Tzuri'el home. The family lived closer to the center of town, while the ben Obed family residence was closer to the gate and the edge of town.

Gently knocking on the door, Leah was surprised to find a tearful woman opening the door and falling into her arms. A kind and wise woman like Leah knew exactly what to do. She gently wrapped her arms around Chazael and stepped up into their home and closed the door behind them.

Seating Chazael at her own dinner table, Leah proceeded to hum her favorite song as she pulled the packet of date cakes she had packed in her satchel and placed them on the table. She then proceeded to pour milk tea into the little pot and place it over the warm coals. Finding the cups on the counter washed and ready to use, she brought them to the table. Deliberately taking her time, Leah was giving Chazael time to regain her composer. Pouring the warmed tea into the cups, Leah said, "I think I can understand your emotions. But please tell me what is going on in your heart."

Chazael began, "I do not want my daughter to marry a Philistine and move away. I thought I did at first, I even encouraged it because Ednah has been so sad. But I have come to realize this might prove to be a wrong choice and a sad choice, for both of us."

Leah thought 'a little late don't you think?' but said out loud, "You may be right about that. Is there anything you can do at this point?"

Chazael's fresh set of tears indicated to Leah the answer was probably no.

"Uzzi has accepted the mohar for her. The betrothal will take place next week, here. Rafi insists that the wedding feast will be in Gath where his family resides," Chazael wiped a stray tear and continued, "Uzzi and I will accompany Ednah to Gath to participate in the feasting."

"How long between the betrothal and the wedding?" Leah gently asked.

"Three weeks!" Chazael exclaimed, launching into a fresh set of tears.

"That is not long," Leah confirmed. "What does Ednah say about all of this?"

"She is overjoyed. Finally, she will have a husband, money, and prestige. It is all she talks about; all she thinks about," Chazael wept.

Leah knew that Chazael and Uzzi had not planted the seeds of righteousness in the heart of their daughter. Not that parents always have control over what their children do with the seeds that are planted, but this family's behavior was evident for all to see.

"Yahweh," Leah bowed her head and began to pray out loud, "we are so grateful that you walk through difficult times with us. We know that you love Ednah, Chazael and Uzzi. We pray that you will guide them on this path."

"Is there anything that I can do for you?" Leah asked, looking into Chazael's eyes and into her heart.

"Will you and Obed come to the betrothal next week?" she asked.

"I will consult my husband on that and see what he says. If I do come, I insist on helping you make and serve the food," Leah offered, wisely leaving the clean-up off the list, knowing Obed would seek an early opportunity to leave, if he consented to come at all.

Chazael smiled, comforted by the kind words and willing help from a true friend.

Obed was not happy at the invitation, but as one of the leaders of the town he could not see a way out. Besides, he knew his wife wanted to help Chazael with the party. He consented to attend, with the stipulation that he and Leah would leave when he felt it was the right time to leave. Leah agreed.

נאמנות יהוה

It was not so much lavish as it was pagan.

Immediately on edge, Obed continually scanned the room. There were quite a few soldiers, friends of Rafi, who had arrived the previous day. Most Hebrew betrothals were simple affairs, leaving the feasting for the wedding. But he should have known this event would be like this.

The wine flowed freely, too freely. It wasn't so much about celebrating, Obed noticed, but more about revelry. It wasn't about looking to the future of a new couple beginning their life together, but about who could have the most fun, in this moment, at this party. Obed tapped Leah's arm. He glanced at Jesse who had his arm protectively around Nitzevet, who had also been invited to the betrothal ceremony.

The women were placed between the two men, second nature for the ben Obed family. Both men knew it was time to make their escape, but they needed to be discreet so as not to draw attention. Nitzevet wisely whispered to Jesse that she and Leah would leave and that the men were to follow one by one, quietly and slowly.

They were all quiet on the way home. Collectively sad as they replayed the events of the evening in their heads. The party was set to be lovely, Chazael had done a lovely job of decorating and Leah was a big part of preparing the delicious food. But as soon as the soldiers arrived, things immediately took a turn.

"Did you see Ednah's face just before we left?" Nitzevet asked her mother-in-law quietly.

"Yes, my dear, there was a hint of fear in her face as she tried to put on a front," Leah sighed.

The men listened, not wanting to add to the sadness, and not knowing really what the women had seen, but they understood.

"I believe for the first time in her life Ednah realizes that what she asked for isn't really what she wanted," Nitzevet said, wisely illuminating what they were all thinking.

Nitzevet could not help but speculate as to what Ednah's life would be like in a few weeks when she moves to Gaza and married Rafi. She could not help comparing her life with what she assumed Ednah's will be like.

Nitzevet longed to talk about this with her friend Rebekah. Her dear friend always made sense of the senseless, but she was very near to giving birth to her second child, so the conversation would have to wait.

25

PREPARATION FOR MIZPAH

SAMUEL HAD BEEN IN THE service of his God since birth, so his mother Hannah told him. But if you asked him, he would tell you all about the day his mother left him at the Tabernacle in Shiloh with Eli and his family. That was the day he began his service to Yahweh.

Thirty-two years later, living in Ramah, he was now a judge over Israel. But if you were to ask him, he would prefer to characterize who he was and what he does by these simple words, lover of Yahweh. It had been many years since Yahweh had appeared to His people, but ever since that first encounter in the Tabernacle as a young boy, Yahweh had been continually conversing with Samuel. He was humbled and honored to be considered worthy to be in the presence of the Almighty God.

But Samuel was tired. It had been nine years since Eli had died and Israel was still suffering under the oppression of the Philistines. Samuel traveled in a circuit acting as a judge and administering justice at Bethel, Gilgal, Mizpah, and Ramah. He consistently called the people to repent wherever he went. It was the only way out of their current situation. They were suffering because of their sin and idolatry.

But today was different. For the first time in his tenure as leader of Israel, the leaders of the people had come and asked Samuel to lead them in repentance before Yahweh. The problem for Samuel was that he knew their history over the past five hundred years. It was a cycle of Israel serving Yahweh, Israel falling into sin and idolatry, Israel being enslaved, Israel crying out to their God, Yahweh raising up a Judge, and then delivering Israel.

Could this be the beginning of a new cycle? The people are feeling the pressure of the Philistines and the hold they have over them. Could this be a moment where they truly repent and seek Yahweh?

Rebekah could tell that Samuel was concerned. While he was a man of few words, he didn't usually spend so much time alone with such a furrowed brow. "My love," Rebekah began, "would you like to take a walk?"

Samuel looked up from deep thought and after gazing at his lovely bride for a moment said, "Yes, I would! It would be good for me to stretch my legs."

Leaving the little ones with their nurse, the two walked through the city gate at Ramah and continued down the path around the town. It was a beautiful evening as the sun was setting over the hills. They appreciated the cool breeze on their faces as they walked.

"What troubles you, my husband?" Rebekah asked. After ten years of marriage, they had learned to understand each other's moods and Rebekah knew that Samuel was brooding.

"Yesterday, several elders from several tribes came to me with a request. They have been meeting with other elders and are collectively seeking to approach Yahweh," Samuel mused.

"Oh!" Rebekah said, a little shocked at the request. While her life with Samuel was one lived in the presence of Yahweh, it was not her experience that the people of Israel were inclined to seek their God. "Why do they want to seek Yahweh? Is this a good thing?" the questions tumbled out.

'Yes! It is good news. They are seeking to repent," Samuel said simply.

"But why do you not act as one who has received good news?" she questioned.

Samuel paused, realizing how his concern must have been written on his face. "Yes, it is good news, but my concern is their sincerity and just how many people are interested in this collective change of heart."

"I suppose that since their request is a good request, that you must let them decide how serious they and everyone else is. I know that Obed and Jesse will be pleased to know that people are desiring to seek Yahweh," she said.

"You are as wise as ever, my love. I will seek Yahweh and see what He tells me to do regarding this matter. Thank you for the walk and the talk," with that he abruptly turned to the fields to wander by himself. Rebekah smiled; she knew this was her cue to exit the scene because Samuel wanted to be with Yahweh. She did not mind sharing her husband with Yahweh. Actually, there was no greater privilege.

Standing for a moment, she watched him wander into the dusk. His long hair reached almost to his waist, there were a few more streaks of gray this year than last. She was grateful for a companion who walked with God.

נאמנות יהוה

"Obed, Obed!" Leah gently shook her husband awake. "Samuel is here in the courtyard waiting to speak with you."

Obed blinked and rubbed his eyes. Having been woken in the early morning from a deep sleep he was just a bit confused. "What did you say? Who is here?" And then after putting the words his wife was saying together, he said, "Yes, yes, let me prepare to meet him. Let him know I will be there. What does he want?"

Leah shrugged her shoulders as she walked through the door to inform Samuel.

Sipping his cup of warm milk, Samuel was excited to tell his friend about the request of the people and what Yahweh had said. There was much to do to prepare for national repentance. "Greetings my old friend," Samuel smiled as he teased his greatest mentor and friend.

"You have no idea!" Obed replied, willing to admit he knew he was old. "What is so urgent you have to wake an old, crippled man so early in the morning?"

Samuel's laugh made the milk come out of his nose. Obed may be old, but not crippled, he was one of the most robust old men he knew. As he gained his composure and began acting like a prophet of their God, wiping the milk from his nose and chin and said, "I have good news."

Obed relaxed.

"Yes, the elders of the tribe of Benjamin, Reuben, Simeon, Issachar, & Zebulun came to me several days ago seeking to bring the people together to repent," he said as he studied the face of his friend.

Obed smiled, "Yes, I have heard the rumors. As one of the leaders of Judah, I was in on the messages and conversation. I hope it is sincere. What do you think Samuel?"

"I told the men to go home and get rid of all of their foreign gods and the Ashtoreths. I did not need to consult Yahweh before saying that. Then I consulted Yahweh. He told me to have them meet me in one month at Mizpah. I am to lead them in a ceremony of repentance where I will intercede for the people there," Samuel replied.

"Have you heard from the leaders of Ephraim, Manasseh, Dan, Naphtali, Gad, and Asher yet?" Obed asked as Jesse approached them, having been roused by Leah at Samuel's request.

"Good morning, Samuel!" Jesse said as he poured himself a cup of warm milk and savored the delicate spices. "What brings you here at this hour?"

Obed filled Jesse in on the details as Samuel listened and then he turned to Samuel and asked, "Should we send messengers to those tribes to let them know of the meeting at Mizpah?"

"Already done!" Samuel said. "I sent the messengers from Ramah before I left to come here."

"I would like for you to bring your family to my home in Ramah, stay with us for a few nights, and then we can make our way to Mizpah on the appointed day," said Samuel.

"Nitzevet would be very happy to do that," Jesse said, knowing his wife would cherish a visit with Rebekah. Obed nodded as he thought 'Leah as well, would not want to miss this event.'

"In the meantime, I would like to meet with the elders here in Bethlehem today and tomorrow and then I will return home to wait for your arrival," Samuel explained.

Jesse, hopeful but cautious, shared the news with his wife as she prepared for the day. "I told Samuel that you would go with me to Ramah and then on to Mizpah, I hope that is alright with you?" He said kindly.

Nitzevet smiled at his gentleness, although as any mother would be she was uneasy leaving her little ones. "I think it would be good. Shammah is already three and Zeruah is a really attentive big sister. The children have many aunts and uncles, and we have friends who act as aunts and uncles. They will be in good hands, and I would love to see Rebekah."

After breakfast, Nitzevet packed up some snacks and her four little ones and they started their walk to the fields. Settling down in the grass she pondered out loud to Yahweh as she watched her children play by the tower "Repentance? Israel desires repentance? I can only be grateful that they are seeking You. I am glad to see it. I pray it is genuine," she said thoughtfully as the words of a poem tumbled out of her thoughts:

> *A hardhearted people seek the face of their God.*
> *A loving and compassionate God turns His face*
> *toward them.*
> *We are blessed oh Lord,*
> *when you look upon us with forgiveness.*
> *We are blessed oh Lord, pushing our iniquities far from us*
> *because of your compassion.*

26

MIRACLE AT MIZPAH

NITZEVET, LEAH, AND REBEKAH STOOD arm in arm as they gazed over the multitude of people gathered in the valley below Mount Gilead. They could not believe their eyes. Truly the people as a nation were seeking Yahweh, the only true God, in repentance. The news had traveled of how the people were destroying the temples of the foreign gods with fire and smashing the idols in the high places. Repentance had swept this struggling yet growing nation. It was hard to believe that it was really happening. Was there hope?

As they gazed into the far distance and their eyes came closer to where they were, Nitzevet noticed the pile of stones next to a standing stone pillar. It seemed that they were not natural to the landscape, they had been placed there. Then she remembered something from history, "Leah," she asked, "is that the witness heap and the stone pillar that Jacob and Laban set up?"

Leah nodded to the women and explained, "Yes, we are at Mizpah the watchtower, where Jacob and Laban set these stones up as a witness between them. As you know it was not a very happy occasion, in effect, they were making a pact with each other. They were saying 'our peace agreement is void if either of us crosses this line toward the other.' It was a solemn and sad agreement between an uncle and his nephew."

"Is this why Samuel chose this place?" Nitzevet suddenly asked.

Rebekah answered, "Yes! Samuel told me that because of the significance of this place and how it stands as a memorial to the pact between Laban and Jacob that it will also stand as a pact between Yahweh and His people."

"So wise," Nitzevet whispered.

Leah leaned close to both Rebekah and Nitzevet and with a gentle voice whispered, "your babies are fine!" Nitzevet smiled at how well her mother-in-law knew her. She had left her 4 little ones in the hands of her capable sisters-in-law, she knew they were fine. They were probably romping through the house with their cousins as they spoke, but she still missed their sweet little faces. Rebekah, also smiling at Leah's perception, had left her two young boys with her mother-in-law Hannah. She knew they were having the time of their lives; Hannah was the best grandmother.

As they were eating their evening meal with the pillar and the heap in the distance, Samuel relayed to the elders of the twelve tribes the plan for the next day. Leah, Nitzevet, and Rebekah quietly served the food they had cooked over the campfire and listened as well.

Samuel began, "When you came to me a month ago, I told you, 'If you return to the Lord with all your hearts, *then* put away the foreign gods and the Ashtoreth from among you, and prepare your hearts for the Lord, and serve Him only; and He will deliver you from the hand of the Philistines.' We are here because you honored my request, and the people were obedient."

After a pause for a few moments to think, the men continued to eat the roasted lamb and Samuel continued, "You are to inform your people that tomorrow will be a day of rest, at sundown tomorrow we will begin a 24-hour fast. On the following day at the third hour, we are to assemble in the open area up against the hillside near the heap and the pillar where I will begin the ceremony. We have often used this hill and valley for large gatherings here at Mizpah because the sound carries, so most of the assembled people will be able to hear," Samuel explained.

The men nodded in understanding and agreement.

Samuel looked around the table and noticed the somber mood and eagerness to comply with his instructions. He was pleased that these men really were serious about their request. As they finished their meal, Obed overheard the men discussing how surprised indeed they were at the amount of people still arriving and assembling. The men began to leave Samuel's tent so that they could tell the people what he had said, knowing it would take quite a while for them to distribute the instructions and for everyone to understand what was required and be able to attend at the third hour in two days. There really were that many people.

On the morning of the third day, Samuel awoke with great expectation, he knew that true repentance meant taking action in our lives to realign our behavior with our hearts before our God. Reconciliation always demands repentance, turning around, and going in the other direction. That is why the first thing they had to do was to get rid of their foreign gods. He was pleased that so many people had acted. The next step was to illustrate to them what it means to be forgiven and move forward. He chose the water-pouring ceremony to illustrate what it means to Yahweh.

Just before the third hour, everyone could see Samuel slowly walking toward the appointed place. Rebekah prayed silently for his courage and strength. She could see the sheepskin full of water in his hand. The men, leaders of each tribe, followed him up and surrounded him. The rest of the multitude silently waited for Samuel to begin.

Samuel, with slow deliberate movements, raised the skin of water and silently poured out the contents on the ground. Everyone watched as the water splashed onto dry thirsty ground and was soaked up as if it were never there. In a few moments there would not even be a wet spot because of the heat of the day and the nature of the dry soil.

"Men of Israel" Samuel began in a loud voice, "as you have witnessed the pouring of this water into the soil we are saying to Yahweh, that our lives are like water, poured out onto the ground, it cannot be gathered up again. Because you have put away your foreign gods and because you have assembled here before your God, you are showing your dependence on Yahweh, your allegiance to him, and your change of heart."

Samuel looked up at the pillar and pointed toward the pile of stones and said, "May this pillar and this heap be a witness between you and Yahweh of your promise, just as it was a witness in the past between Jacob and Laban. May this day be the start of a new era in our nation, where the people seek their God and follow in His ways."

Then Samuel lifted his face toward heaven and began to pray for the people of Yahweh. Every word that Samuel chose was full of meaning and power. His prayer was not long, but the people clung to every word.

Then he said to the people, "Return to your tents today, continue fasting till the end of the day, and seek Yahweh. Tomorrow we will return home," Samuel walked back to his tent where Rebekah greeted him. As he was about to go into the tent to rest, one of the young men who had been instructed to stand guard at the perimeter of the encampment came running into camp.

"Master Samuel", he said in a panic "the Philistines are amassing on the western slope, it appears they are preparing to attack us."

While the Israelites were never without a military contingency as protection, especially when they gathered together, they knew that they could not repel a force as large as the messenger had described. Several of the leaders of the tribes had gathered around Samuel and began to speak out. "You must cry out to Yahweh for us and do not stop, that He will rescue us from the hand of the Philistines."

Samuel looked at the worried faces of the men. He was pleased that their first response was to seek Yahweh and not complain. He looked over the men around him and resting his eyes on the commander of the soldiers said, "assemble your men and place them in formation to our west. He spoke quickly to Jesse who was standing ready to do whatever Samuel asked, "Bring me a suckling lamb."

He then looked at Obed, "gather up the leaders and have them prepare an altar for sacrifice."

Turning to Rebekah he put a hand on her trembling shoulder as she stood next to Nitzevet and Leah, he asked them all to pray and seek Yahweh's face for their salvation. Then walking to the altar that was quickly being assembled, Samuel quickly prepared to sacrifice a whole burnt offering. When he was finished, he lifted his face toward heaven and cried out to Yahweh for their deliverance. There was no other way they would survive the onslaught of Philistine warriors with their chariots and weapons.

As the Israelite people stood still in silence with a united heart, waiting on their God, they could hear the hooves of the horses as their chariots drew near, they could see the cloud of dust and taste the dirt in the air as the mass of soldiers marched toward the Israelite camp. Samuel in quiet confidence stood before the smoldering altar and continued to wait on Yahweh, knowing that even if Yahweh did not save them this day, He was their perfect holy God and worthy of sacrifice.

Then it happened.

As Samuel's eyes were fixed on the last wisps of smoke as they rose from the sacrifice, the loudest bang that he had ever experienced rippled through all the air and shook the ground. Samuel turned to watch the spectacle and it seemed to him as if everything started moving very slowly. The rapidly approaching Philistine chariots were suddenly careening out of control, the soldiers started screaming and turning to run in the opposite direction as if they had witnessed a horrible sight. Samuel knew that Yahweh had stepped in.

Just as their God caused the Midianite army to flee from His presence and Gideon's three hundred men, so these Philistines were fleeing from the Israelites, or something. Nitzevet also watched it play out as if in slow motion. After recovering from the incredible sound, she saw the commander of the Israelite force raise his hand and motion for his soldiers to pursue the fleeing Philistine army. Nitzevet swallowed hard, knowing they would have no mercy on the panicked Philistine soldiers.

נאמנות יהוה

The silence was thick. Jesse stood behind Samuel, processing everything that was passing before him. The people stood around, unable to talk, barely able to understand what was happening. For most of them, Jesse knew that Yahweh had not been a part of their daily thoughts for many years, He lingered in the margins of their life as something their ancestors had believed in but wasn't really for them. Jesse knew this because he often had conversations with his peers. They were always questioning why he was so focused on Yahweh. They couldn't understand why he put so much effort into following Yahweh who they considered an 'absent' God.

It was not lost on Jesse that this magnificent routing of the enemy happened after they had desired to seek Yahweh and put away their gods. A mighty reversal of their fate through the supernatural hand of their God. 'When we seek Yahweh, He will be found.' Jesse thought to himself. Yahweh was always faithful to care for His people, he wanted to draw them to Himself. Jesse knew that the Israelites were going to be thinking about Yahweh a whole lot more in the days to come.

נאמנות יהוה

Passover season was upon them again. This year there was a buzz in the air. The People had been talking about how Yahweh had delivered them from their enemies. The ladies were busy preparing the lamb for the Passover dinner that evening. As Nitzevet pulled the fresh unleavened bread from the clay oven she reminisced with her sisters about the recent event on their minds, "I am so glad Samuel chose Mizpah for the return to Yahweh ceremony, the witness pillar and heap will help us remember" she said looking at Shifra.

Shifra had not yet seen the stone monument that Nitzevet was referring to, she had only heard about it. "I know my sister; I would love to go see the pillar and hear the story of our God's deliverance again. Do you think we could make the journey with our children someday?"

Nitzevet kept forgetting that neither Shifra nor Keturah had seen the event because they were both at home in Bethlehem caring for their children as well as hers. The idea to visit the memorial was a good one and she was determined to make it happen so that the whole family could be a part of what Yahweh had done for them.

Keturah asked, "What is the pillar like?"

Nitzevet thought for a moment how to best describe the monument. "It was a rough stone about five feet in height and three feet wide. It was light-colored and had reddish bands. It was worn and rugged in appearance, but stood up on its end, obvious that someone had put it that way. It is not really a very remarkable stone. But to those of us who witnessed Yahweh's deliverance and the loud noise, we look on it as the most beautiful thing ever. You will too when we go see it and we hear the story again. I will talk to Jesse and ask when we can take our family trip."

The meal was, as usual, a remembrance of what their God had done for the people in Egypt and how He had delivered them from the Egyptians. But this year, it had a whole new meaning, the fresh deliverance from the Philistines infused new meaning on a whole new level into the annual meal. Each member of the ben Obed family lingered on every aspect of the ceremony as if no one wanted to rush the time they had together remembering. Nitzevet sat quietly in the corner holding her little boy pondering all that Yahweh had done for His people. She was so sleepy; it must have been all the preparations for the Passover meal.

Leah looked over at the sleepy Nitzevet and remarked to herself, 'There may be another little one coming.'

27

SHEPHERDS AND SHEEP

NITZEVET'S BELLY WAS SWELLING MUCH faster than before, Shammah had given up trying to sleep on his mother's lap, there just was no more room, not even for a little head. He curled up beside her on the cushions. Leah laughed at the plight of the little one and gently picked up the sleeping child and carried him to his bed in Nitzevet's cool room.

"My dear, it is pretty obvious that there are two in that big belly of yours," Leah said as she came back.

It was Shifra's turn to giggle now, "I have been saying that for weeks Ema! She has four months left and looks like she will give birth any moment."

"I think it is time my dear for you to consider taking it very easy for the next few months. You keep your feet up, tell stories to your little ones, and dry their tears, we will do everything else. That is the beauty of living together as we do. We care for one another," said her very wise mother-in-law. Only three months later, Nitzevet gave birth to her tiny twins after many hours of labor, a little boy that she named Nethanel and his twin sister Abigail. Nitzevet was fine but exhausted. Gila, Dalit, and Leah had their hands full caring for the babies and for Nitzevet. Shifra and Keturah managed the cooking and cleaning. Nitzevet's four older children were with Reu and Shoshannah on a sleepover, much to Jesse's great relief. It was all he could do to worry about his wife, four rambunctious children would have put him over the edge.

נאמנות יהוה

Jesse wept bitterly.

Nitzevet tried to comfort him with her presence and her silence, she knew that nothing she could say would remove or even lighten the grief that Jesse felt at this moment. Such was the profound grief of a son who lost his father who had become his best friend.

Obed had been ill for almost a month. Slowly he lost strength in his legs and his arms. Then he remained in his bed for days until he died. No one knew why, only that he was losing strength and declining rapidly, and they knew something was wrong. His mind was strong, his body was weak.

Leah had asked Samuel to come and pray for her beloved. Not so much that she pretended to know Yahweh's plan or to dissuade him from it, but Samuel's presence always brought calm in the midst of strife and sorrow. Samuel came. He prayed.

Obed was an old man; he was ready to meet his Creator. He was eager to do so. The last few days of his life were full of joy and expectation: joy that he was with his family, talking as they enjoyed the lingering presence of their patriarch; expectation of his entrance into eternity. And then he was gone. Obed simply closed his eyes, took one more breath, and never took another. The family was gathered around, and they all bowed their heads and thanked their God for a remarkable man who loved Yahweh and taught them to love Him just as deeply.

That night Nitzevet gathered her husband in her arms, and they lay nestled together in the midst of their grief for a long time.

נאמנות יהוה

Life seemed to quiet down for a few years in Bethlehem. Nitzevet had two more children Raddai, meaning 'to subdue', and Ozem meaning 'strength'.

Ozem proved to be the easiest baby Nitzevet had ever had, or even imagined. She gazed at his sweet little face as he slept beside her. The pregnancy was easy, the birth was easy and now after eight days of getting to know her new little one, he was just as easy. She knew this was a blessing and she was going to relish it and enjoy every moment.

With four other little ones running around, life was getting busy, she was thankful for her three oldest children.

Nitzevet was also grateful to live in this beautiful home with the ben Obed family. Shifra, Keturah, and Leah were so much help. She knew her mother had worked well with her grandmother, but she did not know that she could enjoy this for herself as well.

Growing up in a little town where everyone knew everyone else's business, Nitzevet had seen some pretty tragic family situations. There were families where the mother of the household was not kind or empathetic toward her offspring and their wives. A few of these disillusioned young women had found their way to Nitzevet's shoulder and cried not just a few tears. It was hard for her to understand their plight at times, having known only the goodness and compassion of Leah, but she could imagine what it was like. It is soon going to be her turn to be the "Leah" to the spouses of her own offspring. Thinking of her children, it seemed that Zeruah was interested in a certain young gentleman.

נאמנות יהוה

Over the past few years, Jesse had begun classes to teach men of the neighboring tribes about breeding sheep. He also taught them the best ways to care for the sheep and everything involved in sheep husbandry. Because this had become widely known in the region as a great place to learn from the best sheep herder in the land, many men came from near and far to participate in the training. Jesse felt the need to build sleeping quarters for these men next to where his own shepherds lived, to accommodate the traveling learners. During the month before the shearing season, the beds would be full of men learning to care for sheep.

This season there was a group of young men from the tribe of Ruben who had come across the Jordan to spend a couple of months learning from Jesse. This tribe was also known for sheep herding in the pasture lands east of the Dead Sea, but they had heard of Jesse's prowess and ability to raise perfect lambs for sacrifice. This is what prompted the men of the tribe to send their sons to learn from Jesse, as apprentices. Among these men was Namir. He was not so much interested in sheep husbandry as he was in getting out of his own town, Bezer, and exploring the other regions of Israel. He was a rather large young man, broad in his shoulders, and yet in spite of his size, he was a very fast runner. Hence his name Namir meaning leopard or panther.

He was not particularly gentle or kind, but Zeruah was smitten. She could only see the rare bright blue eyes, the mop of unruly hair, and his strength. She often pictured him lifting her up in his strong arms.

"Zeruah!" Nitzevet almost yelled her name. Obviously, her oldest daughter was lost in a daydream about something … or someone.

"You need to pick up the pace with that bread, we have a lot of men looking to eat this evening and they will be hungry after working with Jesse all day," she instructed her daughter.

"What are you thinking about?" she asked, already knowing the answer.

Zeruah was not ready to tell anyone quite yet of her infatuation with this young man, unaware that they already knew, so she responded, "Just thinking of how the summer is coming to a close". It wasn't exactly the truth, but it wasn't a lie either. Summer was drawing to its end and Namir would be leaving after the shearing season. This made her sad.

Namir was not oblivious to this vigorous young woman who always seemed to be nearby. Her head was covered whenever she was around, so he knew she was unmarried.

"Who is that young woman over there?" Namir asked his friend one evening.

A big smile came over his companion's face, "Ah, I see you have taken an interest in our instructor's daughter."

Namir was unaware that she was Jesse's daughter. He was not always the most observant of these things, but now that he knew, things were different. She was not only a lovely young woman but had prestige as well. Namir liked that. He really liked that.

The next day, the last day of training, Namir had devised a plan. He was going to ask Zeruah to be his wife. But he did not let on, he needed to go home and return with his father and the mohar. As the day progressed, he paid special attention to Zeruah, taking note of her movements. It was pretty apparent that she was interested in him, as much as he could tell from a chaste Israelite woman. And her attention to him implied that she was not otherwise attached to another. The plan was settled in his mind, he gave her a wink as he caught her eye as she walked by. He could see the lovely shade of pink cross her face when she saw his wink.

Zeruah slowly walked across the courtyard after she saw the wink Namir sent her way. She could feel the warmth in her face and knew he had seen it from his smile. As soon as she reached the doorway to the main house she ran in and buried her face in her pillow. Her thoughts were out of control. This handsome man winked at her; it could only mean one thing. What should she do? In her heart, she knew there was nothing but waiting. But she did have one confidant that she could seek out to share her heart with, her aunt Shifra.

"What?" Shifra said a bit too loudly with a shocked expression on her face. She had surmised that something was going on, but a wink was proof.

"Shhh, Aunt Shifra!" Zeruah cautioned. "Yes, he winked at me."

Shifra smiled; she instinctively knew what that meant as did Zeruah. "We must wait then to see what comes of it. But I will be here waiting with you. Have you told your mother?" She asked.

"No, what if it comes to nothing? What if I am making more of it than it is?" the worries tumbled out.

Shifra wrapped her arm around her usually more than confident niece. "My dear, I can tell you that when a Hebrew man of Namir's age winks at you, it means something. But now we put it into the hands of our God, He will direct his steps. If it is the will of Yahweh, then Namir will propose in the correct manner. I suggest you find time within the next few days to tell your mother, so she is not caught by surprise."

"Thank you, my friend, I am so glad you are my aunt and my friend," she hugged her confidant and then left to finish her chores for the day. The water must be fetched, the food preparations must be done, and the house must be tidied. Life must go on. But it was different, the horizon was broader, and the sun shined a little brighter for Zeruah that day.

נאמנות יהוה

Namir approached his father immediately upon arriving home. "I found my wife and I would like to be betrothed … soon."

Maharai responded with surprise, "Really my son?" He thought that the time for Namir to settle down and provide him with grandchildren would never come. He was pleased.

"Who is this bride-to-be, where is she from, who is her father?" he asked positively, excited and hopeful that the answers would be good.

Namir was glad to report to his father that his desired bride was none other than the daughter of Jesse ben Obed, one of the leaders of the tribe of Judah and the owner of the largest sheepherding farm in Israel. A beautiful young woman, full of grace and who was also interested in him, as much as he could tell. He left that last part off.

His father was truly pleased at this news. "Well, my son, what is to be the purchase price for this beautiful bride?"

Namir and his father left three days later on their journey back to Bethlehem to the ben Obed household to purchase his bride. In tow, they had some beautiful jewelry for the Mohar as well as a young cow for the family. Namir knew that Jesse was a gracious and kind man so he would naturally give the mohar to his daughter. With this knowledge, he and his father chose jewelry as the Mohar so that it could stay with Zeruah. Not only would it be a prize possession, but if anything, ever happened to Namir it would be very valuable, and she would not ever be destitute. The cow was for the ben Obed household.

Jesse was sitting at the city gate with his father when the caravan from Ruben arrived. He had an inkling that this was going to change his life. Nitzevet, having had a lengthy conversation with Zeruah, shared with Jesse that there might be a young man from the tribe of Ruben seeking Zeruah's hand in marriage.

Jesse remembered Namir, not particularly keen on his manner, nevertheless realized that if Yahweh willed and Zeruah desired, he would consider it. As Namir approached the gate, he greeted Jesse introducing his father to the father of the woman he desired. Jesse asked them to sit at the gate while the other men watered their livestock at the well.

"What brings you back to our city so soon?" Jesse inquired, not letting on that he knew.

Maharai spoke first, as was the custom, "I have come on behalf of my son to purchase your oldest daughter Zeruah as a bride for my son Namir."

Jesse was pleased with the attention to protocol and nodded with interest, indicating that Maharai could continue.

"My son encountered your daughter while he spent time here learning from you and desires to take her as his wife. We would be honored if you would except this bride price," at that time, Namir opened the chest of jewels, and a servant brought the young cow forward.

Jesse was again pleased at what he saw. The jewels implied that Jesse was a kind father, so they were giving him something he would have no need of because they knew as a good father, he would give it to his daughter. Realizing that, in addition to this extravagant bride price they brought a cow for the family, which was indeed telling, they respected Jesse.

Getting up from his seat, he embraced Namir again and then his father and said, "I give you permission to take Zeruah as your wife ..." pausing for emphasis and looking straight into Namir's eyes said, "Providing Zeruah accepts." He wanted to make sure that this was not solely his choice as father, but that the burden of acceptance rested on Zeruah.

Namir nodded, quickly understanding what Jesse was saying.

נאמנות יהוה

"I can't believe you are getting married!" Abigail whined.

Zeruah hugged her little sister, "I know my sweet sister, but you knew it would happen sometime, right?"

"I know, yes, I knew. But now that the time is here, it was so fast," she responded.

"We still have six months or so to be together, so let's make the most of it," her big sister said kindly.

"You really have to move to Bezer?" Abigail asked.

"Yes, sister, that is where my betrothed is building our house. You can come and visit. It will be so much fun. You can even help me make my home beautiful. You have inherited your grandmother's eye for beauty," she said encouragingly.

Abigail smiled at the prospect of an adventure and visiting her sister in a new place.

נאמנות יהוה

Resting in the field on a warm afternoon, one of the rare times Jesse and Reu could be together in the midst of the work, they were processing the new extended family they were to soon be inheriting, "so Namir's grandfather was a murderer?" Reu asked.

Jesse wanted to make sure that the truth about Namir's family was precise, "Not exactly. Maharai's father was wrongly accused of murder. He was the only person present when his best friend fell off the cliffs near Moab. As the story goes, Onan, Namir's grandfather, and his best friend were climbing near the cliffs. As Maharai recounts the story that his father told him he says that his father's friend slipped and fell down the cliff. Onan raced to the bottom of the cliff, climbing as fast as he could, but by the time Onan reached the bottom to get to his friend, he had died."

"When Onan brought his friend back to his family, they were deeply grieved as any family would be. Several days later, they showed up at Onan's home accusing him of murder claiming the right of vengeance and calling for Onan's death. A wise brother of Onan quickly got him out of town and off to the closest city of refuge, Bezer, where he was forced to live until Eli died."

"What does the death of Eli have to do with Namir's grandfather and the city of Bezer?" Reu asked, not fully understanding Yahweh's provision with the cities of refuge.

Jesse explained, "When someone is accused of murder, if they did it, then their life is forfeit and they die. But if there is doubt, then Yahweh provided various cities of refuge for Israelites to flee to for a fair trial. Apparently, Onan received a fair trial from the Levite city of Bezer and they deemed him not guilty. They could find no proof that Onan killed or even wanted to kill his friend or cause his friend's death."

"But" continued Jesse, "the law states that even if Onan is pronounced innocent, he has to stay in the city of Refuge, Bezer, until the current High Priest dies. That was Eli at the time of the death of his friend. If he were to leave that city, then the family of Onan's friend could avenge his death and kill Onan. So he stayed, married, and raised his family."

"Why are they still in Bezer?" Reu asked.

"His family loved the city, Maharai told us, so they stayed and built their life. It is a beautifully clean, walled city on the eastern edge of the Reubenite territory. Near Ammon," Jesse said, knowing he was sending his daughter there to live and silently praying for her safety.

Reu spoke the concern Jesse was feeling, "It is safe? Are the Ammonites safe?"

Jesse explained to Reu who the Ammonites were, always forgetting that Reu did not have the basic knowledge of Hebrew history, "The Ammonites are descendants of Lot, Abraham's nephew, in essence, they are our cousins. Safe, maybe, intentionally evil, probably not." Jesse smiled, knowing why Reu was asking these questions, and said, "But our girl is in the hands of Yahweh."

נאמנות יהוה

It was now spring, the flowers in the fields were blooming, the air was crisp and fresh and Passover would soon be upon them. Nitzevet wandered in the fields with her three youngest and Abigail. She loved spending time with her children, whatever age they were, they were truly a blessing to her.

"When will Zeruah leave, mama?" Abigail asked.

Nitzevet sighed, realizing this was probably the best moment to tell her daughter, "We received word yesterday from a messenger that the wedding feast will be seven days after the feast of Unleavened bread," she paused as the reality of letting her daughter go hit hard, "It is about ten Parasang, so about a three-day journey. Maharai gave us instructions to start our journey on the third day after the feast and arrive on the seventh day. Obviously, we will be spending Sabbath on the road."

Abigail had mixed emotions, excitement at the adventure ahead, and sadness at having to leave her sister at the end of it. It seemed life was always like this, full of joy and sadness at the same time. Hard for a young girl to grasp at times.

Nitzevet reached over and hugged her daughter, surmising the emotions that were bubbling up as she watched the expressions flash across her face. "We will make the best of it."

נאמנות יהוה

It was hard for Dalit. She wanted so desperately to go to the wedding in Bezer, but Shelach was not well. He could not travel. So, the loving wife she was, she put on a smile and helped her daughter pack for the wedding of her granddaughter.

"Did you pack the gift I made for Zeruah?" Dalit asked.

"Yes, Ema, I am putting it in the bag now. She will love this beautiful bed cover you made her." She touched the soft wool with beautiful rich colors and said, "Our daughters and granddaughters will always cherish the wonderful bed covers you make for each of them." Gila said lovingly to her mother, knowing, only as a daughter can, that she was struggling with staying behind.

Comforted that she would be remembered, even if it was by the bed covering, Dalit smiled and relinquished her will to Yahweh. The housemaid picked up Gila's bags and carried them to the waiting donkey. Leah, Jesse, Nitzevet, Zeruah, and the rest of their clan would be arriving shortly to add her to the caravan heading to Bezer. Gila kissed her father goodbye and relished each moment, knowing his days on this earth would probably not be long.

נאמנות יהוה

The journey home was exhausting for everyone. While the wedding was beautiful, Namir's mother, Tahliah, had outdone herself with the food and the details, it was seven days in someone else's house, in cramped quarters. It was a long time to be away from home.

"You were pleased?" Jesse finally had a moment to ask his wife her opinion of everything. They walked silently for a moment, Jesse holding Abigail's hand on his left and Nitzevet on his right.

"Yes, I am pleased," she paused as she began to list why, "the town is beautiful and safe, up on the plateau. Zeruah's home is very lovely. I really like how it is attached to the back of Namir's father's house; they have privacy but closeness. Her new mother-in-law obviously is kind and gracious and will be a good friend to Zeruah. She seems to relish Zeruah's confident personality and ambition. I did worry about that, some mothers-in-law might feel challenged by a girl who works hard. Tahliah is not challenged by our daughter and appreciates her very much; I could tell even in such a short time we were there. So yes, Jesse, I am pleased," Nitzevet gave her husband one of those smiles he cherished so much, it was a smile that said, all was good, and the sadness and the blessings mingled together in her heart. Jesse loved that about his wife, she embraced all of life, the good the bad, the happy the sad, and worshipped her God in the midst of it all.

The family was very tired of camping, it was good to be at Gila's home in Efrat for the night. They all went to sleep early knowing that it was one more day's journey till they were home in Bethlehem. Shelach was so happy to see his relatives, it had been a while since he had a conversation with Jesse. "I am sure you will be happy to be home after three weeks on the road," Shelach said.

Jesse smiled, "It was a long journey, and it will be good to be home. Although now that we have a daughter three-day journey away, we will be making this trip often."

Shelach, a perceptive old man, turned toward Jesse and said, "I sense something brewing in your mind, my son?"

Knowing that he could not outrun the insight or intellect of this man, nor would he want to, Jesse shared his thoughts with his grandfather-in-law, "I have been pondering lately what Yahweh's plans are for the future. I know that he promised to redeem the people of the earth, but how?"

Shelach smiled, there was nothing that brought him greater joy than discussing this with his grandson. So he began, "I am convinced that Yahweh's appointed times reveal truths about Himself and His plans that are not obvious to us now, but as they play out in the future generations, they will be unveiled by our God himself."

Taking a long drink of hot tea, Shelach continued, "I know my son that you understand all the festivals of the Lord but indulge an old man as I go through them again and explain some insights."

Jesse nodded and smiled, there was nothing he would rather do. He knew Shelach would not be with them much longer. He noticed that he spoke a little slower than usual and would pause longer than normal. Jesse settled back on the cushions and waited; this was the conversation he had been longing for.

Shelach began, "It was clear that our first ancestor Adam sinned and consequently destined everyone to our current state of sin. But it was also quite clear that Yahweh would make a way to redeem humanity back to himself. What was not apparent was how. But I think it has to do with the appointed times, our seven festivals."

Jesse pondered this for a moment, he knew the festivals inside and out, he had been practicing them his whole life. He waited for Shelach to continue.

"Moses told us that when Yahweh cursed the serpent he said, 'And I will put enmity between you and the woman, and between your offspring and hers; he will crush your head, and you will strike his heel.'[18] This means something. Then Yahweh said to Abraham, "Go from your country, your people, and your father's household to the land I will show you. I will make you into a great nation, and I will bless you; I will make your name great, and you will be a blessing. I will bless those who bless you, and whoever curses you I will curse, and all peoples on earth will be blessed through you."[19] Shelach paused for a moment to catch his breath.

"Jesse, I think that the blessing that is to come through Abraham, Isaac, and Jacob is the seed, the promised One who will redeem humanity. It specifically says he will come from the Hebrews but the whole earth will be blessed," Shelach explained.

A puzzled Jesse asked, "Why would our God choose Abraham or the Israelites? It seems that we are an unlikely people in light of all the rebellious people who died in the wilderness, and even now, after the cycles of disobedience where our people were worshipping idols rather than Yahweh. It just seems we are the most unlikely heroes of the world."

"I understand, Jesse, but Yahweh did not choose us because we are great, but because He is. Think of it this way, if Yahweh can use a people like us for his purposes, despite our behavior and utter sinfulness, then He can save anyone. Do you remember when our God made this promise to Abraham? Do you remember the details of the covenant?" Shelach waited for Jesse to respond.

"I know that according to the ancient custom for cutting a covenant, Yahweh asked Abraham to take five animals, a heifer, a goat, a ram, a dove and a pigeon. Abraham then cut the animals in half but not the birds.

And according to the custom, both parties of the covenant are supposed to walk between the halves of the animals," Jesse outlined.

Shelach asked, "But what happened in this particular covenant between Yahweh and Abraham?"

"Yahweh put Abraham to sleep, and Yahweh alone walked between the animals sealing the covenant with himself alone," Jesse explained, having been taught well by his father.

Shelach continued, "Yes. Both parties are supposed to walk through the covenant ritual to indicate that they will be held responsible for upholding the covenant, and the consequence for violating the covenant is to end up like these animals, dead. But Yahweh did not let Abraham walk through."

"All of this I know, grandfather. But I do not really understand," Jesse responded in a discouraged tone.

"Ah, my son, here is where I may be able to provide insight. Yahweh knew that mankind, any human, even our ancestor Abraham would not be able to keep up their end of the covenant. Just look at our past! Yahweh had to destroy millions of people in the flood because the hearts of man were evil all the time. Yahweh alone walked through the dead animals indicating that He alone would keep the promise and if anyone paid the price it would be Yahweh," Shelach waited for Jesse's response.

Thoughtfully pondering for several moments, Jesse was confused, "Die? Yahweh die?"

"Think about it Jesse, all the festivals that we celebrate require sacrifice. Many animals have been sacrificed weekly and, in several festivals, annually, by everyone. It is as if these sacrifices don't actually accomplish the cleansing of sin but are pointing toward something that will satisfy our God's required payment for sin. And if man cannot and only our God alone can do that, then Yahweh, Himself must die," Shelach had a hard time speaking these words out loud. They seemed so blasphemous. But he knew deep down, they must be true.

"So let me see if I understand this correctly. Man sinned and is stuck because we cannot redeem ourselves as a result of our sin. Consequently, Yahweh put in place, way back in the garden of Eden, a plan to redeem mankind Himself. He made the unilateral covenant with Abraham which Moses wrote down in the Torah, and then He set forth the annual festivals and weekly sacrifices to point towards a time when Yahweh would accomplish this redemption of man by dying Himself?" Jesse outlined all the details.

"But how can Yahweh die?" Jesse asked.

"Oh, my son, that I do not know, nor can I explain. But I do believe that this promised One will come from the tribe of Judah, remember Jacob's blessing to his fourth son? 'The right to rule will not leave Judah. The ruler's rod will not be taken from between his feet. It will be his until the King it belongs to comes. It will be his until the nations obey him.' Jesse, I think the King whom the nations will obey is the Messiah."

Jesse had a lot to think about, he could also see that his grandfather was really tired. He said, "Grandfather, can we continue this conversation another day? It seems that we need to find our beds, and I have a long journey tomorrow to Bethlehem."

Shelach agreed. Jesse went to his bed and laid down softly next to Nitzevet so as not to wake her. His heart and mind were full. The tribe of Judah, his tribe, would produce the Messiah. When? Soon or in the distant future? Jesse hoped it would be soon.

28

THE YEAR OF JUBILEE

IT WAS QUIET FOR THE last two years; it seems that the ben Obed family had developed a routine. Living life in the presence of Yahweh, appreciating the Sabbath rest, especially this last year, the year of Jubilee. It was a full year commanded by our God to rest. Not only themselves, but the land needed rest from cultivating and harvesting. The families in Bethlehem for the most part loved this year. They made a special effort to invest in one another, in relationships and in friendship.

'It was so like Yahweh,' Nitzevet thought, 'to give us a full year every seven years and an additional year every forty-nine years to simply rest. If we follow His law as He specifically dictates, it goes well.' She pondered the beauty of the last year and how refreshed and relaxed everyone seemed now that it was almost over.

Uzzi and Chazael embraced the year of Jubilee. They really enjoyed getting to know their neighbors. Because no one was working and there was only time to rest, there were quite a few dinners and family gatherings where the people told stories and laughed together, building deep relationships.

The Law stated that in the forty eighth year they had to harvest enough food for the Shamita year and the following year of Jubilee. The people all over the land had all worked very hard in that forty-eighth year. For most people this was their first Jubilee year, not for Leah or Dalit, this would be their second, so they knew what to expect. Leah set the pace for the whole town. She gathered the women of the town every few weeks to explain a new way of preserving food. Since there would be no formal harvest for two years, there was a lot of planning and preserving involved in food preparation. Leah's wisdom was a priceless resource for the women of the town, and they knew it and were grateful.

They all knew they could eat directly from the field, so every day when the crops came up on their own and there was produce to harvest, they would take enough for the day. It was a great time together; all the women would embrace the morning sunshine with their baskets and head to the fields to pick a few grapes or stalks of wheat for the day to supplement what they had stored up from the forty-eighth year. This was Nitzevet's doing. Her love for frolicking in the fields never diminished over the years and she brought her unique perspective to the year of Jubilee. The whole town of Bethlehem was blessed by her exuberant celebration of Yahweh's year of freedom.

The year, however, did bring other significant changes. The bondservants who had indentured themselves to a master for wages, or paying back of debt were freed on the tenth day of the year after the Shofar was sounded. This was good for them, but not for the land or business owners. Jesse knew this Jubilee rule, his father had prepared him. Having a few indentured servants, Jesse was glad that the year of Jubilee was a year of no work because he had 12 full months to figure out how he would work his business when the servants were freed from their positions.

Reu never once thought of leaving. Why would he leave his family? This is where he belonged. Besides, Jesse treated him more as a partner in the business than a bondservant. They spent many hours over the Jubilee year pondering how to carry out the tasks that would be coming their way when the year ended. They had it figured out. Jesse told Reu, "It is so like our God to free us. It is evident that Yahweh does not approve of anything that holds humans in bondage ... even us."

"I have never felt freer than in the presence of our God. Some would say that obeying His laws is bondage, but they are not. Those very laws give us freedom. Freedom from the bondage of sin and wrongdoing. His laws free us to have a right relationship with Him and with others," Reu explained from rare wisdom.

Alas, the year was ending. The family was eager to get to work. They had tremendously enjoyed Yahweh's provision of rest, but they also enjoyed His provision of work and were eager to implement all the new plans they had discussed and designed.

The Day of Atonement was approaching, and the family gathered together the day before for a very large feast. They would finish their feast before dusk because the day of Yom Kippur started at dusk, and they were not to eat any food or do any work. They all planned to go to sleep early and sleep in late. The following day would be the first day of work after two years of no work.

נאמנות יהוה

The time had finally come. Time to say goodbye to one of their cherished elders. Shelach had gone to be with his forefathers. Some of the people believed that there was no afterlife, and that belief was becoming more and more popular. Maybe because of the influence of the pagan people around the people of Yahweh, or simply because they were not remaining faithful to their God.

Jesse and his whole family believed wholeheartedly that Yahweh would redeem those who loved him, and who followed him faithfully. Granted, Jesse did not understand how, but after his conversation with Shelach and rereading the writings of Moses he was beginning to gain a deeper understanding of Yahweh and what His plans might be. It was still very confusing. This Redeemer, this 'seed' of the woman, this was going to be a turning point in history. For Jesse, this prophecy was something to be cherished, something to look forward to. In the meantime, they would bury their dead and trust in Yahweh who holds the future.

נאמנות יהוה

The next few days were long as Dalit and Gila packed up their things to move to Bethlehem after living for so many years in one place. It was a sad time. As they talked and processed the past and looked toward the future, their perspective began to change. "It will be so good to be near Nitzevet," Dalit said as the sun slipped over the horizon. She had missed her granddaughter so much over the years. Even though she would see Nitzevet several times a year, she missed the daily interaction with her sweet granddaughter.

נאמנות יהוה

Jesse called the meeting with the elders at the gate of Bethlehem. This time they were in a room located inside the wall of the city. It was a rather small room, so the men were crowded, but the warmth was good on the chilly winter morning.

"Men of Bethlehem," Jesse began, "I have gathered you here to discuss the prospect of a new king."

The sighs of the men were heard around the room, they had all had uneasy feelings ever since the messenger from Samuel arrived the day before with the news that he would be appointing a new king soon at Mizpah. The men crowded in this little room were men who loved Yahweh and considered Him their king. But they had heard rumblings throughout the past few months from other tribes that there was a desire to be like the nations around them with a human king on the throne.

The main reason the people were demanding a king was because Nahash, king of the Ammonites, was attacking the people on the east side of the Jordan River. The Ammonites were a cruel people, they were the descendants of Lot through his youngest daughter. Yahweh had warned the Israelites with these words: "When you approach the territory of the people of Ammon, do not harass them or contend with them, for I will not give you any of the lands of the people of Ammon as a possession, because I have given it to the sons of Lot for a possession". They obeyed their God and the Israelite tribes of Gad, Reuben, and half of Manasseh claimed the territory bordering that of the Ammonites. But that did not matter, the Ammonites harassed them anyway.

Jesse paused for a moment to collect his thoughts, and then continued, "I am concerned as to Samuel's choice, let me rephrase that, Yahweh's choice of king over Israel."

The other men did not know what Jesse was talking about, why would he question Yahweh's choice? But out of respect, they waited for him to continue.

"The new king will be from the tribe of Benjamin," he said as his words immediately hit the ground like a rock and at the same time caused tension in the air.

"We expected the king to come from the tribe of Judah, as was prophesied!" Abner pointed it out a little too emphatically.

"Exactly," Jesse stated, understanding the emotion coming from these men who were from the tribe of Judah. "There is a reason Yahweh chose Saul, and I think it is because He is not pleased with Israel. I have invited Joel from the tribe of Issachar from Jezreel to talk to us about what his people are thinking about Yahweh's choice. Joel, please help us understand."

The men of Judah settled back in their chairs, ready to listen. The tribe of Issachar was well known throughout Israel for their wisdom in understanding the times and seasons of Yahweh's activity. They knew this man would speak the truth and were grateful for Jesse's forethought to invite him to share with them.

Joel cleared his throat and in a soft yet firm voice, he began to explain to the elders of Bethlehem what his and his families' perceptions were as to what their God was doing with this new development. "Yahweh chose a Benjaminite king as a punishment for Israel," said Joel.

The gasps could be heard around the room. They had known there was something up with this development but would have never guessed that their first king would be a punishment.

Joel continued, "Because the people have demanded a King, rather than asking for Yahweh's will, Yahweh is giving us a 'foreign king' in our midst. You all know, more than anyone, that our kings should come from the tribe of Judah. We know the Messiah will come from the kingly tribe of Judah."

Pausing for a moment to gather his words, he continued, "We have concluded that because Yahweh chose Mizpah as the place to anoint Saul, it is a punishment. As you all know Mizpah was first known as the place where the covenant between Laban and Jacob was made. A place to witness a covenant. It seems that Yahweh has used it as such a place ever since."

In case there was someone in the room who did not fully understand or remember Mizpah, Joel explained, "Mizpah is where Laban and Jacob set up a memorial watchtower as a symbol for Yahweh to keep watch between them. It was where the Israelites met to ask Yahweh to deliver the Ammonites into Jephthah's hands, it was where the tribe of Judah led the battle against Benjamin for their sin. It was also the place where Samuel brought the people together to repent eight years ago. Most of you remember that while you along with all the other Israelite leaders were sacrificing to Yahweh, the Philistines came to attack and their God himself alone fought the battle for Israel. This time we are back to Mizpah to again "judge between us". And the judgment this time is not good, nor will we as a people ultimately be blessed by it," Joel looked around the room to see if they understood.

Jesse nodded, "we expected as much. Yahweh is always faithful to His word. Just to be clear, men of Bethlehem, we are not questioning Yahweh or his choice of a king. If our God is giving us what we deserve as a nation, then so be it. We will never waver from our trust in Him and His wisdom. There will be a king from the tribe of Judah someday, but it appears we must wait. Thank you, Joel, for the explanation. May Yahweh continue to bless the tribe of Issachar and your wisdom and knowledge of the times and seasons."

With that the men filed out of the small room and back to their homes, silent and somber as the prospect of a future of judgment loomed large on the horizon.

29

A RELUCTANT KING

THREE DAYS LATER, SAMUEL, ON his way to Mizpah, stopped by Bethlehem to spend the night and drop Rebekah off for a long overdue visit with the ben Obed family. The elders of Bethlehem gathered eagerly for dinner at Jesse's house, which was usual when Samuel came to town. Even more so, in light of why Samuel was coming and where they were all going the next day. Even though the men were aware of the situation with the new king, they were anxious to hear Samuel tell the full story of what Yahweh had asked him to do and how the events of the selection of the new king had unfolded.

"It all started, as you all know when I appointed my sons to follow in my footsteps and participate in leading Israel," Samuel started to explain and grew silent. The men watched as sadness washed over the face of their leader in his grief.

"I am sorry my friend, we know they are not good men," said Jesse, remembering Eli's sons and how Samuel's sons were following that same path. "Could it be that they are too young?"

"Yes, I know, I thought maybe the responsibility of representing Yahweh at a younger age would help to temper Joel and Abijah and mold them into true followers of Yahweh. But I was wrong," Samuel squared his shoulders, sat up straighter, and continued his narrative, "So you remember, I told you a few weeks back that the leaders of the people came to see me and demanded a king. They told me because of the Ammonites as well as the evil deeds of my sons, they wanted a king. I was so angry when I told Yahweh because I felt like they were rejecting me as their appointed judge. But He told me that they were rejecting Him, not me. Yahweh then told me to explain to them everything that the King would take from them, their sons and daughters as servants, their money as taxes, and their land. But they would not listen and wait on Yahweh. They wanted a King," Samuel was again visibly sad and uniquely vulnerable before his friends.

"Then what happened?" Jesse asked gently. All the elders of Bethlehem were eager to hear these details as well. Since they were not a part of this demanding mob, they had no insight into why a king was demanded.

"Yahweh told me that a man from Benjamin would come to see me the next day. When he came, Yahweh indicated this was indeed the man that I should anoint as king. He was very handsome and tall, a rather impressive man, although a little reticent for a king if you ask me," Samuel paused in thought as the details of the scene passed through his mind.

After a thoughtful pause, Samuel continued, "I asked him to eat dinner with me that night at the sacrifice. Then, before he left to go back to his father, I privately anointed him as king. He was a little shocked, as was I, because he was a Benjamite. It was our understanding from the writings of Moses that the 'Scepter would not depart from the tribe of Judah'. We all expected the kings of Israel to be from Judah." Samuel took a few moments to refresh himself with a cool drink and then continued. The men silently nodded in understanding of what Samuel was saying, especially after what Joel from the tribe of Issachar had told them about why our God would choose a Benjamite as king.

Samuel continued, "Yahweh had instructed me to tell this new king Saul a couple of incidents that would happen in the next few days after that so that the People would see that Saul was special. The Spirit of the Lord came upon him, and he prophesied with priests on his way home. I think the Lord was going to use him to attack the garrison of Philistines near Gibeah which would have solidified him as king. But my servants told me he did not. He is there now in Gibeah, waiting for me, for us. As you know I am summoning the people to Mizpah to install Saul as king in three days."

One of the elders responded, "Yes Samuel, the messenger came several days ago, and we are prepared to leave with you in the morning to head toward Mizpah. We have gathered provisions to camp along the way and while we are there. We would be honored if you would stay with us in our camp for the duration of the meeting."

Samuel was grateful for the invitation. He appreciated the friendship of these elders of the tribe of Judah, true leaders, and of Jesse and the safety he felt in their presence.

Nitzevet and Rebekah relaxed outside in the courtyard on the bench beneath the window. They quietly listened as Samuel spoke and pondered the outcome silently. Seeing the tear slip down her friend's cheek, Nitzevet knew Rebekah was grieving over her sons; she hugged Rebekah with an embrace that communicated kindness and empathy. They would talk later.

Jesse rose to indicate that dinner was over and that it was time for everyone to head off to sleep because they would all be up for an early morning departure.

As Samuel lay in the soft bed with his arms around Rebekah awash in the Shalom of Yahweh, he whispered a prayer of gratitude for their room, a warm bed, and gracious hosts.

Early, the next morning, the men left for the installation of the new king. The women sighed in relief and prepared to enjoy the time off alone. While sipping their spiced milk, Leah said to Rebekah, "I am so sorry about Joel and Abijah and their disobedience. We pray for them all the time."

Once again, a tear slipped down Rebekah's cheek as she nodded and sipped her tea, she could not help the feeling of sadness and grief, nor did she want to avoid it here in the presence of her friends.

Moving to a different subject Leah asked, "What do you think about our king from the tribe of Benjamin?"

Rebekah pondered the question as she composed herself. It was not a new thought; she had been pondering it for a while. "I think that Yahweh is stalling."

With a puzzled look, Leah asked, "What do you mean?"

"I mean that when Yahweh is ready to give us a king, he will come from the tribe of Judah. This king demanded of Yahweh, so He is giving us what we asked for," The women were silent, taking in the wisdom they had just heard.

Nitzevet nodded with new understanding and added, "We have always taken Yahweh at His word, even when He seems to be doing the opposite of what He said he would do."

Shifra refilled Rebekah's cup and said, "Yahweh has never disappointed."

Nitzevet looked at her closest friends and said, "You know that we cannot be disappointed in Yahweh's timing. He always comes through in HIS time. I trust my life to Him. And even if what Yahweh provides is not what we expect, but something different, then He still came through because of His love for us."

The women relished these moments together, like-minded and confident in Yahweh.

Glancing over at Shoshannah sitting quietly, Nitzevet said, "I am glad Reu went with them, Shoshannah. He is so good to Jesse and his faith is so strong, I know that Yahweh will use him in Jesse's life to encourage him."

Nitzevet continued, "I need to go check on my grandmother, Dalit was not feeling well this morning and I think she needs something to make her feel better."

נאמנות יהוה

The men set up camp for the night, midway between Bethlehem and Mizpah, well away from the city of Jebus, the Jebusites were not the nicest of people.

The men cherished the time with Samuel. When he was with them, they felt the peace of Yahweh whose presence went with Samuel, and everyone knew it. As a prophet, he was also wise, a result of spending much time with his God.

Jesse sat on a rock ledge at the edge of their camp looking west as the sun was setting. It was a moment of silence to ponder all that was taking place in his life, in his town, in his nation. If there ever was a time that he longed for a conversation with his father or his father-in-law, now was the time. He felt their loss most in those moments.

Samuel sensed that Jesse could use a friend, he himself missed the wisdom of Obed and Shelach, so he could only imagine how Jesse felt. He approached slowly making sure that Jesse could hear his footsteps as he approached. He sat down on the rock ledge a few feet from his friend and waited, as friends do.

"Why do you think Yahweh chose Saul?" Jesse asked after a few quiet moments alone with Samuel.

"I really don't know why; Yahweh did not tell me. But I have a hunch that Yahweh is giving us Saul, not because he is what our God wanted but because he is what the people wanted."

Jesse nodded, respecting Joel even more for coming to the same conclusion earlier. "That would make sense as to why our God did not appoint someone from the tribe of Judah."

"I believe you are correct my friend. Tomorrow we will once again camp at Mizpah and the following day we will gather all the people. Yahweh Himself will draw out Saul by lot and appoint him as king before all the people."

The two men grew quiet, pondering this new chapter in the life of their nation. A king, no one knew what that looked like. Israel had never had a king. They hoped it would turn out well, but whenever human leaders put themselves between the goodness of Yahweh and the people, things didn't turn out well for the people. The only good and true king was their God. After a long time of silence, the men rose and slowly made their way to their sleeping mats and fell asleep.

נאמנות יהוה

The morning after they arrived in Mizpah was crisp and most of the men slept well on the journey. There was something refreshing about sleeping under the stars after eating a meal over a campfire. Samuel, however, was worried. As he had shared with Jesse as they traveled, he did not feel this anointing was a 'joyous' occasion, to him it was ominous, and it showed in his countenance.

After breakfast with his closest friends, Samuel stood up and encouraged them to go stand with the men of their tribes. Jesse reluctantly left his side and stood with the men of Bethlehem among the men of the tribe of Judah, all of whom were in a somber mood. Jesse looked over the multitude of people, mostly men. Some women had come with their husbands to care for them and cook for them, but Jesse was glad that Nitzevet was not here. This was not a joyous occasion; it was judgment, and he could feel it. He was glad that Nitzevet was spared from this, she typically felt these things most deeply.

Samuel motioned for the people to be quiet and then he started speaking, "This is what the LORD, the God of Israel, says: 'I brought Israel up out of Egypt, and I delivered you from the power of Egypt and all the kingdoms that oppressed you.' But you have now rejected your God, who saves you from all your disasters and calamities. And you have said, 'No, appoint a king over us.' So now present yourselves before the LORD by your tribes and clans."[20]

Slowly the procession began with the tribe of Reuben. The leader of the tribe stepped up and presented himself before Samuel and as Samuel paused, listened for Yahweh, and shook his head no.

Jesse saw his new son-in-law Namir standing behind the leaders of the tribe of Ruben. He was glad he was there; he would go speak with him later.

After Samuel rejected Ruben, the leader stepped aside and the next leader from the tribe of Simeon stepped up. Everyone knew that Samuel was the de facto leader of the tribe of Levi, but Samuel had instructed the head of his own clan to step up as a matter of formality and he shook his head, as everyone expected. Then the head of the tribe of Judah stepped up, Jesse. Samuel looked him in the eyes with great sadness and again shook his head. You could hear and feel the gasp of astonishment rush through the crowd. Everyone who knew Yahweh's word knew the prophecy that kings came from the tribe of Judah. Everyone had thought the same thing as Jesse stepped up, 'surely one of Jesse's sons would be the next king!'

Samuel did not let them linger on this point, so the rest of the tribes followed in the same manner: Dan, Naphtali, Gad, Asher, Issachar, Zebulun, Joseph, and then the leader of Benjamin stepped up and Samuel motioned for him to pause. He asked for the leaders of each of the families of the tribe of Benjamin to step up. Matri was chosen. As his sons stepped up Samuel immediately chose Kish and looked behind him and expected to see Saul. But he was not there.

Samuel was really puzzled, because Yahweh was leading him to choose these men, and he knew that Saul was to be chosen, but then Saul wasn't there. Samuel quietly asked his God, "Has he come yet?"

Yahweh told Samuel, "He is hidden among the equipment," Samuel sent the men to look for Saul.

Jesse could tell that Samuel was very displeased. He and the elders of Bethlehem knew that Saul had been anointed. Saul himself knew that this was his big moment, what was going on? Jesse wondered why he did not stand up like a man and present himself. Instead, he was hiding. He whispered a prayer, "Please, Lord, do not let this behavior be indicative of his leadership as our king."

The men who went to find Saul returned to the crowd with him. All the people that looked at this young man standing before them were surprised by his stature. He was taller than everyone.

Samuel walked up to Saul and looked deep into his eyes. Saul saw the flash of disappointment, but that faded quickly as Samuel turned and said to the people, "Do you see him whom the Lord has chosen, that *there is* no one like him among all the people?"

All the people shouted, "Long live the king!"

Jesse was shocked, this was the very tall messenger that had come to their town years ago telling of the fate of the Ark of the Covenant when it fell into the hands of the Philistines.

The newly installed king spent the remainder of the day with Samuel and the heads of each tribe. Samuel explained the details of how kings were to act and how the people were to respond. They were all very attentive since they had never had a king before. Samuel had appointed several scribes to write down everything he said as he spoke so that the people would remember and could reference the details when they needed to.

After several days of this, Samuel sent the people home and Saul returned to his home in Gibeah. Jesse noticed that it was interesting how there were quite a few men whose hearts Yahweh had touched to go with Saul. They were valiant men who knew Yahweh and listened to His prompting. One of those men was Namir, Zeruah's husband. As Jesse watched he knew that his daughter would be moving to Gibeah. It saddened him as it seemed that she would soon be the wife of a soldier.

Jesse took mental note of everything as it played out before him. He wanted to take all the details home to his family and explain to them what had taken place. While he and Reu were walking through the tents of the men who had gathered, they noticed a group sitting by a fire having a rather intense conversation. Jesse motioned to Reu to stop for a moment and lingering in the shadows just outside of their visual range of the light of the fire, Jesse and Reu listened. The young men were not speaking highly of the new king. The most vocal said to his companions: "How can this man save us? Wasn't he hiding among the supplies?"

Jesse realized that they had a point, but that didn't matter. A king had been chosen and Samuel was clear in his teaching over the past few days that the people of Israel were to be loyal to their God's chosen king and not disparage him among themselves. Reu and Jesse continued their walk to their tent, not wanting to share what they heard. Yahweh will take care of this.

נאמנות יהוה

Sadness permeated the little town of Bethlehem again. A few days after Jesse returned their lives were once again in upheaval. Dalit had not felt herself for several weeks. Gila had risen early in the morning to check on her beloved mother who shared a room with her above Nitzevet's room. She knew immediately that Dalit had passed from life to death in her sleep.

Everyone knew Dalit and now they felt the stinging loss of such a wise woman. Gila was the most impacted. Her mother had been her best friend since her husband had died so many years ago. She had played the role of confidant and counselor, encourager and admonisher. Now both her mother and father were no longer with her. Her loss was palpable.

After the women had prepared her body for burial and dressed her in her best dress, the men of the town carried Dalit's body to the family tomb. It was a natural cave that Boaz had renovated to become a tomb for the family. It was not lavish or decorated, just a simple cave with a central room and many alcoves surrounding the central room. As Jesse and Reu placed her body in the designated place, the family stood together and mourned silently for their beloved grandmother. They all knew this would not be the last of them, for there were quite a few older people in their midst. It was natural in this moment for the younger to cherish the presence of the older, recognizing how fleeting life really was.

It was their custom to fast on the day their loved one died. After the burial, the women huddled together on the cushions in Leah's room, sometimes talking, with long moments of silence that did not make any of them uncomfortable. They just relished being together. Shoshannah quietly let herself in the door and joined the women in their silence. Several of the women of the town had volunteered to engage the children, Nitzevet, Shifra, Zeruah and Shoshannah were all grateful for a few moments of silence to collect their thoughts before they had to return to the busy life of raising children.

Other women of the town brought food and placed it on the table so that after dusk the family could eat without having to prepare their own food. The community loved this family and it showed.

נאמנות יהוה

Reu knew it was early, but he had to speak with Jesse. He let himself through the courtyard gate of the ben Obed family and gently knocked on Jesse and Nitzevet's door. Jesse answered bleary-eyed after a few moments, having spent several hours in the night up with his children. "Yes?" Jesse asked, a bit annoyed.

Feeling bad, but also knowing that Jesse needed to know the news, Reu whispered boldly, "We need to talk, a messenger just arrived, and something has happened."

Jesse motioned for Reu to sit in the courtyard and wait. Reu sat down and pondered what little he knew. Apparently, the town of Jabesh Gilead was under attack by the Ammonite king. They had sent messengers throughout the land of Israel to plead for aid and help to fight the Ammonites.

Wrapping his cloak around him to stave off the early morning chill, Jesse stepped out of his home and came close to Reu in the predawn light so he could speak softly and not wake up the entire household. Reu relayed what he knew and watched as Jesse responded by whispering with disgust under his breath, "Nahash".

"What snake?" Reu asked.

Jesse did not hear his question because as usual, he was pondering the situation for a moment. He then told Reu to go wake up the elders of the town and have them meet him at the city gate.

They gathered quickly at the urging of Reu, and Jesse quieted the men down just as the sun was cresting over the hills to the east. They could all feel the subtle warmth of the morning light. "We have a situation. Nahash has attacked Jabesh Gilead," he said waiting for the men to absorb the news.

Reu then understood why he had been confused about the 'snake'. Nahash meant serpent in Hebrew, but it was also the name of the Ammonite king. He was now understanding more as Jesse continued. "Apparently, they told this evil king that they would make a treaty with him and be subject to him, but instead of accepting he gave the people of Jabesh Gilead an ultimatum. 'Die by the sword or everyone must lose their right eye.'" The men were sad but not surprised. Apparently, it was well known that the Transjordan tribes had suffered greatly by the hand of this man. He had removed the right eyes of a lot of Israelites living on the other side of the Jordan.

Jesse was now very glad that Zeruah and Namir had moved to Gibeah, away from the evil snake king, Nahash. He whispered a prayer of gratitude to Yahweh and continued.

"The men of Jabesh Gilead requested a reprieve from Nahash for seven days to ask for help, if no one came, they would surrender. This was the message that arrived from Jabesh early this morning. Apparently Nahash is quite confident that no one will come to their rescue, because he granted their request."

Abner, the eldest and most cognizant of the historical implications asked, "What does our King think?"

Jesse noticed that Reu looked confused, so he whispered, "I will tell you the history later," Reu was pleased that he would finally have some understanding.

Jesse knew immediately what Abner was referring to and replied, "I have already sent a messenger to Gibeah to find out what the new king is thinking. We will know soon. In the meantime, I suggest we ask Yahweh to guide us as He wills, so we do not repeat history. What a nightmare that would be. I have also sent a messenger to Samuel to make sure he is informed as to what is taking place."

As the men got up to go to their homes and work, Jesse announced to the men that he would like all those interested in a history lesson to meet at his home that evening, especially the younger men and women. This was one of those situations where history was very important, and seriousness was lost on those who did not know or understand the history. Jesse agreed that dinner that night would be a corporate event and all who wanted to know the story should come. He wished his father were here, he had always been a great storyteller.

נאמנות יהוה

The food was prepared and ready, the cushions were laid out and the people were assembling. Nitzevet relished the opportunity to host the younger people of the tribe in her home, especially when history and teaching were involved. This was not a story for the very young, too many inappropriate details, but it was a story for the young men and women who needed to know.

After the meal was nearly complete, Jesse stood up and began. "My dear friends, this is not a history lesson for the faint of heart, but it is a necessary one. Before my father Obed was born, there was an incident in the town of Gibeah. There was a certain Levite who lived in the territory of Ephriam whose concubine was from our town. She left her husband the Levite and returned to Bethlehem and he came to retrieve her. After spending a few days here with her father, the couple began their journey back to Ephriam. The servant of the Levi suggested they stop at Jebus but the Levi said no, they would not stay in a non-Israelite town that they would either stop at Gibeah or Ramah. The sun was setting as they approached Gibeah, so that is where they decided to stop. They were sitting in the town square when a fellow Ephraimite encountered them and nervously encouraged them to go home with him where he would provide them with lodging. The couple agreed and went home with the man, to his apparent relief."

Jesse pondered how best to illustrate the next part of his story, asking Yahweh for the right words. "That night a group of men from the town of Gibeah came to the door of the host and demanded that he send out the Levite so that they could 'know' him," Jesse could feel his disgust rising, this was not something he should 'have to' talk about. "Can you see the similarities between this incident and Sodom and Gomorrah?" Jesse said, to help them fully understand what he was saying. The people listening nodded their heads in complete understanding, also disgusted.

He continued, "The host offered to the evil men his daughter, but the Levite sent out his concubine," Jesse shuddered at the thought of treating a woman in such a way. "They raped her and killed her."

Jesse continued with the gruesome tale, "The Levite was very angry, but he needed time to think about what to do. So, he put her body on his donkey and went home. He then dismembered her body and sent it throughout the 12 tribes. This act solicited the desired response. People all over Israel were enraged. They assembled 400,000 men at Mizpah and asked the Levite to explain what happened."

"The Israelites sent word to the tribe of Benjamin to send out the evil men from Gibeah. But they refused. Instead, the tribe of Benjamin mustered 26,000 men to fight against 400,000 Israelites. The Israelites went to Bethel to inquire of their God who should go up first against the Benjamites. Yahweh responded that Judah should go up first. I think we all know the consequences, the tribe of Judah lost 22,000 men that day. The next day they inquired of their God again, and He said yes. That day they lost 18,000 men. At this point, the Israelites decided to repent and offer sacrifice for their sins before Yahweh. And Yahweh said, to go up on the third day that He would deliver the Benjamites into their hands. That day, the Israelites lost about thirty men, but because of an ambush tactic, the Benjamites lost more than 25,000. Not only that, but the Israelites also continued their rampage. They burned the town of Gibeah and killed all the women, children, and livestock and then burned every Benjamite town, killing everyone in them. Only six hundred men that had fled with the Benjamite army had survived because they ran to the place called Rock of Rimmon where they hid."

Reu shook his head at the loss of life, 65,000 Israelite men had died in battle in just three days, plus the thousands and thousands of women and children. That was too much. "Why would Yahweh allow this? Why would he not intervene?" Reu asked with obvious pain in his voice.

Jesse greatly respected Reu's compassion. He explained, "Reu, there was no king in the land, meaning the Israelites did not recognize Yahweh as their king and there was no leader who recognized Yahweh, so the

Israelites did what was right in their own eyes. Our people were walking away from our God, making bad decisions, not following Yahweh's ways, a cycle of disobedience that persists to this day, and our God was punishing us. But it did not stop there."

"After all this had gone down, Israel realized what they had done, they had basically wiped out the whole tribe of Benjamin. And they were very sad. One man, the Levite, had been threatened by a mob and they had killed his concubine. Both very bad and detestable things. But instead of punishing those that should have been punished, the Israelites made one bad decision after another, and many innocent women died at the point of their swords."

Jesse smelled the spices from the freshly brewed tea that Nitzevet was making and decided it was a good time to pause for a much-needed break, "Let's take a break, I know that this is a heavy story from a hard time in the history of our people."

The 'students' got up and stretched their legs. While sipping on the piping hot sweet tea that the ladies were serving, Reu stood quietly by his wife, thinking about the lack of faith and relationship that the past generations of Hebrews had with their God, his God. "Why, Shoshannah, did they not trust Yahweh? Why did they not consult Him and find out how to deal with the sin and the murder of this woman?" Reu asked his young wife.

Shoshannah smiled and thought how blessed she was to be married to such a compassionate man who loved Yahweh. Before she could answer she heard Jesse calling them back to finish the story. She was glad because she did not have an answer for her husband.

Jesse began, "After realizing what they had done, rather than consulting Yahweh, the Israelites continued with yet more bad decisions. Because they had vowed not to give any of their daughters to the tribe of Benjamin, they needed to find women for these six hundred men," Jesse sighed and then said, "Someone got a brilliant idea. If there was a tribe that did not show up at Mizpah when they were called, not only were they guilty of not showing up, but neither did they make the vow about not giving their daughters to the tribe of Benjamin," Jesse shook his head in disgust, thinking of his wife and daughters.

"Sure enough none of the men from the city of Jabesh-Gilead from the trans-Jordan half-tribe of Manasseh came when they were called. These wayward men of the other eleven tribes sent 12,000 men to kill the entire town of Jabesh-Gilead; men, women, children, except the virgins. They spared four hundred young women from Jabesh Gilead and brought them back as wives to the six hundred Benjamite men hiding in the hills. But they were two hundred women short. Another bad idea bubbled up from the pool of sinful men, they told the two hundred lonely Benjamite men to go hide in the vineyard and steal the virgins from Shiloh at the annual Festival of the Lord. So that is what they did."

Nitzevet, sitting in the back, spoke up, "It seems as if they considered their ill-conceived and downright sinful vows more sacred than the very lives of their brothers and sisters."

Reu started to realize a connection. Remembering that Saul was from the tribe of Benjamin and knowing that his home was in Gibeah he said, "Do you think that our new King is descended from the men of Gibeah and the women of Jabesh-Gilead?"

Everyone listening heard Reu's thoughts and realized that he was correct. Jesse smiled at Reu's quickness and said, "Yes!", they had understood the point of the history lesson. "Saul was most likely a descendent of both Jabesh-Gilead and the six hundred men from Gibeah and would feel the pain of the threat on the people of his ancestral city more than most."

Jesse stood up, signaling that the history lesson was over. Everyone walked home quietly wondering how their new king would respond, knowing that the town of his ancestors was being threatened by an evil king.

30

MEN TO BATTLE

LEAH RUSHED INTO NITZEVET'S ROOM trembling with fear, "They are leaving at dawn!" she exclaimed.

"Who?" Nitzevet responded, trying to calm both her mother-in-law and her startled children.

"Jesse and his brothers, Reu, and four hundred other men from our town are going to meet Saul at Gibeah and march toward Jabesh Gilead," she said sobbing into her hands. It is always tragic for a mother to watch her sons go to war and it was no different for Leah. But not as tragic as a young wife with young children.

Nitzevet hugged her mother-in-law as they quietly sobbed in each other's arms. Soon the room was filled as Shifra, Keturah and all of their children rushed in. They were all sad and worried for their men and fathers. Nitzevet spoke through her tears to the One who could help, "Our Lord, Yahweh, we know that you care for us, for your people. We pray that above all else, you will be in the midst of this endeavor. We pray that Samuel and Saul will lead the people in victory over this evil king who desires to harm our people."

Her prayer calmed the women. Everyone sat in silence for a moment until they heard the men coming, they knew they were in for a long night of work, making food and packing it up with other necessities for their men as they went to battle.

נאמנות יהוה

Jesse held his wife as she sobbed in his arms. The children were finally asleep, and this husband and wife were having a hard time sleeping knowing what the morning would bring. "Yahweh will protect us my love. Trust Him," Jesse said as he drew her even closer.

"Yes, I know He will. I have complete faith in Him. But I am sad to see you go," she responded.

"I know, but this is one of the consequences of having a king, when he calls, we go. We have to trust Yahweh to lead him and pray that He will protect us as we obey His chosen," Jesse said with a quiet confident voice.

After a few moments laying in each other's arms, knowing it was the last night for a while, Nitzevet enjoyed the warmth of Jesse's arms and of his love. She asked Jesse, "Was Saul very angry when he heard?"

"Yes, as one would expect when he found out his people were being threatened with such a vial act. Apparently, this evil king has been doing this for a while in that region. There were 7000 men who escaped the latest raid and did not lose their right eyes. These are the men that Nahash is after. But we will prevail with our God's help. Pray for us my love," he said as he closed his eyes and fell into the gift of a deep sleep.

Nitzevet lay awake thinking of what the next few days would bring to their little town. She prayed for each of the women. She knew that Shoshannah especially would be so very sad that Reu was leaving. The uncertainty of his status and his inexperience with battle must be overwhelming her. Then she had an idea, over the past few years, Shoshannah had developed a special bond with Abigail. Even though she was only ten, she was a precious child with a very calm nature. Nitzevet would make plans in the morning to send her second daughter to stay with Shoshannah.

נאמנות יהוה

Abigail was so happy to go and stay with her 'Auntie' Shoshannah. As she packed up her little bag she asked her mother, "Will you be ok without me?"

Nitzevet smiled and said very graciously, "Yes, my dear, we will manage somehow without you. But I think it very important that you go and keep Shoshannah company while Reu is gone with your father, can you do that?"

"Yes, mama, I would be happy to!" she said, and really meant it.

Nitzevet knew that being a twin wasn't always easy, especially a twin of a boy who had several older brothers, girls could not do what the boys do. While she always wanted to be with her twin, it was not always possible and often made Abigail very sad. This, however, was her opportunity to be special with a special task that only she could accomplish.

נאמנות יהוה

News of the pending battle was trickling back to the elders who sat at the gate of Bethlehem where the old men waited not so patiently. Apparently, one messenger told the Elders that Saul was so angry that he chopped up his oxen and sent the pieces throughout the land, reminiscent of some of the details of the original historical account of Levi and his concubine.

It had been ten days since the men left and they saw the runner coming up the road with the message from Jesse. Finally, they would learn the outcome of the battle. The messenger spilled the details as quickly as he could, on the night of the seventh day of the reprieve given by the snake king, Saul planned to attack the Ammonites. When the people of Jabesh-Gilead were told and were elated that they would be saved by their brothers. At the last watch of the night on that seventh day, three divisions of Saul's soldiers broke into the Ammonite camp and killed almost everyone. Only a few scattered men survived.

Abner's first question is, "How many Israelites were hurt or killed?

נאמנות יהוה

Nitzevet heard someone calling her name in the courtyard. It was Abner, the chief elder of the town, hobbling down the path to her home. He had not gone to battle because of his age. Nitzevet knew that something

227

bad would have happened if Abner had come to her personally. She came into the courtyard and offered the elderly man a seat and motioned to Shifra to get him something to drink.

Abner immediately said, "Jesse is fine," knowing that was what her anxious question was. But then he looked at her with sadness and proceeded to tell her the story the messenger had relayed. During the battle with the Ammonites, the fastest runner had been sent from one regiment to the other to relay a message from Saul to the leader of the other regiment. While he was running, he was ambushed by a scout from the Ammonite army and killed. They found his body after the battle.

Nitzevet wept quietly for her daughter. She had only been married for four years and had three young children and lived in a strange town. No family, not even Namir's mother was near her. She had to go; her daughter was still so young. How was she going to cope with this tragedy? Then she asked Abner, "Has the messenger left, has he told Zeruah?"

Abner responded, "He is resting now. He will be leaving at dusk to head to Gibeah to tell Zeruah."

Nitzevet knew what she had to do. Wiping her tears, she thanked Abner for relaying the difficult news she ran into her mother's room and told her the plan. "Namir died in battle; I am going with the messenger to Gibeah to be there when he tells Zeruah. I will wait there for Jesse, and we will bring her and her children here."

Gila was shocked at the news, saddened, it was all happening so fast, but she knew it was the right thing to do, Zeruah needed her mother. "Yes, my dear, we will watch your children, go get your girl, I will tell Leah, and then help you pack.

Gila ran to get Eliab, "Grandson, please go find the messenger from the battle and tell him to wait for you and your mother. You will be traveling to Gibeah this evening with the messenger. Your mother will explain it to you later, go now."

Eliab ran to the city gate where he knew that the messengers had a resting place. He found the elders sitting in the gate and told them that when the messenger woke up to tell him to wait, and that he would have companions going with him to Gibeah.

Eliab then went to the stable and brushed down the donkey. He was going to make sure that his mother did not have to walk the whole way. She would ride for as many of the four parasangs to Gibeah as she wanted.

נאמנות יהוה

Eliab was glad that he was with his mother. While Shammah was the most empathetic of Nitzevet's sons, Eliab was very protective of his mother and understood her concern and grief. Anytime one of her children was in pain, she was in pain.

"Ema, Zeruah will be ok. We will take care of her," He offered simple encouragement.

Nitzevet smiled at her oldest. "Yes, my dear son, she will, and we will."

It seemed as if the journey took forever, as all journeys bringing bad news seem to do. They finally arrived and went straight to Zeruah's home where they knew she would be. Nitzevet told the messenger that she would take care of informing Zeruah and that he could stay at the city gate and explain everything to the elders of the town.

When Zeruah opened the door and saw her mother she knew immediately something was wrong. Nitzevet wrapped her daughter in her arms as Eliab shut the door behind them. There was much explaining and grieving to do.

נאמנות יהוה

Reu returned to Bethlehem with Samuel a week after the battle. They had quite a story to tell the people of Bethlehem about what happened. When the people found out they had returned, they started to gather in the town square and sent a messenger to Jesse's home where Samuel was staying.

Reu joined Samuel in the town square, knowing the people would not rest until they knew what had happened. "My friends and neighbors, please quiet down, we are here to listen to Samuel's words as he tells us how the battle unfolded and what happened after.

All were quiet as Samuel stepped up and began to retell the tale of this magnificent battle.

"As you all know, for quite a while, Nahash has been tormenting the trans-Jordan tribes of Gad, Ruben and half tribe of Manasseh. This is mainly why the people have asked for a king, to make war against King Nahash. Yahweh granted your wish, giving you Saul as king over Israel. And may I say, it saddened Yahweh to know that you desired an earthly king over him, after all he has done for you."

The people were sad about this, quite a few of the people in the crowd were not among those who wanted an earthly king, but they knew that when their voices were few, that the prevailing winds of political desire did not go their way. They grieved alongside their God at the new monarchy and all that would bring.

"A few weeks ago, a month after Saul was appointed king, the king of Ammon led his army to Jabesh Gilead where about 7000 men had escaped his evil campaign and still had both of their eyes. He besieged the city. But the people of Jabesh asked for peace. They begged Nahash to make a treaty with them that they would be his servants."

"Nahash, the evil man that he is, said that it would only be under one condition, they would all lose their right eye."

A young man near the back of the crowd spoke up, "I don't understand, why do they have to lose their right eye?"

Samuel appreciated the thoughtful question, so he explained, "When a warrior fights in battle, his shield covers his left eye. Soldiers mainly use their right eye to see what is ahead of them, where they are aiming their spear, and where to walk. If all of the men lose their right eye, they could no longer see ahead nor fight in battle … it would be a disgrace to Israel."

Samuel continued with the account, "So the men of Jabesh asked the king to give them seven days to see if anyone would come to their rescue, and if no one came, they would submit to his terms," Samuel chuckled, "so the arrogant king, thinking so highly of himself and assuming that no one would come to stop his reign of terror, granted their request. His troops set up camp for a seven-day wait. Meanwhile, the men of Jabesh sent messengers to this side of the Jordan begging for help. One of those messengers went to Gibeah where Saul lives. Saul had been plowing his field. Honestly, I don't know why, it is like he did not take his anointing as king seriously. I gave many instructions and had them all written down, but he went back to plowing."

Realizing that he was getting off track, Samuel continued, "When Saul came in from the field and found the people of Gibeah weeping he asked what had happened. When he heard the message from Jabesh-Gilead he was very angry. He took his oxen, chopped them up, and sent them throughout the land, as you well know with a message "This is what will happen to the oxen of anyone who refuses to follow Saul and Samuel into battle!" That is how I found out what was going on."

"I arrived in Bezek just as Saul was sending messengers to Jabesh-Gilead that Israel was coming to their rescue by noon the next day. I was surprised to see 300,000 men from Israel and 30,000 men from Judah already assembled ready to follow their new king into battle and rescue our trans-Jordan brothers."

Samuel continued, "It was about seven parasangs from Bezek to Jabesh-Gilead. Saul told the people of Jabesh that the Israelite military force would arrive by noon the next day, he hoped that detail would leak to the Ammonite army, and it did. Saul actually planned to arrive in the early morning hours. Saul divided the army into three detachments and attacked from three sides. They did not know what was going on, since they expected us at noon. The Ammonite army was nearly wiped out. Only a few men escaped."

"It was at that time that I knew that Yahweh was going to use Saul. He was turning out to be a good military leader. On another note, there were some soldiers asking around for the men who had questioned Saul's leadership so that they could kill them. That is when I overheard Saul say, 'No one will be executed today, for today the Lord has rescued Israel!' I was pretty proud of him."

"It was then that I took the people to Gilgal to renew the kingdom. In a solemn ceremony before the Lord, the people officially made Saul their king. We offered peace offerings to the Lord and all the men were filled with joy.

I told the people that I had done as they had asked and given them a king. I wanted to clear the record and make sure that my duty was done, so I asked them to testify against me in the presence of the Lord and before his anointed one. Whose ox or donkey have I stolen? Have I ever cheated any of you? Have I ever oppressed you? Have I ever taken a bribe and perverted justice? Tell me and I will make right whatever I have done wrong."

"They said that I never did any of those things. So here is what I told them, and now I am telling you:

"It was the Lord who appointed Moses and Aaron, He brought your ancestors out of the land of Egypt. Now stand here quietly before the Lord as I remind you of all the great things the Lord has done for you and your ancestors.

"When the Israelites were in Egypt and cried out to the Lord, he sent Moses and Aaron to rescue them from Egypt and to bring them into this land. But the people soon forgot about the Lord their God, so he handed them over to Sisera, the commander of Hazor's army, and also to the Philistines and to the king of Moab, who fought against them.

"Then they cried to the Lord again and confessed, 'We have sinned by turning away from the Lord and worshiping the images of Baal and Ashtoreth. But we will worship you and you alone if you will rescue us from our enemies.' Then the Lord sent Gideon, Bedan, Jephthah, and Samuel to save you, and you lived in safety.

"But when you were afraid of Nahash, the king of Ammon, you came to me and said that you wanted a king to reign over you, even though the Lord your God was already your king. All right, here is the king you have chosen. You asked for him, and the Lord has granted your request.

"Now if you fear and worship the Lord and listen to his voice, and if you do not rebel against the Lord's commands, then both you and your king will show that you recognize the Lord as your God. But if you rebel against the Lord's commands and refuse to listen to him, then his hand will be as heavy upon you as it was upon your ancestors.

"Now stand here and see the great thing the Lord is about to do. You know that it does not rain at this time of the year during the wheat harvest. I will ask the Lord to send thunder and rain today. Then you will realize how wicked you have been in asking the Lord for a king!"

Samuel paused for a drink of water, and someone called out, "Did it rain?"

"Yes, it did. The Lord sent thunder and rain. And all the people were terrified of the Lord and of me. So they cried out "Pray to the Lord your God for us, or we will die! For now, we have added to our sins by asking for a king."

"I told them not to be afraid they had certainly done wrong, but I encouraged them to make sure now that they worship the Lord with all their hearts. Don't go back to worshiping worthless idols that cannot help or rescue you—they are totally useless! For it has pleased the Lord to make you His very own people, for His own good name He will not abandon His people."

"I want you to know, as for me, I will certainly not sin against the Lord by ending my prayers for you. And I will continue to teach you what is good and right. But be sure to fear the Lord and faithfully serve him. Think of all the wonderful things he has done for you. But if you continue to sin, you and your king will be swept away."

31

ZERUAH

JESSE, NITZEVET, ZERUAH, AND HER three children Abishai, Joab, and Asahel returned to Bethlehem. Gila and Leah met them as they arrived in the courtyard. It was a rather somber greeting, knowing the depth of Zeruah's sorrow. For a Hebrew woman to lose her husband was tragic. The overwhelming love of her family and the gracious community surrounding them lessened the grief that Zeruah was experiencing.

"We love you Zeruah, your home is here with us, you belong to us," Gila told her granddaughter. These words lifted the burden of Zeruah's grief. A widow was typically destitute in these times. Zeruah knew that had she belonged to a 'normal' family, she would be truly fearful of her future. How would she raise and support three little boys on her own? But this family, the ben Obed family, was different. They were a community of love, and compassion, the very expression of Yahweh's love for those around them. She knew she was blessed.

After a few weeks in her childhood home, Zeruah sat for a moment, resting in the shade while the boys ran wild with their cousins. She smiled at their antics, for the first time since Namir died. Her heart sighed as if saying 'This was good'. There was no place she would rather be than here with her family. Her boys would grow up with their cousins and their grandfather. She missed Namir terribly. He was not very romantic, nor gentle, but he was her love and he was gone. The smile again faded and would not return for a while. Zeruah sighed and said to herself, 'Someday I will smile again, but today I am grateful for Yahweh's provision, my family.'

נאמנות יהוה

The weeks turned into months and months to a year and just as their corporate grief began to lessen a new and fresh tragedy struck the family.

It was Sabbath morning and the family went about gathering up food for their breakfast that had been prepared the day before by their Matriarch and her staff. Nitzevet noticed that Leah was not among them, so she sent Ozem to find his great-grandmother. He returned and stood silently beside his mother.

Nitzevet leaned close and asked him what was bothering him.

The tears spilled out as he explained that his beloved grandmother was silent and cold.

Knowing immediately what had happened, she hugged her son and whispered into Jesse's ear. They knew their lives would never be the same without this woman's presence. They must allow themselves time to grieve and recognize fully what their lives would mean without her.

It was overcast when Samuel and Rebekah arrived the next day. Jesse's first act when his mother died was to send a messenger to his best friend Samuel. When the messenger arrived they immediately started their journey from Ramah to Bethlehem, knowing this precious family needed their presence if nothing else.

נאמנות יהוה

Jesse sat quietly in the field with the sheep. Breathing deeply of the fresh morning air with a hint of moisture from the dew. This was the place where he came to process his thoughts, away from the prying eyes of those who relied on him. His mother was gone. As he slowly let go, he allowed himself a moment of profound grief. He had remained strong over the past few days of mourning for the family, his sisters, his wife, and his children. He had not yet given himself the time or space to grieve for his precious mother. Now was that time.

32

LOSS

NITZEVET BAT ADAEL RAISED HER swollen eyes to the horizon. The sun was coming up bringing a new day, for which she still praised Yahweh. 'There was not much else to praise Him for,' she moaned to herself. Her life was in a shambles. Her past was now scarred by the death of a son. Her future is unsure and without hope, because of the choices of others.

Her precious baby boy had died six months ago. Her seventh son … the apple of her eye, the pride of her old age. He had died moments after birth. Now, she was instructed to forget that he even existed. After carrying this precious life in her womb for nine months.

Nitzevet had always disliked the Hebrew custom of not mourning the death of a child who did not survive past thirty days. It was as if they were erasing the existence and memory of a child. Now, after her own loss, she abhorred the custom. She could not imagine where that came from. It was not Yahweh, for He is the one that knit the tiny humans in the wombs of their mothers. She knew that each precious life was cherished by her God. She knew He mourned the death of each one.

Nitzevet was forced to bury her unnamed baby in an unmarked grave and then she was expected to proceed with life as if nothing had happened. She just couldn't. If only her mother were here. She knew that Gila would have exactly the right thing to say, having lost three babies of her own before Nitzevet was born. Her thoughts immediately turned to her compounded loss. Leah passed from this earth three years ago, then her own sweet mother last year, and now her baby boy. It just seems that tragedy was following her. But in her heart, she knew differently, both Leah and Gila were up there in age, and everyone knew there was one sure constant, death. The tragedy was only so painful because it was compounded. Nitzevet never liked to pile up problems and make them larger than they actually were. But her heart still ached for the loss of her mother-in-law, her mother, and now her son.

She had known that Jesse was suffering too. Never fully recovered from his mother's death and now his son was gone. Being consumed with her own grief she could not remember much of the past six months, but Jesse had not spoken to her for quite some time, weeks maybe months, since shortly after the death of their son.

"Yahweh, where are you? Take this pain from me, numb my heart," pleaded Nitzevet. She proceeded to head to the fields, ultimately to the tower to seek the presence of her God if she could find Him in her sorrow.

Jesse at that moment was pondering his next step. His doubt was great, his faith was small, and his decisions were becoming more and more irrational as he drifted from the One who was his foundation.

He sought out his friend Reu for a conversation, if only he could speak his thoughts out loud, he would get clarity.

As they sat in the fields, listening to the gentle bleating of the sheep, Jesse asked his friend, "Reu, help me process this mess." It was more of a cry for help than a simple request, which left Reu unsettled, but he knew listening was what he should do at the moment.

"When my grandfather Boaz married Ruth who was a Moabite woman, it was an unwritten law that Israelites could not marry Moabite men, and there is still no consensus that Hebrews can or cannot marry Moabite women. I believe this was set forth because when the Israelites were passing through the wilderness, it was the Moabite men who refused them passage," he explained to Reu.

Reu was confused but continued to listen, sensing he should not comment yet.

"I am worried that the death of this little one, my seventh son, was punishment for something I have done. What if, as the grandson of Ruth, I am considered a Moabite man, then marrying a true Hebrew woman would be forbidden? Could I have brought this calamity upon my wife and family because I married Nitzevet? I love her so much, to cause her to continue to sin by being married to a non-Israelite would be wrong." He was speaking mostly to himself at this point, not thinking about Reu and his marriage to a Jewish girl, Shoshannah. Reu knew that Jesse did not mean to offend him and that this thinking was becoming increasingly irrational, spawned by the grief from the loss of his baby son. The Yahweh that Reu had come to know, mostly through Nitzevet and Jesse, would not punish someone so many years later for a perceived sin based on a nebulous ancient rule.

"Jesse, you and Nitzevet were meant for each other. You have had thirty years of a wonderful marriage. Why would you start thinking about these things?" he asked.

Jesse's pain was so great, that he could not listen, in his grief, he had convinced himself of his sin. He would not listen to the one person who was speaking wisdom. So irrationally blaming himself for this sin, Jesse decided what he would do at that moment, without consulting his God, full of grief when his mind was not thinking properly. He would quietly separate from his precious wife, considering this a great sacrifice of his own, but not considering the sacrifice his wife would have to make, nor the stigma that would cling to her.

Despite their love, the years of marriage, and raising a family, despite the history of their family and all that they had accomplished, clouded by the chaos of loss, he decided to inform Nitzevet as gently as he could. A man, seeking to make sense of his deep grief, rather than leaning into the confusion and chaos and trusting the One and only Person who could help, Jesse proceeded headlong into an irrational human choice. He would tell Nitzevet that he would care for her, and support her, and all would seem normal, but they would not be husband and wife. He would explain that this was his meager attempt to 'please' his God.

He found her resting in the shadow of the tower and approached her quietly, "Nitzevet, my love. My precious one. I have some grave news. I have decided that I cannot be your husband, nor can you be my wife." He began with boldness that melted as he watched the bewilderment on Nitzevet's face turn to a flood of tears as the fresh, new tragedy began to dawn on this woman's already hurting soul.

"Please don't cry my love. What if ... the death of our son was a judgment from Yahweh, what if we were wrong in getting married?" he stammered.

This was the last thing that Nitzevet would have ever contemplated. She knew that her relationship with Jesse was strained because of grief, but to doubt their marriage, their family, it was unthinkable.

"What if? … what IF?" Nitzevet's reaction was to scream his words back at him in the midst of her confusion, not understanding where any of this nonsensical thinking was coming from.

Jesse was stunned, not used to this side of Nitzevet, he backed up and gently responded, "When my grandfather married Ruth, he unwittingly doomed me to be considered a Moabite man. That means I am not lawfully allowed to be married to a proper Hebrew woman like you." Despite the wavering in his heart he spoke with a firm resolve, "It will be as I said. I love you but we cannot be husband and wife." And then he left, stumbling away as the ramifications of his choice ran through his mind.

Now in the quiet of the morning, as Nitzevet pondered what had just taken place she felt the remaining morsel of hope drain from her life. Sorrow upon sorrow and grief upon grief overwhelmed her. Usually, mornings were her favorite time of day, filled with the promises of what might come. Filled with the possibilities of joy and love and family. Now she was filled with nothing.

"Oh Yahweh, why?" Nitzevet cried. "I asked for you to help, and you bring greater tragedy," she sobbed into her robe.

Moments, maybe hours, passed when the hint of a memory tickled the edges of her mind. She remembered. So many years ago, in this very place, the messenger from Yahweh had appear to her. As she looked over to the very place he had stood, she remembered his words: "Dear one, I cannot reveal to you what our King has in store for your life, only that you are never alone. All that will come to you comes through His hand and he walks the path with you." It was as if Yahweh brought these words forth from the depths of her memory, for just this moment.

Deep in her heart, Nitzevet knew, because of her faith in her Great God, that her pain and suffering were part of a larger picture. Yahweh was her God; He had never left nor forsaken His people. Punish them, yes. But He loved them. As one of the 'Remnant' she had always felt the deep love of her God and nothing could take that from her, even the news that she was no longer Jesse's wife. The spark of spiritual life, and relationship with Yahweh was still there.

In her pain and suffering, a sad and sorrowful, yet deeply grateful Nitzevet bowed her head and spoke from memory the words of Job from so long ago:

"I know that my redeemer lives, and that in the end he will stand on the earth. And after my skin has been destroyed, yet in my flesh I will see God; I myself will see him with my own eyes I, and not another. How my heart yearns within me!" [21]

Nitzevet only knew one thing to do. Lean on her only friend, her Father who had cared for her through the years, just as Job did so many years ago in the midst of his tragedy. She leaned into His presence, there under the tower where He always enveloped her in His love. She whispered, "I love you my God, my Father." It was in the very character and faithfulness of Yahweh that Nitzevet put her trust. There was no one else.

33

ABIGAIL MEETS HER PRINCE

JESSE WAS SITTING AT THE city gate, he found himself there quite often lately. He pondered the deep sadness of the past few years, that he could never quite shake, since the ill-fated conversation with his wife. 'Was this how the rest of his life was to be, the consequences of choices?'

He noticed a rider coming up the dusty road. As he grew closer Jesse admired the beautiful stead and knew that this rider was most likely in the service of their king.

The young handsome man jumped down from his horse, approached the gate and greeted the elders sitting there.

"Shalom, men of Yahweh. I hope all is well with you. My name is Jether," he said.

Jesse was an observant man, especially of newcomers and noticed a gentle, noble soul standing in front of him. The uniform was tidy and neat and a bit different than the average soldier's uniform. He had heard that Saul had a group of men in his service who were unique, brave, and strong, 'Saul's Mighty Men'. This must be one of them. He also noticed the reference to Yahweh in the man's greeting indicating that he was indeed a man of God. "Shalom!" responded Jesse, "How can we help you?"

Jether bowed to Jesse and lowered his voice a bit so only the elders could hear, "I am looking for someone in your city who would be inclined to learn to be a metal smith, someone who would be willing to work for the King?"

Jesse nodded, with the other elders, understanding the predicament. While the whole world experienced a shortage of tin to make bronze,

241

there were certain cultures that were progressing into new technologies of metal working. The Philistines were in possession of a new metal that was stronger than bronze, creating a significant influence and domination over the Israelites. The Israelites were not allowed by their "overlords" the Philistines to have any metal smiths among them.

Jesse pondered the question for a moment and a plan began to form in his mind. "Jether, would you come to my home tonight for an evening meal? We can discuss the details of your request then after you rest for a bit," Jesse asked, nodding to the other elders that they too were invited to dine with them that evening.

"Thank you, sir, it would be an honor to dine with you this evening. Is there an inn or room I could rent for the evening somewhere in town?" he asked.

"I would not hear of it. You are welcome in the ben Obed home any time, we have a room for you. Follow me and we will get your horse cared for on the way to my home," Jesse said as he led the way.

Jether had heard of the ben Obed family. They were the established central family in Bethlehem. He thought to himself, they are the largest sheep herding family in Israel, that is how I know them. This was going to be a nice evening, for their reputation as followers of Yahweh was widely known.

The pair arrived at the gate of Jesse's home right when Abigail was returning from the well getting water for the evening meal preparation. Jether, without much thought, reached over and immediately took the rather large water jug from Abigail's shoulder as if it weighed a few ounces. Her shock at his gentlemanly kindness registered on her face.

"Excuse me, ma'am, it just appeared that the jug is very heavy, and you are so very small, I hope you do not mind," Jether said.

Abigail recovered quickly, not from the pot but from the handsome man standing in front of her in an impeccable uniform addressing her as if she were the queen of Egypt. "Thank you, sir, that is fine," she smiled graciously and cast her eyes to the floor, not sure what to do next.

"Abigail, could you let the household know that we will have a guest plus the five elders for our evening meal? Also, have a servant make sure the guest room is ready for the evening. Thank you, daughter," Jesse smiled pretending not to notice, but knowing exactly what was going on with her. It was not that long ago that he was head over heels for Nitzevet. All of a sudden a deep sadness overwhelmed him at the thought of his beloved, she still was the love of his life, and he knew it.

"Come, my new friend, let's sit in the shade for a moment with a cool drink." Jesse took his guest to the courtyard sitting area where the shade was deep and thick with a little moisture in the air from the trees and foliage that had grown thick and lush from so many years of care.

Jesse saw his third son walk by and called him over, "Shammah, this is Jether, one of the King's men, he is going to have dinner with us this evening. Could you please go and find Reu and invite him to have dinner with us too this evening? Also, invite Eliab and Abinadab as well as yourself?"

Shammah turned to Jether, "Shalom sir, welcome to our home." then turning to Jesse he said, "Yes, Father I will go now and find him, I believe he is at the Tower with the other shepherds preparing for the shearing that is coming up."

Shammah headed to the tower immediately thinking 'I wonder what is going on. What a fierce-looking man, his uniform was different than any he had seen. Tonight will be very interesting.'

Abigail had slipped away just before Shammah had arrived, hoping that she had gone unnoticed. 'Did he see her blush? Did he know that she was immediately smitten with his stature, his appearance, his uniform ... him!'

"What is going on Abigail, you look flushed?" Nitzevet asked as Abigail walked through the kitchen area.

"No mama, it is just warm out and I brought the water from the well. Papa said that there will be six additional guests for dinner this evening. Shall I let Zeruah know?" Abigail asked.

"No, sweet daughter, you go lie down, cool off, and rest. I will go and tell Zeruah and help her prepare," Nitzevet said as she kissed the forehead of her sweet daughter, not giving it another thought, it was indeed warm outside.

"Zeruah, there will be six additional guests for dinner this evening," Nitzevet called to her oldest daughter as she walked into the kitchen. "Bless you, my daughter, I don't know what I would do without you."

"Yes, Ema, I already know, news of an extremely handsome young man in a military uniform sitting in our patio courtyard travels quickly!" she responded smiling with a wink.

"Oh my!" Nitzevet said, peeking out the window in the direction of the shaded courtyard, "He is handsome!" Then the flush on Abigail's face flashed across her mind and Nitzevet knew what was going on, or at least she suspected. It wasn't that long ago that her face became equally as flushed at the mention of Jesse's name. Her heart still fluttered when she heard his voice. What joy mingled with the sadness that life brings.

נאמנות יהוה

Dinner that evening was interesting on many levels for everyone involved. Reu was pleased to be invited, Shoshannah had come along to help the women serve the meal and because she was curious.

As the guests arrived Jesse introduced them, "Jether, let me present my best friend and yes bond servant, that is a long story, Reu, from Gaza. Reu, this is Jether from the King's men."

Reu bowed slightly showing his respect and responded, "Shalom Jether, it is nice to meet you."

Jether was taken aback by the mention of a bond servant, best friend, and Gaza all in the same sentence. But he recovered and greeted the rest of the elders whom he had met earlier in the day at the gates of Bethlehem.

Jether was happy to answer all of their questions about himself as they ate their meal. He knew they were asking out of genuine curiosity. When they found out he was not "Hebrew", but an Ishmaelite, they were not shocked or repulsed, but even more curious. They talked a lot about Yahweh, as did he. Immediately Jether knew that their God was their bond.

His shock at meeting Reu, who was considered a friend, melted into a deep understanding of love and acceptance. He sat back and watched the family interaction as he thought 'This Hebrew of Hebrew families of the tribe of Judah had welcomed a stranger into their midst and treated him as one of their own.' It is what he longed for. As a follower of Yahweh, he wished he could claim to be a Son of Israel. He could claim to be a son of Abraham, and that had to be enough.

As the meal finished and the women gathered the dishes, Jether continued to explain King Saul's plan to implant a metal worker apprentice among the Philistines to gather information and knowledge into metallurgy. Saul wanted this person to bring back knowledge of this new metal and implement it among the Israelites so they would have the technology as well.

As the conversation continued, everyone knew who this was going to be and why. As a Philistine himself, disciplined, intelligent, and loyal to Yahweh and Israel, Reu was the man for the job.

Jesse turned and looked at his friend, "Reu, could you learn this trade? Could you go back to one of the Philistine towns, not your own of course, but another, and seek to learn the trade?" Jesse asked.

Jesse continued talking about the details, letting Reu ponder the request, "Just for a few weeks, you could apprentice yourself to a metal worker and learn all you can. While you are gone, we will set up a place for you to work here. You could bring back the knowledge and train men here in Bethlehem for our King."

Reu glanced at his wife who was seated in the corner with the other women, she smiled and nodded, he smiled back. "I think that is something I could do. They would not have a problem teaching me, it is only Israelites who are not allowed to work with metals. And it would be an honor to serve the King and Yahweh," Reu said.

Jether looked at these men with gratitude. He had no idea that he would find such a perfect solution and such willing and generous people. He glanced toward the woman and searched for Abigail, she was looking at him and he saw the slight tinge of pink cross her face. He smiled and turned back to the men, "You are all very kind and I know King Saul will be pleased at this plan. If we could establish a base of manufacturing here in Bethlehem, we might be able to turn the tide of war from having the Philistines as our overlords to being on the same level as they are with our weapons and military." Then he added, "as well as what this new metal would do to revolutionize our lives, plowing and woodworking."

Shoshannah was happy and sad, Reu would be gone for a while. She knew she could not go with him; she was Hebrew through and through. If this were to work, the Philistines teaching Reu would need to think of him as a true Philistine. But if this was Yahweh's plan, then she was glad to sacrifice a few weeks of her life away from Reu. Besides, she had Jashobeam and Eleazar to keep her busy. She looked over at her sweet sons playing with Zeruah's children, they were good friends.

Nitzevet hugged Shoshannah in the darkness, "You are a good wife. I am so proud of you."

Nitzevet whispered into Shoshannah's ear, "Did you pick up on the looks between Jether and Abigail?"

Shoshannah responded in a hushed tone, "Hasn't everyone?"

Nitzevet stifled her laughter.

"Jesse, I have noticed that your family and friends are very intentional about obeying Yahweh and following His plans," Jether observed.

Smiling, Jesse responded, "We are not perfect by any means, but Yahweh is the center of our lives. Our lives are not without pain, but the knowledge of Yahweh's love for us means a lot, and we feel as if we owe our lives to Him."

"I am so glad to hear it!" Jether said wholeheartedly as he glanced at the corner where he knew Abigail, the beautiful girl, was sitting. Then he said, "Could I have some more water please?" looking right at Abigail, who jumped up quickly before anyone else could even hear the question. She poured his glass full, and her hand accidentally touched his and she felt the tingle, as did he.

Abigail retired to her room after that. She did not trust herself to not make a fool out of herself. Better that she just goes to bed and forgets the whole thing. How could such an important and impressive shoulder and servant of the King want to have anything to do with her?

Nitzevet, Zeruah, and Shoshannah silently cleaned up after supper while the men continued to talk and make plans. All were lost in their own thoughts, Nitzevet about her youngest daughter's heart, Shoshannah about her own heart and what Reu was stepping into, and Zeruah still grieving from the loss of her love as the prospect of young love was on display before her. Not only that but young love with a soldier. Working together, at a common task as women was somehow healing and comforting at the same time. They were grateful for one another.

Shoshannah and Reu gathered up their sleeping little boys after dinner and headed home, not far, just a few minutes down the road. Jesse escorted Jether to the guest room and shook his arm. There was a bond developing between the two of them that both could sense but not completely understand.

The next morning, Jether was up early. After a quick breakfast, he gathered his horse from the stable, but before he mounted and took off toward Gibeah, he paused as if thinking for a moment and turned to Jesse who had risen early with him, and rather bluntly said, "Would you mind if I courted your daughter?"

"I am sure Zeruah would be grateful," Jesse said smiling, he knew Jether was talking about Abigail.

Flustered and not wanting to insult Zeruah, Jether hemmed and hawed for a moment. Jesse rescued him with a laugh, "Yes, I am sure Abigail would be honored. And Zeruah would be glad to see her sister finally courting someone."

Jether smiled. He liked this man. Heartily shaking his hand, he said, "Thank you, sir, it will be my pleasure. Please don't tell Abigail, I will be back in a few days to tell her myself, when I bring word back from King Saul about our plans," Jesse agreed.

Plans for Reu to go to Ashdod were underway. It was the furthest Philistine town from Gaza where he grew up, to lower the chances of being recognized. Still, it had been over thirty years since he left and he was only ten when he came to Bethlehem, his home. He knew he would not be recognized. Most of the people searching for him were dead or very old. Just to be safe, Jether insisted he use an alias and cut his hair like the Philistines did. He would let it grow again, like the Hebrews once he came home.

Shoshannah was busy making his clothes to match the latest Philistine styles. Abigail was busy helping, she loved to sew, and it was something she could do to contribute to the espionage other than helping Zeruah cook for the meetings.

They expected Jether to be back any day now to let them know the details of the plan and how to proceed. But more than that the women were anxious to see how Abigail would respond. Jesse had shared Jether's request with Nitzevet and Zeruah. The women noticed that Abigail had been a bit reclusive the past few days after Jether left. They knew why and left her alone mostly.

"My precious daughter, come sit with me," Nitzevet said as she handed Abigail a cup of hot spiced milk.

"Ahhh, Ema, you know exactly what a girl needs. This breadmaking has my back-breaking," she laughed at her rhyme.

Rolling her eyes at the lame joke, Nitzevet continued seriously, "I can tell you need a break. I also want to let you know that if you need to talk to me, you can, about anything on your heart, right?" Nitzevet stated and asked all at the same time.

"Yes mama, you will always be the first I talk to," she responded by sipping the delicious aromatic concoction. "Why does this tea smell and taste so very good today?"

"I added a bit more cinnamon and sugar than usual, but then I would think that anything would taste, and smell enhanced to you lately," she said giggling like a teenager.

"Ema!" Abigail admonished, knowing exactly what she was referring to.

נאמנות יהוה

A few hours later, the whole town knew that Jether was back. He was hard to miss striding up to the Bethlehem gate on his beautiful black mount with his shiny uniform perfectly fitting and well-kept.

Abigail's heart skipped a beat as she saw him pass by the courtyard gate. She was sitting in the darkest corner of the patio, behind the overgrown leaves that made the patio the envy of the whole town.

She marveled at his stature and strength and noticed his measured gait and then heard him ask someone in the courtyard for her. She heard him say her name out loud. She trembled at the sound of her name on his lips. The servant looked at her in the corner and it was only then that he saw her.

He strode over to her with that sure and solid gait. Confident, handsome, smiling … Abigail thought she might faint at that moment. But she did not.

"Hi Abigail, do you remember me?" Jether asked, taking her hand.

She laughed. She did not mean to, but seriously, 'remember him' - he is the only thing she could think of over the past few days. He was on her mind when she woke when she went to bed and all day long.

She covered her laugh with a gracious statement, "Of course I remember you sir. It was an honor having you for dinner, I mean serving you for dinner, I mean thank you for coming to dinner."

"Please call me Jether. I have a question for you," he said as he laughed at her mixed-up words.

She looked up at him, not knowing that her big eyes and questioning look made her remarkably beautiful, causing Jether himself to stumble over his next words. He cleared his throat and proceeded, "Will you allow me to court you?"

She sucked in her breath and immediately responded, "You will have to ask my father."

"Already did, days ago, before I left. He said yes," Jether smiled, a little too proud of himself.

"Then ... yes," she whispered as she blushed.

He gently kissed the back of her hand that he was still holding, neither had thought to let go, nor did they want to.

Zeruah's little boys came running in from the fields and everything settled back to reality as Jether gently let go of her hand and in a quick single motion threw one boy over each shoulder. It took Abigail's heart quite a while to settle down. Life had just changed dramatically for her.

נאמנות יהוה

At dinner, Jether laid out the plan that the King's generals had come up with. Reu would infiltrate the town of Ashdod and enquire about the metal trade from a certain merchant named Azmaveth. The intelligence that had been gathered seemed to indicate that Azmaveth was looking for an apprentice and if Reu was compromised in some way, intelligence also indicated that he would be sympathetic.

"Reu, you will leave the day after tomorrow. There is a Philistine caravan that runs along the main highway every new moon. They are always on time. You will be able to join them for the journey to Ashdod. It will be better if you are among people of your own so that some zealous Israelites will not think you a 'lone Philistine' and seek to take revenge on you," Jether explained.

Reu was obviously grateful for the forethought, consideration, and willingness of the King's men to think of all the details including his safety getting to Ashdod and preparing the way for him while there. "Please tell the King and his generals how grateful I am for all the careful planning you have put into this endeavor. I will do my best to learn what I can and bring the trade back here."

"This is a pretty important mission. It means a complete change with how we do warfare in the next few years. It is vital that we think ahead for the years to come. I am so glad that you and your family and friends can be a part of this," Jether said gratefully.

He pulled out a bag of coins and said, "Here is a partial payment. It should be enough for you to leave some here for your wife and take the rest to live on in Ashdod. You will need to find lodging and someone to help you with your daily needs. I am sure you can remember how things were run when you were living among your people."

Reu's eyes filled with tears, for some reason he had expected to fund the venture on his own. But the King had funded the whole thing and provided for his wife and family while he was gone. He was truly overwhelmed and grateful.

Jesse could see that Reu was set back by the generosity, so he picked up the conversation. "We will have him set to go the day after tomorrow," he said to Jether, and then turning to Reu he said, "And we will look after Shoshannah while you are gone. Abigail is going to go and stay at your house while you are gone to help her with the little ones."

"Thank you, Jesse, Shoshannah will appreciate the help and companionship," he said.

נאמנות יהוה

On the day of departure, Reu kissed his beloved wife goodbye and hugged his wiggly little boys. He also embraced Jesse and shook hands with the elders and then off he went on the adventure of his life, back to his people on a mission for Yahweh.

Abigail moved in with Shoshannah. But her life changed more than that. Every week she had a visitor. A tall, handsome, uniformed visitor who became part of the family quicker than anyone could have imagined. It became obvious to everyone why the King had made Jether one of his mighty men. He was witty, kind, gentle, brave, intelligent, full of laughter and mirth, yet serious when needed and wise beyond his years, yet a gentle soul. Nitzevet knew why ... he walked with Yahweh, more than anyone she had ever seen. It was as if Yahweh walked with him. She had no doubts about her daughter falling in love with this man, even if he was another soldier.

One afternoon Jether walked into the courtyard and announced that the betrothal ceremony would be held in Gibeah. Abigail knew that the King was grateful for what Reu was doing for him, so he let Jether come every weekend to see her. But never in her wild imagination would she have guessed that the King himself would request that their betrothal take place in the palace in Gibeah. Apparently, according to Jether, the King wanted to see for himself what had so enthralled his soldier in Bethlehem and had offered to host the ceremony.

Jesse was unsure of the offer of King Saul, but as he pondered it, he realized it was the marriage supper that was most important to his family to have at his home, so he conceded and was grateful to have the betrothal dinner with the King. In the past he would have discussed it with Nitzevet. He longed for her wisdom and insight, but things were strained between them, so he made the decision to go along with the king's plan.

Abigail, Nitzevet and Zeruah set about to plan the trip. There was much to do.

נאמנות יהוה

In the meantime, Reu returned. He was tired and weary and bespeckled with the little burns all over his forearms from the trade of metal working. But no worse for the wear.

Abigail took Jashobeam and Eliazar home with her so that Reu and Shoshannah could spend time alone and talk about all that happened. They needed time to get reacquainted. A sleepover with Zeruah's boys was a treat beyond treats, for all the boys.

Reu, glad to be home, put on his Hebrew clothing, started to let his beard grow and became accustomed to his real home and people again. After his brief excursion back to his birth culture he was grateful to live among the Hebrews and considered himself one even more so. Jesse, true to his word, had started outfitting the metal shop in Bethlehem. There was a small ravine at the very west edge of Jesse's land that was perfect. It was tucked away from the main road so that it was a small clandestine structure that would not draw attention. It was far enough away for Jesse to claim the shop when appropriate and deny its existence if necessary. There was also a long list of raw materials that he would need to start forging weapons. But for now, it was the forge itself that needed to be constructed. The ben Obed shepherds had volunteered to help set up the forge and gather all the volcanic rock necessary for the structure and all the high-temperature coal they would need to fuel the very hot fire in the forge.

When Jether arrived to get his soon-to-be bride, he gladly took the list from Reu for the raw materials. He then presented him with another bag of coins for payment for a job well done. With gratitude from the King himself.

Jether did not see the tear of gratitude slip down Reu's cheek, he was mostly focused on the details of getting his bride to Gibeah for the betrothal ceremony.

34

ANOTHER BETROTHAL

THE FAMILY GATHERED UP ALL their preparations and started off. Jesse, Nitzevet, their six sons, and two daughters gathered at the edge of town. Zeruah kissed her boys goodbye and gave Shoshannah unneeded last-minute instructions for their care while she was gone. Shoshannah knew Zeruah's boys as well as her own but also knew that a mother's heart was always about the care of her children, so she listened to the details.

The distance was about three and a half parasang from Bethlehem to Gibeah. Abigail walked silently behind her father and Jether. Listening to the conversation and grateful that there was a real friendship between the two most important men in her life.

When they finally arrived, Abigail and Zeruah were shocked at the huge room assigned to them. King Saul had built quite a house for himself. The servants left the room after delivering the bags. Abigail and Zeruah were silent, taking it all in.

A knock on the door prompted Zeruah to slowly open it. A sweet little servant girl let her know that the evening meal would be served in two hours and that she was there to draw a bath for the ladies to prepare. Zeruah was unaccustomed to this kind of treatment but let the girl in to do as she said. "What is your name?" Zeruah asked.

"Chana," the little girl stuttered shyly. She was also unaccustomed to such treatment, no one ever asked her name.

The sisters could not argue that it was a rare treat to have a warm bath and special treatment in the palace of a king. But they also knew that the value of their home and their family was beyond comparison to this luxury. They knew what they preferred.

Zeruah helped Abigail get dressed for the special night. She sensed her sister's nervousness and asked Chana what they should expect.

"The women will be seated at the table with the men. Your mother will be seated to the left of Merab who is seated to the left of her mother Ahinoam. King Saul will be on Ahinoam's right at the head of the table and to our King's right will be Jonathan and to his right Abinadab and to his right Malchi-Shua. Jether will come next," Chana graciously explained. "Your father will be to the right of Jether and all your brothers in order of age to the right of your father. Around the table this will go till your youngest brother is seated next to Abigail."

"It will be a rather intimate dinner with only seventeen in attendance, your family and the king's family."

Abigail took mental notes of the details so as to limit the possible missteps. "Do we speak or remain silent?" she asked her.

Chana giggled, "you can talk as much as you like. That is, if you can get a word in with Merab sitting next to you."

I thought you said that she would be between her mother and my mother, Abigail said as she visually worked her way around the table in her mind.

Chana again giggled, "Yes that is the plan, but reality rarely ends up as planned with Merab around. One sight of you and she will be seated next to you."

As Abigail took her seat at the table as instructed, she realized what Chana had meant. Merab had not only taken the seat between her and Zeruah, but she had not stopped talking the moment she saw Abigail. Quite a few years younger than Abigail, but old enough to know a kindred spirit, when she saw one, Merab and Abigail became fast friends.

Jether gazed at this lovely woman sitting across from him. He knew there was something special and unique about Abigail. He whispered a prayer of thanksgiving to Yahweh for allowing him to meet and marry such a beautiful woman inside and out and for being in service to the King of Israel. It was a good day, a good year.

"You did not tell me she was so beautiful, Jether!" King Saul announced as Abigail walked into the banquet hall.

Abigail blushed. Jether spoke up, "Yes, she is a beautiful woman, sitting among beautiful women," glancing at Abigail, Nitzevet, Zeruah then Ahinoam smiling.

"My son, when is the marriage supper?" Saul asked.

"My king, I am not sure. My father died ten years back, so I was hoping that you would play that role and let me know when to go get my bride," he smiled, hoping he had not overstepped his boundaries.

Saul laughed, knowing Jether's bluntness rather well, it is why he liked him so much, he could trust him. "Yes, my son, I will play that role. Let's eat!"

After the abundant meal, the two families adjourned to the more comfortable room, equally as large but there were several very comfortable cushions to sit on.

Saul took charge and led the couple in the ceremony. Playing the role of the groom's father was easy for him. As they each took the cup of wine, Jether smiled and gazed into the eyes of his betrothed "I will not drink again of the vine until I drink it with you in your father's house as my bride."

After they drank the wine, Jether nodded to his friend who was standing in the shadows for this moment. The young man walked up and placed a linen bag in his hand. Jether slowly withdrew the most beautiful necklace anyone in the room, including King Saul, had ever seen.

All eyes were fixed on Abigail as Jether gently and gracefully fastened around her neck a gold necklace with the jewels of green jade, blue sapphire, white jade, emerald jade, sardonyx, sard, citrine quartz, amazonite, olivine peridot, chrysoprase, lavender jade, amethyst quartz. He said, "The twelve stones in this gift to you symbolize Yahweh's family and His leadership as a loving Father over us. As we join our families, my prayer is that we will grow in love as family, friends, and the people of Yahweh."

Abigail wiped the tears from her eyes as did Nitzevet, Zeruah, and Ahinoam.

Jether knew that he would have to explain once the necklace came out of the bag. It was unusual for someone like him to have such rare jewels. "Let's sit down and I will tell you the story of my family. My grandfather was a trader. It is well known that the Ishmaelites were international traders of luxury items. This is one of the things that my father passed down to me from his father. He had always intended it to be the Mohar for my bride. I am pleased to give it to Abigail."

"The rest of your mohar will be waiting for you in your room at your home in Bethlehem," Jether told Abigail.

Saul clapped his hands, not wanting to be outdone by one of his men, although at this point, nothing could top Jether's gift. The king said, "As stand-in 'father of the groom', I am going to set aside the southernmost quarters of this house for you and your bride, Jether. Your responsibility is to prepare them for your bride. When they are ready, I will tell you."

Jether was shocked by the gift. He knew the King loved him, and he knew that asking him to be his stand-in 'father' would be appreciated by the King, but he never knew that the King would truly make him part of his family.

Jonathan, as young as he was, smiled at Jether and said, "I welcome you brother."

Jether already had established a bond with this young man, but now it was clear that Jonathan was special, he was not jealous in the slightest.

As Jether walked his bride back to her room with Zeruah following at a distance, he said, "I hope tonight wasn't too overwhelming for you. I didn't even ask you if living with a king would be ok with you."

Abigail smiled, knowing it was odd for a man to care what his betrothed desired, but it was not odd for Jether, "I will live wherever you live, as long as you are there. I would like to have a room in Bethlehem too, so we could visit and feel at home there as well."

"I have already spoken to your father about that. Construction starts next week on a room addition to your house. Looks like I have two fathers inspecting my building ability."

Abigail laughed and gently touched the precious necklace, "if your building skills are anything like your family's craftsmanship skills, I am blessed."

He smiled, paused a moment then kissed her cheek and slipped off to his room as Zeruah walked up.

35

THE PLAN

"MAMA, DID YOU CALL ME?" Abigail said softly as she stumbled into her mother's room. Early morning was not her favorite, but her mother was precious to her, and she was quite attentive to her moods. For the past few years had been different. It seemed to her that the love between her mother and father had diminished to a flicker of respect if needed. Things were quiet and sad, ever since the baby died.

"No precious one, I was just speaking with Yahweh. The early morning is so quiet, and the sun so warm as it rises above the horizon, it reminds me of Yahweh's eternal presence."

"Can you please go get a jug of water to start our morning? Thank you!" Nitzevet said to her sleepy daughter who had already gathered up the jug and was making her way to the well.

Nitzevet had not mentioned to anyone the decision her husband had made after the death of her seventh son. None of them knew that the joy of life for her was over, although they knew something was different. Her beloved had rejected her and now, life must assume a new perspective. Her only hope was Yahweh.

Even in the early morning, Bethlehem bustled with people and traders. Abigail made her way slowly to the ancient well near the gate.

Abigail noticed as she drew the cool water that her father was at the city gate speaking with the other elders. She knew something was wrong. Although she knew her father loved her deeply, she knew she could not ask for answers that were not hers to know. Yet, at that moment she could not prevent herself from thinking that something bad was happening.

Her father spoke in hushed tones, and she heard one of the elders say, "Another son, really Jesse?"

The oldest of the wise men, Abner stood up abruptly and said, "if you proceed, Jesse, you will bring judgment on your family and even on this town if Yahweh desires." Then he quickly walked away and made a movement of shaking dust from his feet.

Abigail could tell her father was rattled, but there was a determination to his features. She knew he was a holy man; he would never choose to go against Yahweh's will. "I suppose I will have to wait and see what happens and listen," she sighed to herself.

After her typical morning walk as Nitzevet approached her home, she could tell something was up. There was a buzz in the air and as she drew closer, she could see the servants diverting their eyes. She knew that she was the topic of conversation, although how or why she did not know. Quietly, she slipped into her room hoping to go without further notice. "OH!!" she was startled. Her eyes questioned the maidservant unexpectedly standing before her. Pigat answered, "My lady, I have come to honor you."

Nitzevet had no idea why this young maidservant would be in her private room. Zeruah had taken over the management of the house and servants in the last few years. Typically, Pigat was cooking or washing, doing something domestic. But knowing that this young girl was a kind person from the rumors floating around, Nitzevet responded with a kind nod and simple gesture to have a seat. Pigat was obviously struggling to speak. Nitzevet smiled and nodded for her to continue.

"Ma'am, I will be sixteen soon," she blurted out with a bit of sadness. She continued, "I have come to respect you. I watch you and see how kind and gentle you are with Abigail and Zeruah and your grandchildren." She hesitated as she searched for the words, then doggedly proceeded to speak her heart, "Ma'am, your husband has chosen to take me as his wife within a week so that he may have a child of unquestionable ancestry. He says that if he were to emancipate me, our children would become full members of the tribe of Judah. He seems to think I am the one. But I respect you. I cannot do this thing, knowing the pain that it will cause you."

Nitzevet was astonished at both the candor of the maid and the audacity of her husband. She was devastated. From grief to bad choices through a path of ill-fated logic that made no sense at all. It was as if Jesse was blinded by something, preventing him from trusting Yahweh and his plans. 'Yahweh help us,' she whispered.

Pigat noticed Nitzevet's anguish and wiggled in her seat as if there were more to say that might relieve the pain, then she spoke quietly ... "Ma'am, you could take my place."

Nitzevet gave her a questioning look through her tears.

"Remember the stories that you tell the children," Pigat said, "when Jacob married his love Rachel, but then on the wedding night Rachel's father gave Leah to him instead. Then Jacob had to work seven more years to marry Rachel?"

"Remember my lady, how Yahweh blessed Rachel by giving her not only the love of her life but her sons Joseph and Benjamin."

"You can take my place on the wedding night. For sure Jesse will not know, after so much wine, which I will make sure he takes. Maybe you will have the eighth son, that Jesse longs for ... the son to replace the one you lost."

Nitzevet could say nothing. She hugged Pigat and slipped out of the house to walk among the hills ... to seek the face of Yahweh and think. Disgusted with the ways of men, saddened by her grief that once again she must suffer because of what man thought up trying to guess what their God wanted, rather than seeking Him and knowing Him. Why must most men and women for that matter, doggedly pursue their own agendas, when Yahweh is a whisper away, a quiet stroll in the hills, a moment of thoughtful expectancy.

This deceptive plan that Pigat proposed would not fix the pain that Jesse had caused. A young sixteen-year-old girl did not fully understand the emotional scars that women bear at the hands of some people, scars that were not easily erased or fixed. But, deep down, Nitzevet knew this was a good plan. What if, for such a time as this, she was meant to take Pigat's place and in so doing deceive her husband? Truth be told, Nitzevet would be the one doing the 'right' thing saving everyone else from sin. But she knew she would have to bear the truth, the pain, and the scars alone.

Several days passed, and Nitzevet asked Abigail to bring Pigat to her room. Abigail did not question her mother but simply obeyed. Nitzevet took Pigat's hand and let her know that they would follow Pigat's plan. Pigat was impressed by Nitzevet's quiet resolve and unwavering strength; this great lady had remarkable faith in Yahweh. 'Surely, Nitzevet walks with Yahweh', Pigat thought as she hugged Nitzevet and left the room.

Jesse doggedly pursued his plan in spite of the wise warnings. He was a stubborn man, and the death of a son could push a man to his limits. Man in his attempt to fix any problem or provide a solution, doesn't always come up with a good one without Yahweh's involvement. On the night of the ceremony, when Pigat supposedly slipped off to Jesse's room, she actually went to Nitzevet's room and silently rolled up in her bed while Nitzevet slipped into Jesse's room. Early the next morning, the two women switched places, and no one saw, no one knew.

Weeks later Nitzevet knew she had conceived. It was a bittersweet moment when she acknowledged that fact. Not only would she have a child in her old age, a comfort to her aching heart, but confusion would surround his birth and life. One thing she did know was that this little boy or girl would be loved and cared for beyond imagination, by 'most' people.

36

JOY IN THE MIDST OF CHAOS

"WHAT A MESS!" ABIGAIL THOUGHT sitting alone in the courtyard. My mother is pregnant, but no one knows the truth. She is insistent that she will wait until Yahweh reveals the truth about the pregnancy to everyone.

Zeruah sat down gently on the bench beside Abigail handing her a cup of warm spiced milk. "Cheer up my sister, your groom is surely on the way!" She said this to distract her sister from their mother and father's drama.

Abigail's face immediately reflected the joy that filled her heart every time she thought of her groom. "Yes, my sister, he is coming!"

"Do you have everything ready?" she asked, really not needing to ask.

Smiling back at her big sister, and rolling her eyes a bit, Abigail said, "What do YOU think?" She had been staying up late every night, ready to put on her dress when she heard the trumpet sound.

Shoshannah had come over every evening on the pretense of 'trying different hairstyles' with the thought 'maybe tonight.' 'What some girls do when the groom is coming!' Abigail thought.

"I am going to join you and Shoshannah tonight with your nightly hair rituals. I can't imagine how Reu is surviving with the boys, with Shoshannah gone every night till late," Zeruah teased.

"Reu is surviving just fine. Soon I will be married and gone and none of you will see me much!" She responded in a playful pouting tone.

Zeruah laughed, "Yeah, living in a palace with a king! Poor you!"

261

"Oh, I found some beautiful blue Campanula in the field yesterday when Ema and I were walking. I am going to head out with the boys this afternoon and pick a bunch for Shoshannah to try in your hair tonight," Zeruah said and Abigail's heart skipped a beat at the prospect of the 'son' of the King coming tonight.

Abigail sighed contentedly. She knew her family was in a bit of a pickle at the moment. But she was not sad, her groom was coming, he was on his way, she was sure of it.

Zeruah was making bread for the evening meal and told the maids to run and tell Reu to prepare a lamb for supper. The family needed some lighthearted feasting this evening. The thought popped into her mind that that special salad that everyone loved so much would go nicely with roasted lamb and fresh bread. Artichokes, olives, fresh cheese, tomatoes, her mouth watering just thinking of it. While gathering the ingredients for the salad, she noticed the newly cooked chickpeas ready for a fresh garlicky hummus to dip their bread into. That would make it a special occasion. Gathering up the garlic and chickpeas, Zeruah started on the hummus. Cooking was always a pleasant distraction for her, and she had quite a few things in the works for dinner. The maids joined her with their lighthearted banter and helped her finish all the food projects so she could go pick the flowers.

"Don't forget to put some roasted peppers in this hummus!" She called over her shoulder to the kitchen staff as her youngest son burst into the room and she remembered the flowers as he dragged her through the door to the fields. Putting it all behind her, she raced her boys to the tower. Longing, as her mother did to be in the presence of Yahweh, with the problems of life left behind for another time.

Alone at the tower, pondering her plight, Nitzevet had spent the afternoon crying out to her Lord: "Out of the depths I cry to you, Lord; Lord, hear my voice. Let your ears be attentive to my cry for mercy."

'In the midst of my pain,' Nitzevet thought silently, 'I still feel Your love, I still feel Your joy. In the midst of my tears, I sense your presence. I am so grateful, Yahweh.'

Looking up, she saw her oldest daughter and her bouncing boys running toward her. Then they saw her and smiled. "Safta!" they cried.

He knew what she needed at that moment, the joy of children and the friendship of a daughter.

נאמנות יהוה

The men were gathering in the courtyard for dinner. Jesse was there, his sons, their wives, Zeruah had invited Reu and Shoshannah too - so much food, she thought.

"Well girls," Nitzevet said to Abigail, Shoshannah, and Zeruah, shall we present ourselves for dinner tonight? Thank you Zeruah for making such a lovely meal, I am not sure of the occasion, but we are truly grateful, we needed something special."

While they were tidying up the room getting ready to go to dinner they heard it.

Abigail jerked her head up and stared at her mother. No words needed to be said, they all knew what they heard ... the trumpet!

Hands went into swift motion. While Shoshannah finished poking the Campanula flowers into Abigail's hair and winding the small pearls through the braid. Zeruah held the beautiful dress for her to slip into. Nitzevet gently lifted the beautiful twelve-stone necklace from Jether, ready to fasten it to Abigail's beautiful neck.

Slipping on her delicate sandals, she was a work of art. The women were proud. Suddenly there was a knock on the door. Shoshannah rolled her eyes, "that will be Reu, making sure we heard the trumpet. Sweet, but a little late."

Sure enough, Reu stood in the door starting to explain the trumpet to Shoshannah when he saw a glimpse of Abigail and paused, "Jether is going to be so pleased!" Reu loved his brother-in-law and was so happy for the couple.

The commotion was growing in the courtyard, they could all hear it. The servants and staff were busy making more food and pulling together bits and pieces of things that would make this already beautiful feast a true wedding feast. Having lived and served with Leah and Nitzevet for so many years, they knew exactly what to do and how. Tables were pulled together; bouquets of flowers were quickly assembled from Shoshannah's garden. Sauces and dips were being made; candles were being lit as the groom approached.

Then the knock came, and he called for his bride. Zeruah flung the door open and stepped aside as Abigail rushed through the door into her groom's strong and secure arms. Forget the pomp, forget the tradition, forget the litter to 'fly her to the house', she was already here at her house and so was her groom.

Lifting her high, he admired her beauty. Her delicate features with her long silky hair braided with flowers. The dress he had purchased in Egypt the last time he was there, and his family's necklace all made his bride the most beautiful woman on the planet, and she was in his arms. It was rare to see a soldier cry, but this was one of those rare occasions.

Jesse, a very proud father, dutifully shut the door after the last guest had entered. It was a beautiful feast.

37

THE SEVENTH (EIGHTH) SON

SAUL HAD BEEN REIGNING FOR several years, the first human king ever to rule over Israel. The people were mostly happy. Those who wanted to be like other people were happy. But the lovers of Yahweh, the Remnant, were sad. They felt the rejection of a Theocracy by the people was a rejection of Yahweh, in a way it was. Nitzevet felt the rejection more acutely than others, for she loved Yahweh deeply. She had learned of her God's love for His people from Jesse's grandmother Ruth. Although she did not personally know Ruth, she had heard many stories of how a Moabite woman left everything behind to follow Naomi and Naomi's God.

Nitzevet had given birth to her eighth son three years back. She had named him David because he was beloved. She rejoiced at the birth as did Pigat. At the time of his birth only Nitzevet, Pigat, Zeruah, and Abigail knew the true nature of David's lineage and birth. Jesse, however, did not know and as anyone would imagine was not pleased, to say the least, not fully understanding who David's father was.

Unfortunately, Nitzevet's sons rejected her out of loyalty to their father and a misplaced cultural man code that assumed wrongdoing on the woman's behalf without question. But Jesse loved Nitzevet and did not allow them to mistreat her.

Nitzevet firmly believed this course of action was Yahweh's will, yet it caused her an enormous amount of sadness and pain watching others condemn her and reject her. At the same time, her sweet boy was precious beyond words. He was special. She diligently taught David the ways of

Yahweh. She told him how Yahweh loved his people and desired for them to live holy lives. He desired that they choose Him alone above all the other 'gods' that surrounded them in the promised land.

David continued to grow and became a sweet young boy with unruly red hair like his mother and amazingly beautiful blue eyes. It was as if he could see right through a person. Maybe it was his wisdom, maybe it was the pain and suffering that he faced every day from isolation and rejection of his older brothers that made him a young man with an old soul. 'Maybe this was Yahweh's plan, maybe this is what would form David into the man his God wanted him to be as only the crucible of suffering and loneliness could,' Nitzevet hoped.

נאמנות יהוה

Nitzevet taught David to remember. As he grew, he began to bear the brunt of the torment his brothers dished out. He didn't know why their torment was so vehement, and neither did they share with him the reason for their contentious behavior. David knew his mother loved him and he knew his God loved him, and for David that was enough.

"Ema?" called David one day when he was five.

"Yes dear?" She responded.

"Why are you sad, Ema? What can I do to make you happy?" asked David.

"David my dear, you make me happy every day because you are you", she said as she smiled, one of her increasingly rare and precious smiles.

"Ema, you know I love you. You will remember right?" petitioned David.

"Come, David, let us make a remembrance of your love for me, my love for you, and Yahweh's love for us." Nitzevet loved to be opportunistic with her young son, seizing teachable moments. She grabbed her bag and added some cheese and bread and a skin of water and walked out the door, motioning for David to follow.

"A remembrance?" David questioned as he skipped to her side to catch up with her long steps.

"Yes, dear one. After our people, all twelve tribes crossed the Jordan after many years in the wilderness, the Lord God commanded Joshua to make a remembrance out of stones," she explained.

Nitzevet continued the story, "Joshua chose twelve men, one from each tribe to go pick up stones from the middle of the Jordan River where the priests holding the Ark of the Covenant stood. He then instructed them to carry the stones to the other side to where they were going to camp that night."

"What about the rocks Ema?" David demanded to know.

"They then piled them up as a remembrance to serve as a permanent national reminder and a memorial to future generations of the miraculous river crossing. And they are still there to this day!"

"A remembrance of rocks, can we go see?" petitioned David eagerly.

"Someday my son you will see the remembrance by the Jordan river but for today, let's make our own remembrance in this field."

"Here we are, let's choose a rock that represents our God for our foundation stone, and then each of us will put a rock on top."

David wandered the area for a bit, looking for a special rock that would represent his God. He found it and called out to his mother, "I found it!"

Nitzevet was pleased with David's choice, a large foundational rock with a smooth flat surface, a rock that could carry the weight of other rocks and remain level. She looked lovingly at David, so young, and yet he intuitively understood Yahweh.

She brought the rock that she had chosen and put it on top. Then David chose his rock and Nitzevet had to help him lift it into place. They were pleased with their remembrance and sat down to enjoy their meal for a while together enjoying and remembering. David learned the beauty of worship and silence from his mother.

Nitzevet raised her hands to Yahweh and said, "Just as the 12 stones which they took out of the Jordan and Joshua set up at Gilgal, so do David and I set these stones up. Remember Your love for us and our love for you. May all the peoples of the earth someday know that the hand of the Lord is mighty and that Israel will fear the Lord our God forever," David and Nitzevet worshiped God.

נאמנות יהוה

David continued to recognize inconsistencies in his life. The hardest part of his life was how differently some members of his family and certain neighbors treated him. He knew he was an outcast and never fully understood why. His brothers said he wasn't their brother. And the neighbor kids acted as if David was unworthy of their friendship, but why he did not know.

He spent most of his time with his flock in the distant pastures. Rarely did he come home for the evening meal. One time, when David and his flock were near home, he was eating at 'his' table relegated to the corner, a different table than his father and brothers. It was that day David found gall; a bitter herb mixed in his food. He was so angry the only thing he could think of doing was to grab his gear and run to the flock where the darkness became a cool blanket of comfort. Yahweh was there, all around him in the darkness he brought shalom and David felt at home, in the presence of Yahweh.

Although his way of life and relating to his family seemed strange, and was awkward at times, he did not dwell on it or grieve too much. Someday he would ask the burning questions and then he would know, but now, he actually loved the company of his sisters and mother and his father's friend Reu. Their gentleness and kindness were like a refreshing balm on his head.

Reu found David in the southern pasture where he had promised he would be. David and Reu were preparing to take the flock to en Gedi. It was their favorite place, a secret place in the southern part of the land given to the tribe of Judah where they often took the flock. Reu named the area where they were going "the Crags of the Wild Goats." There were caves and fresh running water from cool springs and grass where David's flock could graze. Neither David nor Reu could fully understand why they were drawn to the area. Reu thought it was for the quiet, David for the rich grass, most importantly they both admitted it was far away from his cruel brothers.

Nitzevet had asked Reu, years ago when David was very young, if he could help her educate her son in the things of Yahweh. Nitzevet did a wonderful job teaching David, and he knew more than the average boy. But for David to see another man love Yahweh and speak of him with reverence and respect was very important to Nitzevet. What she did not fully understand was that Reu communicated to David a unique perspective. As a foreigner who was brought into the nation of Israel, accepted and loved, he had a unique understanding of the love of God. He shared this perspective with David on the many occasions they were together.

David often heard Reu quote from the Torah "When a foreigner resides among you in your land, do not mistreat them. The foreigner residing among you must be treated as your native-born. Love them as yourself, for you were foreigners in Egypt. I am the LORD your God."[22]

Even as Reu told David events in his childhood, David understood his own nation better after contrasting it with Reu's description of the Philistine culture and growing up with idols and the cruelty of that culture. It was definitely not a people that cherished and loved their children, not that David really understood that fully. It was almost as if Yahweh was molding David into a special person, the kind of person that only hardship, suffering and special training could produce, someone whose heart longed for God.

Because David and Reu planned to be gone for several weeks, they had a donkey with them to carry the supplies Reu had packed. Reu was the father David longed for, the friend he never had and the spiritual guide that God had purposed for him, a foreigner who understood the love of Yahweh more than most. And Reu loved being with David, whose musical skill was beyond measure and the words he put to music moved his soul. These two souls were knit together in hardship and in love for Yahweh. Time together was a gift from their God.

נאמנות יהוה

Passover was soon approaching; David's twelfth Passover. The feast of First Fruits was the day after Passover. It was a special feast for Nitzevet, she couldn't quite explain why, only that Yahweh had impressed upon her it's importance. Many years ago, her mother had told her the story of Jericho and how it was the perfect example illustrating the Feast of First Fruits. She had never forgotten it. When she began to raise sons, she made it her goal to make sure each of her sons had made the trek to Jericho and were taught the lessons of Yahweh around this feast.

Nitzevet believed it was time to take David to Jericho. David, being the child of her old age, missed out on the earlier journeys. At age twelve, it was time.

"Abigail, dearest?" called Nitzevet one day when Abigail and Amasa were visiting from Gilgal.

"Yes Ema, I am here," said Abigail gently. "What do you need?"

"Let's plan a trip to Jericho. You and Zeruah and all your children with David," she proposed.

"Yes, mama!" Abigail knew exactly what this was about, she was part of that journey in the past and loved the history lesson. She was so excited that her mother was creating this opportunity for Amasa along with David. She loved teaching children all the things of Yahweh, and her son would love the journey.

"Could you tell your father that we are heading to Jericho, all of us. Please tell him to set up the time and the traveling arrangements," informed Nitzevet.

That evening at dinner Nitzevet let David know of the plans. "We will be leaving as soon as your father has set up the details of our journey. I need you to be ready to leave. Remember to take a change of clothes."

"Finally, we get to see the stones of remembrance. How far is Jericho, Ema?" asked David with excitement, "When will we leave?"

"Passover is coming, and we will celebrate Passover here as well as the feast of First Fruits, and then during the week of Unleavened Bread, we will make our journey, Yahweh willing. It is about five parasangs, which means we will sleep two nights under the stars on the way there, two nights at the gates of Jericho, and two nights coming back," responded Nitzevet.

"David, do you have someone to watch the flock while we are gone?" asked his mother.

"Yes, Ema, Eiran will do it," responded David.

Abigail laughed. "Sister, I hear you, what are you giggling about?" asked David.

"Sweet brother, I just think it is ironic that the person you choose to watch your flock's name means 'watchful'. Did Eiran grow into his name or did his name define him from the beginning?" asked Abigail.

"I don't know actually; I am just grateful that he is as watchful over me as he is the flock. He is a good friend," David pondered all that Eiran had done for him. He had taught David some valuable lessons.

When Abigail asked her father to make preparations for the trip, Jesse knew what Nitzevet was planning with David. He was pleased. She took good care of their sons and David was no different. He gladly put out the word that Nitzevet was leading a group to Jericho and that any and all were welcome to take their children and go learn about Yahweh's Feast of First Fruits.

38

A LESSON FROM JERICHO

NOT TOO LONG BEFORE PASSOVER, word came to the elders in the town of Bethlehem from a messenger that Saul had lost favor with his God. The worried look on the faces of the elders really bothered Abigail and Zeruah. For even though women were not included in the discussions of the town, they were not prohibited from listening.

"But what did he do?" asked Elihud, chief counsel member.

"Apparently, while waiting for Samuel to arrive to offer the sacrifice to Yahweh, Saul grew impatient and offered the sacrifice himself," responded the message bearer.

"He's not a Levite!" Manly blurted out. A hush fell over the group of men, for they knew that the rules Yahweh had ordained did not allow for anyone other than a priest or prophet to sacrifice to their God.

"Did Samuel come?" inquired a young man standing nearby.

"Yes, it did not take long for Samuel to find out what Saul had done. Samuel told Saul that "he had acted foolishly because he had not kept the command of the Lord … Saul's kingdom will not continue."

The elders were astonished. Even as old as they were, this was their first and only human king, so they did not really know how things began or ended with a monarchy.

The messenger rushed on, "Samuel told Saul that the Lord had sought out a man after his own heart and had commanded him to be prince over his people, because Saul did not do what the Lord commanded him."

"What happened then?" Jesse asked.

"Samuel left and so did Saul," responded the messenger.

The counsel was stunned. They could not even fathom what their king had done. As they sat in silence their minds were running wild with questions: 'Now what? Who could this new "Prince" be? Who is someone 'after God's own heart'? And what does that even mean?'

Zeruah and Abigail ran to their mother to tell her all they had heard from the council. Nitzevet was also shocked, she knew how important it was to keep all the laws of Yahweh. She knew deep in her heart that the laws were there to show Israel how holy their God really was, and how unholy they were. But to willingly go against these established laws as king, was to dishonor their God in a way that the Israelites had not seen in a long time. Perhaps not since the golden calf incident in the wilderness.

It was now even more important to teach the youth about Yahweh and His principles.

נאמנות יהוה

Abigail, Amasa, David, Nitzevet, Zeruah, Asahel and twenty other neighbors as well as many servants set out for Jericho on the eighteenth of Nisan. Shoshannah and her son Jashobeam came too. A field trip that all knew from the past was one to remember. Many older siblings in all of these families had made the trek with Nitzevet when her other boys were young and had talked of the trip for years after. It profoundly impacted them all to learn of the ways of Yahweh, especially from someone as knowledgeable as Nitzevet, the wife of one of their elders, Jesse. It seemed while explaining the Feast of First Fruits and what that meant to Jericho, she was explaining the heart of her God, it was as if she knew Yahweh personally.

"David, this is the same path that your great-grandmother Ruth took from Moab to Bethlehem," Nitzevet instructed.

"Can you imagine a foreigner, a young widow coming into a new country, a new culture, and a new people? She even embraced Yahweh as her own God with all of her heart," Nitzevet grew quiet at the thought of such a sacrifice.

"Who taught Grandma Ruth about Yahweh?" asked David.

"It was her mother-in-law, Naomi, your father's great-grandmother. Naomi had moved to Moab to escape the famine and lost her husband

and her sons, one of which was Ruth's husband. But in the midst of that, she never lost faith in Yahweh. Ruth saw her mother-in-law; she watched her in the midst of her loss and tragedy. In spite of Naomi's sadness, she clung to her God. He was bigger than her tragedy. Yahweh turns tragedy into promises, just like he did for Grandma Ruth, having brought her to Boaz," Nitzevet explained. She knew David had heard this story many times but retelling it in different ways with a different focus helped children remember, so she never hesitated to retell the history of their family. Nitzevet grew quiet after this explanation, how it resembled her own tragedy and struggle.

Having left early on this gorgeous spring morning, the group was excited to be on a journey. But as the day wore on, they were growing weary. At this point, dusk was upon them the group of weary travelers. They had traveled two parasangs and their scout and guide had found a nice meadow beside a brook. A safe distance from the Jebusite city of Salem, they did not want to attract any attention.

David was pleased, as he took in the details of the land, he was always aware of good pastureland. The nearness to Salem made it too dangerous to bring his flock, but someday if the city ever belonged to the Israelites, it would be a great place for the flocks. After helping his mother set up the tent for the evening, he lay down by the brook as his sisters and the other women prepared the evening meal.

After David's nap and a simple but tasty dinner cooked over the fire, Nitzevet called the young students together to sit before her. The parents and servants gathered behind the youth to listen to what Nitzevet had to say.

"Let me start at the beginning. Yahweh gave us the feasts, all of them, to teach us about Him. Also, to remind us of His principles each year. It is our responsibility to faithfully observe the feasts and to diligently teach them to our children. Remember Moses' words? Let's say them together:

> *"Hear, O Israel: The LORD our God, the LORD is one. Love the LORD your God with all your heart and with all your soul and with all your strength. These commandments that I give you today are to be on your hearts. Impress them on your children. Talk about them when you sit at home and when you walk along the road, when you lie down and when you get up.*

Tie them as symbols on your hands and bind them on your foreheads. Write them on the doorframes of your houses and on your gates." [23]

"The Feast of First Fruits as you all know is the third feast that Moses instructed us to observe and participate in. We finished celebrating that yesterday; however, we are still in the midst of the Feast of Unleavened Bread. Rebekah, why do we celebrate the feast of Unleavened Bread?" Nitzevet asked one of her students.

"We are remembering our people fleeing from Egypt after the Passover, they did not have time to let the bread rise, so they ate unleavened bread," answered Rebekah.

"Exactly! Wasn't our evening meal much easier while traveling because we were able to eat unleavened bread? Can you all identify with our ancestors as they are traveling out of Egypt, stopping for their evening meal and putting up their tent just like we did? Pulling out the flour and water and mixing up our bread as we did and baking it on the hot stones in the fire?"

The students looked back at her with a deeper understanding of her words as she related them to what they had just experienced. Nitzevet knew there was no better teacher than experience. She looked down at one of the sleepy children knowing she needed to wrap it up soon. "David, what is the point of remembering?" asked Nitzevet.

"The point is to never forget what Yahweh has done for us, how He brought us out of Egypt, across the desert, and into this beautiful land," replied David.

Nitzevet smiled, she could see a warm heart for Yahweh in David's eyes. He naturally explained the plans of Yahweh in plain terms, in full confidence of God's love. She silently prayed that he would grow in his wisdom.

"As we go to sleep tonight, I want you all to think about First Fruits and what we did yesterday, as well as all the aspects of the feast and we will talk about it tomorrow night on our second night on the journey."

"Good night sweet ones," called out the teacher as the group began to drag their weary bodies to their tents. "Morning comes early!"

Indeed, the morning came early, and the groans from the young and old indicated that unused muscles had certainly been used the day before.

But a few achy muscles were not going to stop this group from reaching their goal. After a meal of fresh milk and leftover bread and a few dates for energy, the families packed up and set out on the second day of their journey.

David was quiet. He was not used to being around so many people for so long. He had slept in the field a stone's throw from the group. He enjoyed the quiet, he needed the quiet. This morning, he was pondering First Fruits. He knew that it was about giving Yahweh the first of everything in the harvest, even before the rest was ripened. He did not fully understand why. Hopefully, he will find out.

The second day wore on, seemingly a bit longer than the first day, but actually, their guide had shortened the trip a little, having found a lovely spot near the city of Adummim where a fresh water source, bubbled from the ground. Surrounded by lovely, lush green foliage and birds of all kinds, the guide knew his people would appreciate the luxury, so he stopped. Nitzevet immediately knew that this was a special place. The bubbling water, vibrant green plants and the red spots in the rocks, the contrast made it uniquely beautiful.

Quite often Nitzevet would have a premonition of sorts, where she would wonder if someday whatever she was experiencing at that moment would be a profound moment in the future. She had that special feeling now, that this would be a special spot in the years to come.

David once again set up the tent, this time by himself, he was getting adept at mechanical things and knew how to be most efficient. His mother nodded appreciatively with a smile, giving David an extra boost of energy and an idea. He had brought his Lyre. He would play for the women as they cooked and prepared dinner.

Rebekah nudged Abigail, "Ohhh, Abigail, he is getting out his lyre. This is going to be a special evening indeed."

Abigail watched her brother with admiration. Not only was he kind, gentle and full of compassion, he was a very, VERY talented musician. For a boy of such a young age he could play every instrument known to their people and not only that, but he also wrote his own lyrics and melodies. The people of Bethlehem had long known of David's talents but had seldom been the recipients of the pleasure of listening, his sheep most often had that pleasure.

David began to play and the women continued to cook, but silence fell over the group as they listened and truly enjoyed the lovely music coming from David as he played and sang:

> Lord, our Lord, how majestic is your name in all the earth! You have set your glory in the heavens. Through the praise of children and infants you have established a stronghold against your enemies, to silence the foe and the avenger. When I consider your heavens, the work of your fingers, the moon and the stars which you have set in place, what is mankind that you are mindful of them, human beings that you care for them? You have made them a little lower than the angels. and crowned them with glory and honor. You made them rulers over the works of your hands. You put everything under their feet: all flocks and herds, and the animals of the wild, the birds in the sky, and the fish in the sea, all that swim the paths of the seas. Lord, our Lord, how majestic is your name in all the earth! [24]

It was as if David were looking around him and putting what he saw to words and music, and it was lovely.

The small group, so moved by the song, cheered as he finished playing. David blushed, not used to the praise. The sheep did not cheer.

A tear slipped down Nitzevet's face as she cherished this moment in her heart. Surely, David was destined to be a great man, a man of God.

Wiping her tears, Nitzevet instructed the students to get their meal and gather around her. After they were seated, she began by asking a question, "What did we do on the Feast of First Fruits two days ago, who can tell me?"

Jashobeam spoke up first, "We offered burnt offerings to Yahweh."

Nitzevet pointed to Eleazar next who said, "The priest waved grain back and forth over the sacrifice."

Not to be outdone by his cohorts, Amasa's arm was shooting up and down as if he had something very important to say, "my Ema mixed the flour and oil together and then gave it to the priest."

"Very good boys, we did all of those things. We offered a year-old lamb without blemish as a burnt offering. The priest waved the sheaf of grain back and forth. And we offered two-tenths of an ephah of fine flour mixed with oil as a food offering to the Lord. Did we offer anything else?" asked Nitzevet.

It seemed as if everyone had forgotten the last item, so Abigail spoke up, "We offered a drink offering of a fourth of a hin of wine."

"Thank you, my daughter, yes, a drink offering. We were supposed to start doing this when we entered the land, why do you think Yahweh asked us to wait until we entered the new land?" she asked.

David explained as if the knowledge came spontaneously, "Because we did not have land nor grow crops on the east side of the Jordan, it wasn't until we reached this land, the land Yahweh gave us, that we had the time and land to plant and harvest."

Nitzevet, smiling at David's wisdom, continued, "Yes David, exactly. And we obeyed. We have been obeying ever since. Now, before we go to sleep, I will leave you with one question to think about. What does our journey to Jericho have to do with First Fruits? Now off to bed!"

נאמנות יהוה

It was only a short distance to the ruins of Jericho. The little group of travelers got up early and ate quickly the food they had set aside the night before for breakfast. Once they were on the road, the journey went quickly. Nitzevet remarked to herself what a beautiful time of the year for a journey through the desert, early spring was the best. It was not yet hot, and there were flowers popping up everywhere. She pointed out the various types of plants and flowers along the way. Most of which she learned from Shoshannah.

As the group approached the ruins of Jericho in the late afternoon they were overwhelmed with the site. Nitzevet paused for a moment to allow them to take in the view. Even though some of the older people had seen this before, it was always awe-inspiring. Jericho was the oldest and most fortified city in the Promised Land. It had the distinction of being impenetrable among the people of the land. Yet here it has completely fallen down as if from within. Nitzevet nodded to their guide who knew where they were going to set up camp and led them the remaining distance to their place of rest for the next two nights.

After the evening meal, they sat around the fire contemplating the mound of rocks bricks before them.

David asked, "Ema, was this the city that Moses described as "their towns are large, with walls rising high into the sky"?[25]

Nitzevet smiled at David's knowledge of the Torah, "Yes, but as you can see, the height or strength of the wall was no match before Yahweh."

She continued her description, "See if you can picture it as I describe it, and then tomorrow, we will walk around the city and you will understand what I am talking about." She continued, "The cities of the Promised Land were built on mounds or what we call a 'tel'. This is how Jericho was built. However, it had something more than most, its wall was massive and unique. At the top of the city, there was a great wall about twenty feet tall. On the outside of that wall there was a great sloping embankment of earth below that was held up at its base by a stone retaining wall that was about fifteen feet high. On top of that outer retaining wall was a mudbrick wall that was an additional twenty feet high. This made that outer wall thirty to forty feet tall and the inner wall rose above that wall and towered to the sky as if 'up to heaven', as Moses wrote."

"Can you imagine these people having wandered in the desert for forty years, most having never seen a walled city since most were born in the desert? It seemed to tower above them, and they had no weapons or tools or any way of conquering this massive impenetrable city. But they had something that the people within the city did not have. Who can tell me what that was?" she asked.

Looking over the crowd, she could tell from their blank looks that they did not know. Then her eyes rested on David, his smile betrayed that fact that he knew the answer but was not speaking up. She nodded at her son so he would speak up and he said one word with more reverence and deep emotion and love, more than anyone could imagine, "Yahweh!"

The group of travelers remained quiet. They heard how David had proclaimed the precious and intimate name of God as if it were always on his lips, as if He were David's closest and most precious friend. They were humbled and awestruck at the same time.

Nitzevet decided that this was the best time to end the evening, with the name of their God lingering in the air with reverence. She got up and went to her tent and the rest followed.

David, however, took his lyre and went into the darkness, into the fields and began to play a melody that illustrated his love for his Creator. They could all hear the melody as it echoed throughout the hills as if it were proclaiming honor to their magnificent God. Most eyes in the little group were wet with tears as they worshiped Yahweh with enchanting music.

נאמנות יהוה

Nitzevet sipped her milk tea and munched on her date cake in the early morning as she gazed on the great stones of the city. "Thank you, my God, for showing us this amazing illustration of your power and magnificent grace to your people. We did not deserve this, but you gave it anyway. You gave us this land and promised that forever it would be ours. Thank you."

The little group began their march around the city, just as their ancestors, under the leadership of Joshua had marched around the city. Nitzevet had instructed them before they began to remain completely silent as they walked, as our God had instructed their ancestors. They walked in single file all the way around the city once. When they had reached the place where they had begun, Nitzevet broke the silence. "Do you see that section of the wall?" she said as she pointed north to a little section of the lower wall that had not completely fallen.

One of the boys in the group spoke up, "Why did it not fall like the rest of these bricks?"

Nitzevet smiled, "that is where my Aunt Rahab lived. It is where she and all her family were when the walls fell. Does anyone remember why?"

Asahel spoke up, "Because our Aunt Rahab helped the two spies, and our God promised to keep her safe from destruction. And he did!"

Zeruah smiled at her son. "Yes, you are exactly right. She understood who Yahweh was and obeyed his command and he saved her. And you can see the part of the wall that is still standing to protect her and her family."

"Why are the bricks laying all the way down the hill?" a little girl asked, not quite understanding what had happened.

"On the seventh day, the Israelites walked around the city seven times and then blew their trumpets. Joshua had instructed them that when they heard the trumpets they were to shout as loud as they could. And when they did, the wall fell down flat. Outward, the top wall fell down the embankment," Nitzevet pointed to the upper layer of stones, "and the lower wall also fell outward creating a ramp up the retaining wall," she said pointing to the lower wall.

"It is as if Yahweh made a ramp or stairway straight into the city. The Torah says, 'then the people went up into the city, every man straight before him, and they took the city.'"[26]

Nitzevet paused, thinking of the provision of their God, "Can you believe that even the way that the city walls collapsed made it possible for our people to get into the city and take it? They would never have been able to climb over the retaining wall if the upper wall had not fallen and created a ramp of sorts. Yahweh thinks of every detail."

"So back to my question: What does Jericho have to do with the Feast of First Fruits?" she asked.

She knew David knew, so she did not look at him. She wanted the other children to have an opportunity to use their minds. "Wasn't this the 'first' city that they conquered when they went into the promised land?" Eliahba asked.

"Yes!" Nitzevet said as she smiled.

39

DAVID AND THE LION

DAVID LOVED THE QUIET, THE solitude of the countryside. Naturally, he was drawn to the sheep and the pastures where they roamed freely. He felt at home, maybe it was the quiet, maybe it was the absence of the torment his brothers loved to inflict. From a young age, he would pack up his bag of food for a couple of days and a mat for sleeping. Heading out to the pasture he would lead his flock to green pastures with quiet waters in the hills surrounding Bethlehem. Sometimes he would take them to the pasture they discovered on their trip to Jericho, a full day's walk away from home.

It was during these times that David relished his time with Yahweh. Staring up at the stars, David would contemplate the wonders of creation. Remembering and pondering all the things his mother had taught him while he was at home, David added to his knowledge of life through his communion with his Creator. He looked up into the starry night and sang one of his favorite Psalms of Moses:

> "The Lord is king! He is robed in majesty.
> Indeed, the Lord is robed in majesty and armed with strength.
> The world stands firm and cannot be shaken.
> Your throne, O Lord, has stood from time immemorial.
> You yourself are from the everlasting past.
> The floods have risen up, O Lord.
> The floods have roared like thunder; the floods have lifted their pounding waves.

But mightier than the violent raging of the seas, mightier than
the breakers on the shore— the Lord above is mightier than these!
Your royal laws cannot be changed.
Your reign, O Lord, is holy forever and ever ... [27]

"Shhh!!!" David instinctively whispered to his fluffy companions. His sheep knew what this meant from their master and remained quiet as they blinked glassy eyes at him. He gently rose from sleeping to a crouched position. He had heard something. Was it the cracking of a stick under a heavy paw? David's trained ears knew what he had heard. Looking in the direction of the sound he saw the green glowing eyes of what he knew was a lion.

Quickly and quietly, David knew what to do. He knew safety was in swiftness and motion, so before the lion could grab a lamb and run, he must act first. With three giant leaps toward the glowing eyes, he landed next to the startled lion where he grabbed him by his shaggy beard and landed a blow to the lion's temple and in the same motion, David reached for his knife in his belt, and slit the lion's throat.

David sat back for a moment, gently singing to the flock, for he knew they were as frightened as he was and if not reassured rather quickly, they would bolt ...

"In peace I will lie down and sleep, for you alone, O Lord, will
keep me safe." [28]

40

YAHWEH'S REGRET

"SAMUEL ... SAMUEL!" CALLED THE voice of Yahweh. It was as if He were right in front of him and all around him. Samuel could not mistake the voice of his God, once again.

"Yes, Lord?" responded Samuel, sensing an urgency in the call of his Master as he quietly and reverently kneeled before the King of the Universe.

God continued, "I regret that I have made Saul king because he has turned away from me and has not carried out my instructions."

Samuel was distressed. 'Oh no, what did Saul do now?' he thought. He wasn't actually surprised at God's revelation as much as sad. He felt regret, knowing he had played a role in Saul becoming king and had some culpability for Saul's failings. After all, it had been Samuel's own sons Joel and Abijah who by their greedy and ungodly behavior had pointed the Israelites to want a human king.

But Samuel knew he had followed Yahweh with all of his heart and had obediently anointed Saul as the first King of Israel, at the command of his God.

Yahweh continued, "I made Saul king over Israel, I wanted him to obey me in all things. I sent him on a mission, and I told Saul, 'Go and completely destroy the Amalekites, and fight against them until they are exterminated.' Samuel ... Saul did not destroy them as I commanded."

Samuel remembered this very well because he was the very messenger that went to Saul and told him Yahweh's message: "This is what the Lord Almighty says: 'I will punish the Amalekites for what they did to Israel when they waylaid them as they came up from Egypt. Now go, attack the Amalekites and totally destroy all that belongs to them. Do not spare them; put to death men and women, children and infants, cattle and sheep, camels and donkeys.'"

Samuel knew the instructions were very clear and now Samuel finds out from God Himself that Saul did not obey.

Yahweh did not speak further that evening. Samuel assumed that it was because Yahweh knew he needed time to process. He wept before his God all night. Samuel wept for his own failures, and he wept for the failures of Saul the king.

Samuel thought back on the past few months. The downturn in Saul's kingdom began when Saul sacrificed to Yahweh because he was impatient with Samuel. He could not wait for Samuel to arrive, now this. Yahweh was angry.

Samuel rose early in the morning to go meet Saul, he was glad it would take him nearly a whole day to make the journey, he needed to gather his thoughts. About midday, he was met by a messenger from Carmel who told him, "Hello Samuel. I have a message from Saul for you. He came to Carmel, where I had just come from, and set up a monument in his own honor there. Now he is on his way to Gilgal."

Samuel thanked the messenger and sent him on his way. Then, a very disgusted Samuel continued his journey to Gilgal. As he approached the city he could see Saul, coming to meet him. Saul proclaimed jubilantly, "Blessed are you of the Lord! I went on the mission, and I have accomplished all the things that God told me to do."

Samuel stopped, shocked at Saul's boldness in deception, he was seething with anger at this man. In complete awe that this king was so unaware that not only had he not obeyed his God, but he set up a monument to honor himself for his disobedience. His anger was coupled with disappointment, disgust, and great sadness. Samuel slowly lifted his eyes to Saul and said, "What then is this bleating of the sheep in my ears and the lowing of the oxen which I hear?"

Saul was taken aback by Samuel's response, not completely understanding why he was acting this way, and responded rather sarcastically, "Yes of course the men have brought the sheep from the Amalekites, for the people spared the best of the sheep, and oxen, to sacrifice to the Lord your God; but the rest we have completely destroyed."

As Samuel looked up at this tall handsome man, he was not unaware of Saul's chosen words 'they' brought, and 'we' destroyed. Saul had just blamed the people for his oversight, his disobedience. The whole job of the king was to lead, not conveniently put the blame on the people for his own wrongdoing. Samuel whispered for fear of losing his temper, "Stand still Saul, I am going to tell you what the Lord said to me last night."

And Saul, seeing that Samuel was seething before him, became seriously angry himself. He tried to wrestle back control of his petulance and in spite of the fear rising up in him responded to Samuel in the kingliest manner he could muster, "Speak!"

Samuel said, "Although you may think little of yourself, are you not the leader of the tribes of Israel? The LORD has anointed you king of Israel. And the LORD sent you on a mission and told you, 'Go and completely destroy the sinners, the Amalekites until they are all dead.' Why haven't you obeyed the LORD? Why did you rush for the plunder and do what was evil in the LORD's sight?"

Then Saul, still seeking to justify his disobedience and without a shred of remorse, doubled down on his excuse and said to Samuel, "But I did obey the Lord, I carried out the mission he gave me. I have brought back King Agag but I destroyed everyone else. Then my troops brought in the best of the sheep, goats, cattle, and plunder to sacrifice to the Lord your God in Gilgal."

Samuel, shocked at yet another incredulous act of disobedience by bringing back Agag said in a seething tone, "What is more pleasing to the Lord: your burnt offerings and sacrifices or your obedience to his voice? Listen! Obedience is better than sacrifice, and submission is better than offering the fat of rams. Rebellion is as sinful as witchcraft, and stubbornness is as bad as worshiping idols. So because you have rejected the command of the Lord, he has rejected you as king."

Then Saul, realizing there was no way out but to admit he was wrong, confessed to Samuel that he had done wrong. He outlined to Samuel how he knew he had disobeyed the instructions of the Lord. But then he asked Samuel to forgive his sin and return with him so that he could worship the Lord.

But Samuel replied, "No, I will not go back with you! You were arrogant and did not obey your Lord and because of that you have been rejected as king of Israel."

It was Saul's turn to be shocked. He was desperate not to lose his throne and his kingdom and his reputation so as Samuel turned to go, in an impetuous effort to keep Samuel with him he seized the edge of Samuel's robe, and it tore.

Samuel paused for a moment, thinking of the audacity of this man and he said to Saul, "The Lord has torn the kingdom of Israel from you today and has given it to someone else, who is better than you. And, He who is the Glory of Israel will not lie or change His mind; for He is not a man that He should change His mind."

Then Saul said, "I know I have sinned. But please, at least honor me before the elders of my people and before Israel by coming back with me so that I may worship the LORD your God."

Samuel did have compassion for the people who so blindly asked for a human king who let them down. Samuel did not miss the words Saul used and how he referred to Yahweh as 'the Lord your God', it made Samuel deeply sad. He went back following Saul, and Saul worshiped the Lord.

Then Samuel, prompted by Yahweh said, "Go and have someone bring this capture king to me, Agag, the king of the Amalekites." And Agag came to him cheerfully. And Agag was confident that since he had been sent for that everything was going to be fine.

But Samuel said, "As your sword has made women childless, so will your mother be childless among women." And Samuel hewed Agag to pieces before the Lord at Gilgal.

Then Samuel went to Ramah, but Saul went up to his house at Gibeah. That was the last time Saul saw Samuel living. Samuel grieved over Saul. And the Lord regretted that He had made Saul king over Israel.[29]

41

THE CEREMONY

"SAMUEL WAS COMING," REU SAID as he paused at Nitzevet's door. That is what the elders told Jesse this morning. All they told him was that Samuel was coming to 'give sacrifice in Bethlehem'.

"What does it mean?" Nitzevet asked him. What she really wanted to know was if Samuel would bring Rebekah, how wonderful it would be right now to see her friend. She said a silent prayer of hope.

"I don't know," Reu responded simply, "but Jesse wanted you to know so you could prepare Samuel's Room."

Jesse was caught off guard by what he had just heard from his fellow elders, and nervous, as he sat at the gate on this lovely morning. Why was Samuel coming to Bethlehem and why would he specifically invite Jesse and his sons to the ceremony? It seemed so formal. It was a bit out of character for Samuel to arrange a meeting via a messenger. It had been a while since he had seen his friend the prophet. Even though the distance was not far, Samuel was busy working with King Saul, and communicating with Yahweh, while doing priestly duties.

In the years since making his decision to set aside his beloved wife and choose a servant as his wife Jesse had been nervous. He chose this path to guarantee that he was doing the right thing before his God. But he never received the peace he desired from this seemingly well-intentioned choice. The discomfort in his soul was leading him to think that he had made a wrong choice and his family had suffered, especially Nitzevet, his beloved wife.

As Jesse's thoughts wandered, he asked himself ... "Was Samuel coming to punish Nitzevet for her sin of conceiving David? Or ... was

288

he coming to confront me?" For some reason, he had not sought out the company of his friend, the holy man who walked with Yahweh. Life had been rather dull the past few years, the voice of Yahweh was mostly non-existent. Only in the past few years had he recognized the distance that had grown between him and his God. Maybe that is why he did not seek out Samuel, one could not help but feel in the presence of Yahweh when Samuel was around, he and his God were close. Jesse missed the fellowship.

"Jesse ... Jesse!!!" Demanded Abner chief elder of Bethlehem. "Are you listening to us? We are making final preparations for Samuel's visit tomorrow night."

"Yes. I am here. What was it you wished me to do?" asked Jesse.

"Since Samuel has specifically asked to stay with you and that you and your sons would attend the ceremony, we thought your family could host the feast after the ceremony. Your wife and daughters are very good at hosting."

"Yes, my family would be honored to host," asked Jesse. "I have already sent word to Nitzevet." He was reluctant to call her his wife, was she? Oh, it was all so confusing.

He was still nervous as to the reason for Samuel's visit, so Jesse got up quickly and hastened his pace toward home muttering to himself ... "Just wait and see ... wait and see."

נאמנות יהוה

It had been a few months since Saul had disappointed God with his disobedience to Yahweh.

"Disobedient man!" Samuel thought about Saul. His thoughts these days were not always happy. But this was to be a joyous occasion, a new King and he was again privileged to be asked by Yahweh to anoint the new king.

As he walked along toward Bethlehem, Samuel was both nervous about this assignment and excited to find out who could be "a man after God's own heart." For that was how Yahweh had described this person who was to be king. Samuel knew nothing more. Knowing most of Jesse's sons, especially the older ones, he was speculating on which one might be Yahweh's choice. Samuel had not revealed his purpose for the visit to anyone. It could be dangerous for a newly anointed king with Saul still occupying the throne. The fewer people that knew the better until Yahweh chose to reveal His choice.

He turned and smiled at his sweet wife sitting on the donkey at his side. "Are you well my love?"

Rebekah loved the way Samuel cared for her physical well-being as well as her mental state. She could always trust him to guard her heart. "I am well my dear. Just excited to see Nitzevet. It has been so long, and I miss my friend. Do you think she will be surprised to see me?"

"If I know Nitzevet when she found out that I was coming, she sent up a silent prayer that you would accompany me," he responded as he laughed.

נאמנות יהוה

"Remember Zeruah, there are five elders, two priests, our six brothers, and Jether that need to sit at the table," Abigail called after her sister as she set aside the ingredients to make bread. The sisters did not even bother to include David anymore, they cared more for his feelings than trying to include him where his family did not want him.

Their father had just informed them of the special visit of Samuel the prophet that evening, they had so many things to do, to prepare for such a special visit.

"Hello Ema, would you like to help?" Abigail asked as her mother entered the kitchen area. Abigail and Jether were in Bethlehem for an extended visit. Nitzevet and Zeruah were grateful for her presence, she always knew how to make the situation calmer and get things done.

Nitzevet nodded and began to prepare the yeast. "I am so curious Ema, as to why Samuel is coming, aren't you?" Abigail asked, looking into her mother's face to see if she knew anything. Nitzevet simply nodded again. Abigail continued, "I hope that it is for a good thing and not a punishment. After what King Saul did, I am sure Samuel is not pleased. But he is coming, so we should be prepared," Nitzevet nodded, knowing what Abigail was talking about, and smiled at the thoughtfulness of her daughter.

Nitzevet continued to wonder as to the purpose of the visit. She prayed it was not about her. She prayed that she could remain in the background, unseen and unknown. "Please, Yahweh!" She thought, "Please let Rebekah come too," she needed her friend.

It was only two parasangs from Ramah to Bethlehem, it was still early in the morning and the journey would take most of the day. As Samuel walked by his beloved wife, he decided to use this time to pray. When times were hard, Samuel was the first to seek his God.

"Precious Father, bless this family, my longtime friends. The rumors that I have heard regarding how Jesse treated Nitzevet have not been good. Out of respect for this good family, I have not put much stock in rumors and instead, I have constantly brought this situation before You, to work out for their good and Your glory. I pray for Nitzevet, that in her trials you will bless her and comfort her. I ask that you lead Jesse to your path of righteousness and that he will return to leading his family into your presence. Thank you, Father," Samuel grew silent. He loved just remaining in the presence of his God, walking with him, feeling His God surround him.

As the group approached the little town, Samuel could sense the people were nervous to see him. It had been a long time since he had been to Bethlehem. He was sure all the people had heard by now of the deposing of King Saul and it wasn't every day that the Prophet of God and last Judge and kingmaker came to any town.

As was the custom, the five elders came outside the city gates to greet the Prophet. Remembering Samuel's actions with Agag they could not help but tremble a little in his presence. They asked, "Do you come in peace?"

Samuel smiled, a little surprised at the question, and responded with a joyful voice so all around could hear, "Good evening people of Bethlehem, today is a good day," Samuel's words put them at ease. "Today I am here in your town to sacrifice a fellowship offering to the Lord! I am sure you saw my servant walk by with the heifer! Consecrate yourselves and come with me to the sacrifice!"

Samuel then turned to Jesse, embraced his longtime friend, and said with a smile, "Peace be to you Jesse ben Obed!"

Jesse sighed in relief as he gave his longtime friend a long hug. He responded, "Yes, Samuel, it is good to see you, my friend." Then he turned to Rebekah and said, "Nitzevet will rejoice with great joy, for I know she has been praying that you would accompany Samuel."

"Let's get Rebekah to our home to rest a bit and then we can meet your servant at the sacrifice," Jesse said, indicating to the servant with the heifer that he could proceed to the place of sacrifice.

As they passed through the Bethlehem gate and walked Samuel gave further directions, "Jesse, my friend, make sure all your sons are at the sacrifice this evening."

Jesse was still puzzled but responded, "Yes, the messenger mentioned that you wanted my sons to be in attendance, we have made arrangements for them to be there. Can I ask the reason?"

"We will find out in time; Yahweh has not yet fully revealed to me his purposes," Samuel smiled, knowing that Yahweh did not always reveal every detail, He delighted in simple obedience and trust, so Samuel was used to being obedient.

Rebekah could see the joy on Nitzevet's face as they approached Jesse's home. Nitzevet had seen her friend Rebekah sitting on the donkey and could not help herself from running to greet her. Jesse had not seen that much joy on Nitzevet's face in a very long time and the shock was etched on his face with a shadow of grief, Samuel noticed it all.

Samuel, who knew things deeper than most people, and was also a loving husband, perceived what was going on. Coupled with the rumors he had heard, he knew he must confront Jesse, so he looked deep into Jesse's eyes and said, "We will talk later, we must talk."

The women of the town were gathered outside Jesse's home. It was a special feast, and the roasted beef was going to taste so good, they were so excited that they were invited to take part in the fellowship sacrifice, the whole town could smell the roasting meat. There was a lot of it. Abigail and Nitzevet had made an abundance of bread so that when they could, they would distribute some bread along with the meat to their neighbors. The law of the fellowship offering required that the meat be eaten within two days, any leftover past that time must be burned. It was a blessing to be able to share Samuel's feast with those around them.

As Samuel and the elders approached their home after the sacrifice, Abigail could hear Samuel discussing things with Jesse ... "Yes, I have come to anoint one of your sons. God has chosen one of them for His special purpose."

Relieved to finally know the purpose of Samuel's visit, Jesse said with great pride, "We are honored that Yahweh would choose one of our sons." Yet, deep down, he had more questions ... 'what special purpose, which son?'

"Jesse are your sons here?" asked Samuel. He had known Jesse's sons, although not very well. He was trying to count them among the people gathered, he knew there should be seven.

As Jesse led Samuel into the family courtyard he responded, "Yes, they are here. Eliab, come my son," Jesse called Eliab his oldest and most handsome son.

Samuel approached the oldest, he was tall and handsome, and Samuel was thinking, 'surely the Lord's anointed is before him'. Samuel greeted Eliab warmly with an embrace. He then considered him thoughtfully, having known him through the years, he waited on Yahweh. Samuel could hear the voice of the Lord in his spirit, "Don't judge by his appearance or height, for I have rejected him. The LORD doesn't see things the way you see them. People judge by outward appearance, but the LORD looks at the heart."

Samuel stepped back, looked at Jesse and smiled while shaking his head no.

Jesse was bewildered at the rejection of his firstborn and silently glanced from Eliab to Samuel, not knowing what to do.

He finally gathered himself together and announced, "Samuel let me call Abinadab over."

Samuel, again, quietly considered the man standing before him and again shook his head saying, "God has not chosen your second son either Jesse."

Jesse announced, "Samuel, Shammah is talking with his sister, let me bring him over." He stepped aside to wave his third son over, surely Shammah is the one.

Again, Samuel shook his head saying, "Him either."

Seriously puzzled now, Jesse ushered Nethaneel before Samuel, "Nethaneel, my fourth son," Jesse tried to muster the strength in his voice.

Samuel shook his head.

"Raddai, my fifth son," Jesse motioned for Raddai to follow.

Samuel continued to shake his head no.

This was it, the last one, "Please meet my sixth son, Ozem!" Jesse announced proudly, surely this was the one.

"Are all your sons here?" Samuel asked Jesse, knowing immediately that his God had rejected Ozem as well.

"Well ... there is another son, the youngest, but he is with the sheep." Jesse reluctantly confessed; he had secretly never considered David his son.

Samuel noticed that Jesse did not say that this last son was 'his' son. He sighed and patiently said to Jesse, "Send someone to get him, because we will not sit down to eat until he comes here."

Jesse was frustrated that he had forgotten to invite David, surely Samuel was mistaken, and he would go back to one of the others. It was a good thing that David was not too far, just in the next pasture over.

"Quickly!" Jesse said to his servant "Go get David and bring him here, as fast as you can."

The servant ran to the pasture to get David. Fortunately for David, he was just finishing his afternoon swim in the still waters near the pasture. While putting on his clean tunic, he saw the servant running toward him.

"Come quick David, the Prophet Samuel has called for you," the servant said breathlessly.

"Me, why me?" argued David. No one had ever shown any interest in David.

"Go David!" the servant said, shoving the teenager in the direction of the town.

David left the servant to care for the sheep and walked quickly back to the town, reluctantly. Nothing good had ever come of David being the center of attention.

Samuel immediately saw how ruddy David was, and how he had beautiful blue eyes and how handsome he was, it had been a few years since he had seen David. He looked like Nitzevet. As David approached the spirit of God said to Samuel, "This is the one; anoint him."[30]

Smiling Samuel stood, embraced David, took the horn of oil and anointed David in the midst of his entire family.

Immediately, Samuel sensed the presence and power of Yahweh in David. The others gathered there felt it too, but they did not know what they were experiencing. Samuel did. He remembered the first time he had encountered his God, in the still small voice of the night. He thought Eli, the priest who cared for him, was calling him. Three times Yahweh had called, and after asking Eli, his master realized it was Yahweh and told Samuel to go back to bed and if the call came again, answer the call with "Speak Lord for your servant is listening."

This was one of those moments. The Spirit of God rushed upon David and David knew it.

Yahweh had called. Yahweh had anointed.

Nitzevet stood back overwhelmed. As the scene played out before her, she knew what was happening. At first, when all her sons were rejected, she too was bewildered, but then Samuel asked if there was another son, and she knew. She knew David. When he arrived, handsome, sweet, gentle, her kind boy, and she saw the reaction of Samuel, she knew. She understood that the horn of oil meant a special anointing. She, lover of Yahweh, could feel His presence. And She, the mother of David, could see the change when the Spirit rushed upon David.

Her world was changing. Maybe Jesse's was too.

David went back to the pasture. Back to the sheep. Back to the place where Yahweh communed with him. He could always feel the presence of God, but now it was different ... more. He knew that something had changed. He had changed. He had to think, to process, to understand.

נאמנות יהוה

As Samuel lay in bed that evening, he knew what Yahweh had meant when he said, "man after my own heart". For he sensed it in David, even before the anointing. That gentleness of spirit, the kindness in his eyes. There was no guile, no evil, no malice to be found. Just a gentle soul ... an obedient soul.

He was pleased that he was honored to anoint the next King of Israel. However, he did not make that clear. Surely as he anointed David people were speculating, everyone must know he is the kingmaker, but he never actually said that he anointed David as king.

נאמנות יהוה

Samuel knew that Saul had turned to the dark side. There was no question that Saul would seek recompense if he found out that Samuel had anointed the new king. At Yahweh's bidding, he masked his visit as a fellowship offering, and an anointing for special service. He left it at that.

In His time, Yahweh would reveal to everyone who David was and the purpose for the anointing. One must not jump ahead of Yahweh, for His ways are not ours and His timing is not ours. Surely there was a purpose in waiting.

The next morning, Samuel felt prompted by Yahweh to speak with Nitzevet. For being the wise old man that he was, and a father and husband himself, Samuel knew there was something more to the story. Rebekah had stayed up until the wee hours speaking with Nitzevet. But Samuel, being the sensitive, kind man that he was, did not ask questions. He preferred to let Yahweh reveal the truths that he needed to know, in His time and in His way. A handsome, well behaved, wise son to not be invited to the meal was strange especially when Samuel had specifically told Jesse to invite all his sons.

As Nitzevet exited her home, Samuel who was in the corner sipping a steaming hot cup of spiced milk greeted her, "Nitzevet, it is so good to see you. It has been too long, I did not get a chance to speak with you yesterday, it was so very busy. My wife is still sleeping, so I have not spoken with her. I really wanted to speak to you personally because I know there is strife in your household, you must tell me what is going on," Samuel said.

Nitzevet smiled. She was not shocked that Samuel knew. He walked with Yahweh. He solved problems for Yahweh, and she had been asking for a solution for years.

Nitzevet motioned for Samuel to wait for a moment. She knew Yahweh had provided this opportunity to speak with her friend privately. She ran inside the house to get Zeruah to walk with them and then ushered Samuel toward the fields, toward the tower. As they walked, she slowly told Samuel the whole story.

Zeruah was near and heard for the first time, the whole story from beginning to end with all the details. She had long suspected something, but no one had ever explained, and she had not asked. She heard about the rejection of Nitzevet as Jesse's wife. The wedding night switch gave her a whole new view of Piaget. The birth of David and his rejection by his brothers. She silently wept for her mother, for David, for her family. She thought, 'So many years of nonsense went by for what? To pretend to be holy? To hope to please God?' She pondered her father's actions; they had mirrored King Saul's. We think our sacrifice will please God. It is something we can do. But God simply wants obedience over sacrifice. 'What had they sacrificed in their lives and relationships in place of simple obedience?'

Zeruah treasured these things in her heart. She was growing day by day to love your God more and more. In her mother's faith and David's faith she could see that Yahweh was a good God and loved them fully. He had protected their hearts and cultivated a heart of love, kindness, and compassion in David in spite of how he was treated. It was the humans that got in their own way.

42

A MARRIAGE HEALED

IT WAS TIME FOR THE long-awaited conversation between Samuel and Jesse. After Nitzevet had explained it all to him the day before, Samuel had spent the day praying and seeking Yahweh. This was the new family of the king of Israel, he wanted to follow Yahweh's leading in the process of reconciliation. Samuel sensed that the Spirit of Yahweh was urging him to talk to Jesse, he knew that his God would give him the words, so he simply obeyed.

Samuel got up early and went to the cooking area where the servant provided him again with a steaming hot cup of Leah's goat milk tea, so sweet, so spicy, it reminded him of this wonderful lady that was with Yahweh now. He asked for a second cup, knowing that Jesse would be waking soon. Sure enough, he heard Jesse shuffle through the courtyard and Samuel greeted him with the steaming hot cup.

"Bless you, Samuel!" Jesse exclaimed a little too loudly and a little too eagerly. He was glad to have this time with Samuel. After the events of the previous few days, he had a lot of questions. Besides the fact that he had so much chaos in his heart, a conversation with this godly man would clear out the webs in his mind.

They sat down on the bench for a moment to sip their tea. Samuel began to pray, "Yahweh, Lord of Armies, King over all, we praise you for who you are, for who you have formed us to be, and the path you have set us on. We ask that your presence go with us, in our lives, in our activities and in this conversation between two friends. Selah."

"Selah!" responded Jesse.

After a few moments of silence between friends, as they listened to the sounds of the early morning, Samuel drained the last drop in his cup and said, "Shall we walk and talk Jesse?"

Jesse nodded and they stepped out of the gate and walked down the path.

"So, my friend ... what is happening in your life, leave nothing out, especially what is going on between you and your wife?" Samuel asked and then paused to wait for Jesse to explain.

Jesse explained everything. Everything from the past fifteen years came gushing out of Jesse amidst tears, anguish, sorrow, desperation, sadness and the most devastating of all a growing sense of disappointment in himself and his behavior.

Samuel let the silence linger, knowing that words would not comfort Jesse in this moment as much as the silence of a friend.

Jesse regained most of his composure and then asked the burning question, "Why David?"

Samuel looked at his close friend and explained, "Yahweh told me to stop mourning for Saul, to get up, go find Jesse of Bethlehem and anoint one of your sons as king."

Jesse could not believe his ears. Yahweh said David was his son!

"Wait!" Jesse paused and thought to himself, 'What did Samuel say he was anointing David for ... king?' He gave Samuel a puzzled look, as if he did not hear him correctly.

"You heard me Jesse, David will be king of Israel, and yes, he is your son. Yahweh specifically called him, let me see, oh yes, 'a man after His own heart'," Samuel saw that Jesse was still confused and quite speechless on both accounts.

"My friend, do you remember when Saul sacrificed to God rather than waiting for me? It is strictly forbidden for anyone other than a Levite to sacrifice to Yahweh. Saul knew this and was impatient and he did it anyway. That was when Yahweh told me that he had a new king in mind, and he used those words 'a man after his own heart.'" Samuel explained.

Samuel waited a long time and then prompted by the Holy Spirit he gently explained what Nitzevet had shared with him about the conception of David. How and why, David was Jesse's own son. He explained how Pigat had planned fifteen years ago on that fateful wedding night to switch with Nitzevet and how Nitzevet followed through with it feeling that it was Yahweh's will to save Jesse from committing various sins against not only Yahweh but against her and his family. That was the night David was conceived.

It was as if the scales fell off of Jesse's eyes. Once the stigma of Nitzevet's perceived sin in conceiving David was taken out of the way he began to see David differently. Images of his kindness, gentleness, and mercy came up before him. He remembered times when David fearlessly protected his lambs without the need for commendation or recognition. He remembered scenes crossing through his memory of how David loved his sisters and his mother. And then Jesse's thoughts settled on Nitzevet and her lovely face and her sweet disposition and he realized the evil he had done and the pain he had caused her.

Jesse wept, bitterly.

נאמנות יהוה

Samuel knew that Jesse needed to be alone with his God, so he excused himself and went back to their home to pack for his journey home.

Jesse could not fathom how he was going to make amends to his wife. After several hours of confessing his sin and reestablishing his relationship with Yahweh, he knew what he must do. He must find Nitzevet.

Usually, she was out in the fields wandering, doing who knows what. He could not blame her, for he knew he had severely hurt her and grieved her deeply. As he wandered through the hills, he encountered Abigail returning to the city.

"Hello Father, who are you looking for?" she asked gently, sensing from his countenance that he was grieving.

Jesse responded, "I am looking for your mother."

"Oh!" Abigail did not expect her father to be seeking out her mother. "She is by the tower."

Jesse kissed his daughter on her head and smiled. They parted ways and he headed toward the tower where he found his wife. Nitzevet was perched on a rock in the shadow of the Acacia tree, near the tower gazing to the west. You could almost smell the sea breeze from the Great Sea.

She looked so beautiful to him as she sat there, unaware of his presence. He sensed that she was at peace, for the first time in a long time.

He gently approached and she looked up and smiled, for the first time in many years, she smiled. Nitzevet smiled at him. It was a beautiful smile.

Jesse greeted her with a nod and then proceeded to sit beside her and gaze at the horizon. "Hello, my beloved."

It was awkward talking to Jesse, especially when he used such intimate terms. Their relationship had withered into nothingness, as most relationships do when they are neglected. It was just easier that way, the pain was not so acute when there was no semblance of a relationship. But this greeting took her back, back to the pain.

Nitzevet responded in kind, "Shalom, my beloved."

Not knowing where to start, Jesse just blurted out, "I am so sorry. I have sinned against you, against Yahweh."

Something had changed within Jesse. Nitzevet knew it was Samuel at Yahweh's leading who had shared the truth that melted his heart and changed his thinking.

Nitzevet took a deep long breath and began the journey back into a relationship with her beloved. She explained to Jesse all that was in her heart. She had rehearsed this conversation many times. Sometimes it was an angry exchange full of blame and bitterness. Sometimes it was full of tears and sorrow. Today, it was completely different than expected or planned. It was simple, truthful, and without blame or remorse.

Yahweh was here. It was His timing and yes things were changing. "Husband, David is your son. Pigat and I switched places on your wedding night, and it was I that conceived your eighth son."

Jesse looked deep into her eyes with compassion that was beyond words. Then he said with shame and regret, "I know. Samuel told me."

He had sought to sacrifice his marriage, his wife, his happiness for something he thought would be holiness and it was not pleasing to Yahweh. Obedience was pleasing to Yahweh. Honoring the wife of your youth is pleasing to Yahweh. Being faithful to marriage vows was pleasing to Yahweh. 'Obedience, not sacrifice'.

They both were in the moment thinking of King Saul and the story that Samuel had told last night to the crowd. Yahweh had said the same thing to him, 'to obey is better than sacrifice'. They both understood in their hearts the full meaning of that statement. Jesse felt as if he were as guilty as Saul. He was.

Jesse realized that because of the righteous ways of his wife, he was released from the sin he would have committed had his plans with Pigat been followed. How grateful he was.

He looked at Nitzevet, took her hands in his, got down on one knee and begged her forgiveness for his years of foolishness. Nitzevet had never seen this coming in all the scenarios she had run through her mind, and eighteen years ago would have completely withheld forgiveness from this man. But eighteen years in the presence of Yahweh, growing ever closer to a God who understands forgiveness better than anyone, she could not withhold forgiveness. It gushed forth from her heart as if it were the only thing she could give.

As husband and wife embraced, they knew that things were indeed changing. As Jesse sobbed into her robe, Nitzevet could feel the past melting away with his tears. The pain was turning into joy and chaos into peace. Yahweh was here.

נאמנות יהוה

As Nitzevet lay in the arms of her husband that night when all was quiet except for the night creatures she remembered her words to Rebekah many years before, "You know that we cannot be disappointed in our God's timing. He always comes through in His time. I trust my life to Him. And even if what Yahweh provides is not what we expect, but something different, then He still came through because of His love for us."

נאמנות יהוה

David seemed the same from the perspective of most people in the village of Bethlehem. But to his mother and sisters, they were astonished at the change. Not that David was suddenly 'better'; he had always been a good boy. But the presence of the Spirit of God in him was even more evident. Rumor had spread that he had been anointed for a special purpose, but the details were unclear, and no one knew exactly why. His brothers did not bring it up much and gave vague answers when questioned. They were not pleased that David at the age of fifteen had been singled out over all of them, by the Prophet. Eliab was especially out of sorts. As the eldest of the family, the most experienced, the best looking, he is the one who should have been chosen. He was angry and bitter about it.

David felt the sting of Eliab's frustration in his words, for he was the one who had to hear what Eliab said and endure the pain he caused.

"Why don't you go back to the flock where you belong David!" yelled Eliab.

"On my way as we speak!" replied David with extraordinary grace and compassion in his voice.

That is not what Eliab wanted. He wanted a confrontation. He wanted to give David what he deserved for stealing what was his as the elder brother, the blessing. It just wasn't fair. At the same time that he felt such anger and jealousy, he felt shame. 'A man of his age and stature should not be jealous. He was a leader, he should rejoice in the blessings of others, but David! Why David?'

David was so used to the abuse from his brothers, that he did not even falter. He knew his place, and he knew the best location was for him to be out with the flock. Gathering up his belongings he headed out toward the flock. He was so grateful that Yahweh was with him. He never felt alone.

It wasn't long after what came to be known as "the anointing" that David's three oldest brothers joined Saul's army. Eliab, Abinadab, Shammah, may have joined because they were asked by their king, but Nitzevet knew deep down they had felt that David's anointing was rejection by Samuel and wanted to make a name for themselves and their family. She missed her oldest sons from afar. Their relationship had never recovered after the birth of David. She had felt their renewed rejection after the anointing.

Yes, life was changing, some things for the better, others not. She was grateful for what Yahweh was doing in her marriage and in the life of her youngest son. She prayed for her older sons, hoping they would seek Yahweh and learn to love him as she did.

"Let's go Eliab!" called Shammah. As the third child, he was the most independent and quickest to be on the move. His oldest brother, the most responsible, was double-checking their resources, making sure they had everything they might need while in the service of their king.

Abinadab seemed tearful. As the second born, he was the most attached to life as it was. While always up for fun and frivolity the idea of leaving for an unknown extended service in the military was taking its toll on his emotions.

"Take care of yourself, Father. Keep us informed on how you are doing," said Abinadab as he embraced his father. He glanced at his mother. She was standing near his sister.

He strode over to where they were standing and embraced Zeruah as she said, "Greet Jether for us and please tell Abigail of our love." Then Abinadab turned to his mother and in a rare moment of compassion, he embraced her and said, "Take care, Ema." Then he walked away.

Nitzevet was so grateful for a moment with her son. She knew Abinadab was the most hurt by what happened so many years ago, but there was little she could do. Some day he would know the whole truth and would grieve.

43

THE TOWER OF THE FLOCK

DAVID HEADED TOWARD THE TOWER. Just like his mother, it was his refuge in the presence of Yahweh when life became unbearable. Throughout the years, even as a child, his mother would gravitate on their walks toward the tower. He was always pleased when they would stop and eat their bread and cheese in its shadow. In that shadow, they had some of their most lively discussions. Memories flooded over him as he recalled as a young boy the first time his mother had shared the creation story with him. How Yahweh had hovered over the formless and empty dark surface of the deep and then said with the boldness only the Creator of the Universe could have, "let there be light!" and there was light.

He could still see the face of his mother as she related the details of creation, the tears would creep down the sides of her cheeks, not from sadness but from awe and gratitude to be part of a plan instigated by the Creator Himself. David longed back then to have the faith of his mother. He set his goal in life to love Yahweh as his mother loved Him.

Sitting beside the cool brook once again, he remembered the story of his ancestor Jacob who buried his wife Rachel not far from here and then pitched his tent just south of the tower. She died in childbirth of Benjamin, Jacob's twelfth, last, and most beloved son. David felt a connection with Benjamin, the last son.

He looked over at the remembrance pile of stones that he and his mother had built when he was five. He saw the flat solid foundation stone that he had chosen to represent his God. Immediately he realized how significant that was. Yahweh was his rock.

He lay on his back and looked up at the tower of Migdal Edar. This tower, this place, David was sure, would have great significance to Israel in the future, just as it did for him now. Something great would happen here.

נאמנות יהוה

A few days after her oldest sons left to fight with Saul, Nitzevet sipped her tea in the shadow of the tower as the sun was slowly peeking over the horizon. Her favorite time of day. To her, the beginning of the day was all about new beginnings, a fresh start and opportunity. The shepherds, her shepherds had left the fire burning with nice hot glowing coals to heat her small tea pot filled with spiced milk. They were the most gentle and gracious of men, probably from spending so much time with sheep, who were gentle by nature, but mostly because they loved Yahweh as she did.

She could see a figure approaching across the field. She knew it was her beloved, she could tell by his gait. She pulled the extra cup she always brought with her out of her bag and as Jesse walked up, she poured him a steaming cup of her delicacy.

Jesse kissed her check and took the warm mug. As he sat down behind Nitzevet so he could snuggle in and watch the sunrise over her shoulder, he could smell the vanilla and raspberry scent of her hair, that beautiful unruly red curly hair that refused to obey.

"I knew I would find you here," Jesse laughed.

"Everyone knows where I am, they always look here first," Nitzevet giggled, teasing Jesse. "I love this place, Yahweh is here."

Jesse nodded; he could feel the same presence. It was the Presence of goodness and light. He could feel the tears rise to his eyes as he thought of how he had wasted so many years. Years where he had denied Nitzevet his love and affection. He had still loved her, but mistakenly thought that Yahweh wanted something different. How foolish he had been.

Now that their oldest sons had left to be with King Saul, things were different. Jesse knew that David was his, how he had denied that boy true love of a father and yet he is one of the most amazing men. Jesse was ashamed. His behavior, his choices were inexcusable. Yet, he was forgiven. Not only forgiven by his God but by his wife and his son. He was grateful.

He decided at that moment that every moment with Nitzevet would be precious. They would use this time, this morning, to signify a new beginning to their life, their marriage, their family.

He whispered all of this in her ear. But he could not see the tears of pure joy and contentment that streamed down Nitzevet's face as she listened to the words she had longed for and prayed for. His love, his kindness and his desire to make all things right was overwhelming. She silently thanked Yahweh for answering prayers ... for new beginnings.

Jesse listened and marveled as Nitzevet whispered to Yahweh:

> I waited patiently for the LORD to help me,
> and he turned to me and heard my cry.
> He lifted me out of the pit of despair,
> out of the mud and the mire.
> He set my feet on solid ground and steadied me
> as I walked along.
> He has given me a new song to sing,
> a hymn of praise to our God.
> Many will see what he has done and be amazed.
> They will put their trust in the LORD.[31]

The End.

APPENDIX A

CHARACTER LIST

KEY:
<u>Bold Underlined Characters: People Named in the Bible</u>
Bold Characters: People Named in Historical accounts
Bold Italicized Characters: People present but unnamed in the Bible;
Regular Font Characters: These are not present in the Bible but are assumed.
Italicized Characters: fictional characters.

Abiezer	Tower shepherd
Abigail	Hannah's daughter
<u>Abigail</u>	Nitzevet & Jesse's 2nd daughter/sister of David
<u>Abijah</u>	Samuel and Rebekah's 2nd son
<u>Abinoam</u>	Saul's wife
<u>Abinadab</u>	A Levite in Kiriath Jearim
<u>Abinadab</u>	Nitzevet & Jesse's 2nd son
<u>Abishai</u>	Zeruah's son
Abner	*Chief Elder of Bethlehem*
<u>Ahitub</u>	Eli's grandson
Aliza	Naomi's sister / Dalit's Mother
<u>Amasa</u>	*Abigail and Jether's son*
<u>Asahel</u>	Zeruah's son
Asenat	Nitzevet's friend in Efrat
Azmaveth	Philistine who apprentices Reu in Ashdod

Benjamite Messenger	Possibly Saul
Boaz	Ruth's Husband / Naomi's Son in Law
Chana	Servant girl at Saul's Palace in Gibeah
Chazael	mother of Ednah / wife of Uzzi ben Tzuri'el
David	Nitzevet & Jesse's 8th son
Dalit	Gila's mother / Nitzevet's Grandmother
Ednah	Daughter of Uzzi ben Tzuri'el
Eleazar	Son of Abinadab, Priest who guarded the Ark
Eleazar	Shoshannah and Reu's son
Eli	High Priest of Israel
Eliab	Nitzevet & Jesse's 1st son
Elihud,	Chief counsel member.
Elkanah	Hannah's husband
Elimelech	Naomi's husband
Eiran	Friend of David
Gareb	Son of Hannah / Brother to Samuel
Gemalli	Nitzevet's father
Gila	Nitzevet's mother / Dalit's daughter
Hannah	Elkanah's first wife / Samuel's mother
Hophni	Son of Eli
Jacob	Family Patriarch
Jashobeam	Shoshannah and Reu's son
Jesse	Obed's son
Jephunneh	Jesse's brother
Jether	Husband of Abigail Soldier of the King
Joab	Zeruah's son
Joel	Samuel & Rebekah's 1st son
Joel	From the tribe of Issachar
Jonathan	Saul's oldest son
Joshua	Owner of the field where the Ark landed
Keturah	Jephunneh wife / Jesse's sister-in-law
Kohath	Ancestor of Elkanah
Kish	Saul's Father
Leah	Wife of Obed

Maharai	Tower shepherd
Maharai	Namir's father
Manly	Youngest elder of Bethlehem
Malchi-Shua	The third son of Saul
Merab	Saul's oldest daughter
Michal	Saul's daughter
Naharai	Son of Hannah / Brother to Samuel
Namir	From tribe of Ruben, Husband of Zeruah
Naomi	Mother-in-Law to Boaz and Ruth
Ner	Saul's grandfather
Nerhad	Philistine looking for Reu with Rafi
Nethaneel	Nitzevet & Jesse's 4th son
Nitzevet bat Adael	David's mother / Jesse's wife
Obed	Son of Boaz
Onan	Namir's Grandfather
Ozem	Nitzevet & Jesse's 6th son
Paarai	Tower shepherd
Peninnah	Elkanah's second wife
Phinehas	Eli's son
Pigat	Jesse's Philistine Maid
Raddai	Nitzevet & Jesse's 5th son
Rafi	Ednah's Husband
Reu	Philistine friend
Rebekah	friend of Nitzevet / wife of Samuel
Ruth	Wife of Boaz / Naomi's daughter in law
Samson	Judge of Israel
Samuel	Son of Hannah and Elkanah / Priest / Prophet / Judge
Shelach	Gila's father / Nitzevet's Grandfather
Shifra	Vophsi's wife / Jesse's sister-in-law
Shammah	Nitzevet & Jesse's 3rd son / David's brother
Sibbecai	Tower shepherd
Shoshannah	Friend of Nitzevet, Wife of Reu
Tahliah	Namir's Mother/ Maharai's wife

Unnamed	Nitzevet & Jesse's 7th son
Uzzi ben Tzuri'el	Father of Ednah from Tel Hadar tribe of Gad
Vophsi	Shifra's husband / Jesse's brother
Zaccur	Naomi's brother-in-law / Dalit's Father
Zeruah	Nitzevet & Jesse's oldest daughter

DEFINITIONS

Parasang - an ancient Iranian unit of distance of measurement about 3 miles.

Hametz – Hebrew word for Leavened bread - flour or grain that has been combined with water and allowed to sit to produce yeast. This is considered leavened and is forbitten for Hebrews to eat or possess during Passover.

Kiddushin – an engagement contract between a man and woman

Mohar – the price paid by the father of the groom to the father of the bride

Mattan - gift

Seor – sourdough bread

Slicha – Pardon me or excuse me in Hebrew

Teruah – a loud shout either by a crowd or by a shofar

Nappah – someone who uses bellows – a traditional blacksmith

Shabbat – Sabbath day, Saturday

Safta – Grandma

Ema – Mother

Metuka - Sweetheart

STORY INSPIRED BY REAL EVENTS

Everyone knows David, Israel's King David. The Bible outlines many of his relatives including his father, Jesse and his grandfather, Obed. The famous romance of his Great Grandfather Boaz and Great Grandmother Ruth are told across the generations. David's cousins, his aunts, many friends are all relayed in the pages of Scripture. But what do we know about his mother? Ancient Hebrew history records her name, Nitzevet. And David mentions her in his writings, although not by name.

David, a 'man after God's own heart', must have learned that heart posture from somewhere. It is the opinion of the author that he learned this from his mother. This fictional story of David's mother's life is woven into a story of the people of Yahweh using the historical record of the Bible. Along with timelines curated by scholars and theologians, maps and records, the story comes to life giving the reader a better understanding of what life was like at the end of the time of the Judges of Israel.

ENDNOTES

1   Measurement of distance that was equal to 2.4 miles
2   I Samuel 2:2 New International Version
3   Chapter 2: I Samuel 3:1-19 New International Version
4   Psalm 90:1-17 New International Version
5   Psalm 90:14 New International Version
6   Numbers 6:24-26 New International Version
7   Genesis 49:10 New International Version
8   Genesis 12:2-3 New International Version
9   Deuteronomy 4:5-9 New International Version
10   Deuteronomy 4:9 New International Version
11   Numbers 13:1-14:38 God's Word Translation
12   Chapter 14: Joshua 1:1-11 New International Version
13   Psalm 138:1-2 Good News Translation
14   Ruth 1:16-17 Berean Standard Bible
15   Talmud: Ketubot 8
16   Exodus 13:11-16 New Living Translation
17   Leviticus 19:34 New American Standard Bible
18   Genesis 3:15 New International Version
19   Genesis 12:1-3 New International Version
20   I Samuel 10:18-19 New International Version
21   Job 19:25-27 New International Version
22   Leviticus 19:33-34 New International Version
23   Deuteronomy 6:4-9 New International Version
24   Psalm 8:1-9 New International Version
25   Deuteronomy 1:28 New International Version
26   Joshua 6:20 English Standard Version
27   Psalm 93:1-5 New Living Translation
28   Psalm 4:8 New Living Translation
29   Chapter 40: I Samuel 15:1-33 New International Version
30   Chapter 41: I Samuel 1-13 New Living Translation
31   Psalm 40:1-3 New Living Translation

Printed in the United States
by Baker & Taylor Publisher Services